CHOCOLATE

She leaned in closer, seemingly to straighten the knot in his tie, but actually drawing much nearer than was necessary for that. Her voice was fairly a purr as she continued, "I also made those chocolate orange truffles you like so much."

A wide, searing heat licked at his belly, and although he tried to convince himself that it was a result of the chocolatey promises with which she was plying him, he had to concede that there might be just a bit more to it than that. "Oh, yeah," he murmured, the words sounding low and throaty as they emerged from his mouth. "Those are *so* good, Claire. So good."

She nodded, her nearness causing the silky softness of her dark hair to brush against his chin. "And something new," she told him. "Something . . . special."

Somehow, he managed to silence the groan he felt erupting from the depths of his libido. "Lay it on me, baby."

She dropped her voice to a whisper as she revealed, "Something I've named Chocolate M-cubed."

He drew in a slow, languid breath and held it. "Sounds very . . . intriguing . . ."

She skimmed her fingertip slowly across his chin, her voice a bare whisper as she told him, "It's chocolate . . . mocha . . . mint . . . macadamia."

"Oooooh, Claaaaire . . ."

—From "Just Desserts" by Elizabeth Bevarly

ROMANCE COLLECTIONS FROM
THE BERKLEY PUBLISHING GROUP

Love Stories for Every Season . . .

LOVE BY CHOCOLATE

Rosanne Bittner
Elizabeth Bevarly
Muriel Jensen
Elda Minger

JOVE BOOKS, NEW YORK

LOVE BY CHOCOLATE

A Jove Book / published by arrangement with
the authors

PRINTING HISTORY
Jove edition / February 1997

All rights reserved.
Copyright © 1997 by Jove Publications, Inc.
Book design by Casey Hampton.
This book may not be reproduced in whole or in part,
by mimeograph or any other means, without permission.
For information address: The Berkley Publishing Group,
200 Madison Avenue, New York, New York 10016.

The Putnam Berkley World Wide Web site address is
http://www.berkley.com/berkley

ISBN: 0-515-12014-6

A JOVE BOOK®
Jove Books are published by The Berkley Publishing Group,
200 Madison Avenue, New York, New York 10016.
JOVE and the "J" design
are trademarks belonging to Jove Publications, Inc.

PRINTED IN THE UNITED STATES OF AMERICA

10 9 8 7 6 5 4 3 2 1

CONTENTS

Miss Chocolate
and the Law

Rosanne Bittner

A big thank you to my good friend, Bea Kimball,
who winters in Phoenix, Arizona, and who helped me
with some of the detailed information I needed
about that area for this story.
Bea has been a dedicated fan and a good friend
from my very first published novel back in 1983,
over forty books ago!

ONE

PAMELA COULD SEE it was going to be one of those mornings. She had overslept, and who could blame her? She had stayed up half the night revising her résumé, using an old clunker typewriter that belonged to her aunt. She couldn't complain, really. Why would her aunt have need of a modern typewriter or a computer?

She should have known enough to start on the résumé earlier. She hadn't planned this right at all. Aunt Nadene had done enough just by giving her a place to stay for over two weeks now. If she got this job, she could soon move out on her own and leave Nadene and Uncle Bill to their privacy, which they certainly deserved in their old age.

This was all her own fault. Well, maybe not. Maybe it was her mother's fault; better yet, Barry's. That rat! If she hadn't caught him cheating on her, she wouldn't have had to call off the wedding. And if her mother hadn't decided to move to Florida, maybe she could have stayed in Michigan with her for a while. Even before her father died, her mother had never been dependable, a woman who always made rather whimsical decisions that were often self-serving. The woman seemed to have no conception of her daughter's needs.

So be it. She was here in Arizona now and she'd have to make the best of it. It might be easier if it wasn't 110 degrees outside. She stopped her '89 Escort and waited impatiently for a traffic light, then took off again.

"Damn piece of junk," she grumbled. Of all times for the air conditioning to fail! She wanted to look fresh for this job interview, but it was going to be impossible with this heat. She reasoned that if she'd gone with her mother to Florida, things wouldn't be any different. It was hot there, too, and her mother was really no comfort. Aunt Nadene was more of a mother to her, and the sweet woman had practically begged her to come to Phoenix and stay with her for a while. It had been years since Pamela had been here, and she'd forgotten how hot it could get. If she had known before she left the house this morning that her air conditioning wasn't working, she could have borrowed Aunt Nadene's car.

There was no time to go back. She was already late. This, too, she blamed on Barry. She had saved diligently for her marriage. They were going to wait and decide on a new car after the wedding. Most of the time a person could get by in Michigan without air conditioning. There it was heat you had to have. But down here . . .

"I'm going to look terrible by the time I get there," she muttered. She'd left the back windows open, hoping the circulation of air would help. She had not expected it to be this hot at eight o'clock in the morning. Her appointment was for eight-thirty with a law firm in Sun City, and Uncle Bill had explained a back way to get there in order to avoid the early morning freeway traffic.

Bad idea. She had a feeling she'd taken a wrong turn, and now she wasn't sure just where she was. Somehow she'd gotten into an area that was looking more and more uninhabited. This couldn't possibly be the right way. She would be late, a big strike against getting hired, and she would look like a dishrag by the time she arrived, another strike against her. She could feel the life going out of her hair. It was too fine. In this heat it didn't take much for it to wilt into flat, silky strands that just hung there and did nothing. The blow dryer and curling iron she'd used on it this morning had been all for naught. She had gotten ready so fast she hadn't been able to dry her hair thoroughly or hold the curling iron in it long enough.

I might as well turn around and get some directions, she thought. *This whole trip is probably useless, but I might as well show up anyway, try to explain. Maybe I'll get lucky. Maybe they will understand.*

A trickle of sweat began to move down her temple. She turned to get a tissue from a box on the passenger seat, and when she looked back up, an awful chill moved through her blood. Was that a stop sign? She saw only a blur to her right, heard the squeal of tires, decided it was best she keep going if she was to avoid a collision.

She clenched her jaw tightly and waited for an impact, then realized the other car had missed her. She slammed on her brakes, thinking whoever had nearly hit her might have been hurt; but she was going too fast for a sudden stop. The steering wheel seemed to come right out of her hands, and she remembered thinking how glad she was she'd worn her seat belt as the Escort careened toward a ditch.

She squeezed her eyes shut, felt a thud, then realized she was tilted to the left. Her body lay pressed against the driver's side door, and it took her a moment to decide she was not hurt, except for her pride. She opened her eyes and looked down at herself to see the coffee she'd picked up at a fast-food place on the way here had spilled out of the special cup holder and landed in her lap. She groaned. She'd worn a new white suit today.

It was obviously going to be one of those days that she should never have gotten out of bed. She stayed put for a few minutes, gathering her thoughts, making sure nothing hurt. She wasn't even sure she could climb out of the car by herself. Had the person she'd nearly hit just driven on and left her here?

Her question was answered when someone pounded on the right side of the car. "You okay in there?"

It was a man's voice. He managed to open the door, and Pamela looked up. He wore a tan uniform . . . and a badge!

"Highway Patrol, ma'am. I'll help you out. You have a registration with you? Driver's license?"

"Oh, my God," Pamela muttered. Just what she needed to top off the worst morning of her life.

"You ran a stop sign, and you're lucky we're both alive."

So much for the job interview. This is what she got for getting up late, being in a hurry, being too preoccupied with her many woes.

"I'm . . . I'm so sorry," she said. She handed up her purse, then leaned over to open the glove compartment to take out her papers. He took those also. "I can explain," she told him, squirming around to stand up with her feet against the driver's door. "I mean . . . I know there's no good excuse, but this whole morning has been a disaster."

"Ma'am, there is no excuse for what you just did."

"I know. I didn't mean—"

"Ma'am, I asked if you were hurt."

"I don't think so."

"Give me your hand."

Pamela could feel his anger. She reached up. His grip was strong. The wrist she grabbed onto was firm and muscled. He stood with his back against the passenger door to keep it open while he literally pulled her up and out of the seat. She felt her nylons catch on a piece of plastic stripping around the edge of the seat. It had been loose for a long time, and she'd always meant to get it fixed. Now she felt the little tickling sensation of several runs moving quickly up her leg.

She thought what a mess she must look, sweat pouring harder now because of her nervousness, runs in her stockings, the life gone out of her hair, coffee stains on her white skirt. But then, what the hell difference did it make how she looked? This cop was going to hand her a very expensive ticket, no doubt, and she had come close to taking his very life. What did he care how she looked? She spotted her purse and papers on the ground, bent down, and picked them up.

"I'll call a wrecker to come get your car out," he told her. "The dirt in that ditch is pretty soft. Chances are your car isn't damaged. Come get in the squad car. It's cooler."

A bedraggled Pamela followed the man to his squad car. *Good Lord,* she thought. The white police car sat on the wrong side of the road, several hundred feet from the intersection, long skid marks from near the intersection to where the car had stopped. Red and blue lights were flashing to alert oncoming traffic, but so far there was no one else around.

How in hell had she gotten this far into nowhere? "I'm so sorry," she repeated. "So sorry. I don't know what happened. I was looking for a tissue, and . . . it happened so fast." Why did she feel like crying? She hated crying. It was such a typical female thing to do. This obviously ornery and chauvinistic officer would probably love to see her cry. She noticed the blue emblem on the car door as he opened it. She got inside, literally groaning at the feel of the cool air. What blessed relief. It was almost too cold for someone covered with sweat. She shivered as he opened a back door first and reached for something, then got in the front seat behind the steering wheel.

"Here." He handed her a blanket. "I know how it feels to be sweaty when you go into a cold room or get into an air-conditioned car."

She was surprised at his thoughtfulness. "Thank you."

"Let's see your registration and driver's license, ma'am."

He was back to being formal, unfeeling. She was too upset to notice him in detail, embarrassed to look him in the eye, but judging from what she'd seen he was maybe thirty years old, perhaps a little under six feet tall, very solid, like a man who lifted weights. She couldn't really see his eyes because of the dark sunglasses he wore. *What difference does it make how he looks, you idiot?* She was in trouble, plain and simple. She fished out her registration and handed it to him, then opened her purse to get out her driver's license.

"Michigan," he said. "You visiting?"

"No, I . . . well, sort of. I think I'm going to stay."

"If you do, you'll need to register your car in Arizona and get an Arizona driver's license. I'm not sure if they will be eager to give you one after this."

Smartass, she thought. She grabbed her wallet, and her eyes widened with dismay. "Oh, my!"

"What's wrong?"

"Oh, my!" She pulled out her hand, and the ends of her fingers were covered with chocolate. "Oh, no! It's . . . it's everywhere!" Bad had gone to worse. She loved chocolate. She seldom went anywhere without a chocolate bar or chocolate Kisses, anything chocolate. She had already learned you couldn't do that in Arizona in July, but she had meant to eat this candy bar quickly on her way to the job interview and wash it down with the coffee that now stained her white skirt. She'd figured as long as it was wrapped, the chocolate couldn't get on anything, and it would probably stay solid long enough for her to eat it.

But she'd had so much on her mind she'd forgotten about it. "I . . . it's a chocolate bar. It's all over inside my purse, on everything! It must have gotten smashed in the accident. Oh, dear. Do you have a handkerchief or some kind of rag?" She began licking the chocolate off the ends of her fingers, realizing too late she'd gotten chocolate on her left hand also. Now it was on her white skirt along with the coffee stains.

"I might have some wet-wipes in the trunk. You'll have to step back out of the car, ma'am. I can't leave you in here alone while I look."

"Oh, yes, all right." She started to open the door, realizing now she was getting chocolate on the door handle and even getting some on the vinyl behind the handle. "Oh, I'm sorry. I got chocolate on the door—"

"Just get out, ma'am."

Now the tears were getting harder to fight. She got back out, the heat hitting her like an oven. "Damn Arizona," she muttered. Maybe she'd go someplace else, but where? There were too many bad memories back in Michigan, and she wasn't sure her mother even wanted her in Florida with her. Sarah Hiles had met a new man. He'd moved to Florida for business purposes, and she had followed him there. She didn't want her daughter around. In fact, she never had seemed to want her around.

Damn it! This was not the time to cry because she wasn't sure her mother loved her. Besides, July in Arizona might be miserable, but it was twice as miserable in Florida with all that humidity, right? She gritted her teeth and sniffed back tears, absentmindedly wiping at a tear that slipped down her cheek, realizing immediately she'd just smeared some of the chocolate onto her face.

"Here." The officer stood in front of her, holding out a plastic container of wet-wipes. "Move around out of the road, ma'am, over here in the grass." He led her around the car and off the hot pavement.

"Thank you." Pamela's lip quivered as she took a wet-wipe from the container and began wiping off her hands. The trooper pulled out a couple more and left her there, going to the car to clean off the door. Pamela had to use several more of the wet napkins to clean the chocolate off her hands, her arms, her face. The wetness felt good against her face. She rubbed it off her skirt as best she could, but she ended up smearing what was already there.

The policeman returned with a small trash bag and began picking up the discarded wet-wipes.

"I'm so embarrassed. This whole morning has been just awful," Pamela told him, her voice shaky from fighting tears. "Now I'm making such a mess! How am I going to get out my driver's license?"

"Let me try," the patrolman answered. "Sorry about the heat, but we'll have to do it out here to save a mess in the car." He dumped out her purse. "Start wiping everything off. I have to radio this in, let people know where I am. You stay right here."

The words were more of a command, and Pamela began angrily wiping off everything. "What do you think I am, some kind of criminal who's going to try to escape?" she muttered. Her anger helped allay her tears. By the time he returned, she had a clean driver's license ready to hand to him.

"Here," she said with a note of sarcasm. "Go and find out if I'm a wanted killer."

She continued cleaning off other items while he went back to the car to radio in her name and other information from the license. Minutes later the trooper returned, handing her the driver's license and a ticket.

"You might not be a wanted killer, Miss Hiles, but without a stroke of luck you *might* have been a killer after what just happened. Maybe you've had a bad day, ma'am, but that's no excuse for careless driving."

Pamela had laid her belongings on the outside of her purse, figuring she'd never get the inside clean enough to put them all back. She took the license and put it back in her wallet. "I am well aware of that," she answered. "I don't know how many ways I can say I'm sorry." She finally managed to look him in the face. He had a square jawline and dark hair cut very neat. He seemed to be very handsome, but then a lot of men looked great in a uniform and expensive sunglasses. It seemed that out here everyone spent a lot of money on their sunglasses, but then a person needed the best for the Arizona sun. She could feel that sun burning her nose and arms.

"Come back into the squad car while we wait for the wrecker. I can't leave until you're all set and back on the road," he told her.

Pamela stuck the ticket into her wallet and carefully carried her purse and belongings back to the car, setting them inside on the floor. She took the blanket from the roof, wrapped it back around herself, and climbed inside.

Officer Court Barker could not help noticing the long, slender legs of the woman who got into his car, and the short skirt she wore. In spite of the sweat and the coffee and chocolate stains, any man could tell she was a beauty. He noticed she did not wear a wedding ring, then wondered why he'd noticed or cared. He couldn't help feeling a little sorry for her, especially being new to Arizona, but the fact remained the woman had nearly killed him. The entire incident had reminded him of another accident—one he'd rather forget. But he knew he never would. How could a man forget his wife and child? Forget their funeral? Forget their burial? All because of an auto accident.

"My name is Court Barker, Miss Hiles, and believe it or not, I don't enjoy giving out tickets. Maybe this one will force you to be more careful after this."

Pamela just stared forward, glancing at the rifle mounted on the dashboard. "Yes, sir."

She heard him sigh deeply, heard him shift into reverse. She sat still as he backed the car off the road.

"I guess I don't need to leave it where it landed," he said. "I don't need to take measurements and all that, since no one was hurt, and there was no damage. Of course, if you intend to fight the ticket—"

"Why should I? I ran a stop sign, plain and simple. And now I've missed out on an important job interview, and my whole day is totally ruined. My *life* is ruined."

He didn't answer right away. Finally he shifted a little before he spoke. "Believe me, ma'am, there are a lot worse things that can go wrong with your life than getting a ticket and missing a job interview."

Pamela looked over at him. There was pain in his voice when he spoke the words. "I know that. It's just been one of those days."

"Where was the job interview?"

She shrugged. "At a law firm in Sun City. I'm a legal secretary. I need a job so I can get a place of my own. I'm living with an aunt right now in north Phoenix."

He left the car running so it would stay cool. "If your car isn't driveable, I'll take you to your aunt's."

"Thank you." Pamela looked at him again, beginning to realize just how handsome he truly was. Why she was seeing him as just a man and why she couldn't hate him, she wasn't sure, except that sitting with him in the front seat like this seemed somewhat intimate. She stayed as far to the end of her seat as she could.

"I would advise you not to carry chocolate in your purse again, especially if your car doesn't have air conditioning."

"I won't." She felt stupid, awkward. She wondered what he must think of this dumb broad from Michigan who carried chocolate around when the temperature was over a hundred and ten. "I . . . just happen to love chocolate, that's all. In Michigan you can carry it in your purse. Oh, it can get really hot there, too, but most of the time it's nothing compared to this."

"Why the move?"

"I just need to start over someplace new, that's all. I was supposed to be married by now, but I caught my fiancé . . ." She sighed. "Well, I guess it was for the best I found out when I did."

"Seems so, from what little you've told me."

It seemed strange to just sit here and talk to a police officer as if he was just another person. She felt nervous, yet comfortable. Finally the wrecker arrived and Pamela sat in the squad car while her own car was pulled out of the ditch.

"You've got two flat tires, and you ought to have the steering and alignment checked," the man with the wrecker service told her.

Of course. The way this day had gone, did she really expect there would be no damage to her car? The man handed her a business card and told her where he'd be taking the car. "Go ahead and do whatever," she told him. "I'll come by with my uncle after I go home and clean up."

The wrecker left, and Officer Barker put his squad car into gear and drove off. Pamela gave him her aunt's address, and for several minutes they rode in silence, Pamela listening to voices coming over the scanner. She wondered if Barker had ever been shot at.

She stared straight ahead, unaware that behind the sunglasses Court Barker was sneaking glances at her legs.

❤ TWO

PAMELA WONDERED IF she would ever get the dirt out from under her fingernails, feeling like a fool for not wearing garden gloves before helping Aunt Nadene re-pot some house plants.

"Now, things didn't turn out so bad, did they?" her aunt was saying. "I hate to see you move out, Pam."

"I'll only be ten minutes away," she answered. She pressed the dirt tightly around the plant she'd just potted. "The apartments are nice, and there is good security there. I promise to come and see you often. Besides, so far you and Uncle Bill are practically the only people I know in Phoenix."

Nadene chuckled. "It won't take long for you to make new friends at that law firm. You said there are ten lawyers working there. That means ten secretaries and surely several extras. They must have a mailroom and all sorts of extra jobs. I worked in an office for years myself, you know, before I retired."

"I know."

"Of course, I wasn't any fancy legal secretary like you. I was just a shipping clerk, but I liked the work and I made a lot of friends there that I still see."

Pam smiled, thinking a woman like Aunt Nadene couldn't possibly *not* have friends. She was so different from her mother, warm and jolly, totally unselfish. She was a short, stout woman who had never been slender, and with age her arms had grown soft. She still had a pretty, flawless complexion and always wore a spot of rouge on her full cheeks. Her brown eyes were tender, and her mostly gray hair was cut into the same short, curly style many women her age wore. Pamela was glad for her. She seemed to have always been happy living here in Phoenix, where she had moved with her husband many years ago because of his work for a power plant.

"Thank you so much for letting me stay here, Aunt Nadene."

"Oh, it's my pleasure, dear. I didn't want you going to Florida with that mother of yours. I know she's not the most pleasant person to live with. I'll never understand why my brother married her. Here I never could have children, and that woman refused to have more than one. I would have loved to have had one." She sighed. "But the past is past. I hope she finds whatever it is she's looking for in Florida." She looked Pam over. "I'll say one thing you can thank her for. She is a beautiful woman, and so are you, tall and slim like her, lovely features, big blue eyes, blonde hair. You should have gotten yourself into modeling, Pamela."

Pamela laughed, thinking what a mess she was right now, her hair pulled back into a twist to keep it off her neck while working in her aunt's garden this morning. Because it was so fine, several strands had already fallen loose. Her knees were dirty from kneeling in the dirt, and she'd rubbed dirt from her hands onto the back of her pink shorts. Her halter top was an old faded thing she didn't care about, and she figured her face was probably dirty from wiping away sweat with dirty hands.

"Thank you, Aunt Nadene, but I'm sure I'm not the picture of beauty right now." Her smile faded. "Apparently beauty and loyalty weren't enough for Barry."

Nadene sniffed. "You just forget about Barry Hennessey. God did you a favor letting you find out what a scoundrel that young man was before you married him. Having a last fling with an old girlfriend before he tied the knot . . . heavens! I never even got to meet him and I'm glad. I hope to *never* know him! You just put him out of your mind and go on to new things. You're worth far more than a Barry Hennessey, young lady."

"Yes, and I'm twenty-four years old with no prospects."

Nadene rolled her eyes. "Don't be in a hurry. More and more young people today are taking their time, and that's good. In my day a woman felt she had to be married by seventeen or eighteen or she was an old maid. Not that I haven't been happy with your uncle, but there were times when I wondered what I might have done with myself if I'd waited, maybe gone to college first. I spent a lot of years taking in foster children because I longed so badly for children of my own, but I never did have a real career."

Pamela heard the doorbell ring at the front of the house as she answered. "Well, maybe *that* was your career. You have a good heart, Aunt Nadene, and those children needed you. Where would this world be without its Aunt Nadenes?"

Nadene smiled. "That's a nice thing to say, Pam."

Pam's Uncle Bill came out onto the back porch of the modest frame home then, a big grin on his face. "Somebody here to see you, Pamela."

"Me?" She looked down at herself, brushing off her hands over a flower pot, pushing a piece of hair behind her ear. "Who in the world would come to see me? I don't even know anybody yet."

"You know this person." He chuckled. "You're going to be surprised."

"Oh, let's go see!" Nadene said excitedly.

Pamela shrugged, filled with curiosity as she walked through the kitchen and dining room, over old carpeting that needed replacing, although it was clean as a whistle. Aunt Nadene kept a spotless house. She stopped in the arched opening between the dining room and living room, staring at a very handsome young man who stood near the front door. He wore casual pants, a very nice tan shirt, deck shoes on his feet . . . and expensive sunglasses, which he slowly removed as she stood there staring at him. He held something in his hand, but she hardly noticed as she studied his face. When he took off his glasses, she saw soft green eyes surrounded by dark lashes and brows, set in a finely chiseled face. He smiled, his teeth even and white.

"Hello, Miss Hiles. I hope you don't mind the visit."

Good God! "Officer Barker?"

"I guess I look a little different out of uniform. I have today and tomorrow off. I, uh, couldn't quite get you off my mind, hoped you were still here at your aunt's house. I thought I'd bring a little something to make you feel better about what happened a couple of weeks ago, find out how you're doing. Did you finally find a job?"

She slowly nodded. "At a law firm in downtown Phoenix. I just rented a new apartment about ten minutes north of here. I move in next week." *Good Lord, you're handsome!* What was he doing here . . . really? "I got my car fixed and traded it in for a newer one. It's nothing fancy, but at least the air conditioning works."

He grinned more, then chuckled. "Well, I'm glad of that." He held something out. "Here. This is for you."

"Well, glory be!" Aunt Nadene spoke up before Pamela could take the package. "Are you the ornery police officer who gave my poor niece a seventy-five-dollar ticket? You should be ashamed of yourself! Poor Pamela has been through a lot the last few months, and that morning had been a disaster for her. She was a wreck after you dropped her off."

Court reddened a little, not sure what to say to the woman.

"It's all right, Aunt Nadene," Pamela said. "I deserved the ticket. If not for Mr. Barker's quick stop and swerve, I could be dead now. We both could be. I ran a stop sign, plain and simple. You should thank him."

Aunt Nadene smiled. "Goodness, girl, don't you know when I'm teasing someone? Come on in and sit down, Mr. . . . Barker, is it?"

"Yes, ma'am."

"Oh, listen to the way he answered me. 'Ma'am.' I haven't heard that in a long time. You're either very respectful, or it's just the policeman in you talking."

Pamela and Court hardly heard the words. They were

staring at each other. Pamela noticed his gaze moving over her, and she suddenly realized what a mess she was and felt embarrassed. She self-consciously reached up and tried to re-pin some of her hair. "Well, Mr. Barker, it seems you keep catching me at my worst. I've been helping my aunt in her garden and with re-potting some house plants."

Court studied the long, slender legs he'd not been able to forget. She filled out her halter top in a way that made him wish he could touch her breasts, and through all the dirt he saw the most beautiful young woman he'd ever seen. "You look fine. I just wanted to check on you and give you this."

He was still holding out the gift, and finally Pamela took it, leading him to a flowered davenport to sit down. Nadene nudged her husband and motioned for him to leave, and Pamela and Court were left alone in the living room. Pamela looked down at the package, which was gift wrapped. By its size and weight, she had a pretty good idea what it was.

"Candy?"

He laughed lightly. "How could I forget how much you like chocolate?"

She rolled her eyes. "Oh, what a terrible morning. I almost lost my taste for chocolate after that disaster." She tore off the paper. "But that didn't last long." She opened the box, staring down at a huge assortment of chocolate cremes and nuts. "This is very nice of you. You didn't have to do this."

"Yes, I did." He cleared his throat, as though suddenly nervous. "Actually I was wondering if maybe I could take you out tonight, to dinner, a show or something."

As she took a small bite out of a chocolate-covered cashew, she glanced down at his left hand. "I believe that's a wedding ring you're wearing."

He smiled sadly. "I've never taken it off. My wife is dead, Pamela—may I call you Pamela?"

Such manners! "Of course."

"Call me Court."

She nodded, sobering. "I'm sorry about your wife."

"She was killed in an auto accident—drunk driver."

Pamela closed her eyes and looked away. "My God. No wonder you gave me that ticket."

"Oh, I've seen plenty of accidents since then, obviously. You don't do what I do without seeing a lot of death on the highway. Trouble is, I'm the one who found them. Our little boy was with her. He was two."

Her mouth dropped open, and she met his eyes, seeing the pain there. She remembered seeing that same pain a couple of times while they sat in the squad car. "Him, too?"

He nodded and took a deep breath. "It was five years ago. I figured I'd tell you up front so you don't wonder about it, about me." He stood up, sighing deeply again as though to ward off too much emotion. "So . . . to make a long story short, I've dated off and on since, but there has never been anyone serious in my life, and there is no steady girl now—and ever since the day of your accident I haven't been able to stop thinking about you. Will you go out with me?"

Her heart went out to him, but she warned herself not to fall too quickly for a combination most women could not resist—a strikingly handsome man with a tragic past, loneliness, sadness. "Sure. I need to meet new people."

"Good. Dress casual but nice. I'm taking you to the Landmark—best prime rib in town—or steak—or seafood. Whatever you like. Big salad bar, too. It's in Mesa. It won't take long to get there. We just take Fifty-one to Ten and then get off on Apache Boulevard."

Pamela thought how a lot of things around here seemed to be named after Indians. Everything was so different here than in the Midwest. She was growing to like it more and more here, except she still could not get used to the heat. "That sounds nice. What time should I be ready?"

"Six okay?"

"Sure. I have to leave for a while to do a little shopping for furniture, but I can be back and ready by then."

"Good." He looked her over again. Good God, she was beautiful, and she'd agreed to go out with him. His buddies had been after him for years to get on with his life. He'd tried several times, but no one had interested him much. Only recently the pain of losing his wife and son had begun to subside a little, time beginning to heal the wounds. There was something about Pamela Hiles he'd liked, a genuine niceness about her. A woman who looked like that ought to be stuck-up as hell, but she didn't seem to have a snobbish bone in her body. "By the way . . . I guess it isn't my business, but . . . you're not rekindling things with that fiancé back in Michigan?"

She set the candy aside, surprised he'd remembered she had mentioned something about a foiled wedding the day he gave her the ticket. "No. I left a wedding dress and an engagement ring with him, as well as all the unpaid bills," she added with a wry smile. She stood up, folding her arms. "I caught him having a last fling before he entered the prison of marriage. All wedding plans were called off. My mother moved to Florida, and I hate Florida, but I had to get away, so I came here."

He slowly nodded. "Sorry about the messed-up wedding."

She shrugged. "Like Aunt Nadene says, it was probably for the best. Probably saved me a messy divorce."

"Probably." He smiled softly. "I can't imagine any man doing that to somebody as nice and as pretty as you. The man must be the biggest fool in Michigan."

She smiled, a little embarrassed but also flattered. "I like to think so."

He laughed lightly and headed for the door. "See you at six."

"Sure."

Their gaze held a moment longer, both feeling surprising emotions since they hardly knew each other. He nodded and left, and Pamela went to the door to watch him leave. He drove a new Camaro, bright red.

"Well, well," she muttered. She had a date with a state highway patrolman. This was a first.

Court could not get over how she looked. She wore a white halter-top dress that was fitted through the bodice and had a flared skirt. White drop earrings danced from behind her long, blonde hair, and her skin was tanned and so smooth he wanted to touch it. "You look great," he told her aloud, opening the car door for her.

"This is the first time you've seen me that I haven't been a mess," she answered with a smile.

Pamela sensed Court felt the same anxious nervousness she did. She had not dated casually for a long time, and they were still near strangers. "You look nice yourself," she told him when he climbed into the driver's side.

"Thanks."

He wore casual slacks with a lightweight knit shirt and a sport coat. The sun was still bright, and he put on his sunglasses and started the car. The engine rumbled, and when he pulled away from the house, Pamela could feel the car's power.

"Big engine?"

"V-eight, three-fifty LT-one, five-point-seven liter tune-port injection, if that means anything to you. This engine is the same one that goes into a lot of Corvettes."

Pamela raised her eyebrows. "I'm properly impressed. Ever get a ticket with this thing?"

He grinned. "What do you think?"

"I think you could probably drive the wrong way down a freeway and not get ticketed. It isn't fair."

He sobered a little. "Actually I'm a careful driver. I've seen the worst of what speeding can do."

"I know. I'm sorry."

He shrugged. "So, let's talk about something else, like this fiancé of yours. How long had you been together?"

"A couple of years. We knew each other in high school but didn't date until several years later. He was a hometown boy. I thought I could trust him." She sighed. "But when I think back on it now, something about it never did seem right. I guess I was marrying partly because I thought it was about time. The old time clock is ticking away."

He made his way through several stop lights and headed for Highway Fifty-one. "You're only twenty-four. You're not exactly using a walker yet."

"How do you know how old I am?"

"I saw your driver's license, remember?"

She rolled her eyes. "I certainly do."

"I'll make up for the cost of the ticket tonight."

"I certainly hope so." They both laughed. "Tell me a little more about yourself. Have you ever been in a high-speed chase?"

"Sure."

"Ever been shot at?"

"Once. It doesn't happen as often as they make it look on TV. But then nowadays you have to be careful of everyone you stop."

"Did you think *I* was going to pull a gun out of my glove compartment?"

He snickered. "Not really. You learn to read people pretty well. At any rate, it won't matter much longer. I took a test for detective and passed it. I expect to be promoted before too long."

"Really? Well, congratulations. I suppose that means investigating murders and other grizzly crimes."

"Something like that. At least I'll get away from accidents and broken, bloody bodies and drunk drivers. I have a hard time holding back from good ol' police brutality with drunk drivers. If you want the truth, I've had special counseling for it. It was a drunk driver who killed my wife and son. He got off light, spent thirty days in jail, went to court to get back his rights to practice medicine, and he won."

"He's a *doctor*?"

"A surgeon—supposedly one of the best."

Pamela shook her head. "That doesn't seem right."

"You bet it doesn't. There have been times I've wanted to kill him, and in my position I could probably find a way to get away with it."

She could feel his anger, watched him grip the steering wheel a little tighter. "Now you're scaring me a little. I've always heard policemen aren't always a very good choice for a relationship. Maybe I heard right. Maybe you should take me back."

He shook his head. "Jesus," he muttered. He slowed down before reaching the highway and pulled over to stop. "I'm sorry. I'm really, really sorry. That was a stupid thing to say, and I wasn't talking literally. I wouldn't be human if I didn't think about it sometimes, but believe me, I'm over it now."

"Are you really?"

"Really."

She sighed. "I always liked to believe bad cops only existed in movies."

He turned off the car. "You check with my captain, anybody you want. I'm about as straight as they come, a family man, no record ever of any kind of brutality. I was half joking about that, Pam. I don't even care if you talk to my counselor. I haven't needed counseling for almost three years now. I'm okay, and I'm sorry I scared you." He reached and touched her arm gently. "I got us off to a bad start here. I'm really, really sorry. I didn't mean to spoil things."

She looked at him hesitantly. "Take off your sunglasses."

He frowned, removing them. "Why?"

"I want to see your eyes. Eyes say a lot." She studied him intently for a moment. "Okay. I think you really are sorry. You might actually even be a nice guy." She smiled. "And you still owe me a seventy-five-dollar night." She shivered at the way he looked her over and wondered what it would feel like to be kissed by a handsome highway patrolman. Could someone built like he was be gentle? Surely he could. He'd had a wife and son once. Surely he wanted another family someday. She liked that about him.

He grinned, putting his glasses back on. "Okay. You're going to like the Landmark. And they have a chocolate dessert to die for. Do you ever make chocolate desserts?"

She tossed her hair behind her shoulders. "My specialty. My favorite is chocolate chiffon pie—it's chocolate ecstasy."

He cleared his throat. "Chocolate ecstasy, huh? Sounds kind of provocative."

Pamela felt a little surge of desire. "It can be."

"You know what they say about chocolate."

Now she felt the heat rising to her cheeks. "I know what they say."

"Did you eat much of that candy I brought you today?"

"Sorry. Only one piece. I wanted to save my appetite for

tonight. So don't go thinking you've filled me with an aphrodisiac in preparation for this date."

He laughed hard then. It was a nice laugh.

"Oh, woe is me. My plan didn't work," he said, feigning sorrow. "Maybe I *should* take you home."

"Well, we haven't had that chocolate dessert at the Landmark yet."

He nodded. "That's right."

Pamela thought how it wouldn't take chocolate to make her want to know how it felt to be held by Court Barker. She chided herself for the thought. Her breakup with Barry was much too fresh for her to be having such thoughts, but then Aunt Nadene said that all things happen for a reason.

Maybe the good Lord led you down here to find your true love, dear, the woman had told her just tonight. She had carried on about Court Barker, how handsome he was, how she couldn't do much better than a state policeman. But Pamela was going to be cautious this time. She still hardly knew this man. This was simply all too new, the location, the new job, new apartment, new friends . . . a new man. No, she was not about to get serious anytime soon.

"By the way, I don't even know how old you are," she said aloud.

"Thirty-two. I hope that's not too old for you."

She shrugged. "Age doesn't mean much. It's the person himself that counts."

He nodded. "I agree." He pulled onto the highway, then put the car in cruise and reached out his hand. "I really am sorry for what I said earlier."

She took his hand, and he folded it gently around her own. His grip was strong and warm, actually comforting.

"Apology already accepted."

They held hands for several more minutes, saying nothing.

—♡— THREE

PAMELA COULD SEE that Court Barker was a well-known and well-liked man. Nearly every place they went, someone there knew him, and he was always greeted warmly. She felt a little overwhelmed by the many people she'd met in the five dates she'd had with Court, and she couldn't help the warm feelings growing deep inside for him. The man was making every effort to treat her royally, and had so far taken her to only the best restaurants. They had been out dancing, and today they spent the whole day just riding, enjoying the view of the surrounding mountains. Now they were at La Casa Vieja, another wonderful restaurant, this one in Tempe.

"I'm going to get fat if I see much more of you," she told him. "Between the boxes of candy you keep bringing and all this dining out, I'll have to buy a whole new wardrobe." She pulled a piece of meat off her beef kebob.

"You don't fool me. You haven't gained an ounce, and I know you use that treadmill you bought. By the way, I belong to a health club. Want to join? We could work out together."

Pamela swallowed the meat as she pulled off a mushroom. "I'll think about it." This was moving too fast. She realized Court Barker was much more ready for a new relationship than she was. He'd been alone for five years.

She'd broken up with Barry only four months ago, had been in Phoenix only a month. Could she actually already be in love again? Were these emotions only a result of being so deeply hurt that she wanted to prove to herself she could get another man any time she wanted? "This is a wonderful restaurant," she said, trying to change the subject.

"It was built in eighteen seventy-one. Read the back of the menu. This place was originally a port for a ferry service on the Salt River. Then it became a haven for people in need of a meal and a place to sleep. It even tells you here how the town of Tempe got its name. Actually it used to be called Hayden's Ferry. Some Englishman came here one day, and when he looked down on this valley he thought it was so beautiful it reminded him of someplace in Greece—the Vale of Tempe, something like that. It has something to do with mythology. At any rate, he recommended changing the name of the place to Tempe, and that's what they did." He leaned closer. "And quit avoiding the real subject."

She drank some water. "Oh? What's that?"

"Us. This is our sixth date. You've been pretty reserved, Pam. You turn away when you know I want to kiss you goodnight. You never invite me into your apartment. You didn't exactly jump on the idea of joining the health club with me. Are you that turned off by me? I mean, if you don't want me to ask you out anymore, just say so."

She studied her water glass. "Do you *want* to keep asking me out?"

"Hey, look at me."

She met his eyes.

"Would I be spending this kind of money on a woman I wasn't very, very interested in having a relationship with? Most other dates I've had have been a one-time thing. To put it bluntly, I've never felt this way about anyone else since I lost my wife. Of course I want to keep taking you out. Frankly I want more than that. I think I'm falling in love with you, Pamela Hiles." He rubbed at his eyes and leaned back. "There, I've said it."

Pamela's emotions swirled with joy and apprehension. "I don't know what to say."

He leaned closer again. "You could say you think maybe you're falling in love with me, too."

Their gazes held for several quiet seconds, both of them hardly aware of the voices and activity around them. "I think maybe I am."

He flashed a quick smile—oh, so handsome.

"Well, thank God for that much."

Pamela sighed, reaching over and grasping his hand. "Court, I just want to be careful. I don't want to do something on the rebound and wonder later how I got myself into another relationship that might not work out."

"Why shouldn't it?"

"I'm not saying it wouldn't. I'm just . . . scared, I guess. What Barry did hurt me so deeply. I don't want to get hurt like that again."

"I'm not Barry. I never cheated on my wife and never would have."

She smiled wryly. "I've always heard policemen are notorious cheaters. Women have a thing for men in uniform. You must get all kinds of offers. Even if you weren't a cop, you would. You must be aware of how handsome you are."

He laughed, shaking his head and looking embarrassed. "Pamela, for one thing I don't wear a uniform anymore. I'm a detective now, remember?"

She was glad for his promotion, which was part of the reason he had taken her out today, to celebrate. "Detective Barker," she said with a sigh. "All the more provocative."

He let out a little snicker of near disgust. "Quit thinking of me as a cop and start looking at me as just a man, Pam. I'm thirty-two years old, a widower who is tired of being alone. I want a new family. You're the first woman I've met who I feel—I don't know. I feel like we just click, you know? I feel good when I'm with you. You're beautiful, sensitive, smart, have a career. And you believe in fidelity. So do I. I want a deeper relationship with you, Pam. For God's sake, I'd at least like to know what it's like to kiss you."

Pam felt heat rising into her cheeks. She couldn't help being flattered by his feelings, nor could she help feeling cruel by always putting him off. She squeezed his hand.

"The only reason I don't kiss you, Court, is because I'm afraid if I do I won't be able to stop. I want a relationship as much as you do, but I just don't want to be hurt again. It isn't just Barry. I've never had a good relationship with my mother, never felt she really loved me. My father died several years ago, and he *did* love me. I miss him terribly. I just don't want to grab what love I can for all the wrong reasons."

"Are you happy when you're with me?"

"Of course I am."

"Do you look forward to each time you're going to see me again?"

She smiled. "Yes."

"Do you think about me at night?"

Now she did blush, unable to meet his eyes. "Sometimes."

"*Some*times?"

She laughed lightly. "Most of the time. Actually, about twenty-four hours a day."

"Well, there you are. What more proof do you need that we belong together?"

She met his eyes again. "What about you? How do you know this isn't just your own desperate need to be loved again?"

"It's been five years. I think I know my own mind and feelings by now."

"What about that anger inside over that drunk driver? How do I know it won't come out in some strange form down the road, maybe aimed at me? Repressed anger can make a person do strange things."

"My God, Pam." He let go of her hand and leaned back. "You don't really think I'd hurt you, do you?"

"No." She sighed. "I'm just not sure you have truly dealt with those feelings. You have to forgive that man somehow, Court. Don't let it all fester in your soul."

"Forgive the doctor who killed my wife?" He ran a hand through his dark hair. "Okay. I'll think about it. That's all I can say. Just don't expect any sudden miracles."

Pamela poked at what was left of her kebob. "All right. I

know I could never understand how you feel, and I have no right telling you what you should do about it. Neither can you understand my own reservations because of what happened with Barry. This has been kind of a whirlwind affair, Court. I'm still new here, still adjusting. Surely you can understand why I'm afraid to get too deeply involved." She felt sorry for the look in his eyes. "Court, you haven't even told me your wife's name or your son's. I've never been to your house, never seen any pictures. I'm sorry if this hurts, but I think it's important that you tell me more about them."

He slowly nodded. "Okay. Finish your meal, and we'll go to my place right now. The only reason I haven't talked more about my family is because I was afraid you would resent it, maybe feel second best, something like that. I don't ever want you to feel that way. You're very special in your own way and you're really very different from Shiela." He leaned closer. "That was her name, Shiela. And she didn't look anything like you, so don't go worrying I'm attracted to you because you remind me of her. She was dark, part Mexican, but born here in Arizona. She was a vivacious, friendly, beautiful woman. Everybody liked her. She worked for an architect, studied home design in college. But she quit her job when she had our son, decided to stay home with him the first couple of years."

He stopped and took a deep breath, a drink of water, and it was obvious the next words were more difficult. "Our son's name was Enriqué. Shiela named him after her father. We just called him Ricky. He was . . . well, you know how cute little Mexican kids are. He was a damn handsome little guy, bright, sweet." He touched her hand. "It feels good to be able to talk about them. I wasn't sure you would want to. Let's finish eating, and I'll take you home and show you their pictures."

Pamela agreed, noticing he was already through eating. "Actually I'm not that hungry. Let's just go now."

Court nodded, taking her hand and rising. "Lady, I'll do whatever it takes to prove to you I'm ready for a whole new relationship. You name it, we'll do it." He led her to the cashier and paid the bill, then walked her to the car.

Pamela felt a flutter of apprehension as they left the parking lot and headed toward north Phoenix. "Court, are you sure you're ready for this?"

"I'm sure. I might be more ready than *you* are. I hardly realized I hadn't even told you my wife and kid's names. That should prove to you that *you're* all that's been on my mind."

They spoke little for the half hour it took to reach a pleasant subdivision of stucco homes with tile roofs. Court pulled into the drive of one of the modest homes, and it was still light enough for Pamela to see the lawn was neatly cut. A palm tree near the garage swayed in a gentle breeze.

"This is it," Court announced.

"It's very nice," Pamela answered.

He smiled. "Come on inside. I have to warn you, there isn't much of a woman's touch left, but I keep it clean. I finally gave away most of Shiela's things a couple of years ago, packed a few special things into a box in the closet. I did the same with Ricky's things."

Pamela followed him inside, where he led her through a living room furnished in a Southwestern style. He took her on into the dining room, waving his arm then toward a display of pictures on a buffet. "There they are, my beautiful wife and precious son."

Pamela felt a shiver as she walked closer to study the pictures for several quiet minutes. Shiela Barker was indeed a dark, ravishing beauty, and Ricky's sweet smile in his pictures tore at her heart. She began to realize she was falling deeper in love with Court Barker, partly because he had to be a very strong man emotionally to handle the loss of such a beautiful family. She blinked back tears as she finally turned to face him. "Thank you for sharing this with me, Court. It means a lot." She could see his eyes were misty as he drew her close.

"Are you beginning to understand that I am ready to move on with my life?" he asked gently. "I'm pretty damn sure I love you, Pamela. I want to get rid of any barriers to that love."

Pamela felt her resistance weakening. She had wanted to know how it would feel to be kissed by this man almost

from the first time she met him, in spite of the circumstances. "I do, too," she answered. "And I have to admit, I
care more for you than I've let on. Barry Hennessey is far
removed from my thoughts and my heart now. I've been
fighting this relationship, Court, because it has moved so
fast. But it's pretty hard to fight the way I'm feeling. There
is only one thing left I have to deal with."

Court studied her eyes, feeling lost in their deep pools of
blue. He moved a hand over her back, put his other hand to
the back of her neck and leaned closer, brushing her cheek
with his lips. "What's that?"

Pamela felt a surge of desire deep in places that longed to
be satisfied. "The danger."

"Danger?" He pulled back. "What do you mean?"

"You know what I mean. Your job. I'm not so sure I want
to let myself fall in love with a man who could go out and
get shot tomorrow."

He frowned. "I'm a careful man and I've been paired up
with a very seasoned, crusty old detective who really knows
his stuff. His name is Harold Willard—everybody just calls
him Heck. I'll work together with him most of the time.
Hell, the man is in his late fifties and has been on the force
over thirty years and never been hurt. I told you, Pamela, it
really isn't as dangerous as the movies make it out to be."

She moved her arms around his neck. "Maybe not. But it
only takes one lunatic, and God knows nowadays there are
plenty of them out there."

"Sure there are. And we're trained to spot them pretty
damn easy. We also seldom get ourselves in dangerous situ-
ations without plenty of backup. Honey, the danger is out
there in all kinds of forms. I'm the cop, but it's my wife and
kid who are dead. I could get all bent out of shape worrying
about you getting killed like Shiela was killed, but if we
spend our lives worrying about things like that, we might as
well dig a hole and live under the ground."

She rested her head against his chest. "All right. I'm almost ready to give up. But I still think this has all happened
a little too fast. There is only one thing left I feel we ought
to do before getting any more deeply involved."

He kissed her hair. "What's that?"

Pamela looked up at him, and before she could answer, his mouth covered hers in a deep, delicious kiss that made her groan with desire. His embrace was strong but gentle, his lips so warm. He began to search her mouth lightly with his tongue, and she forced herself to pull away. "You don't play fair."

"I don't intend to." He pulled her closer again.

"Court—" How could she resist another kiss? God, it felt good to be in his arms. She ached to know this man fully, to feel him inside of her, to please him, love him. But she just wasn't ready. She turned away from another kiss, lightly pushing herself away from him. "You haven't let me finish."

He rolled his eyes. "Lord, woman, you're going to drive me crazy."

Pamela ran a hand through her hair, backing farther away. "I'm sorry. There is something I want to do before we—before I—completely lose my senses."

"I'd rather you lost your senses."

Pamela gave him a look of warning. "I'm sure you would. I just—I think we should not see each other for about a month, stay away from each other so we can gain some perspective on this. We've been seeing a lot of each other, and now I've learned more about your family. I just need a little time now, Court. I need to make damn sure I'm doing this for all the right reasons, and I can't really think straight when I'm with you."

He sighed deeply, putting his hands on his hips. "All right. Let's not see each other at all for a while, if that's the way you want it. I told you before that I'd do whatever it takes to prove the strength of this relationship to you. You need room to breathe, to think, I'll give it to you. We'll see how long we can stand being apart. That should show you how much I love you, Pam Hiles, because what I really want is to spend every single day and night with you. Being willing to give up seeing you at all is a big sacrifice for me."

She could see in his eyes that he meant it, and she smiled softly. "I love you all the more for this, Court." She folded her arms, afraid to let him embrace her again, afraid one more touch would make her change her mind. "One month apart. No phone calls, nothing. Will you agree to that?"

"You name it."

She shook her head. "I just want more time to think about this, Court. It really has very little to do with you. It's me, my own hang-ups. I need to stop and get my bearings, and I really do need to consider life with a cop. It can't be easy."

He glanced at his wife's picture, back to Pamela. "Life itself isn't easy, Pamela. It doesn't make much difference what your occupation is."

She nodded. "I know. But I still want to do this, Court. Please don't be angry with me."

He shrugged. "I'm not angry. At least I got that kiss." He smiled teasingly. "And at least I know it isn't my deodorant."

Pamela laughed. "You always smell wonderful." *Very manly,* she thought. *Too manly.* There was so much about him to love, so much about him to attract a woman. Sometimes she worried he was just too handsome and too sweet to be true. Maybe Aunt Nadene was right. Maybe God meant this to be. She looked around the lovely home, deciding she'd better get out before he decided to show her the bedroom. "Take me home?"

He turned and held out his arm toward the front door. Pamela hurried past him and outside, and Court followed, feeling crazy with the want of her, yet loving her all the more for not being an easy woman. Her stubborn determination to be sure this was right was one of the reasons he was so attracted to her. But at the same time he was tempted to grab her back inside. Maybe just one more embrace, one more kiss . . . But then it wouldn't be the same. She would always wonder if she had acted too soon, made it all too easy, and that might affect their relationship. Much as he hated the thought of not seeing her for a while, he was determined to let her have it her way, if that was what it took to win her love . . . and finally to share her bed.

He walked out, and she was already in the car. He closed and locked the door, got in the car, and pulled out of the drive. "Actually this is a good time to try this. Heck wants to work pretty closely with me the next few weeks," he told Pamela. "I can concentrate on my new job." He headed toward her neighborhood, only about ten minutes from his own. "Not that it will be easy to concentrate on anything besides you."

"Well, it might be good for you to get me off your mind for a little while. You need to be sure of this, too, Court Barker."

"Miss Chocolate, I'm as sure of this as I am of anything I've ever decided on. I love you. Period. And if you change your mind about a full month, give me a call, and I'll come running."

Pamela had to wonder if she was crazy for doing this, but she was convinced it was right. She watched the passing scenery, and all too soon he pulled up in front of her apartment building.

"You don't need to walk me to the door," she told him. "I might lose my mind and invite you inside."

He grinned, leaning closer. "How about one more kiss?" He glanced around the small interior of the car. "There's no chance of things going too far in this thing. We'd have to be real contortionists."

Pamela felt herself blushing at what he was suggesting. "I guess we could kiss good-bye, since we won't see each other for a month."

"Remember, that was *your* idea, not mine. If you change your mind, you know how to get hold of me."

His lips were so close, his eyes so tender. She closed her own eyes, felt those lips touching her mouth, parting her lips, his tongue flicking suggestively. Pamela had no doubt this man would be very pleasing in bed, and passion fought reason in her soul. She pulled away and opened the car door.

"See you in a month," she said, tears welling in her eyes. She quickly got out, hurrying up the walkway and inside. She turned at the glass door of the lobby entrance to her apartment building and watched the Camaro pull away. Every part of her body yearned for his touch, ached to feel him inside of her, and she wondered how in hell she was going to be able to sleep tonight . . . and every night for the next month.

"You should call him, dear. Such a fine young man. Why on earth are you so afraid to love again?"

"I told you, Aunt Nadene, I just want to be extra sure this time." Pamela set down her glass of iced tea.

"How can you not be sure of a man like that?"

"It's myself I'm not sure of. Maybe I'm just on the rebound. When you've been hurt, you have to be careful of your feelings."

"Of course you do."

Pamela caught the hint of sarcasm in the words, and she glanced at her aunt over her glass of tea. The woman smiled.

"How long has it been now?"

"Three weeks. I didn't come to visit to have you confuse me about Court Barker, Aunt Nadene."

"Didn't you? Oh, not to confuse, just to advise." The woman's naturally rosy cheeks glowed as she broke a cookie in half. "Tell me the truth now. You're dying to call him, aren't you?"

Pamela smiled. "You're too discerning."

The woman chuckled. "You might as well give in, Pamela. He's a wonderful man, a fine catch. You apparently have good chemistry. Isn't that the way they put it nowadays?"

"Something like that."

"Well, you should call him and see him again. You can't explore a relationship being apart this way. The only way to know for certain is to be together. If everyone stayed away from each other for fear of being hurt, there would be no more marriages, no more children. Life would be terribly boring, wouldn't it?"

Pamela laughed. "I'm surprised at how you talk."

"Why? Because I'm getting old? I remember young love, my dear. It's a wonderful thing."

Pamela felt a sudden urge to cry. Yes, she missed Court dearly, and true love *was* a wonderful thing. She'd never felt this way about Barry. "All right," she said. "I'll call him tonight."

"Good girl. Don't be afraid of your feelings, Pamela. You have to sort them out together, both of you. You're a smart girl, and Court is a smart man. You'll know what's right."

Pamela finished her tea. "Either way, I have to leave. I have an appointment to get my hair trimmed a little." She rose and leaned over to kiss her aunt's soft cheek. "Say hi to Uncle Bill for me."

"Of course I will. He'll be sorry he missed you."

Pamela watched the woman lovingly. "Thank you, Aunt Nadene, just for being you and for being here for me. I'm really beginning to like it here. The job is going great, and through work and through Court I'm making new friends. I hardly think about Barry anymore."

"Well, that's good, because he isn't worth thinking about."

Pamela kissed her once more and walked through the house and outside to her car, a '94 Grand Am. Her heart beat a little faster at the thought of calling Court. There was always the chance he'd decided not to pursue the relationship after all. She could have pushed him right into some other woman's arms. But then he *had* sent her another box of candy yesterday, delivered to "Miss Chocolate," apparently his new nickname for her. She smiled at the memory.

"All right, Court Barker," she muttered as she got into her car. "We'll just see where all this takes us. I miss you too damn much to stay away any longer. I hope you don't have plans for tomorrow night." She started her car and drove off, her emotions tumbling inside like a kaleidoscope, for she knew damn well what would happen the next time she saw him. The ache was too deep, the need too great, and her heart pounded harder at the mere thought of being held by him again, tasting his kiss again.

FOUR

❤

PAMELA STUDIED HERSELF once more in the mirror, casual blue slacks, a blue-and-white-print blouse and a lightweight, white crocheted vest. Pale blue seemed to accent her tan and her eyes. She wore a silver concho belt, silver and onyx choker necklace, and sterling silver earrings that dangled from beneath her hair. She'd worn her hair long and loose, the way she knew Court liked it best.

She left the bedroom of her small three-room apartment and went into the tiny kitchen to check on the chicken baking in the oven and the boiled potatoes on the stove. Court had mentioned several times he liked boiled potatoes instead of mashed or fried. He ordered them whenever he could in a restaurant.

She wanted everything to be just right, felt excited at seeing Court again. The excitement in his own voice when she'd called him yesterday told her all she needed to know. She had not lost him just because she'd refused to see him the last three weeks.

She opened the refrigerator and took out a bottle of wine, pouring herself a small amount in a wineglass. She sipped it, wishing the clock would move faster. She checked her chiffon pie again when she put the wine away, dying to taste it but not wanting to spoil it by having a piece cut out of it. She hoped it had turned out as good as it usually did. She'd bought whipped cream and shaved chocolate to decorate the devilishly delicious chocolate dessert, anxious to show her special recipe to Court.

She smiled at the memory of how she'd met Court, that horrible chocolate mess she'd made . . . and him coming to see her later with a box of chocolates. As she thought back on how they'd met, where things had gone from there, she felt more and more right about their relationship; and the thought of seeing him again sent shivers through her.

She drank a little more wine, then set the glass aside when someone knocked at the door. She hurried to look through the peephole to see it was Court. She flung open the door, and for a moment they just looked at each other, hesitant, both suddenly feeling a little awkward.

"You're even more beautiful than the last time I saw you," he told her. He handed her yet another box of candy.

"And I now have a drawer full of candy," she answered.

They both laughed as she took the candy and he came inside. "Am I dressed okay?" he asked. "Just shorts and knit shirt. You said to be as casual as I wanted."

She looked him over. He wore white shorts, and she noticed his legs were muscled and solid like the rest of him. His white knit shirt was open at the neck, showing dark hairs and a thin, gold necklace. "You look just fine. I told you we'd be eating in, so it doesn't matter how we dress."

She turned and set the candy on a coffee table, and Court could not quite get over what a beautiful woman she was, how she always dressed tastefully, was always gracious. "It smells good in here."

"Baked chicken and boiled potatoes. Nothing fancy, but I tried to cook what you said you like. I've made that special dessert I told you about."

He smiled, coming closer. "Chocolate ecstasy?" He touched her cheek. "It's ecstasy just being here with you. I was going nuts waiting for you to call. Thank God I was off tonight."

Their gazes held, both feeling an aching passion. "I'm glad."

He came closer and moved his arms about her waist. "I

have to warn you I'm required to carry a damn pager all the time, in case of a sudden emergency."

"Well, let's hope it doesn't go off tonight."

He kissed her lightly. "Yeah, let's hope."

Pamela traced a finger over his lips. "I wouldn't want anything to happen to you, Court Barker. Not now that I've made up my mind that I love you, and that no matter what the danger, I can't ignore that love or stay away from you." She saw the sudden joy in his eyes.

"That true?"

"It's true."

He breathed a deep sigh of relief. "And I love you, Pam Hiles."

She closed her eyes, felt his lips touch her own, felt the kiss grow deeper, moved her arms around his neck. He pressed her tightly against his solid chest, moving one hand against her back, cautiously moving the other over her bottom.

Oh, yes, this was right. So right! Why had she doubted she should let herself feel this way again? Fact was, it had never been quite this way with Barry. He'd never had this rather commanding air about him, a kind of control over her, that of a man who knew what he wanted and how to get it. She shivered when Court moved his lips to her neck.

"The chicken," she said.

"I'm not sure I could eat first," he answered. "I've missed you too much." He moved one hand under her bottom lifting slightly so that she grasped his neck and moved her legs around his waist.

Pamela felt a mixture of embarrassment and terrific desire. "You move fast once you get permission," she told him. They kissed again, this one hotter, deeper, more demanding. He held her up against him with powerful arms as though she weighed nothing, and he kissed her eyes when he left her mouth.

"Does that mean I *have* permission?"

How could she keep trying to resist the inevitable? "I think you know the answer to that. The chicken can wait.

Let me turn down the oven and the potatoes. They're only partially cooked. They can wait, too."

"I don't want to let go of you. You might change your mind."

"I won't. I promise."

He kissed her again, then gradually, reluctantly let go of her. Pamela moved away from him and turned down the heat, feeling his eyes on her every move. "I'm nervous, you know," she told him. She gasped when he quickly scooped her up in his arms.

"You think I'm not?"

She laughed lightly, resting her head on his shoulder. "I don't know. You seem awfully sure of yourself."

He carried her into the bedroom and laid her on the bed, moving on top of her. "Hey, up to now I didn't much care about the women I was with. Either they were too easy, which turned me off right away, or I wasn't interested enough to want to go this far. You, Miss Hiles, are special. You're careful, thoughtful, responsible, smart, beautiful—"

"You're going to swell my head."

"And I love you," he added. "And I *want* you. I haven't wanted a woman quite this way in years. I don't just want the pleasure of it. I want *you,* your heart, your soul, your devotion, your friendship, all of it."

Her smile faded, and she touched his hair. "I want the same from you."

He met her mouth again, and both knew the talking was finished. She was lost in him. She breathed deeply with anticipation when he sat her up, removed her vest and her shirt, and took down her bra straps. She closed her eyes as he unhooked the bra and pulled it away, laying her back again, exploring her mouth with his tongue as a big, strong hand moved over her breast, gently fondling, bringing out a charge of passion she had not felt for a long time.

"My God, you're beautiful," he groaned, trailing his lips down her throat to her breasts. He gently tasted the taut nipples, bringing fire to her blood. The more he touched and tasted, the more she knew it was right. He moved downward, kissing her belly, loosening her belt, her slacks. She lay still as he pulled the slacks off, along with her bikini underpants, finally taking her sandals with them as he threw everything to the floor.

She watched his eyes and knew he liked what he saw.

"Don't you move." He removed his shirt, got off the bed, and took off the rest of his clothes. He rummaged in his pants pocket for something.

Pamela smiled at the realization he'd brought protection along. "Pretty sure of yourself, were you?" she asked. She glanced at his nakedness and was as pleased with what she saw as he apparently had been with her. He was buck solid, his thighs, his flat stomach, his broad chest, his hard-muscled arms . . . even that part of him that was swollen for her now.

"I figured I'd better be prepared, just in case you finally came to your senses," he told her, climbing back onto the bed. He hesitated a moment to put on protection, and Pamela closed her eyes, on fire with the realization of what was finally going to happen between her and Court Barker.

Court leaned down to kiss her ankles, her knees, her thighs. She drew in her breath when he lightly kissed her most intimate parts, made his way over her stomach, to her breasts again, and finally her mouth.

"I'd love to do more, but I don't want to scare you off the first time," he groaned between kisses.

She shivered with ecstasy as his hand moved between her legs, and with gentle circular movements he brought forth her deepest passions. She wanted him to touch and taste and explore every part of her, he was so good at what he did. In moments, as she lay there buried in his kisses, his fingers working their magic, she could not help a quick climax, could not help groaning his name, opening herself to him as he moved between her legs.

Every part of him was solid as a rock, and she gasped when he invaded her lovenest, filling her to near-painful ecstasy. He raised to his knees, and she found herself wantonly arching up to him to meet his thrusts. She grasped his muscled forearms, hung on tight, deciding sex had never been this great before. Aunt Nadene was right. She'd been led to Arizona for a reason, and Court Barker was it.

He leaned closer and buried himself deep as he wrapped his fingers in her hair, continuing the rhythmic invasion for several minutes of pure ecstasy until he moaned her name in his own climax. He shivered, resting on his elbows so as not to put his full weight on her. "I didn't mean for it to happen so fast," he told her. "I wanted to make it nice for you, but it's been so long—"

"It was great. Besides, we have all night."

He grinned, kissing her eyes, her mouth. "That's right. We do, don't we?" He sighed deeply. "Gee, all this, and we didn't even need to eat chocolate first."

Pamela laughed. "Just looking at you is all the aphrodisiac I need."

"Same here." He gently pulled himself away. "We didn't even take down the covers."

"It's all right."

He rolled onto his back with a deep sigh of satisfaction. "We'll eat that chicken and just lay around and talk and then we'll spend the night together in bed. I could make love to you all night." He turned on his side and fondled her breasts teasingly. "In fact, I could make love to you again right now."

She breathed deeply, feeling guilty for being so happy. "That's fine with me."

He snuggled against her. "This is nice." He ran a hand over her bare hip. "I can picture us waking up like this every morning."

Pam smiled, kissing his neck. "So can I."

"Do I dare say I even want a new family? That I can picture you as the mother of my children?"

Pamela's eyebrows shot up in surprise, and she moved a leg over his hip. "Is that a roundabout way of asking me to marry you?"

He moved on top of her again. "I guess maybe I'm saying I hope that's where this will all lead someday. I know you'd need time to think about something like that, after what you've been through."

She pursed her lips. "I suppose. But I'm not so sure I'd need all *that* much time."

"Oh, yeah?" He met her mouth in another deep kiss. "I'm

happier than I've been in years," he said with a deep sigh of satisfaction.

She traced her fingers over his lips. "So am I. We—"

Her words were interrupted when his beeper went off. Both of them groaned, and Court flopped onto his back again.

"Do you *have* to answer it?"

He sighed. "I'm too new at this job to ignore a page. I could get myself booted right back to highway patrol." He sat up. "Let's just hope it isn't something that will ruin this perfect night." He walked over to search for the pager under a heap of clothes. "It's showing a phone number to call," he told her. "I'll be right back." He pulled a quilt off the foot of her bed and wrapped it around his nakedness, going into the living room to use her phone.

Pamela listened, hoping he could come back and make love to her again, but his voice quickly grew louder.

"Heck? My God, I can't believe it! I'll be right there!"

Pamela sat up when he quickly came back into the bedroom and grabbed up his clothes. "I'm sorry, Pam, but I have to leave! Heck's been shot!" He grabbed up his clothes and hurried into the bathroom to wash and dress.

"Shot! Oh, Court, I'm sorry! I'll go the hospital with you. Where did they take him?"

"He's at St. Luke's," he answered above running water, "just north of here. Look, if you want to come, you'll have to drive separately. I can't wait for you to get ready. I'm sorry, damn sorry, but it can't be helped."

"I understand." Pamela got up and began picking up her own clothes to put back on. "I hope he'll be all right, Court."

"So do I. I don't know all the details, if they got the guy who did it, what Heck was doing at the time, none of it. All these years with the force, and he's never been shot. Some sonofabitch must have deliberately ambushed him. Heck is usually pretty careful." He came out of the bathroom, tucking in his shirt. He buttoned his shorts. "I knew he'd been working on some drug bust, and I half felt like I should have been with him tonight, but it was my night off, and I sure as hell wasn't going to turn down your invitation."

She walked closer. "I hope you don't blame me."

He pulled her close. "Hell, no."

"Personally I'm glad you *weren't* with him. You might have been shot, too."

He searched her eyes. "I hope this doesn't change your mind about me—about the danger of the job and all."

"We'll talk about it later, Court. You'd better get going. I'll meet you there."

He kissed her lightly. "I'm damn sorry. We'll pick up where we left off soon as we can. I might even still be able to come back here tonight." Reluctantly he let go of her, picking up his pager and hooking it to the waist of his shorts. He stepped into his loafers, which he wore with no socks, took one last look at her. "Come as soon as you can."

"I will."

He nodded, looking her over. "I love you, Pam."

"And I love you."

He turned and left, picking up his keys on the way out. Pam walked to the window of her third-floor apartment, which looked out onto the front lawn. There was still a little daylight left. She watched him get into his Camaro and drive off, and suddenly the whole evening seemed unreal.

"Pick up where we left off," she muttered. "Just like that."

Court Barker had just made love to her. She still felt warm from it and wanted more. This sudden leavetaking was almost a shock, and it rekindled her doubts, making her wonder again if she could handle being married to a cop. How often would something like this happen? What happened to Heck only strengthened her fears about the dangers Court faced.

She went to the kitchen and covered the baked chicken with foil to put it in the refrigerator, then drained the potatoes and put them into a bowl to also store away.

"So much for my nice meal and fancy dessert," she muttered.

She hurried back into the bedroom to finish dressing and make herself presentable. Seeing his friend shot was not going to be an easy thing for Court. She should be with him.

❤ FIVE

$\mathbf{P}$AMELA FOUND COURT in the waiting room for emergency surgery. He was talking with some other men, and she hung back for a moment.

"He's already in custody," one of the men told Court.

"Good," Court answered, his hands balled into fists. "I'd love the pleasure of questioning him myself."

"Don't worry. We've got all we need to convict, weapon and all. The guy wasn't very careful, downright stupid, in fact. Trouble is, he got Heck dead in the gut. He's in good hands, though." The man filling Court in put a hand on his shoulder. "You ought to know it's Jim Lance who's working on him."

Court's eyes widened. "Lance!"

"Court, you know that accident wasn't all the doctor's fault. And he happens to be the best there is for things like this. If Heck lives, it will be because of Dr. Lance, and we'll have him to thank for it."

Court sighed, just then noticing Pamela. He left the men and walked over to embrace her. "It looks pretty bad," he said. He turned, introducing her to the two men he'd been talking with. "Captain Carl Stoner and Lieutenant Webster," he said, his arm around her waist. "This is Pamela Hiles, the lady I told you about."

Pamela could not help noticing the pleasure on their faces

as they looked her over. Both were older men, dressed in street clothes.

"Nice to finally meet you, ma'am," Stoner told her, running a hand through his gray hair.

"Same here," Webster said, putting out his hand. "You've got a great guy here in Court. And we all think it's about time he got serious about someone again and got himself settled down. We've heard nothing but good things about you, and one thing we can see Court was right about. You *are* beautiful."

Pamela could not help blushing a little. "Thank you. I'm just sorry about the circumstances under which we're meeting."

"Well, if Heck pulls through, I'll have a big party at my place," Captain Stoner said. "You and Court can come, and the rest of the force can meet you."

"And tease the hell out of Court afterward," Webster added.

They all smiled, but also felt the weight of the moment.

"We have to go, Court," Webster said. "I suppose you'll want to stay here and wait for the results of the surgery."

Court nodded. "Thanks for filling me in. It's best I don't go to the station and see the bastard who did this just now."

"I agree with that one," Stoner put in. "Just don't take your anger out on Dr. Lance. Heck needs him right now."

Court sighed. "Sure."

The two men left, and Pamela walked with Court to sit down, holding his hand. "What did they mean about not taking your anger out on Dr. Lance?"

Court rubbed his forehead. "He's the one."

"The one?"

"The one who hit and killed Shiela and Ricky."

Pamela leaned back. "My God!"

"Yeah. Now Heck's life is in Lance's hands. Lance happens to be one of the best surgeons in Arizona for things like this, maybe in the whole West, I don't know."

Pamela thought a moment. "Did I hear Captain Stoner say something about you shouldn't be so angry because it wasn't all Dr. Lance's fault? Is there something you haven't told me, Court?"

He pulled his hand away and also leaned back. "The man had been drinking, but the level of alcohol was just over the limit. Shiela had run a stop sign when the accident happened. It was basically her fault, but I always felt that if that man hadn't been drinking, he might have avoided the accident—the way I avoided hitting you a few weeks ago."

Pamela was astounded. "My God, the accident was similar to what happened with me!"

He took her hand again. "I guess that's why you stayed in my mind like you did. I couldn't stop thinking about how I could have killed you the same as Doc Lance killed Shiela."

She closed her eyes. "You should have told me all of it, Court. You can't blame the doctor for what happened. Now I understand why he was given a light sentence and allowed to practice again. It basically wasn't his fault."

He stood up and paced. "All I knew was my wife and kid were dead, and he'd been drinking. I hated him. I still hate him. Now the life of a very good man lies in his hands."

Pamela watched him thoughtfully. "Did you ever stop to think that all things happen for a reason? Maybe Heck's gunshot is God's way of bringing you full circle."

"Full circle?"

"You have to face this Dr. Lance someday, Court. The man has probably gone through considerable suffering of his own. He's apparently a man who cares about saving lives. To feel partly responsible for *taking* a life must have been very hard on him. You both suffered in your own way. Maybe this situation is a way to bring you together and help you forgive yourselves and each other."

He sat down again. "I don't know. Jeez, you sound like a preacher."

She touched his arm. "I don't mean to. It just seems awfully ironic to me that Heck's life lies in Dr. Lance's hands. It could even be you in there, Court. It could be *your* life he's saving, and he'd do it, even knowing how you must feel about him."

He leaned forward, resting his elbows on his knees. "I

guess he probably would." He shook his head. "What a damn mess."

She rubbed his shoulder. "They got the man who shot Heck?"

He nodded. "Apparently Heck got a tip that there was cocaine stashed in coffee cans in crates inside a warehouse on the south side of town. He called for backup, but he went in by himself. He'd been told no one is around there after six, and if he wanted to check out the crates, that was the best time. His backup was to stay a block away and wait for Heck to signal him with a pocket signal we all carry for radioing squad cars. I guess someone had been left to guard the place this time. The damn fool caught Heck rummaging through a crate and shot him without any warning, then ran out. The backup heard the gunshot, saw the idiot running, and chased him down. Thank God nobody else got hurt. I guess the guy's gun jammed, and he couldn't get off any more shots." He hit his knee with a fist. "Damn! If Heck lives through this, I'm going to nail his ass for going in there alone like that. I'll bet he knew about this all along and just didn't tell me about it because he wanted me to keep that date with you tonight. It would be like him to do that."

"Well, we'll just have to pray he'll make it without any major health problems."

He placed his head in his hands. "Yeah."

"That means also praying for Dr. Lance."

He shook his head. "I'll let you do that."

They waited, two hours, three, four. More men from the police force came and went. Five, six. Pamela and Court both ached from weariness. How strange that only hours ago they were making love. It would have been so nice to have spent the night together. Captain Stoner and Lieutenant Webster returned and waited with them. Finally, at three A.M., a tall, graying man wearing glasses and a green surgeon's coat spotted with blood came into the room where they all sat. He removed his cap and shook hands with Webster and Stoner.

"You men here about Detective Harold Willard?"

"Yes." Webster nodded toward Court, who had hung back

a little. "This is Heck's new partner, Court Barker. I believe you know him."

The doctor looked surprised, then almost afraid, guilty. He nodded to Court. "Yes, we know each other." He took a deep breath and looked back at Webster. "Mr. Willard will be all right. I had to remove part of the colon, but not enough to affect anything in a long-lasting way. By some miracle no other vital organs were affected. The big thing now is to stave off infection, but we have a lot of ways of doing that, and in spite of his age, Mr. Willard seems to be a pretty robust man. His heart seems good, very stable."

Everyone breathed a sigh of relief. "Thanks," Webster told the doctor. "I don't suppose we can see him."

Lance shook his head. "It will be several hours before he's awake enough to know anybody is around. You might as well all go home and get some sleep. I'm told Mr. Willard was a widower and has no family close by."

"He's got a son in California," Court answered. "I'll get hold of him."

Lance looked at him, a deep sorrow in his eyes. "Fine." He turned to leave.

"Dr. Lance," Court spoke up. "Wait a minute." He glanced at Webster and Stoner, who took the hint.

"We'll see you at the station tomorrow," Stoner said. "Or, I should say, today. I won't blame you if you come in late." He left with Webster, and the only ones in the room were Court, Dr. Lance, and Pamela, who sat down. This was a moment only for Court and Dr. Lance, who stepped a little closer.

"You already told me what you think of me five years ago, Mr. Barker," the doctor told Court. "I don't need to hear it again, and believe me, if you think I didn't suffer myself over that accident—"

Court waved him off, both men studying each other silently for an awkward moment, Court's jaw flexing with obvious repressed emotions. "The lady sitting over there is someone new in my life," he finally told Dr. Lance. "She thinks I should forgive you."

The doctor folded his arms in a defensive gesture. "I don't

expect forgiveness. All I'd like is for you to realize the whole thing has been hell for me, too. I wish it had been me instead of your family."

Court sighed and turned away for a moment. "I'll admit I wanted to kill you for a long time afterward. But life goes on, Dr. Lance, and I guess we have to learn to live with what it hands out to us." He faced the man again.

The doctor rubbed at his eyes. "I'm not sure I could have avoided your wife's car even if I *hadn't* been drinking, Mr. Barker, and that's the God's truth. How I avoided being badly hurt myself I'll never know. The fact remains I *was* drinking, and I'll always wonder, like you, if that might have made a difference. I've dedicated my whole life to saving people, so it wasn't easy for me to accept being partly responsible for *taking* a life, and that's a fact *I* have to live with."

Court nodded. "Heck Willard means a lot to me. It's damn ironic that you're the one who probably saved his life, so now I'm stuck with having to thank you for that. Maybe you were spared so you could go on saving other people's lives. I don't know. I only know I've decided to go on to the future and quit living in the past. Maybe—" He sighed, looking uncomfortable, embarrassed. "Maybe you have to learn to do the same," he said, looking away. "Something like that. I can't say I forgive you, but I don't hate you anymore."

The doctor glanced at Pamela, and she saw the grateful look in his eyes. He looked back at Court. "That helps. I and my whole family have suffered for what happened five years ago, Mr. Barker. My own wife will be glad to know we had a chance to talk."

Court nodded, finally meeting his eyes again. "Sure."

The doctor hesitated a moment, then put out his hand. "I hope you find real happiness again."

Hesitantly Court took the man's hand, squeezing tightly. "I'm trying," he answered. They held hands for a moment, before the doctor turned and left the room. Pamela walked up to Court, putting a hand on his arm.

"You all right?"

He sniffed, and she realized he was quietly crying. She

embraced him, and he held her tightly for a few minutes while he gained control of his emotions. "Something kind of went out of me when I shook his hand," he said. "All the hatred, I guess."

She squeezed him tight. "I'm glad, Court."

He breathed deeply and quickly wiped at his eyes. "Bet you didn't know a big, strong detective could cry."

"Everyone needs release once in a while. Let's go back to my apartment. I'll heat up some chicken, and we can sleep in each other's arms for a while."

He pulled her close again. "That sounds nice. I love you, Pam."

She kissed his cheek. "And I love you. Let's get some rest so we can come back in a few hours and visit Heck. I've never met him."

"Yeah." He kissed her lightly. "How about that chocolate dessert? Is it ruined from sitting so long?"

"Not as long as I keep it in the refrigerator."

He kissed her again. "I'm not sure I want to eat at all. I just want to go back to bed with you. We'll sleep, make love, sleep, make love—"

"You have to get up and go to the hospital and the station sometime, Court Barker."

"I'll make it . . . sometime." He searched her eyes. "What about this shooting? It doesn't change your mind about allowing yourself to love a cop?"

She sighed in resignation. "I'll admit I had second thoughts when you got that call, but then the last few hours I've had time to think about it, and being here with you, watching you . . ." She hugged him tighter. "I can't just walk away because of the danger, Court. You deserve to be loved, to have a new family. And I love you too much to let *any*thing keep us apart. Living with the danger will be easier than trying to live without you in my life at all." She kissed him lightly. "Let's go. I'll follow you."

He held her hand as they walked out of the hospital, and he led her to her car. She got inside and smiled at him as he backed away. "Drive carefully," he told her.

She nodded. "Yes, sir. And I don't carry chocolate in my purse anymore."

He grinned. "Good idea."

"I suppose I'll have to watch the speed limit with you behind me."

"You bet." He turned and left, and Pamela drove around to his car, then drove off with him behind her. She felt better than ever about her decision now. Court was going to be all right. They both were.

CHOCOLATE CHIFFON PIE

I hope you have enjoyed my first contemporary story. I have written over forty novels about the American West of the 1800s, and if you would like to know more about me and my other books, feel free to write me at 6013 North Coloma Road, Coloma, Michigan 49038. Send SASE, please. You can also learn more about my books by contacting my home page on the Internet at http://www.parrett.net/~bittner.

Following is my recipe for Chocolate Chiffon Pie. This is from a recipe book handed down from my grandmother to my mother and on to me. It is almost sixty years old, which is why many of the recipes are for cooking the "old-fashioned" way. The filling is made from scratch rather than just making an "instant pudding" pie.

1   cup evaporated milk
1   cup water
2   eggs (separate yolks and whites)
8   tablespoons sugar
4   tablespoons flour
¼   teaspoon salt
1   teaspoon vanilla flavoring
1   square chocolate
1   baked pie shell (regular piecrust, not graham cracker)

Melt chocolate over hot water. Add flour, six tablespoons of sugar, and salt. Combine milk and water and add slowly to chocolate mixture, stirring constantly. (A wire whisk works better than a spoon.) Cook this mixture over hot water until thick and smooth. The mixture will seem grainy at first, but the longer it cooks the smoother it will become. Once it thickens, add the egg yolks and cook five minutes longer. Continue to stir constantly with wire whisk. Remove from heat and let cool, then add vanilla flavoring.

Poor cooled chocolate mix into baked pie shell. With electric mixer, beat the egg whites and two tablespoons sugar into a stiff fluff (meringue) and spoon over chocolate pie. (For more meringue, just use more egg whites and a little more sugar.)

Bake meringue-topped pie at 325 degrees for about twenty minutes or until meringue browns slightly. Decorate meringue with chocolate sprinkles or chocolate shavings. This pie is so light and fluffy, the chocolate so creamy, you'll want to eat the whole pie in one sitting. Enjoy!

JUST DESSERTS

Elizabeth Bevarly

For Eileen Fallon,
who, like me, never met a chocolate
she didn't like.
Thanks for so many things.

ONE

"IT HAS TO be here somewhere."

Claire Reidling shoved aside an industrial-sized bag of powdered sugar, a white-enameled basket of Bing cherries, a bowl of milk and a half dozen eggs nestled on a linen napkin, catching the last just before they careened off the counter and onto the floor. When the object of her frantic search continued to elude her, she straightened, settling one hand impatiently on her hip while she knifed the other through the dark bangs poking out from beneath her battered chef's hat. Too late, she remembered that her fingers were covered with flour, and now the few threads of silver that had dared to brave appearance in the shoulder-length tresses would be punctuated by premature white, as well.

"I know I was wearing it when I came in this morning," she continued.

She wiped her hand absently on the front of the white uniform jacket that had been a starched, spotless wonder when she'd arrived at work that morning. Now, as the lunchtime rush was winding down, it was splotched brown in a number of places in varying shades of chocolate, and accessorized with a smattering of cherry-juice red and a splattering of butterscotch yellow.

"At least, I *think* I was wearing it when I came in this

morning." She glanced down at the floor, lifting one hiking-booted foot and then the other. Nothing.

"You ask me, it's a sign."

Her tension shifting from anxious to exasperated in less than a nanosecond, Claire turned to her big, blond companion and expelled a noise that fell well short of polite. "I don't recall asking you," she muttered through gritted teeth.

Gus Brody sat on the counter behind her, seeming even larger than his usual six-feet-two, very solid two hundred pounds in the close confines of the restaurant's tiny kitchen. His position was one that might have precluded a very nasty fall in a less balanced, more unfortunate man. But Gus was just about the happy-go-luckiest person Claire had ever met. In that way, as in so many others, he was her complete opposite. In spite of that—or perhaps because of it—Gus was also her best buddy in the world. Her closest pal. Her lifelong chum.

And at the moment, she was wishing he'd choke on the chocolate bombe into which he had jabbed his index finger down to the second knuckle.

"You know," she said, "that bombe was on its way to the freezer when you came in. And after that, it was destined to be dessert for the dinner crowd tonight. But the Department of Health frowns on serving food that's been tainted by the fingers of stockbrokers. They're kinda funny that way."

Gus feigned shock, covering his open mouth with his hand, gasping melodramatically. "Oh, no. Without even realizing it, I've gone and ruined your beautiful dessert. How embarrassing. Whatever will you do with it now?"

Claire made a face at him. "Gosh, guess I'll just have to find a good home for it, won't I?"

He shook his head ruefully. "Well, since *I* was the one who messed it up, I guess the least I could do is take it home with me and make sure it's properly disposed of. Why don't you wrap it up and put it in the freezer, and I'll stop by for it on my way home from work?"

"Yeah, sure, no problem," she muttered. "That's just so very chivalrous of you, Gus. I think I'm almost moved to tears."

He covered his heart regally with one hand. "It's the least I can do."

"It's what you were planning on all along when you stuck your finger into it, you mean."

"Who, me?" he asked innocently. "Why, Claire, you wound me."

She shook her head at him, but refrained from further comment. She didn't mind him stopping by to have a late lunch with her once or twice a week, seeing as how his Wall Street office was so close, anyway. She only wished that once in a while—or even once, for that matter—he'd have the decency to pay for what he ate. After all, it wasn't like he couldn't afford it. Hey, he *was* the boy wonder of the New York Stock Exchange, if one could believe all the gossip one overheard at the bar when one went in search of a bottle of Vandermint.

And it wasn't like Claire owned the restaurant, either. She was just a lowly pastry chef. A pastry chef who happened to be on extremely good terms with the owner to the extent that said owner had asked for her hand in marriage, sure, but that was beside the point.

"You know," she said, "you keep coming around here and sabotaging my desserts like that, we're both in for it. I'll lose my job, and you'll wind up weighing nine hundred pounds, and then no self-respecting woman is going to want to come near you."

Gus smiled at her, then crooked his finger to scoop as much of the chocolate insides out of the dessert as he could. "Sure they will. If I weigh nine hundred pounds, I'll be booked on every talk show in New York, and chicks will be clamoring at my front door trying to take care of me. The cult of celebrity, dontcha know."

Claire wrinkled her nose at him. "You just better hope all those *chicks* can bake. No one could survive on your cooking." She gripped her own throat with forceful hands and stuck out her tongue, executing a last-gasp-for-breath gag as she did so.

He just wiggled his eyebrows playfully at her display. "I've never had to survive on my own cooking, remember?

Not since I've known you, anyway. Why do you think I moved into your building last year? I got tired of driving all the way across town for dinner."

She sighed in defeat, as always, unable to stay mad at him for more than a few minutes. The two of them had been friends for a long time—ever since she bloodied his nose in a Brooklyn schoolyard the first day of first grade when she caught him trying to discover if black patent-leather shoes really do reflect up. Gus had been impressed that Claire didn't fight like a sissy girl, in spite of her lacy panties. And Claire had been impressed by the fact that Gus had been man enough to cry "Uncle," even when he was being bested by a sissy girl in lacy panties. It was the beginning of the proverbial strange and wonderful relationship, one that had survived more than two decades. No matter what happened in her life, Claire knew she could always count on Gus.

Especially on occasions like this, when she was frazzled with a million things to do and needed someone to come in and cause her more trouble than she had already. Gus was especially good at that.

When he shoved his finger back into the bombe for a second taste, Claire smacked his hand with much gusto. "Do you mind?" she asked, her jaw clenched tight enough to grind glass. "I could use a little help here."

Without even flinching, Gus removed his finger, sucking a generous blob of chocolate off the digit. "Perfect as always," he told her with a satisfied sigh.

As if she needed *his* reassurance, she thought with a smug grin.

"But I still like your bourbon balls better."

Her grin fell, and she gaped at him. "I can't believe you. I can whip up a chocolate Bavarian cream lighter than air, almond truffles that have brought men to their knees, and the most wicked chocolate soufflé this side of the Atlantic, and all you ever want me to make for you are those damned bourbon balls I learned at my mother's knee."

He nodded vigorously. "Ever since you brought them to the Senior Valentine's Day party, I've been in love. You may not know this, Claire, but those bourbon balls are what have cemented our friendship all these years."

"And here I thought it was my sparkling conversation. That and my Chocolate Raspberry Debauchery."

He shook his head. "Your conversation is nothing compared to your bourbon balls."

"What about the Chocolate Raspberry Debauchery?"

Gus cupped his chin in his hand and thought for a moment. "A close second to the bourbon balls."

She growled at him. "Well, you'll have to be satisfied with my conversational skills *and* my Debauchery until Christmas."

"But that's ten months away!"

"You know the drill, Gus. The only time I make bourbon balls is at Christmastime, and only because you and dessert heathens like yourself seem to enjoy them."

He frowned at her. "You know, I liked you a lot better in college, when all you were good at was melting down chocolate chips and Jif peanut butter into that dubious mixture you called fudge."

She tried not to be too smug this time when she grinned back. "Yeah, well, I've come a long way, baby."

"Don't forget my birthday is next month," he reminded her hopefully. "And bourbon balls are nothing if not cheap."

She ignored his request and pleaded, "Gus, would you *please* give me a hand and help me find that ring? Ben will kill me if I lose it." As an afterthought, and not quite under her breath, she added, "Again."

Gus jumped down from the counter, and gazed wistfully at the bombe. With one final swipe, he filled his mouth with chocolate and turned to Claire. "I don't know if I should help you," he said as he licked the last remnants of the dessert from his hand. "Any woman who misplaces her engagement ring as often as you do . . . Like I said, Claire. It's a sign."

"It's not a sign," she denied, restlessly shifting her gaze to a row of pastry tubes lined up like sentries near the oven. "And it's not an engagement ring, either," she added hastily as she scattered the tubes in search of the ring. "I haven't told Ben I'll marry him. Not yet, anyway."

For some reason, she felt it necessary to add the *not yet* part, even though she was beginning to wonder if she'd ever get around to saying yes. In addition to being her would-be fiancé, Ben Summers was also her employer. He owned, managed and was head chef of Lumière, one of Manhattan's most prestigious eateries, a restaurant considered to be *the* place to eat when visiting New York City. Claire was Ben's pastry chef, and more than one food critic had suggested that her end-of-the-meal creations—and *not* his entrées—were actually what had created and maintained the restaurant's continued popularity.

Naturally, though, it was a claim that Claire herself had never really bought into. Although she definitely took pride in her work and knew she was very good at what she did, she couldn't possibly presume that the entire future of Ben's restaurant lay in her powdered sugar–coated hands. To even suggest such a thing was, to Claire's way of thinking anyway, just silly. Ben was a superb chef. People always tended to go crazy for dessert and dwell on the way it ended a meal. It was the sugar high, the well-known aphrodisiac quality of chocolate. That kind of thing.

"If you still haven't told Ben you'll marry him, then why are you wearing his ring?"

Gus's question brought her out of her ponderings, but instead of pointing out that she *wasn't* wearing Ben's ring, not at the moment anyway, because she had lost it—again—Claire said, "Because he asked me to."

Gus nodded knowingly. "And you always do what Ben asks, don't you?"

She thrust her chin up defiantly. This was an old argument, one that Gus seemed to delight in perpetuating. Why, Claire couldn't begin to imagine. In spite of their friendship, her love life was really none of Gus's business. And, anyway, he'd never worried about any of her other boyfriends. It was only since she'd started seeing Ben romantically that Gus seemed to have begun to take an extraordinary interest in her social activities.

"I don't always do what Ben says," she assured him, turning her attention now to a stack of copper pots. After clanging them haphazardly one from one and finding nothing inside any of them, she added halfheartedly, "Just sometimes."

"Always," Gus countered. "You're a disgrace to your gender the way you jump when that guy says 'Move.'"

She dropped her gaze to the floor as she said, "Well, he *is* my boss, after all."

Gus Brody sighed and shook his head at Claire. She'd changed since she'd come to work at Lumière. Ben Summers, that jerk, had her so tied up in knots lately that she didn't seem to know what the hell she was doing. He still couldn't believe she was actually considering marriage to the guy. Didn't she realize she was way too good for that schmuck? Hadn't she figured out by now that the only reason Ben wanted to marry her was to keep her in the kitchen, cranking out chocolate mousses—or would that be chocolate meese?—for the rest of her life? Hadn't it occurred to Claire by now that without her, Ben Summers's restaurant would go straight down the tubes, and that was the *only* reason the guy wanted to tighten the tether around her neck?

Gus sighed. No, he supposed there was no way Claire *could* know those things. Except for the part about her being way too good for the schmuck, Gus only knew about those things himself because of what he'd heard as an investment broker from his restaurateur clients. At best, it was nothing more than gossip and not worth repeating. And at worst, it was all privileged information he had no way of revealing to her without having the SEC come down on him for violation of client confidentiality. Either way, he was better off keeping his mouth shut. Just because *he* didn't like the guy didn't mean Ben didn't have some redeeming quality. Something Claire saw hidden in him that was totally invisible to the rest of the modern world.

All Gus could do in the meantime was stew silently and hope that Claire was smart enough to eventually see what a cretin her employer was and never let him become her fiancé. And he supposed it wouldn't kill him if he helped her find that damned engagement ring. If nothing else, his assistance would enable her to return the obnoxious two-carat monstrosity to its rightful owner when she finally did come to her senses. After all, Ben Summers would never love anyone but Ben Summers. *He* should be the one to own his grandmother's antique engagement ring.

"Okay, where was it the last time you saw it?" he asked her.

She tossed him a doleful expression and held up her left hand. "Duh, gee, right here on the fourth finger?"

He gritted his teeth at her and decided to ignore her sarcasm. "You say you were wearing it when you came in this morning, right?"

She nodded, but her expression was anything but confident about the silent response. As if to illustrate further, she said, "I think so."

"But you're not positive?"

She sighed and appeared to be giving the question much thought. Then she snapped her fingers and smiled. "Yes, I'm positive. I remember catching it on the key when I was unlocking the back door."

Gus lifted a hand to rub his rough cheek in thought. "Yeah, that's a pretty major chunk of ice. Seems likely it would get in the way of a lot of things."

He didn't want to ponder further just what kind of things, specifically, the ring would get in the way of, but for some reason, he couldn't quite squelch the sexual ones his brain began to suggest to him. Dammit, Claire's love life was none of his business, he reminded himself. So why did he get gut-wrenching nauseous every time he thought about her and Ben . . . uh . . . having . . . um . . .

"Gus?"

Only then did he realize that Claire had been speaking to him for some moments, and he hadn't heard a word of what she'd said. "What?" he asked impatiently.

"I said, 'Oh, my God.'"

He narrowed his eyes in confusion. "Why did you say, 'Oh, my God?'"

"Because I just thought of something."

He waited for her to clarify, and when she didn't, prodded, "And that would be . . . ?"

Her green eyes wide with panic, she whispered, "What if it's . . . ?" Again, she hesitated and left incomplete whatever it was that was worrying her.

"What if it's what?" Gus asked, his impatience growing.

She glanced over each shoulder, then lowered her voice even more when she pointed at the big mountain of chocolate still sitting on the counter beside them. "What if it's in the bombe?"

He turned to look at the punctured dessert. "What would it be doing in the bombe?"

She stretched her arms out to her sides in something reminiscent of a shrug, but her expression was anything but careless. "Gus, I've looked everywhere I can think to look. That ring is *nowhere*. Unless it's in the bombe. What if it fell off while I was mixing the ingredients and got baked into the pie, so to speak?"

"Only one way to find out." He eyed the confection adoringly. "You hungry?"

She curled her lip a fraction. "Not for chocolate."

He gazed at her, incredulous. "How can you be a pastry chef and not be hungry for chocolate all the time? That's the only thing I've never understood about you, your loving dessert, but not loving chocolate."

"I can't help it. I'm just not that crazy about it, that's all."

His shook his head, clearly disgusted with her. "What are you, a Communist or something? Not that crazy about chocolate . . . sheesh."

"I don't *dislike* it," she said defensively. "You know that. It's just not my favorite dessert in the world, that's all."

He shook his head at her, completely befuddled. "Claire, I've said it before, and I'll say it again. You are one weird dame, you know that?"

She ignored his comment and pointed out, "Besides, it's lunchtime. Who wants to eat chocolate for lunch?"

His disbelief doubling, he said, "Lots of people. I, myself, packed a couple of Ho-Hos, a bag of Oreos and a carton of chocolate milk for lunch this morning. Of course, that was before I decided to come visit you and see what I could filch here."

She made a *tsk*ing noise and waved him off with a negligent swipe of her hand. "Well, that doesn't surprise me at all. You're a chocoholic of twelve-step proportions, Gus. No normal person would eat that much chocolate for lunch."

He shook his head ruefully. "You are *so* naive. And so wrong. Which is good, because if it weren't for chocolate-obsessed people like me, you'd be out of a job."

She sighed. "At the moment, that's not such an unappealing thought. Oh, my God," she added with a quick gasp.

He wasn't sure he wanted to know, but asked anyway. "What now?"

When Claire turned her attention to him again, her expression bordered on panic. "I just thought of something else."

Again, she failed to elaborate on just what exactly had her preoccupied this time, so again, Gus asked, "What?"

"If the ring isn't in the bombe, there's only one other place it could be."

With only a minor hesitation, he asked, "Where?"

"In something else I've created today."

"Claire, could you help me out a little here? What else have you created today?" As an afterthought, he added, "Or should I ask?"

She twisted her hands together fretfully, twining her fingers anxiously. "Actually," she began, drawing the word out over several time zones, "I mean . . . *technically* . . . I've only made three things today."

Gus tried not to sound like an indulgent nanny speaking to her misbehaving charge as he asked, "I assume the bombe is one of those things, right?"

Claire nodded, her expression still clearly worried. "And seeing as how there were no mishaps with the chocolate-cherry cheesecakes we served for lunch, the ring couldn't have been in one of those."

"So what would the third thing be?"

Her knuckles turned white as she squeezed her fingers together anxiously. "The third thing would be . . . um . . ."

"Yes?"

"Um . . . the third thing would be about five hundred single-serving desserts that Ben is planning to showcase at the Death by Chocolate fund-raiser for the Children's Hospital tonight."

Only hours ago, Claire had been blissfully delighted to be working on Lumière's entry for the fund-raiser. Every year, on Valentine's Day, the local Children's Hospital sponsored Death by Chocolate, a one-hundred-dollar-per-head, by-invitation-only fund-raiser that allowed guests to indulge in unlimited quantities of the most decadent chocolate desserts Manhattan's four- and five-star restaurants could create. It was a premier showcase of the city's premier restaurants, an opportunity for each of them to show off and good-naturedly compete. This was the first year Lumière would be included. And Ben was more than a little anxious that his restaurant stand head and shoulders above the rest.

Until that moment, Claire had been confident her desserts would be the talk of the evening. Now that there may very well be a surprise hidden inside one of them—in the form of a molar-cracking, esophagus-clogging gemstone roughly the size of Rhode Island—she wasn't nearly as self-assured.

Gus shook his head and covered his mouth with his cupped palm. "Where are those five-hundred single-serving desserts right now?" he asked from behind his fingers.

She chewed her lip fretfully for a moment, then said, "On their way to the ballroom at the Plaza Hotel."

"Claire, sweetheart," Gus said, dropping his hand to cover her two, completely unsuccessful at prying them apart, "you better hope like hell that ring is in the bombe."

—♥ TWO

IT WASN'T IN the bombe.
As Claire stood over the counter, eyeing the pile of gelid, gelatinous brown goo that had been a beautiful, flawless (until Gus stuck his finger in it) bombe only moments earlier, her heart began to beat rapidly and a wide, whimpering hole opened in her stomach. Ben was going to kill her. Never mind that she had misplaced an expensive family heirloom that rightfully still belonged to him. Never mind the symbolic implications of losing a ring given to her by a man who intended for it to represent a forever-after kind of love. Never mind that she couldn't recall now whether or not Ben had told her the ring was insured.

What *really* worried Claire at the moment was that the ring in question was doubtless sitting inside a chocolate confection waiting to be sucked into the windpipe of someone who had a whole lot of money to spend on legal representation, and enough social clout to besmirch the reputations of both Claire Reidling and Lumière. This could spell disaster for her relationship with Ben. And worse, it might just end her career as a pastry chef forever.

Oh, no, she groaned inwardly, staring at the mess again. How had this happened?

Her hands, like Gus's, were covered with chocolate. But where she simply made matters worse by wringing her fingers together, he was taking great delight in lifting his, one by one, to his mouth, cleaning each with his tongue with all the relish of a cat with an empty tuna can. Bits of chocolate smudged his mouth and jaw, but he seemed not to notice or care.

"Oh, no," she muttered aloud this time. "It's in one of the desserts that are on their way to the Plaza. It has to be. There's nowhere else it could be." She buried her head in her hands, oblivious to the chocolate that streaked her face and hair when she did so. "What am I going to do? What could possibly make this day worse than it already is?"

As if cued by her miserable question, Ben Summers bolted into the kitchen, obviously mired deeply in that singular mood that Claire had long ago dubbed *piqued*. In another man—someone like Gus, say—she would have used words like *resentful* or *outraged* or *mad as hell* to describe such a state. But Ben Summers was never any of those things. She told herself it was one of the things that endeared him to her, the fact that he never got mad.

He did, however, frequently get piqued. And as much as she tried to convince herself otherwise, that did tend to irritate her a little sometimes.

"Claire!" he bellowed, catching sight of her before she had a chance to duck beneath the expo line.

"What?" she chirped, cursing the heat she felt seeping into her face. It was then that she realized exactly what she had done when she'd hung her head in her hands, and that her face was covered with the remnants of what had promised to be a beautiful dessert. She cursed again, this time out loud.

"Dammit," she hissed as she snagged a linen towel from a nearby hook and began to rub ineffectually at the chocolate smearing her face and hands.

Ben approached her quickly, then seemed to forget what he had intended to tell her when he caught sight of Gus. "What the hell is he doing here?" he demanded. "I've told you I don't want anyone other than employees in the kitchen."

"I know, Ben, and I'm sorry," she began. "But Gus was just—"

"Leaving," Gus supplied with a wicked smile and brief wiggle of his chocolatey fingers in farewell.

"Oh, no, you don't," Claire said, collaring him with a sticky fist. A sticky *left* fist.

She remembered then that the normally all-too-obvious ring was missing from her left hand and quickly released Gus for fear that Ben would notice the glaring absence, even through layers of chocolate bombe. Jamming her left hand behind her back, she turned and grabbed Gus's silk necktie with her right instead.

When he gazed down at the small hand clutching his tie, his smile fell. "You know, that's a Hermès tie you're smearing chocolate all over. Not to mention a Hugo Boss shirt."

"Too bad," she snapped under her breath. "You're not going anywhere until you help me get this settled. Sit tight."

"Children," Ben interrupted the byplay. His dark eyes—nearly the same espresso color as his hair—skimmed them both briefly from head to toe and flashed with impatience. Then his gaze wandered behind them, to what was left of the bombe. "Good God, what happened?" His gaze settled on Claire. "I could have sworn I asked you to make that bombe to serve twenty, not to give yourself and your best friend facials."

Claire bit the inside of her cheek to keep herself from saying something she knew she'd regret later, then planted her foot firmly on top of Gus's to keep him from doing likewise.

"Sorry, Ben," she said coolly. "We had a little bit of an accident."

Gus nodded. "Yeah. That bombe exploded. Is Claire good or what?"

Ben narrowed his eyes at each of them in turn. "The dinner crowd will start trickling in within a matter of hours," he told Claire. "I assume you have something else to serve them for dessert?"

Gus leaned close and whispered, "I could run down to the deli real quick for a big bag of Ho-Hos, if you want."

Claire lifted her foot and brought it back down on his—

hard. "It's okay, Ben," she assured her boss. "I'll stay late and fix something else. Those chocolate liqueur cups don't take long. And I'll whip up some white chocolate medallions, too. Those went over well when we tried them before."

Ben eyed her skeptically. "Will that still give you time to get to the fund-raiser tonight?"

"Yes." But it sure wasn't going to give her much time to get there early and search for his ring, she realized dismally.

"All right, then," Ben said. "As long as you're sure you can get there on time, then the liqueur cups and medallions will be fine."

"What was it you wanted to see me about?"

He studied her thoughtfully for a moment, and Claire wasn't sure she liked the speculative little gleam in his eye. Yet he said nothing more to belabor the subject, and she exhaled a small, silent sigh of relief.

"Did those desserts go out to the Plaza?" he asked instead.

She nodded vigorously. "Uh-huh. Mel is driving them over as we speak. I gave him strict instructions on setting up the booth, along with an illustration of how I want the presentation to look. He'll be fine."

Ben nodded back. "Good. I don't have to tell you again how important this is, do I?"

She shook her head. "No, you don't, Ben." But she knew he was going to do it, anyway.

"This could make or break Lumière. It's our big chance to show everyone once and for all just what a superior restaurant this is. Everyone who's anyone is going to be at the Death by Chocolate function tonight—"

"*I'm* not going to be there," Gus muttered. "*I* wasn't invited."

"—and a lot of them," Ben continued blithely, "haven't eaten here, though why they haven't tried us yet, God only knows."

"God only knows," Claire concurred obediently, ignoring the sound Gus made under his breath.

"This could be our one chance to pull them in. It's absolutely *essential* that we make a good impression tonight, Claire. It's vital. It's crucial. It's imperative. It's . . . it's . . ."

"Really, really important?" Gus supplied.

Ben eyed him venomously.

"I understand, Ben," Claire assured him. "And don't worry. I'll be right there the whole time, schmoozing and fawning and singing Lumière's praises. You have nothing to worry about. I promise you."

He didn't look in any way convinced.

"Ben," she cajoled. "Trust me. What could possibly go wrong?"

Gus made another rude sound under his breath, and when she recalled that she was still clutching his necktie, Claire fiercely tightened her grip to stifle any other outbursts he might be entertaining.

Again her almost-fiancé's gaze wandered from one to the other, but eventually, Ben seemed placated by her reassurances. "All right," he told her. "I'm counting on you to take charge of the booth. But I'm going to be there, too, working the crowd. Between the two of us, we ought to be able to pull this off beautifully. But I'm warning you, Claire, if one tiny little thing goes wrong, it could spell the end for Lumière. And for *both* our futures in this business."

"Nothing will go wrong," she said, hoping she only imagined the little squeak in her voice that seemed to punctuate the statement.

"You had better hope so." With that, Ben nodded once and turned on his heel, exiting in exactly the same way he had entered. "Now let's get dinner on the road!" he called out over his shoulder to the entire kitchen staff as he passed through the doors leading to the dining room.

"Nothing will go wrong," Gus mimicked when the other man was safely out of earshot. He turned to Claire, yanked her hand free of his tie and settled his hands on his hips. "Nothing except that some major society matron, who just so happens to be a client of F. Lee Bailey, is going to choke to death on a two-carat diamond engagement ring that belonged to Ben's grandmother, and he's going to have his ass hauled into big claims court dragging you behind him."

"Shhh," Claire bit off loudly. "Will you just . . . shush. Don't *even* say it."

She began to scrub furiously at her face with the linen towel again, glaring at Gus as she did so. He wouldn't be able to go back to work looking like he did. He was an executive at one of the most conservative brokerage houses in the country, and she was fairly certain that having chocolate blotching your hundred-dollar tie, glazing your solid-gold cuff links and smudging your eyebrows were all probably pretty major fashion don'ts. The state of his appearance didn't seem to bother Gus, though. He simply went back to sucking the remnants of the bombe from his fingers quite cheerfully.

When Claire was fairly certain she'd cleaned herself up as well as she was likely to, she found a clean spot on the towel and started swiping at Gus's face.

"Ow," he said, jerking his head away. "Don't be so rough."

"Oh, stop it," she said playfully. "You like it when women rough you up. You told me so yourself." She wet the towel with her tongue and went after a particularly large splotch of chocolate near his lip.

"Oh, gross, Claire," he objected, circling her wrist with one hand and pulling it away from his face. "Cut it out. I wouldn't even let my mother do that."

"Don't be such a big baby. You can't go back to the office all covered with chocolate."

She made another lunge for the stains on his face, but he held her wrist fast and wouldn't let her budge. His gray eyes glittered menacingly, his lips thinned to a tight line and his rough jaw twitched viciously, one solitary time. Claire wasn't sure what she'd done to make him so mad, but there was no mistaking his anger.

"What?" she asked softly. "What did I do?"

For a long moment, Gus didn't say a word. He only met her gaze evenly and frowned at her. Finally, Claire yanked on her wrist again, if for no other reason than to snap him out of his sullenness. But instead of easing his ill humor, her gesture only seemed to increase it. Gus tightened his hold and suddenly jerked her forward, the action making her lose her balance and fall against him.

"Gus . . ." she objected, splaying her free hand open over his chest to steady herself. What she encountered below her fingertips was solid muscle, warm and rigid and in no way yielding. And for some reason, her heart began to hammer hard in her rib cage, erratic, yet somehow rhythmic, rattling her to her very core. What on earth was happening to her?

"Gus?" she asked again, her voice soft and unsteady. "What's wrong?"

"Are you really gonna marry that guy?"

The question threw her, but not because he'd never asked it before. She'd probably heard him voice it at least once a week in the two months that had passed since she'd agreed to wear Ben's ring while she considered his proposal. No, this time what caused Claire to stumble over a reply was the way in which Gus had delivered the question. He sounded almost . . . hurt. Like she'd betrayed him somehow. His voice was quiet and controlled, but there was no mistaking the anxiety there.

"I . . . I don't know," she stammered honestly. "I . . . I'm still thinking about it."

His eyes remained dark and flinty as he asked, "Well, how long are you going to think about it before you give him an answer?"

She scrunched up her shoulders and dropped her gaze, finding that what she saw at eye level was her own hand spread open over his very impressive chest, covering the spot where his heart was beating rapidly beneath her fingertips. And for some reason, the sight bothered her. A lot. So she dropped her gaze again and stared at the floor.

"I don't know," she repeated softly. "I told Ben I'd give him an answer by March."

"That's only two weeks away."

"Yeah . . ."

"So, what are you going to tell him?"

"Like I said. I don't know."

When Gus remained silent to her response, she lifted her gaze warily to his face once again. His eyes were still stormy, and his mouth was still set in a rigid line. He still looked angry.

She knew he didn't like Ben Summers. And she pretty much knew why. Gus had always been more than a little protective of her. Because of their longstanding friendship, he was, in many ways, like the big brother she'd never had, the kind who was always looking out for her welfare. Plus, Ben was fastidious, a perfectionist of the highest order, and had a tendency to get uptight over the smallest inconvenience. Ben was all the things Gus wasn't. And the two men just seemed to rub each other the wrong way.

But Ben could be a real sweetheart, too, Claire knew. At work, he did indeed worry about even the smallest detail, and he did tend to lose his temper easily. But when the two of them were alone, Ben devoted every scrap of his attention to Claire. He treated her as if she were the most delectable, most mouth-watering confection he'd ever had the pleasure to observe, one that he wanted to savor in every way. With the attention he paid her, Ben made Claire feel beautiful and interesting and important.

That was the Ben that Gus had never met, because the only time the two men ever encountered each other was at the restaurant, when Ben was being his professional self. And that was a real shame. Because that other Ben—the personal Ben—was the man that Claire was considering for her potential spouse.

"Well, you better start thinking about what you're going to tell him," Gus told her. "Because Ben's going to be expecting an answer soon."

He released her wrist and cupped her jaw, rubbing his thumb gently, she presumed, over a spot of chocolate she must have missed on her cheek. It was an affectionate gesture, and not at all unlike him. But for some reason, it felt different from the simple touches he normally offered her in friendship. And for some reason, it made her feel strangely warm and gooey inside.

"And so will I," he added softly.

Claire didn't recall him having asked her a question that required an answer, but before she could point that out, he dropped his hand back to his side, and his eyes cleared of their troubling discontent. As quickly as the odd moment had erupted, it disappeared, and everything seemed normal again.

Or almost normal, anyway. Gus sure did smell nice today.

"Is that a new cologne you're wearing?" she asked, tucking her head into the curve that joined his shoulder and neck to inhale an idle sniff.

"I . . . uh . . . I think they call them men's fragrances now."

He took a step in retreat, clearly bothered by her sudden interest, and found himself backed against a convection oven, which was, fortunately, not in use at the moment. When he realized he could go no further, he pressed himself against it as much as he could, obviously striving to put as much distance between himself and Claire as he possibly could.

How very odd, she thought. He'd never done anything like that before.

She took a step forward to match his backward and nestled her head into his shoulder again. "Okay, is that a new men's fragrance you're wearing? You smell wonderful."

"Thanks," he said, still obviously suspicious. "It's called Ravage."

She burrowed closer still, cupping one hand behind his neck. "Mmm . . . it's nice."

She inhaled deeply, rising on tiptoe to get better range, and found that her mouth was rather close to his ear, close enough to whisper sweet nothings to him, if that was what she had a mind to do. Which, of course, it wasn't. Not in the way most women whispered sweet nothings to men, anyway. Why would she want to do something like that with Gus? Her nearness to him now had nothing to do with wanting to . . . well, be near him. She just had a plan she needed to put into action, that was all. And the sooner she got things rolling, the better.

So, with that in mind, she adopted the sultriest tone of voice she could conjure up and purred, "I'll bet all the women at the Death by Chocolate fund-raiser tonight would go wild for that scent."

Too late, she remembered just what a quick study Gus was. Grasping her shoulders, he set her at arm's length and gave her a scolding look any gym teacher would be proud to call his own.

Rats, she thought. She should have known he wouldn't be stupid enough to fall for that one.

"Oh, no you don't," he said. "Now I get it. Now I know what you're up to. And it isn't going to work. I have a date tonight. With that new consultant in Legal. So just knock it off, Claire. I am *not* going to go to Death by Chocolate and help you look for that damned ring."

"Oh, come on, Gus." She folded her arms irascibly over her abdomen.

"Forget it," he finally reiterated. "I'm not going. You got yourself into this. You can get yourself out. I wasn't invited anyway."

"Gu-uh-us," she whined, shaking her whole body with frustration. "You can be my guest. You have to come with me. I need your help. Now that I have to stay here late to substitute something for the bombe for the dinner crowd, I'm not going to have time to get to the Plaza early to check those desserts."

"Too bad."

"Please?"

"No."

"I'll pay your way."

"Uh-uh."

"I can't handle five hundred desserts on my own. I'll get insulin poisoning or something."

"I told you . . . I have a date. With that new consultant in Legal. The big blonde, Claire. Remember her?"

"Yeah, yeah, yeah. I remember. Camille. The one with the big hooters."

"That's the one. I've been trying for weeks to—"

Suddenly, the gist of Claire's comment sunk in, and he eyed her narrowly. "Wait a minute. Did you say you can't handle five hundred desserts on your own?"

She nodded petulantly, her lower lip thrust out like a child's. But her gaze was focused on the fingers she had tangled again in his necktie. "Uh-huh."

Her admission piqued his interest. "As in, you can't *consume* five hundred desserts on your own?"

Again, the nod. "Uh-huh."

"Let me get this straight," he said, needing full clarification. "You want me to come with you to help you *eat* five hundred chocolate desserts tonight?"

Finally, she looked up at him, hope flickering to life in her eyes. "Well, yeah. How else are we going to find that ring? We have to get to those desserts before anyone else does. It's essential, Gus. It's vital. It's crucial. It's imperative."

She smiled at him, dragging the fingers of one hand up and down along the length of his necktie. For some reason, his heart did a funny flip-flop when he witnessed the gesture, and his lungs suddenly seemed empty of air.

"In short," she concluded, "it's really, really important."

This time Gus was the one to nod, but he hesitated a moment before speaking, not certain his voice was going to behave. Man, it was getting hot in here. Then again, they were standing in the middle of a kitchen. Still, there was something very . . . odd . . . about this particular heat. Like, why was he only feeling it in certain parts of his body? Certain, rather intimate, parts of his body?

Pushing the realization away, he focused instead on something more tangible, something more important. "So," he began, "just out of curiosity, which of your delectable little specialties did you prepare for the big chocolate feast tonight?"

She smiled, smoothing out a spot on his shirt where he sure didn't see any wrinkles. "For starters, my Chocolate Raspberry Debauchery, of course."

"Of course."

She leaned in closer, seemingly to straighten the knot in his tie, but actually drawing much nearer than was actually necessary for that. Her voice was fairly a purr as she continued, "I also made those chocolate orange truffles you like so much."

A wide, searing heat licked at his belly, and although he tried to convince himself that it was a result of the chocolatey promises with which she was plying him, he had to concede that there might be just a bit more to it than that. "Oh, yeah," he murmured, the words sounding low and throaty as they emerged from his mouth. "Those are *so* good, Claire. So good."

She nodded, her nearness causing the silky softness of her dark hair to brush against his chin. "And something new," she told him. "Something . . . special."

Somehow, he managed to silence the groan he felt erupting from the depths of his libido. "Lay it on me, baby."

She dropped her voice to a whisper as she revealed, "Something I've named Chocolate M-cubed."

He drew in a slow, languid breath and held it. "Sounds very . . . intriguing . . ."

She skimmed her fingertip slowly across his chin, her voice a bare whisper as she told him, "It's chocolate . . . mocha . . . mint . . . macadamia."

"Oooooh, Claaaaire . . ."

"It's . . . it's a torte."

"Mmmm . . . yessss . . ."

"I just *know* you're going to love it, Gus." She licked her lips before adding, "I made it with you in mind."

"And, uh . . . you . . . uh . . . you say you'll actually pay my way to this thing, too?"

"Of course I'll pay your way. Isn't that the least I could do?"

When she phrased it like that, Gus realized he could think of quite a few things that she could do that might bring him around to her way of thinking, and plying him with chocolate was only the beginning. How strange, he thought further, to be making *those* kinds of plans with Claire.

He grinned, shoving *those* thoughts away, instead making a mental note not to eat anything for the rest of the day, just to be sure he'd have room in his stomach for his half of the banquet that was to follow that evening.

"Well, hell, Claire," he said as he dropped his hands to cover the ones still fiddling with his necktie. "All you had to do was ask me. Of course I'll go to the fund-raiser with you. It will be my pleasure. I'll just tell Camille that we'll have to make it next week. But tell me. Just what does one wear to consume mass quantities of chocolate?"

─♡ THREE

CLAIRE WAS HURRYING out of the restaurant to go home and change when she heard Ben call out her name again. But this time when he beckoned to her, his voice held none of the anger or impatience that had been so prevalent earlier. He was smiling when he caught up with her at the kitchen door, the one that led out to the street, and she hesitated before shrugging into her jacket.

"Claire, I'm glad I caught you before you left," he said, taking her hand gently in his.

Her right hand, fortunately, she noted with relief, shoving her left behind her back as unobtrusively as she could. "What's up?" she asked.

"I just wanted to double check with you on your arrival time at the fund-raiser tonight. I'll be getting there right about the time that the function begins, but I'm not planning to spend much time at the booth. That will be your job."

"No problem," she assured him. "We . . . I mean *I* plan to get there about an hour before the event begins. I'm on my way home to change now."

"Oh, I don't think it's necessary to get there that early," Ben objected. "Take a little time for yourself this evening. You've earned it."

"Thanks. But I'd rather get there early. Just in case. That

way I can take care of any last minute problems that might arise."

His smile fell a little. "I thought you said there won't be any problems."

Nice going, Claire, she thought to herself. "Oh, there won't be," she promised hastily. "Nothing major. But you know how these affairs are. There's always *something* that comes up at the last minute. Besides, I want to make sure Mel created the presentation correctly. I'd like to be there early. Just in case."

His smile returned, and she breathed a silent sigh of relief. "All right. I know how conscientious you are where your desserts are concerned." He squeezed her hand softly and brushed his lips lightly over her cheek, the small contact warming her from fingertip to nose. "It's only one of the many things I love about you."

She smiled back. Ben often told her he loved her. But for some reason, Claire hadn't quite been able to take that step herself. She told herself she did love Ben. She must, if she were considering marriage to the man. But something still prohibited her from voicing it. She wasn't sure what. She supposed she just wanted to be absolutely certain about her feelings before freeing them into the open where everyone could see.

"You're sweet," she told him, cupping her hand gently over his rough jaw before giving him a brief, chaste kiss on the lips.

When she pulled away, her gaze met his, and as always, she was struck by his abundant good looks. Ben Summers was the epitome of tall, dark and handsome; his eyes, the color of bittersweet chocolate, made even more compelling by the presence of long, sooty lashes, his deep brown hair kissed with red highlights and bound at his nape in a ponytail. With his sunken cheeks, his fashionably unshaven jaw and his Versace suit, he might as well have walked out of the pages of *GQ*.

There were times when Claire honestly wasn't sure what a man like him was doing courting a woman like her. Not that she was a slug or anything, she knew, but Ben was just so . . . so . . . so gorgeous. So sophisticated. So self-assured. So different from her. Then again, she reminded herself, everyone said opposites attracted. And why was she worried about his good looks? His looks, of course, were what had attracted her initially. His attentiveness and deep regard for her were what kept her tied to him even more closely.

And her love for him, she reminded herself. That kept her by him, too. Didn't it? Of course it did.

"Look," he began again, "I know I haven't been easy to live with over the past few weeks. But this whole Death by Chocolate thing is an incredible opportunity—for both of us—and I'm very anxious to make a good impression tonight." His voice was gentle when he added, "I mean, I don't have to tell you again just how important this is, do I?"

"No, Ben, you don't."

But, of course, he did anyway. And when he was through, Claire told him, "I understand. I feel the same way about it. It's as important to me as it is to you."

"I know it is, sweetheart. That's the point. I'm sorry if I've been a little rough on you. You know I don't mean it."

"I know."

"You're more important to me than anything in the world."

"I know that, too."

"I don't want to do anything that will risk chasing you away. So I apologize for all of my bad behavior. After tonight, I promise I'll settle down."

"It's okay, Ben. I know you don't mean it when you get stressed out. And I don't take it personally."

"Good." He gave her hand another gentle squeeze, then asked, "Have you thought any more about . . . you know?"

Claire chewed her lip, striving for a suitable stall that wouldn't sound so much like . . . well . . . a stall. "Um, not really. It's like you said," she added hastily when she saw his crestfallen expression. "This whole Death by Chocolate thing has been consuming my thoughts and concentration. I just haven't had much of a chance to think about anything else lately. Even your proposal."

He nodded, but seemed in no way reassured. "I under-stand. But, Claire?"

"Yes, Ben?"

His expression was both hopeful and fearful as he asked her, "You'll give me an answer by March, won't you? You did promise, after all."

When Claire had promised him that, March had been more than two months away. Now it was scarcely two weeks away. And she was no closer to a decision now than she had been before.

In spite of that, she forced herself to say, "By March, Ben. I promise."

Later that evening, when Gus walked down the two flights of stairs that separated his West Village apartment from Claire's, he wasn't thinking about a lot of things. He wasn't thinking about lost rings or blondes with big hooters or idiot fiancés or even the way Claire's green eyes earlier that day had seemed so full of . . . what? So full of something strange and wonderful when she'd been trying to flatter him into helping her eat her way through the Lumière booth at the fund-raiser tonight.

What he *was* thinking about was chocolate. Mountains of chocolate. Rivers of chocolate. Or, at the very least, five hundred single-servings of chocolate, half of which— maybe more—he would be required to inhale in the name of friendship.

Was this a great country, or what?

And when Claire opened her front door and stood before him in just about the most form-fitting, least skin-covering, itty-bitty black dress he'd ever seen, there was something else Gus wasn't thinking about. He wasn't thinking about how she was his best friend in the whole, wide world and he had no right to be wondering what she was wearing under-neath that dress—if anything. Instead, he was thinking he should be ashamed of himself for the ideas parading through his head.

"Thanks for getting here early," she told him. "We really do have to hurry if we're going to get there early enough to check those desserts." As she turned her back to him and strode into her living room, her posture offered him an even more remarkable view.

The seams of her smoky-black silk stockings were perfectly in line, delineating very well what he realized were surprisingly nice gams. He'd never noticed before what long legs Claire had. She was such a tiny woman—a good foot shorter than he—that long legs had just seemed an impossibility. Now, Gus understood he'd been paying her a grave disservice all these years.

She had a nice back, too, something else that he'd never noticed before, but something that the dress revealed quite obviously now, thanks to the transparent film of black fabric covering her arms, shoulders and upper back. Somehow that sheer scrap of see-through shading seemed more revealing than no fabric at all would have been. With her normally loose hair woven into a tight French braid and bound at the bottom with a big black bow, and with her eyes and mouth made seemingly larger—and more succulent, he thought strangely—by the enhancement of cosmetics, Gus scarcely recognized her.

Usually, Claire was the queen of flannel, a woman who claimed more plaid shirts in her wardrobe than a lumberjack, a woman to whom dress shoes were anything that didn't lace up above the ankle. She was the earthiest woman he'd ever known, one who bypassed the brightly lit makeup counters of department stores without even noticing them, and only held charge cards for Eddie Bauer and Land's End. He'd never known her to even *own* a little number like the one she was wearing now, let alone actually put one on with the intention of going out in public.

"Uh . . ." he began eloquently as he crossed the threshold into her living room and closed the front door quietly behind himself.

Claire spun back around to face him, fixing a big, silver hoop in one ear. "What's wrong? Are my seams crooked?"

She glanced back over one shoulder, an action that caused her back to arch and her breasts to thrust forward. Normally, Gus would have looked away rather than risk seeing Claire in such an erotic, provocative pose. It was nothing personal. He just didn't like to think of her in such a ... such a ... well, in *that* way. This time, however, he was helpless to do anything but ogle her.

It was that damned dress, he thought. A freakin' goat could be wearing that thing and it would make a man question his impulses.

"Uh ..." he tried again.

"Gus?" she asked, turning her attention back to him, her expression puzzled.

There was that voice again, he realized, squeezing his eyes closed in a fruitless effort to shut out the images the sensual tone evoked. It was sultry and slow and sweet, and it made him want to roll naked and sweaty on the floor with its owner. It was the same voice Claire had used earlier that afternoon when she'd been trying to coax him into coming to the fund-raiser with her. At that time, for just the briefest of moments, he'd almost fallen for it. He'd almost believed she was actually entertaining thoughts about him she had no business entertaining. Of course, it hadn't taken him long to figure out what she was really up to and realize she was faking the whole thing and playing him for a sap.

But she had him now, sap that he was, melting like butter in the palm of her hand, ready to follow her to the ends of the earth. Why was she using that voice again? Just what the hell was Claire up to? And why was he suddenly wishing she'd use that voice more often?

"Uh ..." he began a third time. He gave himself a mental shake and forced himself to say, "Your seams are fine. You look ..." Helplessly, he lifted his hand to his forehead, as if trying to ward off a fever. "Claire, you look incredible."

She smiled brightly. "Thanks. You look pretty amazing yourself."

He glanced down at his charcoal Alberto Briani suit, his white Armani dress shirt, his Valentino necktie and his Gucci loafers. There had been a time in his life when his flannel shirt collection had rivaled Claire's and denim was the only other fabric with which he was familiar. Nowadays, it seemed that every article of clothing he wore had a name. An

Italian name, at that. And although he would have preferred something considerably more no-nonsense, like Butch or Duke or Hank—or even Levi Strauss—there didn't seem to be any fashion designers who preferred those monikers. Even his Breitling watch sounded just too-too posh for an otherwise regular guy.

"Thanks," he responded as he glanced up again, wondering for the first time in years when he'd started feeling so comfortable in such clothing. "But it's nothing special. It's the same thing I wear to work every day."

"You still look amazing," she told him. "You're a handsome guy, Gus. Deal with it."

"You don't have to flatter me, Claire. I've already promised to go with you."

She made a face at him. "I'm not flattering you. I mean it. You look really nice."

Still suspicious, he nevertheless replied, "Thanks. So do you."

Her expression turned anxious as she rolled her shoulders uncomfortably. "Feels funny to be wearing something like this. It itches. But I had to buy something for the fund-raiser. You don't think this dress is too much?"

She spread her arms open wide, the gesture hiking the tight skirt even higher on her thighs than it was already. Suddenly, Gus wanted nothing more than to rush right to her, and lose himself forever in the embrace she seemed to be offering.

Try *not enough*, he thought. "No, no," he said quickly. "It's great. You'll be the talk of the party."

Her smile fell some. "Yeah, I just hope it's not because I get taken out in handcuffs when someone chokes on Ben's ring. I mean, I don't think the organizers of this party meant for Death by Chocolate to be taken literally."

He crossed the room to stand in front of her, dropping his hands to gently cup her shoulders. The fabric of the dress was cool, but the skin beneath it was warm, its easy heat seeping into his fingertips like welcome rain after a long drought. Gus tamped down the errant thought and tried to smile reassuringly.

"It'll be fine, Claire," he said softly. "We have more than an hour before the thing gets started. We'll find the ring before anyone even gets there, and no one will ever be the wiser."

"Yeah, but all those little holes from our fingers will just ruin the presentation."

He squeezed her shoulders encouragingly. "If that actually becomes necessary, we'll just poke everything from the bottom. No one will ever know. I promise."

She chewed her lip and met his gaze evenly, and he wondered why he'd never noted the tiny flecks of color that radiated from her pupils into her irises, a starburst of gold against green. He noted too that she smelled wonderful, a light mixture of sweet and spicy that seemed perfect for her somehow.

When he realized he was pressing his fingers into her shoulders and pulling her closer, he immediately dropped his hands to his sides again and strode toward the kitchen, tossing over his shoulder a request for a beer that he didn't even want.

"Sure," she told him. "There's some in the fridge. But hurry, okay? We have to get going."

"Quit worrying," he reminded her again as he reached the kitchen. "I'm ready when you are."

"Just give me another couple of minutes," she called out.

Gus used the distance and momentary separation to gather his thoughts, forcing himself to stand in front of the open refrigerator door for some moments on the outside chance that the frigid air wafting from inside might cool the heat winding through his body. Even though he had no desire for one, he bent to snag a long-necked bottle of beer from the bottom shelf. As always, he took the cold brew's presence for granted even though Claire didn't drink beer herself—she just always kept some on hand for him. He pressed the sweaty brown bottle to his forehead, thought about Claire's lips, and sighed heavily.

It was going to be an interesting night.

When he returned to the living room, she was nowhere to be seen. He heard drawers opening and closing in her bedroom, so he moved to the sofa, figuring she was going to be a while, in spite of her repeatedly uttered need to rush. Women always took a long time when the occasion called for massive bodily maintenance. At the moment, she was probably trying to shove as much of her bathroom as she could into one of those little black purses that were barely the size of an electron. Suddenly, he was grateful for his beer, after all.

Her return was much faster than he'd guessed it would be, but she was indeed carrying a tiny black bag, along with a lightweight, black velvet coat, both of which Gus assumed must be other recent additions to her wardrobe. Without asking, he plucked the coat from her grasp, holding it up to help her into it, and an odd thrill of delight wound through him at the brilliance of her answering smile.

"Thanks," she told him. "Gee, you're so chivalrous. This is actually beginning to feel like a real date."

For some reason, he felt it vitally important to put an immediate halt to any kind of misinterpretation she might be entertaining in response to his gestures. So, as he settled her coat carelessly over her shoulders, he responded, "Hey, you *are* paying my way, after all. And if I'm going to be such an expensive date, the least I can do is make sure you get your money's worth."

He'd meant for the statement to be light and jesting, but when Claire turned around to face him again, she wasn't smiling. Instead, she almost looked as if he'd hurt her feelings somehow.

"Yeah, well, just find that ring for me," she said unhappily, "and we'll consider it even."

"We'll find the ring, Claire. Don't worry."

She expelled a sound of utter dread, and her expression became even more troubled. He hated seeing her so distressed, and without planning to, he dropped his hands to her shoulders again, this time surrendering to the impulse to draw her close. For God's sake, he told himself. It wasn't like the two of them had never hugged.

But somehow, before they even completed it, he knew there was going to be something different about that hug.

And he was right. As everything else had been since that afternoon, holding Claire close now felt . . . funny. Not funny ha ha, but funny strange. And as hard as he tried to figure it out, he couldn't quite pinpoint when the changeover had occurred. It may have been mere hours ago, or it may have been weeks ago. Perhaps even before then. But suddenly, somehow, an odd friction had erupted between them. And he couldn't for a moment understand it.

Gently, he set her at arm's length and tried to smile, but he knew instinctively that his face never quite managed the display. So he gave up trying, and instead retreated to an old, familiar action. He fitted his hand to the small of Claire's back, then wordlessly guided her to the front door. As they passed through it and into the hallway, he draped his arm casually over her shoulder and lightly around her neck to playfully pull her close, the way he used to do, back when they were in college. In response, Claire looped her own arm around his waist, falling naturally into the familiar embrace. That action, more than anything else, seemed to comfort them both.

But try as he might, as they approached the stairs, Gus still couldn't make himself sound encouraging as he said, "Will you please relax? There's nothing to worry about. We'll be getting there early, after all."

♡ FOUR

T HEY DIDN'T GET there early.
    In fact, thanks to the heavy Manhattan traffic, a double-parked delivery truck and some unexpected roadwork in a place where there had been none only a day before, Gus and Claire arrived fifteen minutes after the appointed time for the event's unveiling. Fortunately, it being a society function—New York society at that—very few people arrived on time. And because Lumière's booth was situated on the side of the ballroom opposite the official entrance to the affair, only a handful of the restaurant's desserts had been sampled by the time the two of them bolted across the room to position themselves like sentries in front of the table.

A table that looked absolutely splendid, Claire realized with a sigh of both relief and satisfaction as she approached it. Her assistant chef, Mel, had followed her instructions to the letter, and the desserts were arranged in just the right way that would show them off to their perfection. The chocolate orange truffles were tucked into shiny foil pastry cups and looped about in an elaborate coil. The portions of Chocolate M-cubed were nestled on white paper doilies and scattered in a seemingly haphazard arrangement. Behind the single servings was an example of the torte as it looked when whole, a gorgeous two-tiered cake with chocolate lattice trim, topped with a pile of fresh mint leaves and a scattering of macadamia nuts. Beside that, her famous Chocolate Raspberry Debauchery was a sight to behold, a cloud-light confection dusted with powdered sugar, each serving topped with a fresh, dewy raspberry.

She really, really hated what she was going to wind up doing to that table tonight. If she and Gus didn't find Ben's ring immediately, then by the time they were finished, the whole arrangement on the table was going to look like World Chocolate War Three had broken out. Maybe she should have made another bombe. Somehow, it just seemed appropriate for the occasion.

As she drew nearer the table, she realized that even though she and Gus weren't *that* late for the event, unfortunately they were still too late to stop a rather rotound woman dripping with midnight blue sequins who was reaching for a sample of Chocolate Raspberry Debauchery. As she came up behind the woman, Claire had to force herself not to slap her jewel-encrusted hand in an effort to make her release the confection. She was tempted to tell the woman that she was a representative from the Health Department, and that they'd received an anonymous tip that there was a potential for rat droppings in the dessert, but she managed to clamp her mouth shut just in time and force a smile instead. Her false cheeriness must have been convincing, because the woman actually smiled back.

"You'll love it," Claire promised her.

"I've heard so much about Lumière's desserts," the woman said before taking a generous bite of Debauchery.

Around the mouthful of chocolate, she sighed dramatically, then rolled her eyes to the back of her head and lifted a hand to her heart. Claire was about to spin her around and administer the Heimlich maneuver, until she realized the woman's reaction was one of ecstasy, and not asphyxiation.

So Claire held her breath to see if the woman would chip a cap instead. But when she just closed her eyes and murmured a lengthy *mmmmm* in response, Claire managed to release the breath she hadn't been aware of holding.

"Oh, that's scrumptious," the woman said after swallowing. "I must take one to my husband."

This time, Claire was unable to help herself as the woman reached for another serving. This time, she did indeed smack the woman's hand, then slapped her other hand over her own mouth in horror at her reaction.

"Oops," she muttered. "Um, I mean . . ." She tried to smile again, knowing her expression was anything but happy. "Uh . . . that is . . . just one serving to a customer," she finally finished lamely.

The woman frowned at her. "I thought this was all-you-can-eat for the price of entry."

"Uh . . ." Claire hedged.

"A rather hefty price of entry, too, I might add, even if it *is* for a good cause."

"Yeah, well . . . you see . . ."

The woman arched her penciled-in eyebrows and pursed her overly outlined lips in thought. "Perhaps I should take this up with the event coordinator," she said, turning in a huff. "Or even the manager of Lumière."

"Oh, no." Claire stopped her, taking the woman's wrist lightly in her own. "Here."

With her other hand, she plucked one of the larger servings of Debauchery from the table, hoping the woman didn't notice when she shoved her index finger into the side facing her in a last ditch effort to find Ben's ring. Unfortunately, judging by the incredulous gape the woman threw her in response, Claire figured she'd been nowhere near discreet when she'd performed the action.

"I'm sure your husband will love this," she said half-heartedly, extending the confection toward her.

The woman threw up her chin in regal disgust and yanked her wrist free. "I think not," she said as she moved on to the next table.

Claire watched her leave, then eyed the dessert in her hand. No use letting it go to waste, she thought, as she popped the confection into her mouth. As a precaution, she bit down carefully, rolling the tasty delight around on her tongue for a minute before swallowing, just to be sure it wasn't doubling as a jewelry box. The smooth, raspberry-flavored chocolate melted in her mouth as easily as butter, the faint traces of Chambord warming her throat and insides as it settled in her belly.

Perfect, as always, she noted as she sucked the last bit of chocolate from her thumb. Okay, so maybe she could see why people loved chocolate so much. As Claire had told Gus earlier that day, it wasn't that she disliked it, just that there were other sweets she liked better. Like key lime cheesecake, for instance. And creme brulée. And banana Popsicles. Of course, she'd never admit that last one to anybody. Other than Gus, anyway, who knew all of her weaknesses.

The moment the blue-sequined woman was out of sight, Claire heard his not so muffled chuckle behind her. "Oh, nice going, Claire. That was real professional."

She spun around to find him shaking his head at her in disappointment. But, unwilling to have a repeat of the encounter she'd just botched completely, she moved behind the table and began to lift the desserts one by one, hastily inspecting each to see if any bore obvious signs of having a surprise inside that might prove shocking.

"Get over here and help me out, will you?" she demanded. She lifted a serving of Debauchery in one hand and a chocolate orange truffle in the other, shifting both hands up and down as if weighing the two desserts. "See if you can tell if any of these are a carat or two heavier than they should be. Maybe we won't have to resort to sabotage after all."

She watched as he pulled back the sleeves of his jacket and shoved up his cuff as far as he could without unbuttoning them and making himself obvious. Gus really did have the nicest hands, she thought idly, forgetting for a moment that she was supposed to be thinking about Ben and his ring. Gus's hands were big and blunt-fingered and utterly masculine. In spite of his working behind a desk and in front of a computer terminal, they weren't soft or fleshy. Thanks to a very active athletic life, his hands had been beaten and bound on more than one occasion, and he still harbored a number of faint scars from school-yard mishaps.

Claire had always been of the opinion that a man's hands were great indicators of his social and sexual prowess. She'd always known Gus to be socially gregarious. Funny, though, that she'd never much considered his sexual skills.

Not since that bizarre New Year's Eve seven years ago, anyway. But then, that had been an extremely unusual circumstance, one brought about by too much champagne consumption for both of them and not enough contact with the opposite sex for either of them. It had been an occurrence that neither Claire nor Gus had ever had the inclination to repeat. And really, when she got right down to it, not all that much had happened. Not really. Just a kiss. Just one innocent little kiss, that was all.

Okay, not so little, she conceded quickly, dropping her gaze from Gus's hands. By the time they'd come to their senses and put a stop to that one kiss, the two of them had been half-undressed and gasping for breath, with Claire straddling Gus's middle in a way that was anything but innocent. But in the scheme of things, it really wasn't that big a deal. Not really. Not much. Still, they'd both agreed to never think about or discuss it again, and they hadn't.

At least, Claire hadn't. Hadn't *talked* about it, anyway. Not at length. And certainly not with Gus. She hadn't thought about it, either. Not more than a few times, at any rate. Not lately. And since Gus hadn't mentioned that night—not to her anyway—she assumed he didn't think about it, either.

So why was she thinking about it now, when she had a far more important quandary facing her? And why, suddenly, did she want to put more into that night than had really been a factor at the time?

"Well, what was I supposed to do?" she hissed under her breath in response to his earlier question, pushing her other errant thoughts away. "Risk having her choke to death?"

Gus eyed one of the truffles, then evidently not wanting to take any chances, shoved it whole into his mouth. "No," he said after he'd swallowed it. "But you might have at least done something more convincing and less obvious than smack her hand and shove your finger into her dessert."

"Like what?"

He picked up a piece of the Chocolate M-cubed and sent

it on the same trip the truffle had taken, swallowing it with a heartfelt sigh. "Like fake a stumble and let the thing go flying," he said afterward. "That's what I would have done."

She continued to survey her desserts, but expelled a derisive chuckle. "Oh, right. A food fight. That's exactly what we need to do. Turn this event into a Three Stooges movie."

He, too, continued to study each of the sweets instead of meeting Claire's gaze. "Oh, and what would be so terrible about that, I'd like to know? That's the problem with you women. You just don't appreciate good slapstick."

"Not when it could cost me my job—and maybe the man I'm going to spend the rest of my life with—no. You're right."

"Oh, and you don't think sticking your finger into someone's dessert isn't going to show up on your employee evaluation? Even if you *do* agree to marry Ben, he's not likely to let you get away with something like that."

She had been holding a serving of Debauchery up to the light, but tossed it back onto the table to settle her hands on her hips instead. Then she glared at Gus with all her might.

"Why do you always do that?" she demanded.

He, too, stopped what he was doing and turned to meet her gaze, glower for glower. "Do what?" he snapped back.

"Why do you always adopt that tone of voice whenever you mention me being engaged to Ben?"

"What tone of voice?"

"That totally sarcastic, contemptuous tone of voice."

"I don't—"

"Yes, you do. And I want to know why."

When he said nothing in his defense, she crossed her arms over her midsection and glared harder at him. "You were never bothered by any of the guys I dated before. Jeez, you always got along great with all the guys I dated before. But Ben's presence in my life has turned you into a rabid watchdog. Why do you constantly go out of your way to malign Ben?"

He set his mouth rigidly, as if trying to keep his response from flying out of his mouth against his wishes.

"Gus?" she asked. "Answer me."

"Because . . ." he hedged.

"Because why?"

He expelled an exasperated breath of air and said on a rush of words, "Dammit, because you've never threatened to marry any of the guys you dated before, that's why."

She arched her brows in surprise. "What?"

The one-word reply was all she could think to say. And by the time she did come up with something more elaborate— namely, and rather lamely, *What do you mean?*—another philanthropic chocolate lover approached the table and reached for a serving of Debauchery. A serving of Debauchery that Claire hadn't yet inspected.

"Oh, no," she said, halting the man's hand as it hovered over the dessert. "You don't want that one. You want . . . uh . . ."

She glanced about frantically, then snagged a piece of Chocolate Mocha Mint Macadamia from Gus's hand. When she realized she still had no idea if it contained the ring or not, she panicked. In spite of the fact that she was standing stock-still, she faked a stumble and sent the confection flying across the room. She had rather hoped she would lose sight of it in the light of the crystal chandelier sparkling overhead like a cache of diamonds, and not have to worry about where it landed. Instead, she saw it hit a white-haired woman squarely in the back of the head.

"Oops," she murmured sheepishly, ducking behind Gus when the woman spun quickly around, her hand flying to the back of her coiffure.

"Nice shot, Sandy Koufax," Gus whispered beside her. "I think you're ready for the World Series now."

"Miss . . . ?"

Claire and Gus both had forgotten the tuxedo-clad man who looked like he might be the CEO of a very important company—or maybe the president of the bank that held Ben's mortgage for Lumière—and who had picked up a serving of uninspected dessert despite her protest. And when they both turned to look at him at the same time, they both remained silent, as if each had forgotten the question.

"Yes?" Gus finally asked, having indeed forgotten what the man wanted to know.

The man eyed him warily in return, then cocked his head toward Claire. "She said I didn't want this. Why not? Is it unsafe?"

Gus thought fast. "Uh . . ." Well, maybe not as fast as he would have liked. "Um . . . no . . . no, that's not it at all. Everything here is safe. Perfectly safe. As safe as . . . as . . . as the vault at Tiffany's." He heard Claire wince at his analogy, but ignored the response. Instead, he reiterated, "Of course these desserts are safe. It's just that . . ."

"You look like more of a truffle kind of guy," Claire interjected.

Gus threw her a withering look. No man in his right mind *ever* wanted to be referred to as a "truffle kind of guy." It did nothing to impress the chicks.

"What my associate means," he tried again, "is that this—" He picked up a serving of Chocolate M-cubed that he had earlier squeezed and managed to remold into its original shape—mostly. "This is something completely new. We're very anxious to get the public's opinion."

Claire's expression when she looked at Gus indicated she clearly was impressed with his response. The man's expression when he looked at the dessert indicated he clearly was not impressed with it.

"I'd rather have this," he said, nodding at the chocolate he still held.

Gus reached across the table, snatched it from his hand and slapped the mangled confection down in its place. "Trust me," he cooed. "You'll love this."

The man lifted the dessert Gus had forced on him, wiped his thumb over his index finger at a smudge of chocolate left behind, and then moved along to the next table. As he went, and without bothering to even try and hide his action, he dropped the serving of Mocha Mint Macadamia onto the floor and kicked it beneath the table.

"Well, I never . . ." Claire began indignantly. She spun around to face Gus. "Did you see what he did with my dessert?"

"I saw."

"Did you get a chance to check it for Ben's ring yet?"

He nodded.

"Oh. Okay." She returned her gaze to the table and sighed heavily. "The crowd is starting to pick up. We've already missed the opportunity to check a dozen desserts that people have picked up too quickly for me to stop them. So I guess there's only one thing left to do."

"Yeah," Gus told her as he noted the figure cutting a very quick, very deliberate swath through the crowd toward them. "Run away."

She glanced up at Gus, then followed the direction of his gaze. "Oh, no," she muttered, dropping her head into her hands.

"Oh, yes," Gus assured her.

Coming right toward them at a pace just under Mach speed was Ben Summers, dressed to the nines for the occasion in his designer tuxedo and black collarless shirt, sans tie. A sapphire stud winked in his right earlobe, and his long hair was swept straight back from his forehead with some kind of shiny goo and caught in a ponytail at his nape. He looked cool and intent and professional.

But he did *not* look happy.

—♡ FIVE

OKAY, SO BEN Summers was a good-looking guy, Gus conceded as the man approached the table, his gaze clearly fastened on Claire and no one else. But Gus still couldn't see what she found in Ben that might cause her to consider marrying the guy. Simply put, he just wasn't her type.

"He's staring at you," Gus said. "I don't think he's seen me yet, so I'll just . . ."

Without completing the sentence, he dropped to his hands and knees and crawled beneath the table, yanking the skirt of the tablecloth closed behind him. He sure as hell hoped Claire appreciated what he was doing for her. No way was he spooked by or hiding from Ben Summers. He just figured his own presence at the function would cause Claire more trouble than she already had, and if hiding meant Ben went a little lighter on her, then the least Gus could do was retreat for a little while.

Not to mention his new position would afford him an opportunity to consume all the servings of chocolate he'd inspected and been able to fashion back to their original—more presentable—states. He reached into his jacket pocket for a handful of truffles, bit indelicately into the first, then settled himself in to shamelessly eavesdrop on the conversation that quickly escalated above him.

"Claire, what the devil have you been doing over here?"

"I don't know what you mean, Ben."

"Mrs. Singleton just approached me and said you put your finger in her dessert before serving it to her."

"Oh, don't be silly. I'd *never* do something like that. My finger slipped. It was just an accident. It could have happened to anyone."

"But it didn't happen to anyone. It happened to *me.*"

What a jerk, Gus thought, peeling the foil away from another truffle. He shoved his thumb into the dessert down to his knuckle, and when he encountered nothing but creamy chocolate, popped the confection into his mouth like Little Jack Horner.

Claire's voice was tight as she replied, "No, Ben, it didn't happen to you. It happened to *me.*"

"Well, it might as well have been me. Anything that happens to you is a reflection on me. How could you let that happen?"

Blah, blah, blah, Gus thought, tuning out the verbal exchange as he bit into a rather large portion of Chocolate M-cubed. He closed his eyes and enjoyed every second as the confection melted its way down to his belly. Boy, Claire sure did have a way with chocolate. Too bad she couldn't judge men the same way she did her recipes.

What the hell did she think she was doing, considering marriage to a guy like that? How could she even be *attracted* to someone like Ben Summers, let alone think about spending the rest of her life with him? She'd never gone for guys like Ben— all preened and pruned and prissy and perfect. Guys who got manicures once a week and who said they loved Marcel Proust for his symbolism and who only listened to fusion jazz, whether they understood it or not.

She'd always preferred regular guys. Guys who played rugby in Central Park on the weekends and who thought they *might* have heard of that Lord Byron guy—he played basketball for UNLV didn't he?—and who were die-hard fans of The Band. Guys who Gus had liked a lot.

Or rather, guys who had been a lot like Gus.

And that's when the crux of his problem with Ben Summers hit him. Hit him like a ton of bricks. What bothered him about

Ben wasn't just the fact that he wasn't anything at all like Gus. It wasn't just those obvious differences of opinion that rubbed Gus the wrong way. Hell, he didn't mind if people went about their lives differently. To each his own, and all that.

No, what really bothered Gus was the fact that, for the first time since he'd met her, Claire had made clear that what she liked in a man—liked well enough to consider marrying him—bore absolutely no resemblance to Gus. And that didn't sit well with him. It didn't sit well at all.

Crouching there in the dark beneath a chocolate-laden table, munching absently on a serving of Claire's Debauchery, Gus forced himself to reevaluate his motivation in harboring such a hefty resentment toward Claire's would-be fiancé. Just what did it matter to him who she married? he demanded of himself. Why should he care who she chose for her permanent mate? Unless, of course, Gus just didn't want to see her married. And the only reason he could fathom for why he might not want Claire married was that maybe, just maybe—

"Ben, will you please calm down?" he heard her voice rise above the table, sending his admittedly jumbled thoughts scrambling into even more erratic pieces.

"Calm down?" Ben sputtered in response. "Claire, look at these desserts. They look horrific. What have you been doing to them?"

"Um . . . I think Mel might have gotten sideswiped in the van on his way here. That's the only reason I can come up with for their . . . uh . . . their rather unusual condition."

"Unusual?" he barked. "*Unusual?* Claire, they've been mangled beyond recognition. Some even have holes in them, as if someone's been sticking their fingers into them."

"Wow," she said, her voice way too overflowing with disbelief. "You're right. I didn't notice that. Who do you think could have done such a thing?" After a telling pause, Gus heard her add, "I bet it was one of the other pastry chefs, trying to sabotage our entry."

Ben sounded more than a little doubtful as he muttered, "What on earth are you talking about?"

But Claire was obviously warming to her hastily formed theory, her voice dripping with enthusiasm as she said, "Yeah, that's it. That new guy over at Starling's—Jean-Michel, who's been claiming he's Cordon Bleu, but I sincerely doubt it—has been badgering me about this event for weeks."

Gus waited to see if Ben would go for it, then heard the other man's thoughtfully uttered, "Has he?"

"Yeah. And you know something else?" Claire's voice was very animated now, as if she were really getting into the lie.

"What?"

"He's not actually French. Not many people know this, but he's from Quebec. He even speaks French like a Canadian. But that doesn't stop him from telling everyone he learned his trade in the *petit boulangerie* in Nice that's been in his family for centuries."

"Are you saying he's a liar?"

"And evidently a saboteur, too."

Gus shook his head ruefully. If Claire didn't stop laying it on so thick, she was going to wind up with a defamation suit on her hands.

"I'll go talk to him," he heard Ben say.

"No, wait!" Claire cried.

"What?"

"Maybe . . . maybe you should let me handle this, Ben. Jean-Michel and I go way back."

"Oh?"

"Yeah. Waaaaaaaay back. Ever since cooking school, when my Chocolate *Bête-Noir* completely overshadowed his mango chutney pork loin during finals."

"All right then." Ben's voice was surprisingly calm. "I'll let you handle it. But, Claire . . ."

"What?"

"I don't have to remind you again how important this is, do I?"

"No, Ben."

But Gus knew Ben would anyway. And he did. So Gus used the time to finish off the last of the chocolate he'd pilfered from the table, waiting an extra couple of minutes after Ben's voice trailed off before sticking his head out from beneath the table again.

"Is he gone?" he asked as he emerged.

Claire frowned at him. "Yes, he's gone. No thanks to you."

Gus rose and rolled his shoulders around, arching his neck to work out a few kinks. Then he brushed himself off, straightened his necktie and muttered, "Man, I thought he'd *never* leave."

"Gus . . ."

Before she could do or say anything that might alter his focus from the task at hand and return him to the very strange workings his mind had been experiencing a few moments ago, Gus interrupted her. "You're right about the crowd picking up. It's twice the size it was when we got here. If you want to find that ring, Claire, there's only one thing left for us to do."

Her expression clouded, and she lifted a hand to rub at the furrows forming on her forehead. "What's that?"

"We're just going to have to start eating our way through all this chocolate before anyone else has a chance to."

She glanced down at the table where hundreds of desserts still sat harmlessly awaiting consumption. "I was afraid you were going to say that. And I've already been eating two for every one that I poked my finger into. I'm going to have chocolate overload if I eat any more."

"Here," he said, picking up a serving of Chocolate Raspberry Debauchery. "Have some more of this. This stuff is fabulous."

She glanced first one way and then the other, as if fearful that Ben were still watching her from a hidden roost. Then she met Gus's gaze levelly and took the dark, rich confection from his hand. "I know it's fabulous," she said softly. "Not only have I had about ten servings of it tonight, in case you've forgotten, I created it."

She bit delicately into the dessert, though whether because she feared breaking her tooth on a two-carat diamond, or because she revered the confection as sacred, Gus wasn't sure. Probably the latter, he decided as he consumed another serving for himself. Chocolatiness really was next to godliness in his book.

Next she reached for a generous helping of Chocolate M-cubed, sampling it with a bit more gusto than she had the Debauchery. He watched as her eyelids fluttered downward over her green eyes, and something in his gut tightened when her tongue darted from her mouth to catch a crumb that lingered on her lower lip. Oh, man, he'd been hoping to help her find that crumb himself. With his own tongue.

The realization stopped him in his tracks and stayed his hand as he reached for another truffle. He hadn't had a sexual thought about Claire since that New Year's Eve debacle seven years ago. Well, not really. Nothing *too* licentious, anyway. Not very often. Not recently at any rate. But suddenly, sex and Claire were linked uppermost—and irrevocably—in his mind. When the hell had that happened? And why?

Shaking his head to clear it, he grabbed the truffle he'd been aiming for and shoved it whole into his mouth. He remembered then that he hadn't eaten anything since lunch. That must be the explanation for why his thoughts were so jumbled tonight. Yeah, that was it. He was starving, and his brain was addled as a result. Therefore, the solution was to eat. Eat until he was completely stuffed, and all the synapses in his brain were functioning properly again. And how convenient that he had an entire table before him set with some of the most delectable delicacies ever created.

"Mmmmmm," Claire murmured beside him, holding up a truffle she'd just bitten into herself. "Oh, wow. These turned out even better than I thought they would. Try this."

Even though he'd just consumed one, Gus opened his mouth obediently when Claire held up the chocolate for him to sample, the bite already taken from it suddenly the most erotic sight he'd ever beheld. She skimmed the confection lightly over his lower lip before tucking it into his mouth, the brief, seemingly harmless gesture pooling heat in his groin like he'd never felt before. When her fingers followed the chocolate into his mouth, he clamped his teeth down gently on them, skating the tip of his tongue over each of her fingertips before closing his lips over them entirely, exerting just the tiniest pressure as he tried to suck them further into his mouth.

Claire's cheeks flamed bright pink at his gesture, her pupils expanding nearly to the edge of her irises. God, why had he done that? he demanded of himself as he slowly, reluctantly, opened his mouth to release her hand. It was as if he hadn't been able to help himself. As if what he'd just done were something he did all the time. *Oh, hi, Claire, how are you today? Want to go for a cup of coffee? Mind if I suck on your fingers?*

"Yeah, that really is good," he murmured when he managed to swallow his share of the truffle. "But this," he added, his eyes never leaving hers as his hand fumbled across the table for a serving of the Chocolate M-cubed, "this is even better."

He lifted the dessert to his own mouth first, taking a bite as Claire had done. Then he plucked the sprig of mint from the top and brushed it gently across his mouth, running the tip of his tongue idly over each of the fragrant leaves. Without a beat of hesitation, he extended it to Claire's mouth and raked it leisurely across her lower lip.

Her eyelids fluttered closed again, and her lips parted fractionally. "Oooohhh," she moaned. "That *is* good."

"But you haven't even tasted it yet," he said softly.

"Yes, I have," she whispered back.

Gus shook his head slowly, even though he knew she couldn't see him. "Not the way you should. Not the way you're going to."

She opened her eyes at that, and they seemed different somehow. Heavy-lidded, larger, more expressive, brimming with something Gus couldn't quite identify. He lifted the half-bite of torte to her mouth then, cupping his free hand beneath her chin to catch any errant crumbs. He felt his own lips parting as she bit into the dessert, and all he could do was wish that it were him, and not the sample of torte, that she was consuming whole.

And then, just as he had hoped, a stray crumb did tumble into his palm. Immediately, he scooped it up with his thumb and lifted both to Claire's mouth again. Without resistance, she parted her lips and he tucked the crumb inside, and when he did, she nipped the pad of his thumb with her teeth. The gesture was completely unexpected and utterly arousing. He felt himself grow hard and heavy, and all pretense and playfulness fled.

Their gazes had locked intimately, and he found that he couldn't look away. His heart kicked up a funny rhythm as he realized that all he wanted to do right now was crawl under the table again. Only this time, he'd pull Claire under there with him, figure out how that little black dress unfastened and—

"Um, Claire?" he asked, interrupting his own train of thought, his voice sounding strangled and not a little desperate, a reflection of the tumultuous uproar currently rocking him to the very edge of his being.

She seemed not to notice, though, because he could tell by her own expression that she was every bit as distracted as he. "Yeah, Gus?" she replied, her voice low and husky and full of something he was afraid to speculate about.

"I . . . uh . . ."

An idea erupted into his brain, and with his gaze pinned to hers, he raised one hand to eye level for both their inspections. Then, with the other, he began to wrestle free one of the cuff links from his shirt. While Claire watched, he dropped it onto the floor, where it *ping-ping-ping*ed for a moment before rolling under the table.

He smiled. "I think I lost a cuff link on the floor when I was under the table. Would you mind giving me a hand to look for it?"

Claire smiled back. Evidently no longer bothered by the specter of the missing ring—or maybe having even forgotten about it completely—she nodded eagerly, her eyes growing darker, the pink stain on her cheeks deepening to two bright spots of red.

"Sure, Gus," she said softly. "Sure. No problem. Under the table, you say?"

He curled his fingers around her wrist and lowered himself to his knees, pulling her down alongside him. "Yeah, I think it was over in this direction somewhere . . ." he began, moving them both toward the gap in the tablecloth. "Under here . . ."

The darkness beneath the table beckoned to him. And so did something about Claire. Slowly, Gus moved forward, tugging an unresisting Claire along behind him, still not quite sure where he intended to take either of them, but in a very big hurry to get there.

♥ SIX

THE MOMENT GUS had her close enough, he pulled Claire into his arms, the motion so quick and adamant that he fell backward onto the floor, pulling her down on top of him. He felt hard and warm beneath her, and she splayed her hands open over his solid chest to steady herself. Then she realized she didn't need steadying, because Gus had lopped one arm soundly around her waist, had cupped his other hand behind her nape, and was pulling her head down to his. For one long, searing moment, he only met her gaze levelly with his, his gray eyes turbulent, as if giving her the chance to push him away if she wanted.

She didn't push him away.

Instead, she lowered her head to his even more. But before she could make contact, he closed the distance himself by lifting his own head to meet her, fastening his mouth over hers. Without warning, a rush of memory overcame her. That one night, that single solitary encounter the two of them had shared seven years ago, raged up in her mind and her libido with the speed and ferocity of a raging bull. She remembered what Gus tasted like, what he felt like, what he sounded like when he was aroused. Then she realized that what she was experiencing wasn't a memory at all. It was real. It was now. It was Gus.

She wrapped her arms around his neck and held him as

close as she could, almost fearful that he would try to pull away once he realized what was going on. She wasn't sure what madness had come over her to suddenly want him in such a way, but she was helpless to stop herself. His lips were warm, moist, yielding. His mouth was hot and tasted so sweet. He smelled vaguely of some fragrant, spicy after-shave and strongly of chocolate. There was no way she could resist him.

His mouth on hers was masterful, his lips fluid and deft and utterly arousing. He dragged his tongue along her lower lip, pausing to taste the corner of her mouth before delving deeply inside her. She gasped at the intrusion, an action he used to his fullest advantage, then she tangled her tongue with his, as eager to consume him as he seemed to be her. His hand at the small of her back spread open, then dipped lower, skimming down to cover her fanny and push her more intimately into his waiting warmth. When she felt him ripening hard and full beneath her belly, she was helpless to stifle the groan that bubbled up from somewhere deep inside her.

The small sound was Gus's undoing. He still couldn't believe he was holding Claire so intimately, still couldn't understand the suddenness or nature of whatever had overcome them both, still couldn't get enough of her. As close as he held her, she still seemed to be too far away, as if the thin barrier of their clothing was a wall three-feet thick instead.

So he urged his hand lower, opening his palm over the warm silk covering her thigh. Yes, that was definitely better. His fingers danced over her soft flesh, dipping first one way and then the other, finally settling at the hem of her dress. He played with the soft fabric for a moment, mustering his courage to follow his instincts, fearful that if he made one wrong move, Claire would pull away from him forever. He tore his mouth briefly from hers and met her gaze, his breathing ragged and undisciplined, his heart rate climbing to a dangerous level.

But when her gaze met and lingered on his, he could see that Claire had no intention of stopping him from doing whatever he wanted to do next. Her green eyes were vivid with unquenched desire, her lips wet with the passion they'd done nothing to assuage and everything to enflame.

Those lips moved then, forming a silent direction Gus couldn't quite understand. His confusion must have shown on his face, because Claire lowered her head until her mouth was right beside his ear. Then, in a whisper so soft he almost didn't hear her, she told him, "Do it."

As if acting of its own accord, his hand ducked beneath the hem of her dress, then pushed the fabric up along her thigh until he encountered the lacy tops of her stockings. God. Not pantyhose. Stockings. Bare, heated flesh met his fingers as they passed further upward, until they halted their forward march at the edge of her silky panties. Strangely, the only thought that wound through his head then was a curiosity about what color they were. Then he ceased to think at all, because Claire shifted her body, her leg, to offer him an access that sent his thoughts spinning into a rampage.

Her panties were damp and warm where he touched them, indicating quite nicely thanks that she was as ready for him as he was for her. Gus had to bite back the guttural sound of need he felt clawing at the base of his throat. He wanted to strip those panties away and bury himself so deeply inside her that neither one of them would be able to think straight again. But there was no way he was going to start something like that underneath a table in the ballroom of the Plaza Hotel while hundreds of wealthy society icons milled around discussing the stock exchange and the Dior spring collection.

Not unless he had time to finish.

And, unfortunately, he knew his and Claire's time was limited. So instead of following through with what his libido commanded, Gus slowly withdrew his fingers, dragging them down along her thigh, smoothing the fabric of her dress back into its original position. Unable to help himself, though, he shifted their bodies until they lay facing each other on their sides, curling his fingers over her hip, then inching them slowly to her flat belly.

As he drew his hand up along her torso, she moved closer

to him again. Her lips hovered against his for one long moment, and he could feel the damp whisper of her breath caressing him. She covered his mouth with hers at the same moment she cupped her palm over the hard ridge that had risen in his trousers, stroking her hand up and down the length of him. In response, he covered her breast with curled fingers, thumbing her stiffening nipple to life with a sure, circular motion.

For a long moment, they simply lay gasping and groaning, holding each other, melting into each other. The sensation of being joined in such a way was so sweet, so delicious, so all-consuming, that neither of them paid much attention to the rough clearing of a throat overhead. Not even when it sounded a second time. Or a third.

Not until it was followed by a rather loud, rather obvious, "Hello? Is anyone there?"

Gus and Claire sprang apart at that, eyeing each other as if neither remembered exactly what had happened over the last several minutes. Their breathing was an identical mixture of quick bursts and heavy sighs, and both scrambled at the same rapid pace to gather their wits and rearrange their clothing.

"Oh, my God," Claire gasped, running a shaky hand through her bangs. "What happened?"

Gus scrubbed both hands through his pale blond hair and said, "I don't know. I . . . we . . . it . . ." He surrendered to his confusion, and simply shook his head mutely.

"Hel-loooo?" the voice beckoned again.

Claire wiped a hand frantically over her mouth, her lips feeling swollen and heavy beneath her fingers. She hoped like hell her lipstick wasn't as messed up as it probably was after a mouth-to-mouth session like the one she'd just shared with Gus. What on earth had happened? How could they . . . ? How could they have . . . ? How could they have done . . . *that?*

"Excuuuuuse me?"

With a final jerk of her dress down over her thighs and a quick pat of her hair, Claire scuttled out from beneath the table, leaving Gus to cope with the aftermath alone. Considering the way he'd felt beneath her—and she had to fight off the heat that consumed her at such a consideration—he was probably going to need a few minutes to . . . collect himself. Or whatever guys did when that sort of thing was interrupted.

When she crawled out from beneath the table, it was to find herself being evaluated by an elderly couple standing on the other side. For a moment, they only watched her warily, as if they weren't quite certain she could be trusted. Claire tried to smile, but just as she managed to complete one, Gus's hands appeared from beneath the tablecloth, clamping down hard on the tabletop beside her. Then he heaved himself out from beneath with a heartfelt groan, clawing the tabletop with both hands as he emerged. He was still on his knees when he noticed that he and Claire weren't alone, and he, too, tried to smile.

Oh, boy, Claire thought. If her effort was as weak and unconvincing as his was, they were really in trouble.

When Gus finally shoved himself up to standing, he ran his big hands through his hair once more, craned his neck to straighten his necktie, then rolled his shoulders with a casualness that suggested this kind of thing happened to him every day.

"I . . . uh . . ." he began. He rolled his shoulders again, this time with less conviction. "I lost a cuff link," he mumbled, holding up the object in question for their approval.

The elderly couple eyed them both even more warily, but still said nothing. Claire looked at Gus, and Gus looked at Claire, then they both turned to the couple again.

"What is it?" they chorused as one, their impatience and frustration rising to the fore.

Both the man and woman took a step backward at exactly the same time, as if the move had been choreographed. And at precisely the same moment, their sweet expressions fell, to be replaced with mirror images of discomfort. Claire supposed when you'd been together as long as those two obviously had, you did that kind of thing automatically. Then she realized just how rude she and Gus had been in their response to the couple, and she tried once again to smile. Unfortunately, as hard as she tried, she never managed to make a smile appear.

With a restless sigh, she smoothed a hand down over the front of her dress, noting that her heart was still pounding fiercely behind her ribs and that the breast Gus had held in his hand was still throbbing and unsatisfied. She told herself not to think about it, cleared her throat and tried to smile again.

But it was no use. She didn't feel like being polite or solicitous right now. She didn't feel like being nice. And she didn't feel like looking for Ben's damned ring in what was left of her desserts. What she *did* feel like doing was ripping Gus's clothes from his body and running her hands and mouth over every inch of him. What she felt like doing was running out of the ballroom with him in tow, driving to JFK and hopping on the next flight to wherever it was dark and hot and isolated.

Her patience finally at an end, she sounded in no way polite when she clarified, "I mean, what can we do for you?"

The woman's smile had begun to return, but it dimmed some at Claire's uncooperative tone of voice. "We . . . er . . . we had rather hoped to try some of that Chocolate Raspberry Debauchery we've heard so much about."

No longer able to tolerate being courteous when her hormones were in such an uproar, she located two servings of the dessert, made no effort to hide the way she shoved a finger into each one, then scooped them up and shoved them across the table to the couple. When she noted the puzzled expressions in response to what she'd done, she forced a brittle smile.

She held up each of her index fingers, still smudged with chocolate, and wiggled them. "Haven't you heard? It's the secret ingredient," she said. "It's what makes the dish so special."

Both the man and woman nodded, but neither seemed convinced. Nevertheless, they gingerly picked up their portions and turned away from the table, scurrying off, heads bent together in conversation.

Dammit, Claire thought. She'd had enough. There was no way she could go on like this any longer.

"That's it," she said. "I've had it. There's no point in even continuing with this charade."

"You're right," Gus said beside her. "It's about time to face up to this like adults."

She nodded. "I'm just going to have to tell Ben what happened."

"Yes. You will. Or, rather, *we* will."

She turned to look at him, puzzled by his offer. "Why 'we'?"

His expression would have been the same if she had just stuck her finger in his eye. "Why we?" he repeated.

She shrugged. "Yeah. This doesn't have anything to do with you. It's all my fault. "

"Excuse me, Claire, but I think I had something to do with it."

"No, you didn't."

"Yes, I did."

She narrowed her eyes at him. "Wait a minute. What are you talking about?"

He narrowed his eyes back her. "What are *you* talking about?"

"Ben's ring," she said. "I'm going to have to tell him I lost it and face the consequences. What else would I be talking about?"

Gus's eyebrows shot up in obvious surprise. "What else?" he echoed. "Gee, I don't know. Maybe the fact that you just crawled out from under a dessert table after a nice round of touchy-feely that left your hair a mess and your panties in a twist and your mouth looking like . . . like . . . well, never mind what your mouth looks like . . . and the guy who wants to marry you wasn't even there. How about that for a 'what else'?"

Claire dropped her gaze to the table. She'd been rather hoping all of that had been some kind of bizarre, sugar-induced hallucination. Now she realized what had happened beneath the table had been all too real.

"Oh, that," she muttered.

From the corner of her eye, she saw Gus's expression sour. "Yeah, that."

"I . . . um . . . I don't know what to say."

"I have a suggestion," he was quick to supply. "How about, 'Let's get out of here, Gus. Take me back to your place and make wild monkey love to me all night long.'"

She bit her lip, amazed that she could feel like laughing after what had just transpired. "No, I don't think that would be an option."

"Why not?"

"Because it's just not."

"Why?"

"Gus—"

She honestly didn't know what to say. She couldn't think of a good reason why she should put Gus off, she only knew that she should. It was just too weird, what had just happened between them. It was just too new. Too strange. That New Year's Eve seven years ago, she'd been able to blame their unusual behavior on the festive occasion and the magnum of champagne they'd consumed. But there had been no champagne to blame tonight. Tonight, there had only been—

A festive occasion. And chocolate. Lots and lots of chocolate.

Of course, Claire thought. Chocolate. That explained everything. It was common knowledge that chocolate was an aphrodisiac. And considering how much they'd had to consume tonight, it was no wonder they'd become so . . . aroused. So agitated. So easily and completely overcome with passion. It all made sense now.

Still, was it really possible for chocolate to generate *that* much desire in a person? she wondered. Hey, she knew her desserts were good, but she didn't know they were *that* good. Maybe it was about time for her to strike out on her own . . .

Claire pushed the errant thought away and focused on the more pressing of her concerns. Unfortunately, having an explanation for her actions this evening did absolutely nothing to make Claire feel better. On the contrary, the knowledge that what had just happened between her and Gus had been the result of a chocolate-induced frenzy, and not an honest, heartfelt lust fest, was more than a little disheartening. Nevertheless, she knew it was essential that she make Gus realize what had just happened. That way they could be on their guard to make sure it never happened again.

Although *why* it was so important that such an event never occur again, she wasn't entirely sure at the moment. She only knew there could never be a repeat of the episode. She was an almost engaged woman, after all.

"You don't realize what just happened here, do you, Gus?"

He continued to eye her intently, levelly, lasciviously. Her heart rate doubled when she noted the tiny smudge of smeared lipstick that still stained one corner of his mouth. When she automatically lifted her hand to rub the spot of red away, he gripped her wrist fiercely in one hand.

"Oh, I think I know exactly what just happened here, Claire."

He pulled her hand away from his mouth, but as if he knew what she had intended to do, he scrubbed his own fist over his lips instead. Yet he didn't let go of her wrist, and continued to eye her with displeasure.

"But don't tell me," he said evenly. "Let me guess. You're going to tie it all up nice and neat and then toss it over your shoulder without a second thought, right? You're going to explain it all away with a snap of your fingers and then pretend it never happened." After a telling hesitation, he added, "Just like you did on New Year's Eve seven years ago."

She lifted her chin, telling herself the gesture was not defensive, but merely an attempt to meet his gaze. "We just got a little carried away," she said softly. "It was no big deal."

He laughed, but there wasn't an ounce of humor in the sound. "Oh, I'll say we got carried away." He tightened his grip on her wrist and jerked her forward, until she had no choice but to fall against him. "But I beg to differ," he added in a vicious whisper, his anger obvious. "I think it was a *very* big deal."

"It was the chocolate," she said lamely.

He narrowed his eyes at her. "It was what?"

She nodded. "It was the chocolate. It was. It's common knowledge that chocolate is an aphrodisiac. After all we've had to eat tonight, is it any wonder we . . . um . . ." She felt her cheeks flaming with embarrassment. "That we responded to each other like that?"

Without warning, Gus bent his head and fastened his mouth to hers again, heedless as to who might be watching them. The embrace lasted only a few seconds, but when he pulled back, Claire was as breathless and unsteady as he was. He released her wrist with enough force and fury to make her hand slap against her thigh, then glared at her.

"Here's a news flash for you, Claire. It wasn't the chocolate. And seven years ago, it wasn't the champagne."

"That's silly," she said, the words coming out weak and thin. "Of course it was. What else could it have been?"

He shook his head at her, for some reason looking as if he were disappointed in her. "Oh, gee, I don't know. Just a shot in the dark, but . . . maybe it's because we turn each other on. Because we've turned each other on for years. Because we'll keep turning each other on until we do something about it."

His voice had gradually risen in volume with every sentence he completed, and it grew even louder as he relentlessly continued. "And maybe even that won't stop it. Maybe, just maybe, Claire, we'll be turning each other on for the rest of our natural lives!"

They'd attracted an audience, Claire noted from the corner of her eye, though thankfully Ben didn't seem to be among the people surrounding the table. Nevertheless, there was no reason why she had to let Gus's tirade go on any longer. He was clearly suffering from sugar shock. There was no other way to explain the outrageous thoughts exploding in his addled brain.

"Are you finished?" she asked quietly.

He gazed at her, but said nothing.

"Good," she said, deliberately turning her back on him for its symbolic significance. "Then you won't mind helping me pack up these desserts. I think it's safe to say this night has come to an end. And none too soon."

She heard Gus shift restlessly behind her and prayed silently that he would let the subject drop. At least until they were in a setting that was more conducive to exploring the strange new avenue their relationship had just taken. There was nothing like standing in the middle of a crowded ballroom with hundreds of eyes boring into one to inhibit one's conversation just a trifle. If Gus was still insistent tomorrow that their embrace had been more than a chocolate kiss, she promised herself she'd keep an open mind.

But that was tomorrow. Tonight, she still had to face up to Ben Summers and tell him about the ring.

When she turned back around, she found that Gus had pulled an empty box from beneath the table and had started to fill it with truffles. For each one that he put in the box, however, he was popping one into his mouth. Just what they needed, she thought. More chocolate. As if her desserts hadn't caused enough trouble for one night.

"Ben's never going to forgive me for this," she muttered under her breath, doing whatever she could to try and alleviate some of the tension that still burned up the air between her and Gus. "And he may well fire me. But I'm just going to have to tell him his grandmother's ring is inside one of these desserts, or about to be discovered by some unwitting guest."

"Claire—"

"No, Gus, don't try to stop me," she interjected. "It's pointless to continue this way."

"But, Claire—"

"I mean, so far tonight, we've managed to alienate enough people that word of mouth alone could spell the end of Lumière."

"But, Claire—"

"Not to mention completely destroy any future relationship I might have with Ben."

"I found the ring."

"It's not so much the job I care about. I just—"

Gus's announcement finally sunk in then, and she spun around to find him gritting his teeth at her. Gritting his teeth around one of the most obnoxious, ostentatious, offensive pieces of jewelry she'd ever had the misfortune to encounter.

And for some reason, she was in no way pleased by the new development.

─♥ SEVEN

"YOU FOUND IT?" she repeated, her voice sounding very, very small.

Gus plucked the ring from his mouth, swiped at the chocolate coating it, and nodded. For some reason, he didn't seem quite as angry as he had been before. But he still didn't seem any too happy.

"Yep. That sucker was hiding in one of your truffles." He lifted his hand to his mouth and jiggled a canine with his thumb and forefinger. "Little bugger damn near broke my tooth, too."

"Oh, Gus," Claire whispered as she seized the ring from his hand and shoved it down over the fourth finger of her left hand, chocolate and all. She swallowed a miserable lump in her throat and squelched a sob. "You've . . . you've made me the happiest woman alive."

Funny, though, she realized. She didn't sound very happy. She didn't *feel* very happy, either. For some reason, she was wishing the ring she'd just taken from Gus had been one he was offering himself, and not one that had been given to her by another man.

Another man who seemed to have been conjured out of thin air by the recovery of his grandmother's ring. The moment Claire slipped the ring down over her finger, Ben Summers appeared behind her and placed a chaste kiss on her

•

neck. He was saying something sweet, something nice, something about how much someone had liked one of the Lumière desserts. Then he saw Gus, and his voice turned sour.

"What the hell is he doing here?" Ben demanded.

It occurred to Claire then that the dubious greeting was the same one Ben always offered to Gus, and it was really beginning to annoy her. Then, what registered in her mind was Ben's kiss. Ben's little kiss. The chaste little kiss. The chaste little kiss that had done nothing to make her blood rush as fast and furious as a hot, raging river.

It hadn't been anything like Gus's kiss at all.

And that was when Claire knew she could never, not in a million years, marry Ben Summers. He just wasn't the man for her. Chocolate or no chocolate, the right man was the kind of man who could make a woman feel the way Gus made her feel. At once warm and cozy and hot and bothered. Content one minute, confused the next. Sometimes winsome, sometimes wanton. But always, no matter what, wonderful.

Gus, she realized then, was the right man. At least he was when they were both overcome by chocolate. Now all she had to do was see if they could recreate that passion without the added enhancement of dessert. But how was she supposed to get Gus to give up chocolate?

Knowing she had a far more pressing dilemma to attend to first, she turned around to meet Ben's gaze and tried to smile.

"Hi, Ben," she said, attempting to inject a lightness she didn't feel into her voice.

Gus, on the other hand, didn't even try to mask his animosity when he told the other man, "Nice to see you, too, Summers. I'm here because Claire invited me."

This time, Ben turned his frown on Claire. "Why?" he asked sharply.

She scrunched up her shoulders as she wrinkled her nose, as if by shrinking her body in such a way, it might just be possible to make herself disappear. "I thought he might have a nice time?" she said lamely. Before Ben could comment further, she prodded him, "What were you saying about Lumière's booth going over well?"

Her ego stroking seemed to do the trick, because Ben's expression softened some. He turned his back on Gus and focused his full attention on Claire. "We're a hit," he told her. "In spite of a few . . . um . . . unfortunate occurrences, Lumière is being praised right and left tonight." He took her hands in his and kissed each one. "And it's all your doing, Claire," he added softly. Impulsively, he rushed on, "I can't wait two more weeks. Give me your answer tonight. Right now. Tell me you'll marry me."

She could feel Gus tense behind her, and she glanced over her shoulder to look at him. She had no idea what must have shown on her face, but whatever her expression held, Gus evidently didn't like it. Before she had a chance to say a word, he spun on his heel and strode deliberately away, crossing the ballroom with sure, unwavering strides. He didn't hesitate, and he didn't look back, and all she could do was watch as he disappeared into the crowd.

Her instincts commanded her to follow him, but Ben had just offered her the perfect opportunity to give him the explanation she needed to give. So she turned back around, gently removed her hands from his, and restlessly twirled the ring on her left hand with the fingers of her right. But she couldn't quite find the words to say what she needed to say.

"Claire?" Ben prodded, clearly puzzled by her lack of response.

"Ben . . ." she began, her voice containing none of the self-assurance she tried to force into it.

"Yes, Claire?"

"I . . . um . . ."

"Yes?"

"Ben, I . . . that is . . ."

"Yes?"

She bit her lip, commanding herself to just say it and be done with it. She continued to twist the ring on her finger, finally with enough force to dislodge it. It slipped over her knuckle so easily, so painlessly, so effortlessly, that it gave her the needed boost to speak.

"Ben, I can't marry you."

She had expected him to be disappointed. She had expected him to be upset. She had even been prepared for the possibility that he might be a little piqued. What she hadn't expected, what she wasn't prepared for, was for all the color to drain from his face and for his lips to start twitching violently.

In spite of all that, his voice was deceptively calm as he asked, "You what?"

For the first time since meeting him a year ago, Claire felt unsettled by Ben. She'd never seen such a reaction from him before. So subtly outraged, so silently furious. Granted, she conceded, he'd been under a lot of pressure lately, and being turned down after hoping for a positive reply for two months was enough to make anyone feel a little angry. But still . . .

Maybe there was a side to Ben that Claire hadn't seen before. After all, every day there were new stories on the evening news about guys who were just so smooth and so charming until they got a woman to marry them, and then it turned out they were serial killers wanted in seventeen states and the Republic of Togo for doing in dozens of wives. Not that Ben was necessarily quite that bad, but there was something—some unidentifiable *something*—about him that had bothered her ever since he'd proposed. It was what had kept her from saying yes right away. And it was still bothering her now.

But before she could put her finger on it, and as quickly as it had arisen, Ben's quiet choler evaporated, to be replaced by a very definite demeanor of desperation. Sweat broke out on his lips, his pupils shrank to mere pinpoints and his entire body began to tremble.

"Okay, Claire. That's all right. I understand. I do."

"Thanks, Ben," she said cautiously, still not sure what to make of this new development. "That's big of you." When his body began to shake even more, she asked, "Are you okay?"

"Sure. Sure, I'm fine. Fine. But, um . . . you'll still stay on at Lumière, right? Just because you're not going to marry me, that doesn't mean you're going to quit, does it? You wouldn't do that to me, would you?"

Understanding began to dawn on Claire then. Dawned like a good solid blow to the back of the head. "Just what are you trying to say, Ben?"

He shook his head. "Nothing. Nothing at all. I just . . . I just want to make sure you're not going to leave me."

She bit her lip delicately. "I thought that was what I just did."

He nodded, the gesture too quick, too hasty, too confident. "Yeah, I know. But you're not going to . . . you know . . . *leave* me, too, are you?"

She narrowed her eyes at him. "You'd actually want me to stay on at Lumière after telling you I won't marry you?"

Panic. That was the only way to describe the expression that overcame him next. "Of *course* I want you to stay. You *have* to stay." For the first time, he touched her, gripping her upper arms with enough force to bruise them. "Claire!" he cried desperately. "You *have* to!"

"I don't *have* to do anything, Ben. Now let me go."

Immediately, he released her, smoothing his hands carefully up and down her arms. "I'm sorry. I didn't mean it. I just . . . Don't go, Claire. Please stay on at Lumière. Please? With chocolate-covered strawberries on top?"

"I'm not sure it's a good idea, Ben. I—"

"But if you leave, my clientele will go with you. Your desserts are the only reason anyone comes in."

"Oh, I don't think that's—"

"If you go," he interrupted, some of the color returning to his face, making it a very odd shade of purple, "my restaurant will be ruined. I'll be washed up. You have to stay, Claire. You just have to. Otherwise, I'll be out of a job."

His reaction told Claire all she needed to know about her ex would-be fiancé. No, he wasn't a serial killer. He was just a big jerk. And either way, she was better off without him.

She took his hand in hers and turned it palm up. "Um, thanks for asking, Ben," she said, "but I think I'll try my hand freelancing for a while. Maybe I'll even open my own place." She dropped his grandmother's ring into his hand

and closed his fingers over it. "I'll call it Just Desserts. What do you think?"

Ben gazed down at his closed fist and sighed heavily. "I think," he said with resignation, "that my life is over."

Claire thought about Gus, about the times they'd shared in the past, about the most recent incident under the dessert table, and about the way the two of them had parted. And she wondered what it was going to take to get them back to where they were before.

"And my life is just beginning," she said as she pushed past Ben and made her way into the crowd. "I hope."

Claire waited until late Sunday afternoon to call Gus. For one thing, she wanted to give them both at least thirty-six hours to make sure all the chocolate—and its consequent aftereffects—were well and truly gone from their systems. For another thing, she had a little shopping to do.

Nothing major—just a few things from the gourmet grocery across the street. Oh, okay, and maybe one or two items from that little lingerie shop on the corner. She had plotted out a plan that she was fairly confident would succeed, but a woman didn't want to have to rely on flannel shirts and cotton underwear where true love was concerned. Better safe than sorry, she always said. And better red—red lace anyway—than dead.

When she finally did call him, the phone rang six or seven times before Gus picked it up. And when he did, he sounded groggy and cranky and less than willing to talk to her.

"I was wondering if you'd like to come down for dinner," she said in spite of his surliness.

"Me?" he asked. "Why do you want to have dinner with me? Why don't you call Ben instead? I think you've made it clear you prefer his company over mine."

Oh, how cute. He was being petulant. Claire smiled. It was a very good sign. "I don't want Ben to come for dinner," she told him. "I want you."

"Why?" he demanded. He still sounded angry.

She inhaled a deep breath and released it slowly before saying, "Ben and I split up."

There was a moment's hesitation from the other end of the line, followed by a quiet, and very wary, "You did?"

"Mm-hm. And I quit my job at Lumière, too."

There was another pause before he repeated, "You did?"

"Yeah. I'm thinking maybe I'll open my own place. A little pastry shop here in the Village. I've got some money saved up, and I could do a little catering on the side to bring in some extra cash flow. What do you think?"

His response was yet another hesitation, then what sounded like a very cautious sigh. "You, uh . . . you split up with Ben?"

"Mm-hm."

"You're not going to marry him?"

"Mm-mm. But the shop, Gus. What do you think of my idea about striking out on my own?"

His voice softened some when he asked, "Striking out on your own professionally? Or personally?"

Just to get a rise out of him, she replied, "I don't know. Maybe both. The men in my life have been acting very strangely lately, after all. It might be better to just fly solo for a change."

His response this time was a noncommittal "Mm."

"But if I *do* open my own place, I'm going to have a lot of competition," she went on quickly, before he had time to make up his mind about things one way or the other. "So I've been experimenting with some recipes. I need a second opinion. You free for dinner or not?"

"I *guess* I could make time."

"All I'm fixing are desserts."

"We're going to have *just* desserts?"

She bit her lip to keep from laughing at the appropriateness of his query. "I hope so. So what do you say? Can you come down for dinner? I promise it will be better than Ho-Hos and chocolate milk."

"I'll be right there."

As she hung up the phone, she muttered to herself, "I thought you would."

_♥_ EIGHT

IN SPITE OF his assurances of immediacy, it was actually a good half hour later that there was a knock at her front door. When Claire opened it, she found Gus standing on the other side—freshly shaved and showered by the clean, spicy smell of him—and looking nowhere near as confident of the evening as she had been feeling herself. He was dressed as he used to dress all the time, in faded Levi's and an equally faded, long-sleeved T-shirt that had once probably been a deep, rich, navy blue, his hiking boots identical to the ones she usually wore, except that they were a whole lot bigger.

"Hi," he greeted her.

"Hi," she replied.

For the first time in two decades, an awkwardness seemed to arise between them. Claire had been so sure of herself only seconds ago, before she'd twisted the knob of her front door. But faced with Gus now, looking so handsome and boyish and uncertain, she couldn't quite remember what she had planned.

Seduction, a little voice at the back of her head reminded her. _You were going to ply him with dessert and lure him into your bed._

Oh, yeah. It was all coming back to her now.

"Come on in," she said, stepping aside to allow him entry.

He lifted his nose into the air as he crossed the threshold, then smiled. "Something smells wonderful."

She smiled. "Dinner. Or, rather, dessert."

"I thought they were going to be one and the same tonight."

She hoped her smile wasn't too lascivious as she promised, "Oh, they will be."

Gus eyed Claire curiously, wondering, among other things, why she was wearing her chef's uniform at home, but he offered no indication of his suspicions. Instead, he crossed the tiny living room of her loft apartment in a few long strides and made his way to the even tinier dining area.

Claire's furnishings were as practical and no-nonsense as she was, and hadn't changed much since she'd graduated from college. A colorful quilt covered the old sofa, hiding the places where the stuffing had begun to peek through the cushions. The windows were draped by gauzy fabric that pooled on the gleaming hardwood floor beneath, turning the late afternoon sun shining through into a filmy yellow glow. Her coffee table was a steamer trunk tipped on one side, her metal chairs more suited to a patio than a living room. Area rugs in just about every color under the sun were scattered haphazardly about, and the museum posters that had once been taped to the walls were now framed and covered with glass.

Her dining area, on the other hand, Gus realized as he approached it, looked like something from *Victoria* magazine. She'd covered the scarred mahogany table with a lace table-cloth, then had set it with the Limoges and Irish crystal she'd inherited from her great-grandmother, both items having been packed away in cardboard boxes for as long as she'd owned them. She'd accessorized the soft colors with fresh flowers and gently flickering tapers. Then she'd filled every serving dish she had with a dozen different kinds of desserts.

Chocolate desserts.

Just what the hell was Claire up to now?

"Oh, Claire . . . ?" he began.

He spun around quickly, only to realize too late that she

had followed him over and stood directly behind him. His action caused him to turn right into her, and when he did, she grabbed his upper arms with both hands to keep herself from falling backward. Without even thinking about what he was doing, he cupped his hands over her shoulders and urged her closer. Then slowly, very slowly, he lowered his head to hers. But before he could pull her into his arms, she spun away from him and fled to the opposite side of the table.

"Just what are you up to?" he asked.

She lifted a hand to the top button of her chef's jacket and began to fiddle with it a little anxiously. "Up to? I'm not up to anything. What do you mean?"

He shook his head slowly. "I've known you a long time, Claire. I know when you're up to something."

She, too, shook her head, much more vigorously than he had. "No, I just . . . Before you dive head-first into all this, I need to point out that there's more to enjoying dessert than just the flavor of what's on the menu."

"Oh?"

She nodded, another vigorous gesture that told him she was more than a little nervous. "Of course. Any chef worth her salt will tell you that presentation is also very important."

"Presentation?"

"Mm-hm."

Her response came out a little strangled, piquing Gus's curiosity even more. "And just . . . um . . . just how did you plan to *present* all this stuff?"

Instead of answering him verbally, she unfastened the button she'd been playing with on her jacket. Then she moved her hand to the second button and unfastened it, as well. Then the third. Then the fourth. As Gus watched fascinated, his complete attention focused on the comings and goings of her hands, Claire finished with her jacket and reached for the drawstring of her white pants underneath. Unable to quite convince himself that she was actually doing what she appeared to be doing, he stood motionless, his heart pounding hard and heavy enough to stop traffic, as she shrugged out of both garments.

Under her uniform was a little scrap of red nothing that she was almost wearing. Her breasts were full and high and straining against the lacy fabric, a fabric that sort of covered her flat belly and nether regions. The high cut of the teddy showcased her legs in a way Gus sure never would have considered fantasizing about them, and all he could do was stare.

"Well?" she asked anxiously, and he could see that she wasn't entirely sure of the reception she would receive.

He tried to tamp down the almost uncontrollable urge to leap across the table and wrestle her to the floor, and instead cleared his throat with some difficulty and swallowed hard. "That, uh . . . that's some presentation, Claire."

"Do you like it?"

"Uh, yeah. Yeah, I think I can safely say that you're definitely onto something here. I'm just not sure how the cops are going to feel about having a pasty—I mean, *pastry*—shop like yours in the neighborhood."

She smiled, her expression still a little nervous. "I guess I still have a few kinks to work out."

Gus smiled back. "I'll be more than happy to do what I can to help work your kinks."

"You, um . . . you still haven't tasted anything yet." Her hands were trembling when she snatched up a piece of what appeared to be very dense chocolate cake and shoved it toward him.

"Here, try this first," she said, her voice none too steady when she spoke. "Instead of Black Forest Cake, I'm calling it Black Foremost Cake. What do you think? Pretty clever, huh?"

His eyes never leaving the expanse of soft, creamy skin that beckoned to him, Gus took the piece of cake and bit into it, all but oblivious to the smooth, chocolatey flavor that rolled around on his tongue. She could have handed him a snow shovel to taste, and he would have told her it was delicious.

"Tastes great," he said. "And the presentation is . . . exceptional. But why don't you just call it Black Forest Cake? Is that copyrighted or something?"

"No, I just wanted something different. You like it?"

He took another few bites without replying, his gaze fastened on the shadowy line between her breasts. "Uh, yeah. Yeah, it's terrific."

He started to move around the table, but she stopped him by reaching for something else that appeared to be chocolate pie and extended that toward him. "It's Chocolate Dream Pie," she told him.

Obediently, he took a hasty bite, then set the dessert down and began to move around the table again. "Dreamy," he told her. "But why not call it chocolate *cream* pie?"

As he drew nearer, she held up her hands palms out in a silent indication for him to stop right where he was. Then she reached for another sample from the table, handed it to him and said, "This is the best of the bunch. Baked Yukon."

With an impatient growl, he stopped within inches of her and obediently took the dessert. "Instead of Baked Alaska? Clever. But why are you changing all the names of traditional desserts?" he asked.

He bit into the Baked Yukon, the sweet coldness of it doing nothing to alleviate the heat that had been pooling in his midsection and groin since she'd whipped off her chef's uniform.

"I told you," she explained, "I just wanted something different."

"Oh, this is definitely different."

She started to reach for something else, but Gus closed what little distance remained between them and stayed her hand over a rich-looking chocolate torte. "Why aren't you having any?" he asked.

"I've already tasted them all."

"So taste them again."

"But—"

He glanced down at the table and saw that she had even fixed him his favorite—bourbon balls. So he picked up one of the chocolate confections dusted with powdered sugar and popped it into his mouth.

"Oh, Claire, these turned out even better than usual."

She smiled. "You think so?"

"Mmmm. Try one."

He scooped up another piece of the candy and held it to her lips, but she made no move to open her mouth to receive it. "Thanks," she said a little breathlessly, "but I've been eating this stuff as I go all afternoon. I'm full."

"Come on, Claire," he coaxed. He curled his fingers around her nape for a moment, then traced a slow, delicate line around to her throat. Her pulse exploded beneath the pad of his finger, her flesh felt hot and alive. "Just a little nibble. You know you want to."

She started to shake her head, but he held the candy to her mouth again. So she bit into it, her tongue stumbling over the sweet, still managing to catch a few stray pieces that threatened to fall. Gus's fingers clenched convulsively over the chocolate, crushing it into crumbs. A spot of powdered sugar lingered on Claire's lips, and without even thinking about what he was doing, he leaned forward to kiss it away.

His lips on hers were soft, seeking, solicitous. Claire felt herself melting into his kiss as easily as butter combined with cocoa. There had been a few moments there when she hadn't been sure exactly how Gus would react to her obvious overture. But the moment she'd taken off her jacket, she'd seen sparks of heat ignite in his eyes, and she'd known he was every bit as eager as she to explore this new development.

He pulled away from her for a moment, gazing down into her eyes as if wanting to put voice to a question. But before she could ask him what that question might be, he dipped his head forward again, kissing her more insistently, arousing her to every edge of her being. The hand at her throat was joined by his other, his fingers dancing over her skin like the flutter of butterfly wings. Then he cupped her jaw in his hand, and skimmed the fingers of his other hand down along her shoulder, tracing an unsteady path to her breast.

Claire sucked in her breath when he covered the billowing flesh with his hand, palming her breast gently, kneading it with sure fingers. He rubbed his thumb confidently over the fabric housing her swollen nipple, then ducked his head to drag open-mouthed kisses along her throat and shoulder. When his mouth encountered the wispy strap of her teddy, he shoved it and its mate on the other side down over her shoulders, urging the garment to her waist. Then he moved his mouth to her breast, tasting her with the hunger and finesse of a gourmet long deprived of his favorite delicacies.

"You're so sweet, Claire," he whispered, intoxicating her with the headiness of his voice. "So delicious. I don't know if I'll ever have enough of you."

She tangled her fingers in his silky hair and held him to her breast, her legs growing weak as he intensified his attentions. "You'll have a lifetime to find out," she managed to gasp. "If that's what you want."

He seemed oblivious to her offer, having moved to her other breast, suckling her thirstily as he rolled her other nipple between his thumb and forefinger.

"Oh, Gus," she whispered, "I can't take much more of this."

As if understanding her unspoken demand, he scooped her into his arms with the obvious intention of carrying her to the bedroom.

"Wait," she said when he started to turn away.

"Wait?" he repeated incredulously.

"Bring some of the Baked Yukon," she instructed with a salacious wiggle of her eyebrows. "And some of those dipped strawberries."

He smiled. "You're right. We're going to need our energy."

Juggling Claire with one arm, he reached for the desserts she'd ordered and handed them to her. Then he kissed her all the way to her bedroom and settled her reverently in the middle of her bed. As he undressed, she idly sampled the dipped strawberries one by one, rubbing them gently over her lips before sinking her teeth into the juicy fruit. She saw Gus's pupils—and other parts of him, too—grow large with wanting every time she swallowed a bite.

"My turn," he said when he joined her on the bed.

Claire took her time ogling his naked body, and her heartbeat quickened with every inch her gaze covered. He was solid and beautiful, muscles rippling poetically along his torso and arms and legs, the sinew defined more completely by strong veins and tendons. As he lay on his back beside her, she curled up on her knees, then dangled a strawberry over his lips.

"Delicious," he said when he swallowed, the word emerging in much the same way that it had earlier when he'd used it to refer to her.

"Mmm," she agreed. "They are, aren't they?"

His gray eyes gleamed almost silver as he said, "No, I meant you."

An erratic thrill of heat wound through her body, exploding in her belly like a ball of fire.

"I love you, Claire," he said softly. "I think I've loved you since I was six years old."

She smiled. "Are you sure that's not just dessert talking?"

Her question seemed to throw cold water on the fires that had been burning inside him. Immediately, he turned over onto his stomach and gazed anxiously at her.

Oh, God, was Claire right? Gus wondered morosely. Could it be possible that what he was feeling now wasn't love at all? Could what he was feeling not even be lust in its most basic form? Was it just the chocolate? Was that really possible? He'd never been more turned on in his life than he was right now, and he'd never experienced such an incredible sense of well-being. And all because of a chocolate overdose.

"You were right," he said sadly.

"About what?" she murmured.

"I guess it *was* just the chocolate that made us act so crazy Friday night . . . that's making us act so crazy now."

He was surprised to see her smile at his hypothesis. "You think so?" she asked as she dragged her fingers down the length of his spine.

His skin burned along the path she'd drawn, and he felt like crying at the knowledge that his reaction was nothing more than the result of too much chocolate. His voice was unsteady when he replied, "Well, isn't it obvious? I mean, here's all the evidence we need right here. We're wallowing in chocolate and the beginnings of what promises to be just about the most incredible sexual experience I've ever had.

Don't tell me you're not convinced the two aren't entirely related. You're the one who suggested it in the first place."

Her smile broadened as she lay down beside him, making him even more confused. "Didn't I tell you?" she said. She propped her head on one hand, and with the other, lifted his fingers to her lips, licking at a stain left behind by one of the strawberries.

He swallowed hard, but managed to ground out, "Tell me what?"

"This isn't chocolate."

His heart trip-hammered in his chest as he asked, "It's not?"

She curled her tongue around his index finger, and he felt himself swell to rock-hard readiness. "No. It's carob."

"Carob?"

She nodded, turning his hand so that she had better access to his thumb, then leisurely licked at another smudge of chocolate—or rather, carob, he realized.

"Yeah, carob. It's sort of a healthy substitute for chocolate. I've been experimenting with it for a while now, thinking I could introduce it at health-food restaurants. It's why I wanted your opinion on the results. I figured if a chocoholic like you liked it, everyone else would, too."

"It wasn't chocolate?" he asked again.

"No, sorry. I guess we're only doing this because . . ." She shrugged playfully. "Because we're in love with each other maybe?"

His insides began to grow warm and watery again. "Do you love me, Claire?"

She seemed to give the question a lot of thought, then smiled. "Yes. I believe I do. And I think I have for a long, long time."

He lifted his head to kiss her, then said, "Good. Because I love you, too."

"You're not mad at me for fooling you?"

He laughed, shook his head and gathered her close, pinning her beneath him. He buried his head in the hollow of her throat, chuckling and kissing and tasting. When he lifted his head, the fire of desire was raging like an inferno once again.

"Frankly, Claire," he said quietly, "I couldn't be more pleased with the results."

"Really?"

"Really. You may not believe this, but in my opinion, there are actually one or two things that are more important than chocolate."

She feigned a shocked expression. "Why, Gus. I never thought I'd live to hear you admit something like that."

"Okay," he amended. "Maybe not *two* things more important than chocolate. But I can easily think of one."

"What's that?"

"You."

The smile that curled her lips this time was warm and tentative and soft. "Me? Really?"

He bent his head and brushed his lips lightly over hers. "You. Really."

She leaned into him, snuggling closer to tuck her head under his chin. As she trailed her tongue along his throat and shoulder, she pushed him back and over until their positions were reversed. Then she tangled her fingers on the coarse blond hair scattered across his chest and flattened her tongue over his nipple. Gus groaned out loud when she completed her ministrations and began to venture lower.

"Oh, Claire . . ."

"Hmmm?"

"I don't know how much more of this I can take without having another taste of you."

He heard her chuckle as she placed her cheek gently against his flat belly. "Serves you right. It's your just desserts."

"Yeah, and lucky for me, nobody does just desserts like you do."

As if to illustrate that point, Claire moved back up to his mouth and kissed him again, kissed him hard and deep and long. And Gus decided that, just like chocolate, he'd never be able to get enough of her. Fortunately for him, chocolate and Claire seemed to go hand in hand.

Never had just desserts seemed like such a wonderful fate.

GUS'S FAVORITE BOURBON BALLS
(Courtesy Helen Bevarly—Hi, Mom!)

24   small vanilla wafers
1   cup chopped pecans
1   cup powdered sugar
2   tablespoons cocoa
1½   tablespoons corn syrup
2   ounces bourbon whiskey

Roll wafers until fine and mix with powdered sugar, cocoa
and pecans. Dissolve corn syrup in whiskey and add to dry
ingredients; mix well. Form into balls and roll in more powdered sugar. Chill and keep cool.

SWEET NOTHINGS

Muriel Jensen

♡ ONE

MAGGIE CHARLES APPROACHED the lattice-work arbor woven with pink ribbon and decorated with cupids and hearts. It was placed at the head of the gang-plank that lead aboard the *Bahama Duchess*. The words "Chocolate Valentine Cruise" arched over the top of the arbor in silver foil.

Maggie withheld a prayerful roll of her eyes, and, dropping her suitbag and briefcase to the gangplank, she focused on the festive greeting with her Nikon and immortalized it on film.

Then she picked up her things again, slung them over her shoulder, walked under the arbor and stepped aboard the ship.

"Maggie Charles with *Sweet Indulgence* magazine," she said to the white-uniformed cruise staffer who took her photo as she in turn took his.

"Hey!" he teased. "Your photo will be posted on the wall outside the dining room for you to purchase as a memento of your cruise. What do I have to pay for mine?"

She laughed. "Just the price of the magazine. The July issue, I think."

"All *right*." He handed her a map of the ship. "You have your cabin assignment?"

"Yes." She consulted the folder her editor had given her at the last moment. "126, Lagoon Deck."

He pointed to the elevators in an area behind him that looked like the lobby of a Vegas hotel. "One deck down and aft."

Aft. "The back?"

"Right." He grinned. "First cruise?"

"Yes," she admitted. "As a reporter for a foods magazine, I usually end up in a kitchen. This will be a new experience."

"The forward lounge on the Atlantis Deck has been set up as a Chocolate Bake-off newsroom for this cruise."

"Thank you." She headed for the elevators.

The Lagoon Deck bustled with activity. Men and women moved past her in both directions carrying luggage, shepherding children, calling excitedly to each other. The passageway walls were decorated with the same cupids and hearts that adorned the arbor.

Maggie tried to ignore the isolating experience of being alone in a throng of happy little groups. One family of three wore matching red and white shirts, another held hands even as they skinnied past her, single file. Another young couple, honeymooning, she guessed, by the way they stared into each other's eyes, sidled through their cabin door, gazes still locked.

She distracted herself by reading cabin numbers as she made her way down the passageway—102, 106, 110—but memories came to mind anyway.

She and Mike would have been that couple if he hadn't been more devoted to work than to her.

She pushed the thought away. "Get over it," she told herself sharply. "That was two years ago. Single women have come into their own. It's all right to go your own way. The world's on your side."

She watched another couple go by hand in hand and felt as though she had somehow been placed on Noah's Ark. Intellectually, the world might be on a single woman's side, but physically it threw the two-by-two, yin and yang principle at her at every turn.

126. Thank God. She pushed her way inside.

Her suitbag bumped and banged against the chest of drawers as she made her way past a closed door on her left and through the narrow space to a sofa upholstered in dark blue under a square window.

She was disappointed that the window was not the traditional round porthole, but pleased there was a window at all. An inside room of such small dimensions would have made her positively claustrophobic.

Her eyes focused on the view of Port Canaveral, Florida out the window, she stubbed her toe on something just before she reached the sofa, and fell forward. She held the camera up and out of harm's way in her left hand as she landed with a thud on her bag and briefcase.

She turned to see what had tripped her and stared in stupefaction at an enormous pair of men's tennis shoes—not the thick-soled, athletic variety, but the clean and simple, pristine white deck style. There was a small scuff on the toe of the right one, probably from the sole of her sandals.

Then she noticed other telltale signs of occupancy. A wallet, keys, and a handful of change lay atop the dresser, and a pair of socks and a white T-shirt had been tossed at a door she presumed to be a closet.

A rush of sound that she identified as running water came from the closed door she'd passed upon entering. The bathroom, she concluded. And judging by the shoes, there was a man—or a very, very large woman—in it.

All right. No cause for panic. She would call someone and get this straightened out. But first she would check to make sure she was indeed in 126.

She tiptoed past the closed bathroom door, opened the outer door, and studied the numbers carefully. 1 – 2 – 6.

Good. She *was* in the right room. She started back toward the sofa, prepared to hold her ground when the usurper emerged from the bathroom. Then she passed the chest of drawers with the personal items on it and noticed the wallet. Her heart lurched against her ribs, sank to her stomach, then bounced and rose to lodge somewhere in her throat.

No. It couldn't be.

She closed her eyes and opened them again, but the wallet

was still there, monogrammed with an M and an L she'd had burned into the brown leather. M L for Mike Lawless, the man who'd been her lover, her best friend, her everything, until Valentine's Day two years ago when he'd thrown her out of his kitchen and out of his life. God.

No. It was a coincidence. The wallet must belong to some Murray Longstreet or Milo Lang. Maggie calmed herself with all the reasons why it couldn't belong to Mike Lawless.

He lived in Connecticut. He ran a catering business called Cookin' Good and never left it for anyone—including the woman he purported to love. And she'd given him the wallet that Valentine's Day. He would have tossed it away, the way he'd tossed her.

The bathroom door opened, she spun around, prepared to confront Murray or Milo—and discovered that all her careful reasoning had been in vain.

She saw rich brown hair wet from the shower and mussed by the towel now suspended in a hand frozen in midair. She saw dark brown eyes looking as startled as she felt, and a tall, well-muscled body that was . . . well . . . splendidly detailed.

Mike Lawless was here, all right. In the flesh. Quite literally.

Mike recovered from shock to grab for a towel and wrap it around his waist. He had no idea what in the hell Maggie Charles was doing here, but after she had ruined his life, she was *not* going to see him react to her with the same old lust and longing.

He took a minute to collect himself. He let his eyes wander over her startled cocoa-brown gaze, her dark red lips parted in a gasp, her short mahogany-brown hair tucked behind her ears, long spiky bangs skimming her eyebrows, and realized grimly that he didn't feel collected at all. The same old need and wanting boiled up in him despite the anger that rose as well. But he managed to suppress both, outwardly, at least, and pretend to be unaffected.

"Maggie." He leaned a shoulder in the doorway, enjoying her complete fluster. "Came to find me?"

Her eyes ignited. He used to love to make that happen in

the old days, but not this way. He'd had an entirely different technique then.

"No, I did not come to find you," she said, anger simmering in her voice. "What are you doing here?"

"Cookin' Good is a contestant in the bake-off. What are you doing here? I heard you were living in Manhattan."

She closed her eyes for a moment as though struggling to maintain her composure. "I am. But I meant—what are you doing *here*—in my cabin?"

"Your cabin?" This promised to be interesting. "This is *my* cabin."

She shifted her weight and folded her arms. "Pardon me, but I was assigned this cabin and I have a reservation to prove it."

She went to the folder on the sofa beside her briefcase, yanked out her copy and held it up in front of his face. "See? 126. Says so right there."

He reached to the dressertop for his receipt, consulted it, then held it up to her. "Well, it was assigned to *me* three months ago. Your reservations were made . . ." He leaned over her sheet. "A week ago. Hah! Mine takes precedence."

"Is that so?" She drew a steadying breath. Her small breasts rose and fell under a silky blue blouse. He did his best to ignore it. "Obviously we need someone from the cruise line to arbitrate this dispute."

"Obviously."

Silence pulsed between them.

"Aren't you going to do something about it?" she demanded.

"As I recall," he replied, thinking back over the argument the day they'd parted, "You once said I take too much upon myself. That I have to supervise everything, fix everything, know everything. That I never delegate because I don't consider anyone else competent to do a job as well as I would."

She arched an imperious eyebrow. "And what about that can you possibly refute?"

He smiled. "None of it. But in this case, I delegate you to straighten out the problem with the cabin while I get dressed."

She opened her mouth to object, then her eyes skimmed over his naked chest and she marched across the cabin to the phone. It required only four steps, but it afforded him a four-second view of the neat flare of her backside in a pair of white slacks. He turned back into the bathroom before the towel could no longer conceal that two years without her had done nothing to diminish her appeal for him.

"How," Maggie demanded of a harassed-looking young woman in the white uniform of the ship's staff, "could you reassign a cabin that had already been booked?" The young woman wore a badge that said she was "Julie Baldwin, Purser."

The three of them and a small, dark-featured, balding man who was their cabin steward, were crowded into the tiny room. Mike and the purser sat on the sofa, Maggie paced the few feet from wall to wall, and the steward stood in the narrow area between the bathroom and the outer door, looking distressed.

"I can't apologize enough," Julie Baldwin said. "Our reservations printout for last week showed Mr. Lawless registered to this cabin, but somehow, in the update, he was erased, or dropped, or caught in some glitch that showed this room empty. When your magazine made your last-minute reservation, you were assigned it."

Maggie tried to be reasonable. "I see. Well, I presume you can rectify the mistake and assign one of us to another cabin?"

Julie met her eyes and held them, her own apologetic but resolute. "I'm afraid not. This cruise involves chocolate and Valentine's Day. We're booked down to the last closet. The best I can do is promise you a make-up cruise."

Maggie put a hand to her eyes. A pain was beginning to throb between them. "Julie, I'm here to cover the bake-off. Mr. Lawless is here to *participate* in it. A make-up cruise will help neither of us!"

"I can refund your money."

"That won't help either."

"I'm sorry." The words were sincere but final.

Maggie dropped her hand and sighed. "So, because of the cruise line's error, one of us has to *leave* the cruise, or share a room the size of a bathtub?"

Mike smiled as her voice rose a fraction. He thought that an interesting complaint, considering they'd often actually shared a bathtub—and with little protest on her part.

Her dark glance berated him for smiling. He presumed that was because she was remembering that detail, too.

"Or Lupe can find a cot for you," the steward offered smoothly and took a step toward them, his small, round body exuding a placating goodwill. "If Señor Bandido is cooking," he pointed out reasonably to Maggie, "and you . . ."

"Señor *Bandido*?" she interrupted in puzzlement.

"*Si.* Señor Miguel . . . eh . . . *como se dice*?" He looked to Mike for assistance.

"I think it's a sort of free translation of Lawless," Mike interpreted. "*Bandido.* Bandit. We agreed upon it when I came aboard. Go on, Lupe."

"If he is cooking," the steward began again, "and you, Señorita, are taking *photographias,* then you will be here only at night, and I will find a comfortable cot and pillows, and you will not have to . . ." He pointed to the bed and waggled his eyebrows in a very Latin gesture. ". . . together."

Maggie spread her arms helplessly, then dropped them in frustration. She turned to Mike. "Can you come up with an alternative?"

"I think delegating means I have to accept your handling of the situation."

She groaned. "Please, Señor Bandido. This is no time to be retiring. Can you live with a cot in the room?"

He grinned. "I don't know. Will you be able to keep your hands off me?"

Her cheeks flushed. When they'd been together, she'd often initiated lovemaking. She was probably remembering that, too.

Maggie gave him a frosty glance. "It'll be easy." She turned to Lupe. "All right. Get the cot, please."

The steward was gone in an instant, but Maggie stopped Julie as she tried to follow. "As I recall," she said wryly, "the

Julie on the *Love Boat* had better solutions than you've been able to come up with here."

Julie accepted the rebuke with a gracious smile. "If I had someone offscreen to write my lines, I'm sure I'd do better, too. Meanwhile, I promise to bend over backward to see that you both have what you need."

Mike walked Julie to the door, then closed it behind her. He turned to face Maggie, who stood at the opposite end of the room—only about ten feet away.

Her eyes reflected the same wary acceptance he felt.

"I thought you always considered cook-offs a waste of time," she said.

He acknowledged the truth of that with a nod. "But April first finds me with a balloon payment due on a business loan and a van that doesn't always get us where we're going. The cash prize would bail me out. But I'm sure you're not interested in my business problems. Why are you working for a magazine?"

She unzipped her suitbag and pulled out a small stack of white silky things. "You're not the only one who has to meet your bills, you know."

He dragged his eyes from the pile of lingerie, fighting an overwhelming sensory memory of her against him in silk and lace. He frowned into her eyes. "But you're a pastry chef. Not someone who writes about pastry chefs."

"Please," she said with sudden sharpness, marching toward the chest of drawers. He sidestepped to give her room. "Don't pretend it matters to you." She opened a drawer, encountered his T-shirts and briefs, slammed it shut, and opened a lower one. She found it empty and dropped in the little silky squares, then pushed it closed with her knee. She turned to confront him. "This will work only if you forget there was ever anything between us. I have."

He looked into her imperious dark gaze and saw something she was apparently hiding from herself. She hadn't forgotten anything.

This should prove interesting, he thought grimly as she turned away from him to continue her unpacking. Because he hadn't either.

TWO

T HE COT WAS not the easy solution it appeared to be at first thought. Mike had left the cabin, and Maggie was coming to the conclusion that the only place to put the makeshift bed in the small cabin positioned it directly in the path to the bathroom, or to anywhere else in the room, leaving a very small space on either side of it for the nighttime wanderer to pass by.

The only other alternative was to place it directly beside the sofa bed, and that defeated the purpose of it altogether.

It was late afternoon, they'd just left port, and she imagined everyone else was leaning over the rail, throwing confetti and waving to friends while she moved furniture.

She finally settled on placing the cot right against the chest of drawers. Mike's wallet and keys were gone now, and in their place was a basket of fruit and a bottle of champagne Julie had sent in apology.

The cabin door opened and Mike walked in with an amiable smile. "Sorry. Forgot my brochures. You going to be comfortable on that?" Mike held onto her shoulders as he sidled past her, his thigh rubbing across her backside as he negotiated the small space. The air around her became a cloud of Drakkar Noir.

Awareness and the sharp clarity of midnight memories startled her into stiffness and made her temporarily mute.

Impressions of his touch flashed across her mind, his lips to her forehead in his kitchen in the Connecticut woods, his gentle hand on her cheek at dinner, his strong arm around her shoulder on the patio as they watched the sunset, his fingertips against her in an intimacy that had been passionately possessive, yet infinitely tender.

She'd closed those memories away for the past two years, but they came vividly to life now that she was confined with their creator in this cursedly tiny space.

Loss and longing tangled inside her and made her put a hand to her stomach as she drew a deep breath.

Mike reached for a briefcase leaning between the sofa and the wall. He straightened and noted her stricken expression.

"Seasick?" he asked gently.

"No." Her reply was ill-tempered and dispirited. "I'm just sick of . . ." What? Writing about cooking when she really wanted to be in a kitchen? But being in a kitchen had reminded her too much of being with him, so she'd turned to writing instead, and managed to support herself for the past year and a half.

But she couldn't tell him that, and he was watching her, waiting for her to explain precisely what it was she was sick of.

"Chocolate," she said, and made a production of fluffing the pillow Lupe had brought. "I mean, let's face it. We've dipped everything in it from ants to roses. We've used it as a crust, a filling, a topping, and made it the snob-appeal treat of the century. Why do we need an entire cruise dedicated to it? And a bake-off?" She punched the pillow and tossed it at the head of the cot. "Haven't we beaten it to death?"

He studied her in mild surprise. She knew he wasn't buying it. And what was worse, he was analyzing her, trying to figure out what had really gotten her going.

"I can't believe that's what's bothering you," he said, putting the briefcase down and helping her spread the blanket. "You're the one who'd take a bath in Godet if we could find you that much and who ate so many of her own chocolate roses for that reception in Mystic that she had to stay up half the night making more."

Her eyes lost focus and she felt a smile come to her lips at that thought. He'd stayed up, too, boxing the other desserts. They'd finished after three A.M. and ended up in the hot tub.

The notion of hot water brought her back to reality. She was going to be in it if she didn't get herself and her camera out there among the contestants preparing for the competition.

"I've given up Godet," she said, sidling past the foot of the cot to where she'd left her camera and briefcase. The white-chocolate cognac liqueur was too expensive for her current budget.

He smiled knowingly, hands in his pockets. "You were always seductive and a little aggressive after a glass of it. It made you want to be on top, as I recall. Couldn't the other men in your life take that?"

She scorned him with a look. "On the top or on the bottom, the men in my life are very happy." Or they would be if there were any. "Excuse me, but I have to get to work. And I thought *you'd* take the cot."

He eyed it skeptically. "It's a foot shorter than I am."

That was true. She sighed in exasperation. "I don't care where you sleep, Michael, just please stay out of my way."

"Two years ago," he complained good-naturedly, "you grumped because you said you didn't see enough of me. Now you've got me all to yourself and . . ."

She slammed the cabin door before he'd finished.

Despite the registration snafu, Maggie found that she *was* assigned a seat at dinner, and that it was not at the same table where Mike was seated. She felt herself begin to relax. She'd gotten good shots of several of the contestants resting on chaise longues or walking around and getting acquainted before the serious job of paring the ten contestants down to three finalists. The ship would dock at Freeport on Grand Bahama Island, and though most of the guests would probably go ashore, the contestants would be hard at work. They wouldn't have free time until the ship stopped at Nassau the day after next.

She'd jotted down a few thoughts and observations when she went back to the room to change, grateful that Mike was out.

This might be a blessing in disguise, she told herself as she found her assigned dinner table. If anything could help her get over Mike Lawless, the constant aggravation of his nearness should do it. All she had to do to get through it was stay focused on her work and remember that her relationship with "Señor Bandido" was well and truly over . . . even, she thought with a bolstering sip of wine, if it didn't feel like it was.

"We're the Bertoluccis. I'm Carmen, he's Salvatore." The feminine half of a cheerful, portly middle-aged couple seated beside her introduced herself and her husband. "Everybody calls him Sally." She smiled lovingly at the balding, blunt-featured man. "And this is our granddaughter, Isabel. Isn't she a doll?"

Isabel, about nine, was dark-featured and pretty but very plump. She was also completely oblivious to the conversation as she focused all her attention on the fruit and cheese plate her grandparents had ordered as an appetizer. According to Maggie's calculations, Isabel had eaten a pound and a half of Gouda and several hundred grapes.

"Isabel loves chocolate." Sally beamed, patting his granddaughter's head. "So we brought her along as an early birthday present."

"Say hello, Sweetheart," Carmen prodded.

Isabel made an unintelligible sound around a large hunk of pineapple.

"We're Tammy and Neil Goldbeck," a pretty redhead interposed. Maggie recognized the couple she'd guessed were honeymooning. "We were married yesterday afternoon."

Carmen made a slow sound of approval. "Isn't that nice, Sally? Newlyweds at our table."

Sally smiled, happy with his lot and obviously happy for them.

Julie, the purser, looking stunning in pink silk, sat next to Sally, and beside her was an older man more interested in pursuing the menu than in getting acquainted.

"Bill Gardner. Widowed. Retired," he said gruffly, then retreated behind the large white square.

Seated between Maggie and the Goldbecks was a young man Maggie guessed to be about Mike's age. He had buzz-cut light brown hair and clear blue eyes.

"Warren Anderson," he said, his posture military, his manners flawless. He inclined his head to the ladies and gave the men a courteous nod. "I'm representing The Lightning Creek Bakery of Tulsa, Oklahoma, in the competition."

Sally laughed. "Well, I'm slipping. I took you for a Marine on leave."

Anderson grinned. "Close, sir. Just got out a month ago after a tour in Bosnia."

While Anderson was barraged with questions, Maggie perused the large dining room with what she told herself was simple interest in her surroundings. She wasn't looking for anyone in particular, she was just looking.

She spotted Mike two tables over in earnest conversation with Paula Livingston from *Table Talk* magazine. She looked away immediately, fighting the beginnings of anger in the pit of her stomach.

He was certainly entitled to speak to whomever he wished, particularly someone seated beside him at the dinner table. But knowing Paula, Maggie couldn't help but wonder what kind of personal machinations had placed her there. Paula had been placing herself in Mike's path for as long as Maggie had known him.

They'd been an item and broken up long before Maggie had come on the scene, but even after Maggie had become a part of Mike's life, Paula was always trying to claim his attention. It looked as though she'd finally done it.

Maggie let her eyes drift back to them and saw that now Paula had looped her arm in his and was leaning toward him as she laughed, her neat cap of blonde hair almost touching his shoulder.

That was fine. What Mike did no longer affected her.

Maggie noticed Danny Campbell on Mike's other side. He happened to look up, checking out the room as she was doing, and caught her eye. She smiled and waved. He grinned broadly and waved back.

Danny had joined Mike's staff while Maggie worked for Cookin' Good, and she'd been impressed with the level of his skill. He had the knowledge, the imagination, the attention to detail and the long-fingered dexterity for the fine finishing work so essential to proper presentation of desserts. Even Mike had coveted Danny's rock steadiness.

Despite her resentment toward Mike for making her love him, then loving his business more than he loved her in return, she could admit that Mike was the most brilliant chef she'd ever seen, man or woman. And her father had owned and operated one of New York's finest restaurants. She'd grown up in the business, watching chefs come and go.

Some chefs, she learned, were brilliant, but too temperamental to function smoothly with a staff for the timely production the busy lunch and dinner periods required. Others had the social skills, but were only moderately talented and creative. Some were so fussy the food never got to the table; some not fussy enough.

Some simply couldn't deal with the daily grind of long preparation time, four or five hours of hell on a roller coaster while orders came faster than it was humanly possible to fill them, followed by cleanup and the kitchen inventory so that fresh food could be brought in the following morning, allowing the procedure to begin again the following afternoon.

But her father was a restaurateur who'd made cooking and hospitality art forms. She adored him.

She'd worked in the kitchen with him since her mother had died when Maggie was ten. She'd grown up convinced that no other man could match her father's sweetness, his sense of humor, and the great pleasure he took in his work—and in her.

He'd loved her, indulged her, and wept when she'd graduated from culinary school and told him she wanted to come back to Chez Charles and work with him.

"I was so afraid some high-rolling yuppie would take you

away from me," he'd confessed, "and move you across the country."

She'd laughed and told him, "You're the only man I'll ever love, Daddy."

Then one day Mike Lawless walked into her father's kitchen, and she discovered that one man could possess all the qualities her father had—all the skills a fine, efficiently functioning kitchen required.

He'd graduated from the Culinary Institute of America, had ten years experience in some of the most respected hotel kitchens in New England. He was innovative, "inspired" her father called it, relaxed, and—as long as he believed you were willing to give him one-hundred percent of your best effort—a joy to work with. There was always laughter in his kitchen.

He left her father's restaurant a year later to open a catering business in Connecticut and she'd gone with him, so in love she couldn't see straight. Even her father had approved.

But somehow, she'd failed to make the connection between a man who loved his work and was willing to extend himself in all directions to see that it was completed perfectly, and what that could ultimately mean for the woman who loved him.

She'd learned the following year that it meant working long hours with an almost psychotic attention to detail to cultivate a successful business. It meant that every discussion either began or returned to the business. That every penny went toward it, every ounce of energy, and—on his part, at least—every dream.

For the pampered and indulged apple of her father's eye, Maggie found that a difficult adjustment.

And then came the confrontation on Valentine's Day. They'd catered a party that night for a New Haven socialite that had involved every intricate dish known to man. They'd packed up well after midnight and come home to several hours of cleanup because they had a luncheon in Hartford later that morning.

She'd been exhausted but filled with the Valentine spirit.

Mike, however, had been riding the crest of a successful job and talked about nothing else while they cleaned up.

Still inspired with notions of a romantic interlude, she'd presented him with the wallet and a card filled with effusive sentiments.

He'd given her a red rosebud she recognized from the centerpiece he'd used on the New Haven socialite's table.

And Maggie had gone postal.

In this case, she thought, the single rose was not the testament of a loving man's wordless adoration. It was the make-do minimum gesture of a man who hadn't been willing to separate himself from his work long enough to put a little thought into a Valentine's Day gift for the woman he claimed to love.

She'd thrown the rose down to the carpet and told him she was leaving.

"Ma'am?"

"Yes?" Maggie came back to awareness to see that everyone else at the table was eating except her and the young man at her side. Chicken in an herbed Dijon sauce steamed aromatically on a gold-rimmed plate in front of her.

"You all right, ma'am?" Warren Anderson asked.

"I'm fine, Mr. Anderson," she replied, picking up her fork. "I was daydreaming."

He cocked his head in the direction in which she'd been staring. "About someone at that table? The big guy with the blonde?"

She fought an instinctive blush, unsure whether it was embarrassment or anger with herself at being caught staring at Mike.

"No," she replied, picking up her utensils and sawing with more force than necessary on the succulent chicken. "He's just someone I used to know."

"In the biblical sense?"

She looked around to see if anyone else had heard his question. Mercifully, everyone was raving over the cuisine and comparing side dishes.

"That's a very personal question, Mr. Anderson," she replied quellingly.

He simply smiled and took a sip of wine. "Don't people talk seriously over dinner where you come from?"

"Not to strangers."

"We're going to share this dinner table for the next few days, ma'am. And I make friends in a hurry."

"Friends, Mr. Anderson," she said patiently, leaning toward him to keep her rebuke quiet, "usually respect each other's privacy."

He leaned on an elbow, meeting her halfway and looking unrepentant. "My name's Warren, ma'am, not Mister. And I've been out of circulation for four whole years. If I'm going to find a wife on this cruise, I don't have time to waste."

Maggie stared at him a moment, surprised to discover she was as intrigued by his directness as she was appalled.

"Mister . . ." she began, then corrected herself when he frowned at her. "Warren. Courtship requires subtlety."

He shook his head. "No time for that, ma'am. I—"

"Maggie."

"Maggie. When I get home after the cruise, I'm taking over the bakery from my uncle, who isn't very well, and I'll need a wife to work with me. I want one who's willing to have children, 'cause I grew up alone and I long for noise and laughter around my dinner table." He smiled. It was, she thought, a charming and inviting smile. "A bakery is hard work, but I'd do right by my lady. When the day is done, I'd make her happy. His eyes perused her features. "You have a nice smile. I want a smilin' woman."

She turned to him, prepared to ward him off kindly but firmly.

He shook his head, forestalling her with a raised hand. "You're spoken for—I know. I can see that. That big guy, am I right?" He tipped his head in Mike's direction.

She shook her head. "No, that's over. I don't want anybody for a while."

"Why not?"

She lifted a black lace shoulder. "I think maybe because I'm not sure I know how to be in love."

He looked surprised. "I think it just happens, Maggie. Without you having to think about how to do it."

She patted his shoulder. "You've been out of circulation for four important years, Warren. We're thinking about everything now. And a lot of women have their own plans that don't include husbands and children."

"Sure. I know that." He rested his knife at an angle across the edge of his plate and speared a bite of red potato. "There's always somebody who's happier on their own road, but I know there's a woman somewhere on this boat lookin' for a man who'll love and protect her and do his best by her. It's a Valentine cruise, isn't it? And chocolate is an aphrodisiac."

Maggie wasn't sure what to do in the face of such naive optimism but support it.

"I'm sure you're right, Warren. And you know what? I'll keep an eye open for you."

"I'd appreciate that, Maggie." He popped the bite of potato into his mouth, chewed and swallowed. "I'll be pretty busy tomorrow with the competition, but the next day we'll have off until the finalists compete on the way home the day after that. So once I find her, I'll have a whole day to woo her."

Woo. Maggie repeated the word to herself. She had to admire the man who'd use it, as well as the self-confidence that let him believe he could employ the principle it defined on a woman—and in one day!

"Anything I can do for *you*?" he asked.

"Yes." She held her glass up as he poured more wine. "I'd like to schedule an interview with you tomorrow for my story. Will you have time?"

"I'll make time for you, Maggie," he said with a broad grin. "Has to be in the morning while we're setting up and doing our dry runs. Formal competition starts at one o'clock."

"Is ten all right?"

"Perfect."

Maggie looked up to check on her companions and found that the Goldbecks and Bill Gardner had drifted away, that the Bertoluccis were trying to pry Gardner's leftover dessert away from Isabel, and that Julie, chin resting on her hand, was frowning at Warren. Maggie concluded that she'd heard his sort of retro-nouveau approach to women.

Finally giving his dinner his full attention, Warren didn't notice.

⸺♡ THREE

MIKE FOUND MAGGIE asleep on the cot when he returned to the cabin. She'd left the light on in the bathroom and pulled the door partially closed so that the room was in semidarkness, but his path to the sofa was clear.

He entertained himself for a moment with thoughts of why she'd chosen to consider his comfort over her own by leaving him the sofa. He wanted to believe she still had feelings for him. It didn't seem possible that all the love and passion they'd shared could simply disintegrate.

His feelings for her were certainly very much alive, but all entangled with anger and wounded pride. Though two years had passed, he couldn't remember her throwing the rosebud on the carpet that Valentine's Day and stomping down on it without wanting to shake her until her teeth rattled.

Yet, something inside him was trying to work past that, because watching that kid from Oklahoma bend her ear had made dinner seem interminable. And he'd had Paula talking nonstop in his other ear.

He had finally escaped before dessert on the pretext of checking out Danny's work area for tomorrow's preliminary competition. But he'd slipped off to the Sundance Lounge instead for a Bahama Mama and the replay of the Knicks game.

He wondered what might have happened if he'd come back to the cabin and found Maggie undressing for bed. Fanciful images played across his mind, but he let them go with fatalistic acceptance. If he'd come back, she'd have beaned him with a blunt object and taken the sofa.

Mike slipped out of his clothes, leaving his T-shirt and shorts on in deference to Maggie's presence, gauged the distance to the sofa, then turned off the bathroom light.

He proceeded cautiously but quickly, remembering the narrowness of the space afforded him.

He stopped in his tracks suddenly when there was a sleepy sound from the cot, the rustle of bedclothes, and a movement he sensed but couldn't see.

Then something soft and warm—he guessed it was her hand, connected with the bare flesh of his thigh, slid gently over his knee and down his shin until it finally stopped halfway to his ankle.

Sensation roared through him like a conflagration, armed with clear and instant memories of how it used to be between them. He was exhilarated by the knowledge that she wanted that back as much as he did.

Until he realized in the stillness that followed that she'd simply stirred restlessly in her sleep, flung an arm out, and connected with his raging libido. That was all it was.

With a sigh of bitter disappointment, he reached down cautiously, found the soft, warm inside of her arm, traced it lightly to her wrist and lifted it to replace her arm across her waist so that he could pass.

He reached the sofa with a feeling of having run the gauntlet. He climbed under the covers and gave his pillow a savage punch, wondering what in the hell had ever made him think a chocolate bake-off aboard a cruise ship could solve his problems. So far, it was only multiplying them astronomically.

Maggie awoke to a firm rap on the door.

"Ah . . ." She sat up abruptly, wondering where she'd left her robe, when Mike leaned out of the bathroom. He was barefoot in stone-colored slacks. The muscles in his bare back rippled as he reached out to open the cabin door.

"Morning, Lupe," he said cheerfully, turning to point his razor at Maggie. She saw that half of his face was shaven, the other half still covered with creamy lather. All of it, she thought, looked fresh and handsome. "For the lady," he said, stepping back into the bathroom, raising his voice to be heard. "She's grumpy if she doesn't start the day with an orange and a raisin bagel!"

Lupe came toward her bearing a tray that held precisely that, the orange peeled and pulled open at one end like a blooming flower, the bagel on a paper doily with a rosette of butter, a scoop of cream cheese, and a pot of jam. A teapot and cup were also crowded onto the tray.

Lupe looked at the sofa with its tangle of sheet and blanket, then to the narrow cot where she sat, the blanket clutched to her chest, and shook his head regretfully. He placed the tray on the low table against the wall.

"You slept well?" he asked solicitously.

"Yes," she lied with a phony smile. She'd awakened after an unsettling dream where she'd run her fingertips over Mike's naked body, then been unable to go back to sleep. She'd lain awake, listening to Mike's slow, even breathing, and finally drifted off as day began to dawn.

Now sunlight showered down on her shoulders. She could hear activity outside and knew the ship must have docked at Freeport.

"The cot is very comfortable," she told the steward as he studied her doubtfully. "Thank you. And thank you for breakfast."

He bowed and took several steps backward as though she were royalty. "It is my pleasure. Señor Bandido said you would prefer tea to coffee, is that right?"

She nodded. "That's right."

"Very well. If you need anything else, ring for me."

"I will. Thank you again."

"Thanks, Lupe," Mike called from the bathroom.

Maggie spotted her robe on the closet doorknob and

pushed herself out of the cot and yanked it on before Mike could see her in her thin cotton gown.

She poured a cup of tea from the plump china pot and took a cautious sip. It was hot and restorative.

But before she could proceed to the bagel and the orange, priority one was to get the cot out of the middle of the floor to give them room to move around without colliding with each other. Lupe had set it up last night, but it should be an easy matter to take it down.

She concluded five minutes later that she'd been hopelessly optimistic. The five and a half feet of canvas with its wooden legs and supports, some of them attached and foldable, some of them slipping in and out of fitted slots, seemed to have a life and will of its own.

It had wrestled her to the carpet and had her in a half nelson when Mike emerged from the bathroom, pulling on a pale blue cotton sweater.

She was distracted from her struggle by the sight of his dark eyes emerging from the sweater's neck. Unguarded, the canvas and wood collapsed atop her head.

She heard him hurry to help her.

"How can someone with the dexterity to make chocolate roses," he asked, laughing as he pulled her free, "be so hopeless with simple fold-and-fit principles?"

He'd pulled her to her feet and they were laughing into each other's eyes, forgetting for a moment the animosity between them. Then his eyes grew serious suddenly and darkened to jet. "Although, I remember," he said softly, absently, "a specific fold-and-fit principle . . . at which you were brilliant."

Sensation bumped up her spine as her mind replayed images of their lovemaking. She would have sworn she could see the same pictures reflected in his eyes.

Then he seemed to come out of the trance they had induced and shook his head at her as though something about her—or *them*—confused him.

"I've got to go," he said abruptly. With a few twists of his hands, the cot became a neat, compact package that he placed in the bottom of the closet. "I'm meeting Danny for breakfast at the pool before we get to work this morning."

"Sure." She sat on the edge of the sofa and picked up her cup of tea, striving for steadiness, normalcy. "I'll be interviewing all the contestants for my story. Do you think he'll have time to talk to me before the competition begins?"

"What time?"

"Eleven?"

"I'll tell him." He opened the door, stopped to look at her for a moment with that same frowning puzzlement, then raised his hand in a wave. "See you then."

"Bye." It wasn't until he was gone that she remembered she hadn't thanked him for ordering her breakfast.

"You find a wife for me yet?" Warren, wearing a chef's hat and coat with the cruise-line logo on them, asked as he looked up from his work table to grin at her. Contestants had been set up at a long series of tables under a tent on the Rainbow Deck, and the press was free to wander among them for several hours before the cruise's guests not visiting ashore were allowed in at noon.

Maggie found it a little painful to turn her back on the resort hotels, coconut palms and white sand beaches visible from the ship's rail, but promised herself she'd get back to this island one day as a tourist.

In Warren's hand was a rolling pin and on the table, something under a piece of waxed paper.

"Not yet, Warren, but you're my first stop this morning." She raised her camera and focused as he worked the rolling pin diagonally across the waxed paper. Something under it crunched. "What have you got under there?"

He lifted the waxed paper to reveal crumbled chocolate sandwich cookies on a second piece of waxed paper.

She shot the picture.

"This is part of the bottom layer of Lightning Creek Bakery's world-famous Wild-Man bars." He lowered the paper and reapplied the rolling pin.

"*World* famous? Really?"

"Well . . . maybe that's promotional talk. But I'm sure they're famous wherever Oklahomans are."

"A family recipe?"

"Yep. From my great-uncle. He started the bakery in the twenties."

Maggie dropped the camera around her neck to take notes.

"Came here from Sweden," he added. "Met my great-aunt on the boat. Told you a cruise is a great place to find a wife."

Maggie simply smiled as she made a note of that. She wasn't about to try to point out the differences in romantic points of view between men and women emigrating in search of new lives and opportunities and men and women seeking pleasure and distraction on a chocolate cruise.

A throaty giggle from down the line of chefs brought her head up. Paula Livingston was trying to lure Mike into a shot she was taking of Danny at work, but he seemed to be resisting.

She laughed and tugged on his shirtsleeve. He smiled in amusement, but took her firmly by the shoulders and turned her so that her camera was aimed at Danny. Then he held her in place until she'd taken several shots.

Maggie's insides were smoldering, though she looked away and pretended to take more notes. In Mike's defense, she had to admit that that was probably the only tactic that would have worked with her, but he'd probably enjoyed employing it. She guessed the woman had a few fold-and-fit skills herself.

She saw that Warren had raised his head to follow sounds of Paula's laughter. She pointed her pen in that direction. "You're not thinking about her as wife material?"

He considered her uncertainly then went back to work. "Don't think so, ma'am. A smilin' woman's one thing. A laughin' woman's somethin' else entirely. Got to attract attention to herself. That can be trouble . . . unless a man can figure out what she needs."

Smart man.

"Tell me what else goes into Wild-Man bars."

He recited a list of ingredients that sounded heavenly. It

included macadamia nuts, coconut, bittersweet chocolate chunks, and all the other wonderful ingredients that produced a fudgey cookie. "Then you drizzle chocolate and caramel on top and one bite turns you into a wild man."

She grinned. "Does it work for women, too?"

"Yep. Makes them wild, too." He looked up from sliding the cookie crumbs from the wax paper into a square pan and winked. "And a smilin' *wild* woman is about all any man could hope for. Be sure to come back for a sample, you hear me?"

"I will."

Maggie interviewed an Italian woman who owned a restaurant in Brooklyn and was making cannolis stuffed with chocolate cream, a woman who owned a candy shop in Denver who was making the most aromatic brownies flavored with espresso, and a baker from Wisconsin who was filling hollowed-out cupcakes with apricot cream. There was a gateau, a cream pie, another variation on the brownie, and a chocolate bird's nest with a raspberry filling that was spectacular but looked more ornamental than edible.

And all the time, she did her best to avoid Paula and to keep her eyes from straying toward Mike, who hovered protectively around Danny and did all the talking with reporters.

When she interviewed Danny in—she consulted her watch—twenty minutes, she would be businesslike, she resolved, and avoid those searching looks and the ripe, double entendres.

The fact that a playful fate had placed a couple who'd once been very much in love on the same ship—and in the same room—after two years of being apart meant only that life could be cruel. It wasn't some star-crossed, karmic reunion. It was an accident—a computer glitch, pure and simple.

And the fact that she was experiencing a sort of resurgence of romantic interest in Mike Lawless meant only that she hadn't been smart enough to learn her lesson the first time.

She drew a deep breath, squared her shoulders, and

marched toward the buffet set up on the Constellation Deck, determined to use the next few minutes to get a refreshing drink and look over her notes.

Then she spotted a tall, balding gentleman in shipboard whites and the affectation of a blue paisley ascot tucked into the V neck of his white sweater. She stopped in her tracks. He was William Spalding, the former chef at the Ritz Manhattan who'd retired several years ago and written several best-sellers on entertaining.

It was well known in the business that he loathed reporters and food critics. He wasn't involved in the bake-off in any way according to the information provided her, so she could only guess he'd come simply to enjoy the proceedings.

Convinced an interview with him would lend texture to her story, she started after him, digging out her tape recorder. His long legs ate up the deck, however, and she soon found herself dodging lounge chairs, waiters with trays, couples dawdling in the February sunshine, just to keep him in sight.

He disappeared through an open door and she followed. She caught up with him as he waited for an elevator.

"Mr. Spalding!" She stopped beside him, breathless, and held out her hand. "I'm Maggie Charles with *Sweet Indulgence* magazine."

He looked her over with blatant male interest. "The supermarket rag of culinary reporting," he said disdainfully, though his eyes settled on her nicely formed but generally unimpressive breasts.

Yuk! she thought, but tried to keep the good of the story uppermost in her mind. She had to keep her job if she was going to continue to sock money away so that she could quit and open her own tea shop. The logic was twisted, she knew, but she was desperate to get her life on track again without her father's help.

"Actually," she corrected graciously, "many of our subscribers are restaurants, caterers, food distrib—"

"Do you want an interview, Miss Charles?" he interrupted.

"Yes," she replied, happy to cut to the cleanup.

The elevator doors parted and he stepped on, then put a hand out to hold them open. His eyes met hers directly. "This is a pleasure cruise for me," he said, and the implied message was clear. "Would you like to talk in my cabin?"

All right. So there were times when the good of the story did *not* have to remain her priority.

She drew a breath and smiled sweetly. "I'm sure a man like you can find pleasure all by himself—and probably often does."

She waved as he dropped his hand in indignation and the elevator doors closed.

Repulsed, Maggie turned away from the elevators. "I wish *I* was here for pleasure," she muttered as she rounded the corner of the passageway—and collided with something tall and solid—Mike.

He held her arms to steady her and grinned. She judged by the gleam in his eye that he'd heard that last grumble.

"Say the word," he suggested quietly, "and we can change business to pleasure in a heartbeat."

The suggestion was not that different from Spalding's, but her mind and her body expressed a definite preference for Mike's. Still, she drew away from him, concealing the instant interest the suggestion sparked in her.

"Yeah, right." She readjusted the straps of her briefcase and camera, trying to remember that he was trouble. "Take the whisk out of your hand and you begin to hyperventilate and lose your sense of identity.

She tried to move past him but he took a step to the side. In the small passageway adorned with those thematic hearts and cupids, that was all it took to block her path. "You don't remember correctly," he said. "It was *you* who made me hyperventilate."

The compliment shook her resolve, but she folded her arms and remained firm. "What are you after? Is a good review in *Sweet Indulgence* that important to you?"

He put his hands in his pockets and leaned his weight on one foot. The grin disappeared and his expression grew speculative. "Don't be mean, Maggie. You know you always regret it later."

"Mean? Me?" An emotional knot was loosening in the pit of her stomach. She thought absently that this was a strange time for a settling of accounts, in a narrow passageway decked out in fussy Valentines on a cruise ship bound for paradise, but it didn't seem to matter. She'd swallowed this emotion two years ago and it had lived like an ulcer inside her all that time. "Which one of us could never think about anything but the business?" she demanded. "Which one of us spent every spare dime to buy the other a romantic Valentine gift, and spilled her guts in a mushy card—and was given in return one of the roses someone else bought *wholesale* for a client's centerpiece, and held out as an expression of *his* undying love? Who, please God, is the mean one?!"

She saw the anger flare in his eyes. This Mike, she realized, was a slightly different man than the one she'd known. It had been almost impossible to rile the other one.

"Who," he demanded quietly, "ground her pretty little heel into the rose?"

"I did!" she shouted back at him. "I did! Me! Maggie! And that wasn't mean because what I really wanted to do was grind my heel into your nose! Or your chin! Or whatever else protrudes from your body and could do with a good kick!"

"You're saying the rose wasn't expensive enough?" he asked. Against her shouting, the question sounded like a whisper.

She punched him hard in the shoulder. "Are you really that testosterone-poisoned and blockheaded? A rose you'd bought just for *me* would have been different." She pointed to herself as she spoke, desperate for him to understand. "It would have shown that you'd thought about me, that you cared! But you just plucked one out of a bouquet you bought for a client and gave it to me as an afterthought—because I'd bought something for you out of the deep love I had for you—and you hadn't even remembered me! So to cover yourself at the last minute, you snatched the rose."

She hated that she was losing control. She'd always

prided herself on remaining in charge, even when angry. But this was bubbling up out of her and she seemed powerless to control it. And strangely, there was something comfortable about simply going with it.

That curious sense of comfort was challenged an instant later when she saw something shift in his eyes. Something that betrayed . . . pain?

"You're sure about that?" he asked flatly. He glanced up at the ring of the elevator bell, and when he looked at her again, that betraying pain had been effectively concealed.

She studied him, everything inside her sharpening. "What do you mean?"

The elevator doors opened and expelled two laughing couples. Mike and Maggie moved against the wall to let them pass.

"Well." He leaned one shoulder against the striped wallpaper and shrugged the other. "I mean that you'd spent all that afternoon in the kitchen while Danny and I ran around trying to round up the extra red pedestal mugs the client had to have at the last minute. How do you know that all I got you was the rose?"

She stared at him for a moment, rocked by a possibility she'd never considered. Then she steadied herself and gave him a pitying look. "Mike, do I look like a noodle? I know that stolen rose is all you got me, because it's all you *gave* me."

He nodded his agreement. "That's right, because you threw it down, stomped on it, I took exception, a fight ensued, and you left. It was all I had time to give you."

"You threw me out," she corrected.

He expelled an amused breath and shook his head. "You called me a workaholic Neanderthal with the manners of a pig. Did that mean you wanted to stay?"

She studied her feet uncomfortably, remembering. "I was upset."

"At least."

She looked up at him, her eyes pinning his, deciding he would not make her feel guilty. He was the one who'd given her a rose he'd snitched from his client.

"You're telling me," she asked, her tone openly skeptical, "that you'd bought me something else?"

"What did I give you for Christmas the year before?" he asked.

That seemed like a non sequitur, but she humored him. She didn't have to think about that but the word "Christmas" brought back instant memories of them around the tree at his mother's with his sister's children running around on their Big Wheels while she opened a shirt box that contained, "A laptop computer," she said.

"And for your birthday?"

Her birthday. She didn't have to think about that, either. They'd been in New York for a foods conference. "You took me to see *Evita*," she said. "And you bought me that Judith Leiber handbag I lusted after."

"So. Is it likely that I'd give you only a stolen rose?"

It was a trap. She analyzed the doubts he'd planted in her mind, wondered with a growing sense of panic if she didn't deserve to fall into it.

"It's what you gave me," she insisted, unwilling to admit anything yet.

He sighed, straightening away from the wall. "But, it was more."

"More than what?"

"More than a rose."

She studied him in confusion, unsure whether to believe him or not. Not that he'd ever done anything that had ever made her doubt his honesty. His love—yes. His honesty—never.

"What?" she demanded, annoyed by the subterfuge, irritated by the suggestion of a possibility that she'd reacted harshly and had been wrong. "What was it?"

"I don't know that it matters now," he replied, pulling her out of the middle of the passageway as the elevator expelled more people. Then he went toward it and held the doors open. "You stomped all over it. Going up?"

She looked into the innocent expression on his face and knew he'd enjoyed toying with her. She did her best not to betray the enormous frustration she felt.

"No, thanks," she said amiably. "I'm on my way to interview Danny. See you there."

"Sorry," he said. "Something's come up." He pushed a button and the elevator doors closed.

She turned away, wondering what he could have meant by the rose being something more. Had there been something in it, or on it that she'd missed in her anger? A little niggle of concern took up residence inside her at that thought. Had she thrown away the love of her life in a fit of pique over a situation in which she'd been mistaken?

As she made her way back up the quiet passageway, she remembered what Mike had said. "You stomped all over it." She had a feeling he hadn't meant the rose.

♡ FOUR

W E'RE PREPARING LOVE Word Cookies," Danny
said, as he cut out heart shapes with a floured cookie
cutter. He glanced up at her with a shy smile even as he cut
away the surrounding dough with a sharp knife. "I seem to
remember the recipe is something you and Mike worked on
together."

That was true, she remembered, distracted from her note-
taking. They'd been catering an engagement party and the
mother of the bride-to-be had wanted something special for
every guest.

Mike had been working on a recipe using hazelnut liqueur
for flavoring. They dipped the cookies in melted chocolate,
and she had traced the edges of the heart shape with icing,
intending to add a rose or something else decorative in the
center.

But Mike had winked at her from across the table while
he snapped off bites of the bare cookie, analyzing it for flavor.

Impulsively, she'd written "kiss me" with icing in the
middle of the cookie and walked around the table to hand it
to him.

"Want to check the chocolate coating?" she asked.

But his eyes had gone to the written message and he'd

promptly followed the instruction. He'd checked the coating only after a considerable interlude.

And the cookie had become a staple of their engagement party menu. She fought a tug of wistful longing as she remembered how hopeful and bright her world had seemed then. She indulged it for a moment, then shrugged it off. She was older and wiser now. Well, older, anyway.

"Yes." She focused her camera on Danny as he transferred the unbaked cookies from the table to a cookie sheet lined with baking parchment. "It's kind of nice to know I have an investment, so to speak, in the cookies. If you become a finalist, will you have to prepare a different recipe?"

"Nope." He worked the cookie cutter across the dough with an almost machinelike efficiency. "We prepare the same one again. Any chef can be brilliant once, but most chefs and caterers have to produce the same menu day in and day out under heavy pressure. So we do it again to prove that we're not one-shot wonders."

"Isn't that the truth." Maggie took notes.

Danny put the pan in the oven behind him, set the timer, wiped his hands on the towel over his shoulder, then went to work on a second pan.

"You have an investment in the boss, too, haven't you?" he asked, his tone carefully neutral as he cut out more shapes and moved them onto the pan.

She lowered the camera, surprised by the personal remark. And the mild suggestion of censure in it.

"I'd say that investment can now be considered a loss," she replied coolly. "And if you don't want to appear on the cover of *Sweet Indulgence* with your eyes closed or your mouth open, don't come out on his side when you don't know what happened."

He leaned floured hands on the board and looked up at her, his green eyes direct. "But, I do know what happened. I was with him that afternoon."

She wondered if she was losing her grip or if there truly was a kind of Bermuda triangle in which sanity was lost. "We had the argument that *night,* Danny."

He nodded. "Over what he bought that afternoon."

"The rose?"

"No."

Here she was again. Déjà vu over the *je ne sais quoi!* "What? What did he buy that afternoon? All I got for Valentine's Day was a rose he stole from our client's bouquet."

He shook his head. "That you stepped all over. I know. He told me when I wrestled him for the bottle of Scotch he was having for breakfast the next morning."

"He gave me a rose," she said slowly, desperate to make him see the slight in the gesture, "that he'd bought for the client's bouquet. Valentine's Day is supposed to be dedicated to gestures of love and devotion. All that gesture showed was carelessness and lack of forethought."

Danny leaned toward her, his eyes grave. "He was giving you more than a rose, Mags."

"You mean the rose was supposed to *represent* more?"

"No. I mean the rose *was* more."

"What?"

He gathered up the tornaway dough and worked it into a ball, obviously retreating from the confrontation. "You should ask Mike."

She looked around, making an exaggerated point of Mike's absence. "He stood behind you like a guardian angel when all the other reporters interviewed you, but I understand that now, something's come up."

Danny met her eyes reluctantly, then looked away. "He got a call from home. There's some kind of problem with the party for Senator Roland this weekend."

"Of course." She refocused the camera on him as he moved the filled cookie sheet aside and pulled a plastic-wrapped package of prepared dough toward him. "Silly of me . . ." she said absently, concentrating on getting a tight shot of his hands. They were lean and elegant despite their coating of flour. ". . . to think he could focus on the matter at hand when Cookin' Good is calling him."

Danny's hands were suddenly out of the picture and his eyes were glaring at her through the lens. "He's a caring and responsible employer who would never leave his people out on a limb because he's on a cruise."

She lowered the camera and forced a smile. "Thank you for your time, Danny. Good luck this afternoon."

"Thank you, Maggie."

"You're welcome."

The civil exchange did nothing to relieve her ill temper, but she forced herself to put Danny's remarks out of her mind.

She toured the rest of the contestants' work stations, got good photographs and interesting tidbits on how their recipes were developed. The reporter in her was pleased with her notes, but the chef in her itched for a day alone with a stove and all the right ingredients.

They left Freeport late that afternoon headed for Nassau.

The bake-off finalists were announced at dinner, and included Mama Majorino's, whom Maggie recognized as the creator of the spectacular bird's nest, Warren Anderson of the Lightning Creek Bakery and . . . she found herself holding her breath . . . Cookin' Good Catering.

She applauded with everyone else at her table—except Isabel, who was buttering a roll. She glanced at Mike's table and saw him and Danny and Paula exchanging hugs and handshakes.

Warren Anderson danced with her after dinner. "Your Wild-Man Bar," she told him, "is marvelous."

"Grand prize marvelous?"

"Maybe. It's awfully hard to beat the combination of macadamia nuts and chocolate in my estimation." His bar cookie concoction had tasted heavenly, but by the nature of what it was, fancy presentation was limited. And many of the other desserts featured candied flowers, glazed fruit, swirls of whipped cream, webs of spun sugar.

Across the room, she saw Mike with Paula in his arms, talking and laughing as they glided across the floor.

The rose was more, she thought, feeling as though she were Jane Marple trying to solve a tricky puzzle. What more could it have been? He'd given her a tightly closed rose bud. There'd been no place to conceal a gift of any kind.

Except . . . something very small. Her heart thudded

against her ribs with the possibility. She wouldn't even let her brain form the word.

Instead, it replayed the image of her flinging the rose to the carpet and bringing the black pump in which she'd worked that night down onto the flower with all her might while spewing venom at Mike.

No. She was jumping to conclusions. They'd talked about marriage but he'd been putting every spare penny back into the business. He'd bought a used but serviceable van that year, a new microwave. He hadn't had money for . . . No. He couldn't have.

Maggie noticed Julie talking to the Goldbecks. When the couple turned into each other's arms to dance, Julie wandered off. Maggie waved to catch her eye, then beckoned her over.

In a pale green toga-style gown, Julie was elegant and beautiful. "Warren, have you met Julie, our purser?" She turned her dance partner around. "Julie, this is Warren Anderson, a finalist in the bake-off."

Julie gave him her professional smile and extended her hand. "Hello, Mr. Anderson. Congratulations."

"He's on the lookout for a woman with a smile."

Julie blinked. "Why?"

Maggie winked at Warren. "Why don't you explain while I get some fresh air." She stayed just long enough to see Julie fit into Warren's arms as the music swelled, then ran lightly for the door.

Maggie found a solitary spot at the railing where she could watch the moonlight on the water and contemplate the status of her life and her career.

Both, it seemed, were going nowhere or at least not in directions that excited and enthralled her. Working for the magazine had its interesting and exciting moments, but she longed to get back into a kitchen, though she wondered if it would ever be as exciting as it had been when she'd worked with Mike.

He'd been interested in everything, enthused about everything, and he made a kitchen feel like a lab where brilliant discoveries were being made. Everything he prepared was imaginative and delicious. And her own abilities had been charged by his. She'd done the best work of her career while cooking with him.

And then dissatisfaction had crept in. He worked so long and so hard, she'd begun to feel that their relationship was something he now took for granted, and that the pressures of work were always his priority.

She'd planned a romantic weekend in the Poconos, hoping to draw him away from work, and discovered he'd booked a party for a Broadway star weekending in Connecticut.

Her father invited them to New York for the reopening of his lounge after a renovation, but Cookin' Good was catering a bar mitzvah. She'd finally gone by herself with Mike's blessing and a strawberry cassis cake he'd baked especially for her father, but she'd resented having to go alone.

She scaled down, planning a romantic evening at home complete with oysters Rockefeller, Mike's favorite pepper and cheese biscuits, a bottle of Perrier Jouet and candlelight—and he'd fallen asleep.

She'd been about to give up on him when the approach of Valentine's Day cajoled her into giving it one more try. She'd shopped for a special gift, worked beside him all evening, waited patiently through the cleanup, which always had to be done immediately, poured champagne, presented him with the monogrammed wallet—and been given the rose.

The rose she was sure he'd taken from the client's bouquet. The rose he'd insisted had been more than a rose.

But what?

She supposed it didn't matter. He'd said whatever it was no longer applied to them.

She sighed and watched the water embroidered by moonlight and thought that though she was on a very large ship, she felt as though she were adrift. Unsuccessful past. Uncertain future. And a here and now she had absolutely no idea how to handle.

Except—if she had been wrong and climbed all over

Mike unfairly—she had to rectify it. She couldn't change what had resulted from that night, but her own conscience demanded that she discover the truth and—if she'd been wrong—admit it.

Yes. She had to do that.

___❤___ FIVE

MIKE WAS NO longer on the dance floor with Paula.
Danny was dancing with her now, and Warren and
Julie swayed to the music, engrossed in conversation.

Maggie checked the lounge, the contest tent, did a quick
tour of several decks, and when she didn't find Mike staring
moodily out at the water, she wondered if he'd gone back to
the cabin.

He had. He'd left the bathroom light on as she'd done the
night before, pulled the door partially closed, and was curled
up rather pathetically on the cot. It was at least a foot too
short for him, and his knees were bent awkwardly.

"Mike?" she whispered.

He didn't want to have to deal with this now. He'd decided
it was safer to come back to the cabin rather than risk in-
dulging the impulse to punch out the kid from Oklahoma.
He didn't know what his problem was tonight.

Delayed reaction over seeing Maggie again, maybe. All
the old dreams resurrected, all the old rejections replayed,
reexperienced.

He'd always prided himself on being open enough to take
a chance on anything once, but then he liked to think he was
intelligent enough to learn from his mistakes. If something

hurt him, he didn't do it again. It was a lesson two-year-olds learned.

But here he lay with memories of Maggie in his arms. Maggie, who'd stomped on his rose.

And now she was here, the sound of her voice coming out of the near-darkness, running over him like a touch. His insides raged for her, but he knew that was foolish.

He pretended to be asleep.

He heard her come closer. "Mike?" she whispered again.

Despite itches and clamoring twitches, he remained resolutely still.

Then he heard the rustle of silk right beside him, her spicy floral scent surrounded him, and he felt her fingertips brush at his forehead, touch his cheek.

Everything inside him turned to mush.

She said his name again.

He slapped her hand away as though swatting at an annoyance in his sleep, hoping to discourage her from whatever her mission was.

He should have known better. Maggie, once resolved, could not be discouraged or even distracted.

She slapped his arm. He'd have had to be dead not to feel it.

"What?" he asked without opening his eyes.

"I have to talk to you," she insisted.

He might be able to deal with that if she was quick. "All right. I'm listening."

She pushed at his shoulder. "I want you to look at me."

Hell. He opened his eyes. She was kneeling on the carpet in the narrow space beside the cot. Her eyes were wide and troubled.

He braced up on an elbow, reluctance turning to concern. "What's the matter?"

She was very close. He could see the dark depths of her eyes, the redwood highlights in her hair, the soft uncertainty in her bottom lip.

"Nothing right now," she said quietly. "But . . . there might be something in the past I have to fix."

He wanted desperately to discourage that. He lay down

again. "It's called the past because it's over. It's done. It is no more."

"But, it affects the present. And the future. If I was wrong about . . . about the rose. I want to tell you that I'm sorry."

"Great. Apology accepted. Go to bed."

He heard the rustle of silk and guessed she'd gotten to her feet. He was congratulating himself on sidestepping a soul-searching discussion when the lights went on and the blanket was yanked off him.

He propped himself up on his elbow again and pinned her with a glare, still clinging to the hope he could intimidate her. "You want to repair the past by being a total pest in the present?"

"If that's what it takes," she said impenitently. Her eyes ran over his body, thinly clad in briefs and a T-shirt. Her cheeks flushed, and she tossed him a pair of sweat bottoms he'd left on the foot of the cot. "I promise not to plague you with a soul-baring discussion on how we felt about each other, or what life's been like since then. I just want to know what happened."

Mike pushed himself off the cot, pulled on the sweats and confronted her, hands resting loosely on his hips. "Okay," he said. "To the best of my recollection I offered my love and you stepped on it."

She nodded, accepting that. "This morning you said you'd given me more than a rose."

Hell and damn. "Yes." It appeared he wasn't going to escape this, so he braced for the inevitable. "I did."

Despite her insistence on an answer, she took a step back as she posed the question. "What did you give me," she asked, "that I didn't see?"

He pulled up the cot with one hand and began to fold it up, desperately needing room to move. "It's in my wallet," he said, tilting his head in the direction of the dresser. "In that wad of tissue where the bills go."

He leaned the cot against the closet door and sank onto a corner of the sofa as she took the few steps to the dresser and picked up the wallet she'd given him that night.

•　•　•

Maggie unfolded the wallet and saw the small but permanent bulge made in the bottom corner of the leather by whatever was kept inside. The size of the little bulge was an instant clue. Gooseflesh prickled on her scalp. Oh, no.

She peered into the bill compartment, pushed aside several twenties, and found the quarter-sized knot of tissue. Dismay and real grief over the two years that had been lost welled up in her. She knew what the tissue contained even before her fingers peeled it back.

A small circlet of gold was attached at an odd angle to a heart-shaped diamond about half a karat in size. It sparkled brilliantly against the crumpled tissue, one prong broken, the setting bent back inside the ring, the obvious victim of considerable abuse.

Tears fell before she could stop them. She looked up at him as they slipped off her chin. "Was it . . . tied to the stem?" she asked.

He pushed himself off the sofa, as though he felt edgy, restless. Then he folded his arms. "No. In a moment of uncharacteristic romantic fervor, I pushed it inside the rosebud. I thought you'd sniff it. You always sniffed the flowers when you made the centerpieces. One of my fondest memories of you . . ." He sighed, then was silent for a moment as though changing his mind about sharing the confidence. Then he finally added, "Is that time we used star-gazer lilies and you had your face in them, like one of the blossoms."

She couldn't remember that. Her mind was consumed with pain and guilt. He'd given her a rose that had contained a diamond, and she'd ground it under her heel.

"And you didn't say anything," she guessed, tears now streaming down her face, "because by that time you were probably deciding you'd escaped a pretty ugly fate."

"I'm not sure why I didn't say anything," he admitted candidly. "I've thought about that a lot in the intervening time. I think there might have been a little relief there."

She uttered a self-deprecating laugh. "I can well imagine."

He took the maimed ring and the wallet from her and put them on the dresser. Then he caught her arm and pulled her with him to the sofa. He pushed her down in the middle of it and sat down facing her with a small distance between them.

"You hurt my feelings and wounded my pride," he said, the words brutal but gently spoken. "No doubt about it. But I knew your reaction was because you thought I'd ripped off the rose from our client and that made the gesture thoughtless to you. Not because you wanted something bigger or more expensive."

She sniffed, her expression perplexed. "Then why *didn't* you tell me?"

"I guess because succeeding had always been so important to me. My father had left town owing everybody, and I was always trying so hard to live down his reputation—even with people who'd never heard of him. I thought making my business a success would somehow redeem me. Striving to be more had always defined me. And suddenly . . ." He looked her in the eye, his expression a curious blend of affection and accusation. "There you were, distracting me from my goal. For someone who'd always had focus, I was unsettled by your ability to cloud my concentration. Still, I knew I couldn't live without you so I was going to propose. On that busy Valentine's Day with one of the biggest parties we'd ever done, I went out and bought a ring."

She wept freely now, but made herself listen as a sort of penance.

"Anyway—in the flush of Valentine's Day schmaltz I hid the ring in the rose and presented it to you."

"God!" she said, putting a hand over her eyes to blot out the memory. "And I killed it! I'm so sorry!"

She experienced a kind of agony over the enormity of what she'd done. Then she felt his hand in her hair, stroking gently. She looked up at him in tearful surprise.

His dark eyes were kind and strangely free of condemnation.

"It was easy to blame you," he said. He cupped her cheek in his hand and swept a tear away with his thumb. "Your reaction had been so vehement, so impetuous. It was satisfying to tell myself you were spoiled and selfish. And a man hates it when he's done something . . . sweet." He said the word with amused distaste. ". . . and it blows up in his face. So I found it easier to play the martyr and let you take the blame, when deep down . . . I think I saw a chance to back out and took it."

Maggie didn't know what to feel. The knowledge that he'd bought her a ring was exhilarating; the fact that he'd been eager to change his mind about proposing was both painful and confusing. But relieving her of at least some of the responsibility and the guilt was a kindness he hadn't had to offer and she was grateful.

But there was something she had to know. "Have you regretted it?" she asked.

He leaned forward to kiss her lightly on the lips, his eyes grave. "Every day for the last two years."

"Me, too!" she wept, wrapping her arms around his neck. She buried her face against his throat. "I'm sorry, Mike. I'm so sorry."

He held her close and kissed her cheek. "So am I, believe me."

They clung to each other for a long time, she relishing the warm comfort and security his arms provided, he wondering if this was real or if he was simply living the dream he'd entertained nightly since she'd left.

If was Mike who noticed the tension first. Gradually, the peaceful, restorative quality of their embrace was replaced by an awareness of how she felt in his arms. The tips of her breasts had beaded against the cotton of his T-shirt, and when she'd wrapped her arms around him she'd hiked herself up into his lap. The soft curve of her hip now sat precisely where frustration and his raging libido were concentrated. Her breath puffed against a pulse at his throat. Her hair tickled his ear. The fragrance of flowers and warm feminine flesh was about to send him over the edge.

Caution required that he push her away. The moment was fragile. If they succumbed to passion when thought was called for, they could repeat the same mistakes.

But he'd never operated cautiously, he'd always believed in seizing the moment, and he'd never regretted his mistakes when they taught him something.

And the last mistake he'd made with her had taught him to make sure she knew where he stood.

Maggie felt the sudden edgy tension and pressed her hands against his chest to wedge a space between them. He freed her only as far as the loop of his arms would allow.

She saw a new purpose in his eyes that caused a little frisson of sensation along the back of her neck.

She felt drawn toward him as though he were magnetic north. But was that wise? The last time they'd moved too fast, thought too little. It was important to think now, she told herself, but his eyes were stroking her, drawing her, and thought was quickly giving way to complex sensation.

"We should . . . talk," she managed to whisper as he leaned closer and kissed her lips. His were warm and artfully mobile.

"You're right," he said, planting kisses along her jawline to her ear. "But not now."

She sighed as he dipped his tongue inside her ear and every nerve ending reacted. At the heart of her femininity, desire swelled to fill her with a warm and liquid weight.

"But . . . we didn't allow much time . . . the first time," she tried to reason as he moved to trace kisses down the line of her throat. "We . . . we . . . worked together a few days, went to Federico's for dinner and criticized the Seviche, then we became . . ."

He'd reached her mouth again and she was forced to stop.

"Lovers," he finished for her, opening his mouth on hers, dipping his tongue inside.

She clung to him as he delved deeply, drawing out of her a response that remembered and rejected the loneliness of the past two years, that recaptured and renewed the dreams they'd once shared.

When he finally freed her, the breath she gasped was his name.

"Make love with me now," he whispered into her ear even

as his fingers pulled at the zipper of the lace dress. "Now. Right now."

She tried to remember why talking first had seemed so important and couldn't. She dissolved against him and tugged at the hem of his T-shirt.

—♡ SIX

MIKE PULLED MAGGIE to her feet, then applied a tug and a push to open the sofa into a double bed, and then he went back to her, offering her a hand to steady her as she stepped out of the dress.

She pulled a silky black slip up and off and he felt the old astonishment come over him again as she stood before him in black lace pantyhose and bra. He'd always thought she was perfect, her hips and breasts a little too round for a fashion runway and just round enough to make him wonder what he'd done to be so blessed with her.

While he stared at her, mute with reverence, she walked into his arms.

Her small hands worked under his T-shirt, and he felt her fingernails graze up and over his ribs as she pushed the cotton fabric up. He raised his arms obligingly, and when she could no longer reach, he yanked the shirt off himself and tossed it aside.

She unhooked the front fastening of her bra and pulled it off.

He splayed a hand between her shoulder blades and pulled her to him. The first flesh-to-flesh contact drew a little cry of pleasure from her and a groan from him. It was as though he'd been holding his breath for two years, he thought, and was finally able to exhale.

Maggie felt the softness of her breasts mold themselves to the muscular solidity of his chest and swore she could feel her world right itself. It had been off kilter, out of orbit in the time they'd been apart, and now it seemed to fall into place.

And with that came a sort of personal renewal. She could feel the breath moving in her body, the blood pumping in and out of her heart; every little receptor in her body was now alive and waiting . . . waiting.

She put her lips to Mike's breastbone, to his throat, to his chin, and stood on tiptoe to reach his lips. His arousal pressed against her and she felt embraced suddenly by the warm familiarity of all they'd once shared. She wanted desperately to be filled with him now. Right now.

The urgency in her communicated itself to him as she ran her hands over his shoulders, across his pectoral muscles, over his ribs and to the hollow of his belly.

He caught her hand before she could reach her goal.

"I want to touch you," she whispered against his mouth, her hand pulling against his.

He held firm and drew her fingers behind her back, holding her tightly to him.

"I want to make you wait," he said, nipping at her bottom lip. "I want you to pay . . ." He nibbled along her jawline. ". . . for depriving me of you all this time."

She gasped a little laugh against his cheek. "But I want . . . to touch you. To give you pleasure."

He slipped his free hand inside the back of her panties and traced her right buttock with the palm of his hand.

"It gives me pleasure," he said, as she squirmed against him, "to remind you that we're in this together. That I want some things, too."

"What?" she pleaded in a whisper. "Tell me."

Maggie wondered if it was possible to die of waiting. Her emotions were coiled so tightly she was afraid release, if it ever came, would fling her out into space—or into the endless stretch of ocean beyond their window.

"Tell me, Mike," she prompted, the possessiveness of his touch insidiously robbing her of any desire to be apart from him in any way.

"I want you," he said as he kissed her shoulder, "to tell me how much you've missed me."

She tried to run her free hand, caught over his shoulder, down the middle of him. "I want to *show* . . ."

He caught it and held it behind her with the other in one hand.

"No," he insisted. "I want you to *tell* me." With his other hand he tugged her panties down and explored the contours of her bottom.

He felt her sigh against his chest.

"I turned to . . . to writing . . ." she said breathlessly, "because working in a . . . in a kitchen without you was too . . . painful. And no fun at all. Mike, please . . ."

"Go on." His hand swept up her back, lingered in the small of it, then swept over the swell of her hips, first one, then the other until she felt robbed of air, of mind.

"Days were lonely, though crowded with people," she said in a rush. "Nights were black and endless . . . endless." She said the word a second time and with a sincerity that echoed what he'd felt in his darkest hours.

He freed her hands and framed her face to kiss her soundly, with comfort and promise.

"Can I touch you now?" she asked when he freed her lips.

"No," he replied and scooped her up into his arms.

She frowned into his eyes and asked with an edge of humor, "Has it been so long that you've forgotten how we used to do this?"

He grinned. "I haven't forgotten a thing. But we broke up your way. We're coming together again my way."

She went limp in his arms with a mournful groan.

When he dropped her in the middle of the bed and walked away, Maggie sat up indignantly, prepared to argue if he'd suddenly decided to talk instead. But he went only as far as the lightswitch. The room went black and he was back with her in an instant.

He pulled her panties off, rid himself of sweat bottoms and briefs, then pulled her astride him.

She leaned over him, her heart filled with love, with joy

doubled by the anguish of their separation, and with a desperate need to finally . . . finally . . . take him inside her.

"Now?" she asked.

He pulled her down on him, stroked her thighs with a strong sweep of both hands, then held her to him and dipped a finger gently inside her. He kissed her cheek. "No," he said. "Because there's so much I want to give you first. And the minute you touch me, it'll be too late."

"But . . . but . . ." A hundred noble protests sprang to her lips. "But I want you to have pleasure, too. This first time together again we should both . . ."

But he was stroking her, delving inside then retreating, circling . . . circling . . . and she lost her ability to form words.

But not her ability to move. His concentration solely on her and the rapidity of her breathing, on the little sounds she made that came to his ear like music, he lost track of her wayward hand.

Then it was on him, caressing him, enfolding him, driving him to madness.

The only option left him was to lift her onto him. She laced her fingers with his and danced atop him, like an ivory goddess in the moonlight from the window.

The power of their climax astonished him. He was indefatigable and she kept pace with a wild fervor that left them entwined and exhausted as dawn began to color the horizon.

Maggie lay against him, amazed that what had begun as heartwarmingly familiar had turned, as the night wore on, into something new and wonderful.

He'd been even more tender, more possessive, more generous, and she'd strived to be more giving, more responsive, more . . . just more.

Was this a principle she'd missed the first time around, she wondered. That giving more got more, which inspired more giving and ultimately more receiving?

She leaned her forearm on Mike's chest and looked into his eyes with a shiny newness in her own.

"I feel as though it's my birthday," she said, resting her

chin on her hand. "And my gift is that our love survived for two years, even without us."

He brushed her bangs out of her eyes and smiled. "The stuff has a remarkable shelf life, hasn't it?"

She frowned suddenly, moodily, and moved to lay down beside him. She settled into that familiar and comfortable spot in the hollow of his shoulder. "I mean, what if it had been—say—two years and one month. Maybe it wouldn't have survived. Maybe you have to do something with it within a certain amount of time or it . . ."

"Expires? Like milk or medicine?"

"Yes." She felt stricken suddenly by the possibility that she might have found herself in the same cabin with Mike, looked into his eyes, and seen nothing there—no desire for her, no evidence that he'd carried memories with him as she had of their time together. "What if we'd been too late?"

He heard the sadness in her tone and held her closer. "No point in considering that," he said lightly. "We've obviously caught *us* before the pull date. All we have to do is decide how to put *us* to use."

It occurred to her that that was what had gotten them into trouble the first time. But she was too delirious with what they'd just shared to believe in anything but happily ever after.

"We can talk it over while touring Nassau," she said, snuggling against him. "What time are we supposed to go ashore?"

"I'm not sure. I think we dock at seven."

She closed her eyes. "Good. We can still get close to eight hours."

There was a moment's silence, then he asked in distress, "Of sleep?"

SEVEN

"WHAT ABOUT THIS one?" Mike pointed to a colorful woven purse on a rack with dozens of them in Nassau's famous Straw Market. They were literally surrounded by woven goods of every description.

The air was fragrant with the unique smell of straws and grasses in the market and the heady perfume of wandering ocean breezes.

Maggie turned away from the rack of bags she'd been studying to look over her shoulder at Mike. She dismissed the bag with a shake of her head. "It has to have a pocket."

He peered inside the bag. "It does," he reported, "with a zipper."

She came to join him and kiss his cheek. He carried all the souvenirs she'd bought that morning—slippers, a hat, a local artist's scenic painting of Prince George Wharf for her father. "Thank you for helping, but it has to have a pocket on the *outside*."

He rolled his eyes. "I'm helping because I'm beginning to take root in this spot. Why does the pocket have to be on the outside?"

She noticed a bag on the bottom of the rack and pulled it off the hook. "For my keys," she said. The bag was brightly colored in a horizontal pattern and had a roomy pocket fastened with a loop and a little wooden knob. She undid it and placed her hand inside, checking the size.

"Your keys?" He pretended shock. "What? Is this an attempt to organize Maggie's Pandora's box? Oh, I don't think I could deal with that. I mean, it wouldn't be right if I didn't have to stand behind you for twenty minutes in the dark while you dig for house keys in the bottom of your purse. Or search for theater tickets while the natives are getting restless behind us, or change for the parking meter, or . . ."

She looked up from her examination of the purse, liking the idea that he was imagining them together in the future. She teased him with a raised eyebrow. "I get the point, Lawless. I'm trying to rectify the problem."

"Okay," he said doubtfully, humor alive in his eyes as he made a point of peering into the large leather pouch over her shoulder. "But you could upset the delicate balance of the ecosystem in there. You're probably harboring undiscovered life forms who've never seen the light of . . ."

She caught the front of his shirt in a fist and pulled him down until they were nose to nose. "Let me inform you," she said firmly, her eyes filled with laughter and adoration and playful severity, "that my purse and I are an even closer unit than you and I."

The amusement in his gaze flared with something else, something dark and velvet and all-consuming. He dropped the packages to the ground, careful to lean the painting against the nearby stall, then opened his mouth over hers and kissed her hotly. Her hand on his shirt slackened, but his hand at her back held her to him so that every curve of her body was pressed into every muscled plane of his.

His hand slid down to her bottom, and for her it was suddenly last night again. This busy little marketplace had faded away; they were back in their cabin, body to body, a fit so perfect it had to be cosmically ordained.

"Closer than this?" he asked, nipping at her lip.

"Well . . ." Intoxicated with his attention, she required a moment to reply. "Maybe not closer," she conceded with a grin, her voice breathy. "But a working woman's relationship with her . . . with her purse is a special thing. She has to take her man the way he is, but she can select a purse from a wide assortment to make sure she gets one she can live with."

He studied her in interested surprise. "You haven't been to a singles bar lately, have you? Women do select men from a wide assortment."

She turned the purse over to study the back, giving him a smiling glance. "Some of us aren't fortunate enough to have a choice. Your heart calls to another heart, and that's all the say you have in the matter."

That was how it felt, he thought. As though he'd had little choice. He'd seen her in her father's kitchen under a rakishly angled chef's hat with perspiration on her upper lip and the devil in her eye and he'd been lost. Or found. There had been times when it was hard to tell which. But this time he knew. She was his. He was hers. Forever.

"Okay." He fitted the small packages into the bigger ones to make his burden less awkward. "What you seem to be forgetting is that your man can take you places your purse can't."

She handed the purse to the clerk and came to help him as he picked up the packages again. "Really." She took advantage of his arms being full and stretched up to kiss his lips. "My purse has taken me to Saks Fifth Avenue, Bloomingdale's." She grinned. "Baskin and Robbins."

He was happy to let her have her way with him. He waited until the clerk had handed back her package and she'd turned to him, asking with a glance if he was ready to go.

"Has your purse ever taken you to a quaint goldsmith on Bay Street to have your diamond reset?" he asked.

She stared at him in stunned surprise. He loved it. The fragrant breeze swirled her cotton skirt around her knees, made the off-the-shoulder ruffle on her blouse ripple, stirred her spiky bangs.

"You . . . really want to do that?" she asked. "After the last time?"

She looked so regretful. He wanted to erase all guilt on either side. "Of course. But we don't have to rush to the altar. If you need time, we'll take time."

She came to wrap her arms around him with a little sigh that said volumes. "I don't need time," she said, looking into his eyes with adoration in hers. "I just need you."

And she kissed him slowly, sweetly.

"Ah, a heart shape." The goldsmith frowned at the diamond in the mangled setting, then looked up at Mike and Maggie, their dark heads together as they leaned over the black velvet on which he'd placed the ring. All around him were glass cases filled with brilliant stones of every cut and color, burnished pearls, gleaming gold and silver. He grinned. "A stormy relationship?"

"A misunderstanding," Mike corrected.

The man, who was small, round and bald, held the ring up. One prong stuck out awkwardly. "After which one of you drove over it with a tank?"

Maggie leaned her forehead against Mike's forearm, embarrassed.

He laughed softly and patted her hand. "Can you reset it?" he asked the goldsmith.

"Of course. Something plain so as not to distract from the stone?"

Mike looked at Maggie.

"Yes," she said, "please."

"Can you have it ready in the morning?" Mike produced a credit card. "We're on the *Bahama Duchess*, and we'll be leaving in the afternoon."

"It will be ready at eleven."

They bought a "take-away" lunch and ate it at Rawson Square, where they had a perfect view of a replica of a tall ship on the jewel-blue water, of tugs and fishing boats and puff-sailed pleasure boats.

Then Mike rented a room at a small mansion-cum-hotel and they made love all afternoon with the windows open to the sunny afternoon and a perfumed breeze blowing the gauzy curtains.

"Let's stay the night," Mike suggested when the waning

sun seemed to set even the ocean aflame. "We'll have an elegant dinner then come back here and nibble on each other all night long."

"But I have an interview at eight in the morning with the judges," she complained regretfully, wishing she and Mike had no one to answer to but themselves. "And my skirt and blouse are pretty rumpled."

"No problem," he said. "We'll go back to the boat for a change of clothes, then I'll get you back aboard in time for your interview. I'll have to check on Danny anyway, make sure he's got everything he needs. How long will the interview take?"

"A couple of hours."

"Good. After that, we'll come back and pick up the ring."

"I love you," she said fervently.

He swatted her bottom as she climbed out of bed. "It's about time you came around."

They dined at the Buena Vista, another old mansion turned to profitable use. They gazed into each other's eyes across the candlelight. Maggie wore a pale blue dress with a halter top and a glow on her face that turned heads in her direction.

Mike's dark good looks were an impressive counterpoint to the white linen suit he wore with the ease of a Rick's Cafe Bogart. Unused to seeing him relaxed, Maggie leaned her chin on her hand and admired the picture he made.

"So you *can* put the business on hold for a little while," she observed.

He pushed his empty plate away and leaned toward her. "I concentrate on business," he said, "only when it needs me. Unfortunately, when we were together it was new and it needed me all the time. It's a little better now."

"Only a little?"

He made a so-so gesture. "When you're dealing with people—employees or clients—crises crop up all the time. If you care about keeping both of them happy and about keeping a handle on quality control, it takes a lot of time."

"I can deal with that," she said, reaching across the table

to cover his hand with hers, "if I know that you love me as much as you love being in the kitchen."

He scolded her with a look. "I love you more than anything. I could go back to working in a restaurant, but then you'd be gone all day for the magazine, and I'd be doing dinners and not getting home until after midnight. That doesn't sound like much of a life, either." He shrugged. "And with my own business, when kids come along, I can have them in the kitchen with me instead of at a sitter's."

The picture in her mind's eye of Mike in the kitchen with a baby carrier at his elbow crowded out all doubts about her ability to adapt once again to the life he led. Tears filled her eyes. "I like that idea."

He turned his hand to catch her fingers and stood to lead her onto the dance floor where horns and violins played something poignant and sentimental.

He took her into his arms and she wrapped hers around his neck and leaned into him.

"I like it, too," he whispered, then kissed her ear.

She tipped her head back to look into his eyes. "I want to come back to work for you."

He held her to him as another couple got too close on the crowded dance floor. "Of course," he said with a smile. "Danny's worked to a nub. But why do you want to? Isn't reporting more glamorous than baking?"

She made a small sound of feigned indignation. "I didn't get into reporting for the glamor. I got into it to get out of the kitchen."

That apparently made no sense to him. "But you're a natural in the kitchen. A magician."

She steadied her gaze on him and dropped every defense. "I love cooking. But after we broke up, I worked for two months in a hotel kitchen and thought I'd die from missing you. I mean, it was bad enough to miss you at home, but we worked together every day, and being without you in a kitchen was like being lost on the moon. I hated it."

Mike stopped moving to the music and drank in the sadness in her eyes. Then he kissed her soundly to chase it away. "I lost half my staff the first few months you were gone because I turned into Frankenstein—only I made *myself* into a monster. But those days are over. Here we are together again . . ." He looked around them and added with displeasure, "In the middle of a crowded dance floor. Let's get back to the hotel where I can really show you how glad I am to have you back."

EIGHT

M AGGIE SANK ONTO a deck chair in the sun aboard
the *Bahama Duchess* and kicked off her espadrilles.
She lay back and closed her eyes against the tropical bright-
ness but opened her arms to it, inviting it to warm and renew
her body.

Heaven knew she'd gotten precious little sleep the night
before, but she wouldn't have changed a second of the delicious and inventive ways in which she and Mike had dealt
with insomnia.

She smiled absently at the thought that the fragrance of
poinciana and a slowly turning ceiling fan would forever be
aligned in her mind with the taunting approach of climax.

She forced her mind back to business. This would be her
last feature, but she had to make sure it was well done.

The three judges she'd just interviewed were a mixed bag
of backgrounds and subtle prejudices, and she couldn't for
the life of her even guess which contestant they would favor.

One judge, a woman, had begun a small operation out of
her kitchen providing pies and cakes to local coffee shops.
A reproduction of her face was now on the packaging of her
product in every grocery store freezer on the east coast.
She'd spent most of the interview promoting a new cream
pie she was adding to her lineup.

One of the two men on the panel was a former food critic

for the *New York Times* who'd retired several years ago to write cookbooks and seemed to be bored with the proceedings. The other was a pastry chef from the French Quarter in New Orleans on whom she'd had to concentrate closely to understand.

No one had been willing to suggest a favorite.

The bake-off would take place that afternoon as the ship sailed for home.

Maggie felt herself relax as the sun began to permeate her pores. The warmth inside her rose to meet it so that she felt almost like a new creation, as though a love renewed and the balmy tropics had reshaped her somehow into a new entity.

Her body felt stronger, more supple, and when she concentrated, she could still feel Mike touching her with that tender but possessive confidence that was comforting and exciting all at once.

Her mind felt free. She knew where her life was going now. She and Mike were going to work together and raise their babies in the kitchen. The thought filled her with a radiating glow.

She got to her feet and headed back to their cabin, where she was to meet Mike for the quick trip to the goldsmith's.

She changed quickly into a brightly patterned skirt and top she'd bought yesterday morning on Market Street, combed her hair and freshened her makeup. She was about to become engaged. Excitement filled her.

She looked about the tiny cabin and thought about how she would miss its confining dimensions. In the hotel last night, she and Mike had laughed about how odd it seemed not to have to sidle past each other to move about—though they had anyway by choice rather than out of necessity.

She wrapped her arms around herself, feeling girlish and new. She wished Mike would arrive. Three hours apart was beginning to seem like an eternity.

When the clock read eleven-thirty, she began to pace. When it got to twelve, she began to worry. Something was wrong. A crisis with the catering staff at home, she guessed. Well. She promised to try to turn over a new leaf and be less upset about all the times business interfered with her life.

Cookin' Good was Mike's life, and she wanted Mike. She had to learn to live with it. But she couldn't help a grim disappointment that business was interfering when they were about to reclaim their life together.

A sudden rap on the door sent her flying to it to yank it open. Lupe stood in the passageway.

"Señorita Margarita," he said with an expressive widening of his eyes. "Thank goodness. I have a message for you, but it is very late. Señor Bandido called at ten-thirty, but you were in a meeting, then the *diabla pequena*, Isabella, she was lost and we were all looking for her."

Little devil Isabel. It wasn't difficult to figure out who that was.

"Is she all right?"

"She stole a cake and a bowl of strawberries from the buffet on the Constellation Deck and she is now being very sick in the infirmary. But she will be all right."

"Good." The child was out of control, but Maggie had to admit that only a very fine veneer of adult civility had prevented her from swiping things from the tempting buffets. "What did Señor Bandido say?"

"Oh, yes. He says to tell you he is very sorry, but there had been an emergency."

Her heart bumped against her ribs in alarm. She'd known something was wrong. "What kind of an emergency?"

Lupe frowned, as though trying to remember the details. "He says, a man who works for him called this morning . . ."

Maggie fought an instinctive annoyance that the staff at home couldn't function without him for one day. They didn't know he was planning to be engaged today, of course, but they had to know that the bake-off's final round was this afternoon. The winner of the contest would be named today.

And it was Valentine's Day, for heaven's sake. Didn't they have romances of their own to distract them from work and keep them busy with other things?

She acknowledged with fatal acceptance that Mike didn't run that kind of a business. Of course their minds were on the next party. That was the only kind of employee he retained.

She quelled personal disappointment and tried to remember that it wasn't Mike's fault that an untimely emergency at home had claimed his attention. And his insistence on handling it personally was representative of a responsible and caring nature and that she loved him for it. Mostly.

All right, she decided, shouldering her camera. She would go down to the contest tent to see if there was anything she could do for him. If not, she would employ herself photographing the finalists.

She was walking the main deck, heading for the tent, when she collided with Julie, who had an armful of flowers pressed against her uniform jacket. She looked befuddled but happy.

"Hi," Julie said vaguely, as though her attention was elsewhere.

"Hi." Maggie held her in place and backed up to frame Julie's face and the flowers in her viewfinder. "What's happening? Your birthday?"

She shot the picture and lowered the camera. Julie shook her head, looked into her bouquet then back at Maggie with a startled little laugh. "No. I've just been proposed to."

Maggie ignored the irony of the situation. That was supposed to happen to *her* today. "Congratulations," she offered, delighted that someone was focusing on romance on this Valentine's Day. Then it occurred to her who that someone might be. "Warren Anderson?" she asked.

Julie nodded, looking stunned. "Yes. I think he's crazy, but I guess I must be, too, because I'm considering it. I'm going home with him to meet his family."

"All *right*!" Maggie hugged her. That was how love should be, she thought. Spontaneous, risk-taking, heroic.

"We talked until three A.M. when you introduced us," Julie said. "And spent all day yesterday touring Nassau and discovering that though we have very different backgrounds, we have a lot in common." She giggled girlishly. "He likes my smile. Imagine. In this day and age—my smile."

She walked away, looking like a woman in a dream.

Maggie sighed over her obvious pleasure and turned wryly in the direction of the chocolate tent.

So her own proposal had played second fiddle to a business crisis. So it had been held in abeyance for two years and been reborn as the result of a computer glitch. It was just as real. It just wasn't as romantic. She could live with that. She hoped Mike had remembered to call the goldsmith and asked him to deliver the ring to the ship.

Maggie peered over the railing for something to photograph, and her thought about love was followed suddenly and immediately by a freezing of all bodily function. Then pain burned its way through, leaving a large hole where all her dreams had been.

Running along the pier toward the gangplank, hand in hand, were Mike and Paula Livingston. As though watching actors on a stage, Maggie saw them stop halfway up the ramp, turn into each other's arms, and exchange a few urgent words. Then Paula leaned into Mike's shoulder, he held her tightly with an intimate cheek-to-cheek squeeze, then they pulled apart and hurried off in opposite directions. It occurred to her darkly that Mike had probably forgotten the ring completely.

♡ NINE

SHE TOLD HERSELF it wasn't an urge to die she was feeling as she followed Mike from a safe distance, but rather a wish to kill.

He hurried down a passageway in a smoking section of the Lagoon Deck, then unlocked a door and went inside.

So he'd kept two rooms. Interesting. Or was this one Paula's? She followed him in.

The room was tidy and just like the room she and Mike had occupied, except that the sofa was green.

Mike had opened the closet door and was removing something when the click of the closing cabin door made him turn to her in surprise.

"Maggie," he said. His eyes were troubled, his manner vaguely preoccupied.

Big surprise, she thought.

"Lupe told me there was an emergency," she said, leaning a shoulder against the wall in the narrow space near the bathroom. "Silly me. I thought it was a business problem and was extending myself to try to be understanding."

He was studying her warily, his eyes narrowing on hers as though he were trying to read her mind and not liking what he saw.

She decided to make that unnecessary, making no effort to hide what she was thinking and feeling.

"But I guess if it required Paula Livingston to help you handle it, the emergency couldn't have been business, could it?"

She saw the anger take shape in his face. She guessed because he succumbed to it so seldom, he was magnificent in a temper. There was no sneer on his face, no angry tick, no gritting of teeth.

Every elegant feature remained smoothly, coldly in place. His eyes darkened under an even ridge of brows, his mouth and jaw set in firm, hard lines, and he looked as though no natural force could move him.

A corner of her mind not occupied with her own anger, wondered what *he* had to be mad about. Unless it was the fact that he'd been discovered.

He draped a hanger with kitchen whites over his arm, closed the closet door and came toward her. He stopped several inches from her, that mask of cold anger in place, and said quietly, "Get out of my way, Maggie."

She returned his stare. Her face wasn't as impressive, she knew, but the fury raging inside her had to give her an edge.

"I just want to take a moment to tell you that I was willing to accept that business had gotten in our way yet again. I know I was demanding and selfish last time, but I was determined to be more tolerant and sympathetic today. But your standing me up to run into Nassau with Paula the morning we were supposed to become engaged is a little more than I can let slide. Or did you pick up the ring for her? Ah!"

A cry of alarm escaped her when he tossed the hanger aside, yanked her forward out of the narrow space and lifted her up into his arms. The gesture was far from gentle, and she began to struggle.

He set her down in the closet and held her there with a firm hand right in the middle of her chest. "You should be locked up where you can't hurt yourself or anybody else," he said, his voice vibrating with a cold and quiet fury. "Do yourself a favor and don't come out until you've given me time to get far away from you."

Then he closed the door in her face.

She screamed at him through the door, then yanked it

open, rage, pain, disappointment, disillusionment all roiling inside her like a fatal flu.

She raced for the door, determined to find Julie and tell her that she had to find her another cabin for the night or she would stay in Nassau tonight and fly home from there. She was not spending another night confined with Señor Bandido Bastardo.

She yanked the door open and looked into the very concerned face of a young steward. "Have you come for Mr. Campbell's things?" he asked.

She had a little difficulty shifting her mind from traumatic fury to that curious question.

"Mr. Campbell?" she asked, wondering what Danny or his things could possibly have to do with this room. Then she remembered the white kitchen jacket over Mike's arm. So. This wasn't Paula's room. It was Danny's. That didn't change anything.

"Yes," the steward replied. "Mr. Lawless said someone would be here to pick up his things. He asked if I would pack them."

Maggie was trying desperately to get a handle on the conversation. "Pack Mr. Campbell's things? Why? Where is he going?"

The steward studied her a moment and she got the definite impression he was beginning to think her simple.

"You haven't heard about the accident?"

A warning signal shut off all her other concerns and focused her attention on the steward. "No," she replied flatly. "What accident?"

"He was hang gliding this morning and got caught in a crosswind and landed in a tree. He fell out and broke his leg. He'll be several days in the hospital, so we'll be sailing without him."

A part of her anger shriveled and collapsed. "Is he all right?" she asked, imagining smiling Danny in a hospital bed.

"Mr. Lawless said the doctor assured him it is a simple break but that he is in great pain and should be still for several days."

Maggie's virulent emotional flu collected new ingredients. Concern for Danny and confusion. Major confusion.

Had that been the emergency Mike had left the ship to deal with? But he'd still taken Paula with him instead of her. Of course, she'd been keeping an appointment with the contest judges.

With a sense of burgeoning dread, Maggie stepped aside to let the steward into the room.

The doorway was blocked again immediately by a very puffy-faced Paula. She took one look at Maggie, wrapped her arms around her and burst into sobs.

"Oh, Maggie. Isn't it awful? Poor Danny! I'm the one who talked him into hang gliding. I feel so guilty!" She drew out of Maggie's arms to dab at her nose with a shredded tissue. Her blue eyes were tear-filled and anguished. "Thank God it was just a broken leg. I mean that's bad enough, but when he lay there so pale and lifeless, I thought for sure I'd killed him. I don't know what I'd have done if I hadn't been able to reach Mike."

Major, major confusion. "You were with *Danny*?"

Paula nodded with a roll of her eyes. "I've been dogging his footsteps for a year, hoping to get him to see me as someone other than that annoying woman who keeps having Cookin' Good cater her parties so that she can see him." She sighed. "Anyway, we were dancing the other night. Talked a lot about what we like and what we want. He was surprised to learn that I like Fellini films and hockey and birdwatching. We stayed on the island together last night."

Danny's eclectic interests had been a source of good-natured ribbing when they'd worked together. Who'd have guessed that Paula liked the same things? It was said there was someone for everyone.

Maggie was beginning to believe, though, that that didn't apply to her.

"Anyway," Paula went on, sniffing and pulling herself together. "I'm leaving the ship to stay with Danny and fly home with him."

Guilt and a sense of abject stupidity clouded Maggie's

ability to think. Then simple charity took over and she offered to help Paula pack Danny's things.

She saw Paula off the ship and into a cab and was hugged gratefully for her efforts.

Back in her own cabin, Maggie paced restlessly in the small space allowed her, wondering how on earth she could explain her behavior to Mike when she'd figuratively taken his rose and ground it into the carpet a second time.

She remembered the handsome symmetry of anger on his face and knew an apology wasn't going to do it this time. What she'd just done might be irreversible.

She could still see Mike's face in her mind's eye, read the anger and the disappointment there. She groaned as she paced, wondering what to do.

Then she focused on the bakery jacket Mike had held over his arm and she realized with sudden impact that he was dealing with a business crisis here, as well as the personal one she'd dumped on him with both hands.

Danny was in the hospital. That meant Mike himself would have to prepare the recipe this afternoon for the competition. But as fine a chef as he was, he hadn't Danny's fine-fingered dexterity with the all-important decorations.

And if he didn't win the contest and the cash prize, he wouldn't be able to pay off the bank and buy a new van.

Despite all the time she'd resented it in the past, she knew he worked like a fiend to make financial ends meet while still providing his clients with the finest possible dishes and his employees with a comfortable wage and good benefits.

The need to help him tore at her.

Then inspiration struck. She stood still, afraid to breathe, as she considered it. She smiled grimly to herself, imagining his reaction when she suggested her solution. Perhaps she should go armed.

M IKE WIPED OFF his work station, checked his ingredients again. The competition didn't begin for another hour, but he was doing his best to psych himself up for
it. He could do this, he told himself, though he'd completely
lost interest in whether he did or not.

With a bum for a father, he'd always pressed himself to
prove himself different from the man who'd abandoned wife
and family. But his mother had often stopped him in the
middle of his working frenzies to remind him that life was
not about winning or losing, but simply about showing up to
compete.

And that was all that directed him now.

He loved a madwoman. It was difficult to think seriously
about the just outcome of anything—even a baking contest—when one was dealing with a fate that had made him
fall in love with Maggie Charles. The odds had to be against
him.

But going on in the face of adversity was what he did.
He'd done it at twelve when he'd delivered two paper routes
to help his mother pay the rent, he'd done it in the first year
of his business when expenses had outdistanced profits and
he'd taken a second mortgage on the house and cooked from
five A.M. to ten A.M. for a short order restaurant to meet the
payments before reporting to work for himself.

He'd done it two years ago when the business was thriving, but Maggie took exception to the time it took and ground his rose into the carpet.

He tried to ignore the beginning of a major migraine and remembered in all fairness that he'd accepted part of the blame for that. Then he recalled her accusations of an hour ago and decided that fairness could be damned.

"You don't stop rubbin' that table," the kid from Oklahoma said with a grin as he leaned an elbow on it, "and you'll be down to legs and nothin' to work on."

The kid handed him a steaming paper cup. Mike took it with grudging gratitude. It smelled like Turkish roast coffee.

He'd learned in the last few days that Warren Anderson was genuine and disarmingly cheerful, and he didn't want to be talked out of his acute depression.

"You shouldn't have stopped me." Mike toasted him with the cup and took a sip. Thank you, God, he thought. It *was* Turkish roast coffee. "It'd narrow the field for you if I had nothing to work on."

Anderson shook his head. "Nah. I been readin' the judges and I think we're both doomed."

Mike looked at him over the rim of his cup with only moderate interest. Doom held no horror for him. He already knew how it felt.

"I think they'll be partial to Mrs. Majorino." He pointed to the third finalist on Mike's other side, a wiry, dark-haired woman of middle age who'd produced a nest made of chocolate strands and filled with a mousselike mixture, which she then decorated with sugar birds. "She does pretty work, but how often could you turn out something like that? How could you pack it in a lunch?" He shook his head philosophically. "We've got the taste, but I think she's got 'em with the razzle dazzle."

She looked to Mike as though she should be on Prozac. Schwarzkopf must have looked that intense when he planned Desert Storm. Then he felt his own glowering countenance and thought with wry perception that she might simply be in love with a man who made her crazy.

Mike shrugged off any suggestion of disappointment. At this point all he wanted was to get through this and go home.

"Nothing ventured, nothing gained, right?" he said, downing the coffee.

Warren smiled. "That's right. You and Maggie work everything out?"

Mike frowned at him in surprise.

Warren kept smiling. "Oh, she told me it was over a long time ago, but it ain't over in her eyes. Or in her smile. She smiles at you when she thinks you aren't lookin', did you know that?"

Mike swirled the last mouthful of coffee in the bottom of his cup. "No, I didn't."

Warren straightened away from the table. "Man's got to have a woman with a smile," he said, tossing his cup into a plastic-lined trash basket under Mike's table. "Good luck, Lawless."

Mike extended his hand. "Thanks. Good luck to you, too. And thanks for the coffee."

Warren took his hand in a solid grip. "You're welcome."

Okay. Mike tried to refocus his attention on the matter at hand. He pulled out bowls and tools, lined his cookie sheets with baking parchment, then took out a sheet of the same paper to make the tube he'd use to decorate the cookies after he'd iced them. That's where he'd go down. He knew it. But he wasn't going down without giving it his best.

He drew a breath, trying to push away the anger he could still feel in his hands, in his body, behind every thought. He closed his eyes against a mental image of Maggie.

When he opened them again, she was standing there on the other side of his table and he thought for a moment that he was still imagining her.

Then she folded her arms and gave him a pugnacious glare and he accepted grudgingly that she was real. "Take off your clothes," she said.

God. He *was* fantasizing.

"I'm going to stand in for Danny," she went on, coming around the table to look him in the eye. She tried to hand him a sweatshirt, then put it aside when he ignored her. "I've already cleared it with the judges."

She was real, all right. No other woman in the world could be so outrageous and expect cooperation.

He turned away from her and went to the stove. "Get out of here, Maggie," he ordered quietly. Anger was still ablaze inside him and he didn't want to upset his already flimsy chances in this competition by throwing her overboard.

"You can't do this," she said, leaning around his arm, trying to look into his eyes. "Your hands are too big. You've said so yourself."

He cast her a disdainful glance as he searched a drawer beside the stove for an offset spat. He found it and held it up threateningly. "Well, your mouth's too big, and I don't want anything to do with you, so get the hell out of my kitchen."

He looked for hurt in her eyes; he really wanted to see it there. He caught the beginnings of it, but she squared her shoulders and tossed her head and it disappeared.

"You're going to let me do this," she said firmly.

"No," he said, turning back to the table. "I'm not."

"You have to. Or you won't get the new van or pay off the bank."

"That's life."

"It doesn't have to be. You can't beat Mrs. Majorino, but I can."

He finally dropped the bowl he'd been fiddling with. It wobbled on the table, sounding like the echoes of a gong. Warren Anderson and Mrs. Majorino turned in his direction.

He grabbed Maggie by the arm and pulled her to the back of the tent behind his stove. Her eyes were wide, her skin pale in the shadows.

"You are a spoiled pain in the butt," he said, punctuating that assessment by giving her a small shake. "And I wouldn't have your help on a plate!"

She stood unmoving under his hands. Her mouth firmed and her eyes filled, and she did that toss of her head again. "I'm sorry about this morning," she said. "Paula told me what happened."

He shook her again. "Yeah, well that's it as far as I'm concerned. You want to be treated like the little princess your father turned you into, but you don't give the servants any slack. Things don't go the way you want them to and you blow up without waiting for an explanation. Well, I'm not signing up for that again, so don't think you can make it all better by being heroic with a frosting tube. Day-to-day life takes a little more work than that."

That hurt her. He exulted in the pain that darkened her eyes—for about two seconds. Then guilt squeezed his insides like a giant fist and he barely stopped himself from taking it all back.

Distracted for a moment, he let her shake off his imprisoning hands. She took a step back, drew a deep breath, and her face cleared of all signs of distress. A curtain had closed in her eyes and her lips were steady.

"You're absolutely right about all that," she said, "and to tell you the truth, I don't want back into your life after all. *You* could have straightened out the problem this morning by simply explaining to me what had happened. But it was obviously more satisfying for you to act like a martyr."

She shifted her weight, but her eyes never left his. "My father may have turned me into a spoiled princess, but when your father left he ruined you, too. You seem to think you don't have to explain yourself to anyone. You just go your heroic, wounded way, the poor suffering kid who made good. And it makes you more heroic if you don't end the suffering, doesn't it? Only now you sort of have to manufacture the pain, don't you, because you *could* be happy with me, and that would spoil everything. You'd be just like everyone else then—just a poor working stiff with nothing special about him."

She began to unbutton her shirt. "I'm not doing this for you and me, Mike. This is for Cookin' Good so that you can get out of debt and get the van." The shirt was completely unbuttoned and he could see the tiny white ribbon bow that decorated the middle of her bra. "You'd better take me up on this," she said, her eyes dark and sad and challenging. "You're damn well going to miss me in your life, and you'll need your work to keep you going. Are you going to give me your jacket?"

He didn't bother to think. Her words had been a hit below the belt and he couldn't even sort out what he felt to analyze it. He quickly unbuttoned the white jacket and helped her into it. They stared at each other wordlessly for a moment.

"Remember to chop the hazelnuts nice and fine," he said briskly. He busied himself with cuffing back the too-long sleeves.

She raised an eyebrow at him. "*You* always puree them. I helped develop this recipe, remember. I can be trusted to do it well."

The judges had arrived and were touring Mrs. Majorino's station. The tent had been opened and guests were pouring in, excited murmurs filling the air. Mike turned back Maggie's other sleeve. "I've got a heating pad for the coating chocolate," he said softly, glancing over his shoulder at the gathering crowd. "It's in that box under the table."

She rolled her eyes. "I like the double boiler better. I'll just . . ."

He took the hat off his head and placed it on hers. "Keep the pad on medium," he said, ignoring her protest. "If that seems to hot, just put a towel under the bowl. All right?"

She wanted to ask him impatiently who was doing this, him or her, but he'd unconsciously framed her face in his hands and every negative feeling inside her dissolved. She wanted to do this for him so that Cookin' Good could be everything he wanted, because knowing he was happy was the only thing that would keep her going when she resumed her job with the magazine.

She wanted to think about him filling a bright new van outfitted with racks and trays. And when she was brave enough to endure it, she would imagine what he'd look like working in his kitchen with a baby in a carrier at his elbow.

A sob caught in her throat.

She took his wrists in her hands and pulled them off her. "You'd better go," she said briskly. "I'll be fine."

And, somehow, she was. The judges came to greet her, asking about Danny's condition and remarking on how things had changed from that morning when she'd been representing the press.

She thought dryly that they had no idea how much things had changed in the intervening time.

They offered her the special privilege of a few more moments to prepare or send for more ingredients since she was a last-minute replacement.

But she'd checked things over quickly while they'd still been with Mrs. Majorino and saw that Mike, in his flawlessly organized fashion, had prepared everything as far as possible, and she had only to begin.

She winked at Warren as the judges moved on to speak briefly to him and wondered how things would work out for him and Julie. Such optimism and generosity, she thought, had to be rewarded with success.

She, on the other hand, deserved what she got. But she could make it through if she knew she'd won the cash prize for Cookin' Good.

At the signal to begin, she measured the dry ingredients—a fairly standard mixture for a rolled cookie—flour, cocoa, salt and baking soda. She sifted that concoction, put it aside, then ground a half cup of hazelnuts and roasted them in a shallow tin in the oven to bring out their flavor while she creamed unsalted butter and sugar.

She added an egg, heavy cream, hazelnut liqueur, vanilla and the nuts, then gradually mixed in the dry ingredients.

Mike had pulled on the Cookin' Good sweatshirt she'd brought him to replace his chef's jacket and watched her work with a knot of emotion in his throat that had nothing whatever to do with whether they won or lost.

She was a demon when she concentrated. He'd never known anyone who could apply themselves to a task under pressure, with an audience watching every move, and not compromise a single step. Except Maggie.

The dough appeared to be the perfect consistency, and she divided it into four balls and flattened each ball between her palms with an ease and skill that produced four perfect discs. He guessed if anyone had taken the time to measure, they'd have found the discs to be a perfect quarter-inch high.

She wrapped and refrigerated the mixture, which had to sit for an hour.

On one side of her, a very relaxed Warren Anderson was grinding macadamia nuts for his multilayered bar cookies. On the other side, Mrs. Majorino was working feverishly, threads of chocolate taking the shape of a nest.

Mike went to a pot of coffee that had been set up on the far side of the tent, poured two cups and brought one back to Maggie. The rules required that he stay out of her work area, so he simply placed it on her table.

She glanced up to thank him as she broke squares of semi-sweet chocolate into a bowl.

He left the tent, knowing nothing of consequence would happen for an hour and that she certainly didn't need any help from him.

He went to stand at the railing and look out at the peaceful blue ocean. Everything she'd said to him played over in his mind and settled inside him like truth. However unconsciously he'd done it, he'd behaved like the man he so despised.

This morning all his thoughts had been for the friend and employee who'd been hurt and for Paula, who'd been changed by Danny's accident from the cool, efficient businesswoman to a trembling bundle of hysteria.

While he'd been waiting for an assessment of Danny's injury, he'd thought about Maggie repeatedly, but he'd remembered her interview, so he'd left the message with Lupe. He smiled wryly at the bright horizon. He should have known better than to hope for an accurate retelling of events from a man whose English was enthusiastic but hardly fluent.

As he considered it now, Maggie's reaction was understandable. The plan had been to take her to the island to pick up her engagement ring, after all. And after he'd failed to meet her and she'd waited an hour, presuming business had interfered with their lives again, she'd found him hand in hand with a former girlfriend.

But he'd had his own concerns at the moment, had presumed she'd gotten his message about Danny, and had hoped for encouragement and support from her.

Instead, she'd shouted accusations at him—and feeling abused and rejected, he'd found it easier to let her believe what she wanted rather than explain. He'd found it easier to hurt *her*. He straightened away from the rail, finding that a difficult truth to accept about himself.

And still, she'd come to apologize for that morning and to help him in the competition. But he'd rejected her and tried to push her out of his life.

If it wasn't for her singleminded stubbornness, he'd be holding an icing tube in his ham-sized hands right now, losing the contest.

He closed his eyes and said a prayer. He didn't want to be like his father. Not at all.

Then it occurred to him that one action didn't dictate a lifetime. One stupid move could only become habit if one allowed it to.

He downed the rest of his coffee and went back into the tent.

♥ ELEVEN

M AGGIE, COMFORTABLE AMID all the tools of the trade she'd abandoned out of cowardice, cut the dough she'd removed from the refrigerator into perfect heart shapes and placed them into the oven to bake. The scraps of dough she'd put aside were redolent of the rich cocoa and the hazelnuts. The cookies, she felt sure, would be delicious.

While the cookies cooled, she melted chunks of semi-sweet chocolate in the double boiler rather than on the heating pad as a gesture of defiance.

She dipped the cookies into the coating chocolate, then smoothed the rough edges with a spreader. When she'd coated all the cookies, she placed the tin in the refrigerator to set the chocolate. Then she prepared royal icing and stuffed it into a handmade paper tube. She rolled down the paper end of the tube to force the icing toward the tip, then snipped off a tiny end of the tip to give her a piping point.

Warren, whose bar cookies were cooling before he put on the finishing glazes, moved to the farthest end of his work station to watch her. The judges, too, closed in.

On the other side of her, Mrs. Majorino was dolloping strawberry cream into a perfectly formed chocolate straw nest.

Maggie did her best to ignore the breathtakingly beautiful dessert and concentrate on her own Love Word Cookies.

Taking a breath to steady her hands, she began to write on her cookies with the icing in the tradition of the candy hearts everyone had eaten as children. "Light My Fire," she produced in neat script on one cookie. Then she worked her way down the line. "Love Me," "Kiss Me," "Oh, You Kid!," "Lover Boy."

Laughter rippled among the judges and was picked up by the audience, who pressed closer. Encouraged, Maggie kept writing.

When she'd finished, she trimmed them with a swirled edge. She carefully moved the cookies to a doily-covered plate Mike had prepared and decorated the plate with a few strawberries he'd put in the refrigerator.

She placed it on the judging table where Warren's bar cookies, now glazed with a rippled line of chocolate and one of caramel, had been placed.

The bird's nest appeared beside them looking, Maggie thought, as though Fabergé himself had made it as a haven for *his* eggs.

Maggie looked up into a sea of faces watching her and the other contestants, then instantly looked away. She didn't want to find Mike's face there. She'd done her absolute best for him—both by way of apology for that morning and because she loved him with all her heart.

But he didn't want to know that, and she didn't blame him. If she won, she didn't want him to feel beholden. If she lost, she didn't think she could bear his disappointment.

The tasting seemed to take forever. Then the judges laboriously praised all of them, cited the glories of the desserts they'd produced, then declared Mrs. Majorino's bird's nest the winner, gave Maggie's cookies second place, and Warren's bar cookies third.

Maggie put herself instantly on automatic pilot. Smile. Losers had to smile. Losers had to congratulate. Mrs. Majorino was trembling as though on the brink of apoplexy. Maggie hugged her and pushed her onto a stool. Warren pressed a cup of coffee into her hand.

Warren hugged Maggie and she hugged him back. They

all shook hands with the judges, accepted congratulations and praise from the guests, smiled for photographs.

Photographs! Remembering suddenly that she was supposed to be recording this for *Sweet Indulgence*, Maggie wondered how she could slip away to get her camera when she saw that Mike had it and was doing everything she, the reporter, should be doing.

So the moment she could manage it, she ducked away. She ran through the quiet ship and back to the cabin where she made a phone call to her father, then quickly threw her clothes and story notes into her bag.

Stupid, stupid! she accused herself as tears of acute disappointment and despair coursed down her cheeks. She'd lost her man, lost the contest for him, probably lost her job because she didn't know how she'd ever be able to put this story together for the magazine the way she felt now.

Oh, you can do it, she told herself as she ran into the bathroom to collect her soap and shampoo. It'll torture you with memories that'll haunt you for a lifetime, but you can do it.

She stuffed her makeup bag into a pocket of her suitbag, zipped it and snapped it closed, then hurried for the door. Julie would find her somewhere else to sleep tonight. She had to. And while she was at it, she'd get her to pick up her camera from Mike.

The cabin door opened before she could reach it and Mike walked in, taking up all the space in the narrow area between the bathroom and the wall. She backed up several paces, her heart pounding as his eyes went to her suitbag then up to her face.

"I'm sorry," she said, moving aside and holding her bag against her so that he could move past her into the room. "Maybe I should have kept my nose out of it and left it to you. Anyway . . ." She stepped even farther back, but he didn't seem inclined to move into the wider part of the room. He simply stood at the end of the narrow space, a hand braced against the wall, blocking her escape.

"I . . . ah . . . called my father and told him what happened, and he said he'd be happy to lend you the amount of the prize without interest and you can pay him back when you can."

"Where are you going?" he asked, as though he hadn't heard her.

That seemed like a strange question to her in light of what had happened. "Well . . ." She pointed toward the door, hoping he'd get the message that she was trying to leave and move aside. "Julie's going to find me another room for the night."

"Really." He held his ground and she stepped back, holding the bag to her like a shield. He was going to yell about the cookies. She was ready. "You're planning to run out," he accused, "when you *owe* me?"

She blinked at him, a little surprised he'd taken that tack. He was right of course. Had *he* made the cookies, he might have won. Who could be sure?

"I know," she said urgently, emotion welling up to lodge in her chest. Her voice came out high and strained. "Maybe I should have gone with melting the chocolate on the heating pad, but I was more comfortable with the double boiler and . . ." She was feeling desperate, close to tears, and the last thing she wanted to do was burst into tears in front of him. "Maybe that wasn't what they didn't like anyway. That bird's nest lady is scary. That thing came out looking like a piece of jewelry. I'm good, but I guess I'm not that . . . good." The last word came out low and breathy. She swallowed and tried to explain again. "Anyway, Daddy says he can't think of anyone he'd rather invest in, so he'll lend you whatever you . . ."

He wrested the suitbag from her and tossed it aside. "I don't want his money," he said, that symmetry of anger on his face.

"Mike," she said, trying to hold onto her purse and camera as he took those, too. "This is no time for pride! He's happy to lend you . . ."

He caught her shoulders, backed her up to the wall and held her there with a hand on either side of her head. "I don't want his money," he said again, his eyes looking into hers, dark with purpose. "I want his daughter."

It took a moment for that to sink in. But she was sure she was misinterpreting him. "Oh, yeah," she said. "Well, what makes you think I want you?"

"Because you just worked your heart out for me." His eyes softened as they went over her face, and one of his hands moved to brush the bangs out of her eyes. "I'm sorry I didn't explain this morning. And I'm sorry I jumped all over your apology this afternoon. I'm going to be a better husband than I've been a lover, I promise."

She wondered for a moment if she was hallucinating. Then he leaned over her to seal that promise with a kiss, and she knew she was very much awake.

"You still . . ." she asked in disbelief when he raised his head, "want to marry me?"

He took a small square box out of his pants pocket, opened it, and held it in front of her eyes. It was the heart-shaped diamond in a simple gold setting, one slender thread of gold crossing over the heart from the middle of one side to the center. "I picked it up on the way back to the ship from the hospital. I knew we wouldn't be able to get back for it together before the ship left and the competition started. Do you still want to do this?"

She held her left hand up to him. He tossed the box aside and slipped the ring on her finger.

"Well," he said, carrying her hand with the ring to his lips. "Here we are. Two years later to the day. I love you, Maggie."

She wrapped her arms around his neck and held on as he lifted her off the carpet and crushed her to him. "Oh, Mike, I love you, too. I'm sorry I lost."

He put her down to kiss her soundly and smile into her eyes. "Does this feel to you as though we've lost anything at all?"

LOVE WORD COOKIES

2   cups flour
½   cup cocoa powder
¼   teaspoon salt
¼   teaspoon baking soda
½   cup + 2 tablespoons unsalted butter, room temperature
¾   cup granulated sugar
1   egg
1   tablespoon heavy cream
2   teaspoons hazelnut liqueur
½   teaspoon vanilla extract
⅓   cup toasted hazelnuts (filberts), chopped
16 ounces white, milk, or semisweet baking chocolate

Combine flour, cocoa powder, salt, baking soda and toasted
hazelnuts in a small bowl. Set aside. Place butter in large
mixing bowl. Beat with electric mixer until light, thirty to
sixty seconds. Gradually add sugar and continue beating for
two to three minutes until mixture is light in texture and
color. Add egg, cream, hazelnut liqueur, and vanilla extract.
Beat until combined and light, approximately three minutes.
Scrape sides of bowl frequently. Add half of flour mixture
with mixer on low speed until combined with butter mixture. Add rest of flour. Mixture will be stiff. Divide dough
into four balls, pat each between hands until dough is flat.
Wrap in plastic wrap and place on cookie sheet in freezer for
forty-five minutes. Remove sheet from freezer and place in
refrigerator.

Heat oven to 350 degrees. Remove one round of dough, un-
wrap and place on a sheet of floured waxed paper. Cover
with another sheet of waxed paper and roll out to quarter-
inch thickness. Using either a 2″ or 3″ heart-shaped cookie
cutter, cut cookies out and place on a cookie sheet that has
been sprayed with shortening. Bake for eight minutes or

until no impression remains when tops are lightly touched. Remove from pan onto cooling rack.

Refrigerate cookie sheet and cover with aluminum foil. Melt sixteen ounces of baking chocolate (milk, semisweet, or white) and coat cookies, then place on refrigerated sheet. Let coating set and write love words with royal icing or piping gel.

Thanks to Diane Hankins—friend, food columnist, and creator of the Love Word Cookies recipe.

THE KITCHEN
CASANOVA

Elda Minger

M ISS SINCLAIR, THERE'S absolutely no chance of your attending this particular cooking class."

Jessica Sinclair stared at the elderly receptionist in dismay. The woman seemed to have a will of iron. But she couldn't let this woman prevent her from doing what she had to do.

"I don't want to cause any trouble, but—you don't understand. I don't have a lot of time, and I *have* to learn how to—"

"What seems to be the problem, Emma?"

Jessica turned at the sound of the deep, concerned voice and looked up into a face so alive and vital she took in a deep breath, steadying herself. Dark green eyes. Black hair. And the type of bone structure that made film directors and modeling agencies weep, yet radiated absolute masculinity. A real stunner.

Caught off balance for only a few seconds, she regained her equilibrium and remembered what she had to accomplish.

"I have to take this class," she said, gazing up at him. Then she turned her attention back to the harried receptionist. Now she knew who the woman reminded her of. Mary Poppins, straight out of the P. L. Travers book. Just like the illustrations, bun, nose and all.

"I can't lose the time, waiting for the next block of cooking classes. I have to take this six-week series."

"I don't think you understand," the receptionist said, her voice calm as if trying to soothe the feelings of a tired toddler throwing a tantrum. "This is a class for men. Bachelors. They want to learn to cook fabulous, romantic, Valentine's Day dinners so they can seduce the women of their dreams." She paused, eyeing Jessica. "And frankly, I say that the more men the boss can teach to cook, the better off this world will be. Do I make myself perfectly clear?"

If this woman reminded her of Mary Poppins, then Jessica was feeling more like Jane or Michael by the minute. What now?

"Hang on a minute, Em."

Jessica glanced back at the man who had been referred to as "the boss." Perhaps he had more pull with the management. She had to take this class. She couldn't call her fiancé, James, tonight and admit to another defeat, not when it was this important.

"Please," she began, hating the frustration that was causing tears to well up in her eyes. "Please, you have to let me attend." She couldn't bear the thought of telling James that she'd failed yet again.

"How did you register in the first place?" he asked. He didn't seem to be condemning her, just wondering how she'd gotten into an all-male cooking class.

"Over the phone."

"Jesse," the receptionist said wearily. "Jesse Sinclair. I thought she was a he."

"An easy assumption," the man said. He held out a hand. "Nick Kellaher."

Jessica's eyes widened. "You own the school. And the catering business."

"I do."

"Can you please make an exception? Just this once?"

His eyes were so warm as they studied her upturned face. "I think we'll take a vote. Follow me."

Emma, the receptionist, snorted in disgust as Nick turned

and walked down the gleaming hallway. Jessica, realizing that she might be given a chance after all, raced after him.

He had a great walk. Very sure of himself, yet she hadn't gotten the impression he was conceited at all. She'd thought a cooking school teacher would show up for class in the requisite formal white chef's uniform, but Nick wore a pair of faded jeans that molded to his muscular legs and a blue chambray shirt with the sleeves rolled up past well-developed forearms. Must be from kneading all that bread, she thought.

"Now, tell me why you have to take this particular class," he said.

"James—that is, my fiancé—asked me to take a cooking class as soon as possible. Several, in fact. He says I need to learn all the secrets of preparing fine cuisine because I'll be supervising his staff and arranging dinner parties for his business. So I have to know what I'm doing, don't you think so?"

"Do you like to cook?" He'd stopped now, and she almost ran into him. She had to look up to meet his gaze, but found she wasn't intimidated by his sheer strength and size. The top of her head came up to his shoulders, and they were quite nice shoulders. The sort of shoulders a girl could lean on if she needed to have a good cry and a little comfort.

Jessica blinked, not at all sure where that thought had come from and decided to focus on the question at hand.

"I've—I've never really had to learn. Until now. So—I guess—I don't really know. If I like to cook, I mean."

"Fair enough." He smiled down at her, then continued walking along the long hallway toward a door at the end on the right. Voices floated out from the room. Jessica followed close behind Nick, catching glimpses of colorful posters on the wall detailing various cooking competitions and tours, recipes and culinary classes.

They entered a large room, the huge glass windows overlooking Fisherman's Wharf and, on the far end, a spectacular view of the Golden Gate Bridge. Today, a sunny spring day with the most vivid blue, cloudless sky, perfectly set off this particular view. It looked better than any traveler's postcard.

Two men stood at each raised island, and Jessica quickly took in an incredible array of bowls, spatulas, mixers, pots and pans surrounding each pair. Bags of flour, boxes of spices. Fruits and vegetables and a chicken sat on the surface at every station, along with gleaming knives and interesting-looking whisks.

This cooking class was dead serious stuff. Now, it would be up to the various class members whether she had to tell James she'd succeeded or failed.

"We've got a bit of a problem," Nick called out as he walked to the front of the classroom. He strode up to the raised platform, then stood in front of a large blackboard.

Everyone looked up, immediately interested.

"We have one Jesse Sinclair, alias Jessica Sinclair, who registered for this particular six-week class without realizing it was a male-only seminar. Now, I don't have a problem with her taking this class if you don't. She'll simply learn all our secrets of seduction." He directed a reassuring smile toward her. "And perhaps try a few out on her fiancé."

"Awww," said one burly redheaded man in the far corner in a blue plaid shirt. "That was my next question, Nick. I was going to ask you if the little gal was single."

"Nope. Unfortunately, she's spoken for."

Masculine murmurs and bits of conversation reached Jessica's ears as she studied the various cooking students. Men, ranging in age from one nervous student in his early twenties to several in their thirties and forties, to one elderly man who seemed to be somewhere in his seventies, were stationed at the various islands.

"You'll like this class," the elderly man called out. "Nick is a terrific teacher."

"So," Nick said, a smile on his face, "we don't have a problem with Jessica in this class?"

A chorus of noes greeted this statement, and Jessica felt herself relax for the first time in days.

"You need to be clear about your internal time line," Nick said later that afternoon. "That way you have plenty of time to spend with your guest, and everything's already prepared.

So far, you've got the salad chilling in the fridge along with the dressing, the shrimps are ready for the broiler, another side dish that just needs to be heated through, and drinks on ice. Now, for the *pièce de resistance*—"

"Dessert!" one student yelled.

"Truffles," Nick said. "But chocolate is so terribly temperamental, I've decided to teach you tempering and dipping in another separate class. We'll meet back next Saturday at ten. Questions?"

Jessica listened to the questions and Nick's answers as she and her partner, the seventy-eight-year-old man named Ben, cleaned up their station and gathered their hastily scribbled notes.

She'd learned a lot in the three-hour class, the main piece of information being that Nick Kellaher was both a gifted cook and teacher. If there was anyone in San Francisco who could take the mystery—and fear—out of cooking and presenting food, it was Nick.

"He's a nice guy," Ben said, rinsing one last bowl and setting it in the dish drainer.

Jessica, dish towel in hand and drying one of several spatulas, nodded her head.

"Shame he isn't married," Ben said in that same conversational tone. "He'd make someone a wonderful husband."

"He would." She thought of Nick, of the way he'd coaxed and encouraged. Of the way he'd urged them to set aside their fears and go with their instincts. He wanted cooking to be fun, never a chore.

She stopped by the front office and spoke briefly with Emma, apologizing for any upset she might have put the elderly woman through. The woman seemed surprised she would do such a thing, but pleased. Then Jessica let herself out into the spring sunshine, proud of herself and all she'd accomplished that morning, barely able to restrain herself from calling James immediately. He'd be so surprised.

Nick watched her leave.

Jessica Sinclair. Of the infamous and incredibly wealthy Sinclairs of San Francisco. A week didn't go by without one of the family members in the paper. Charities, fund-raisers, benefits, premieres, gallery openings—the list was endless.

Jessica Sinclair. A delicate blonde, with enormous blue eyes that looked perpetually worried. A sugar-spun princess. She'd totally leveled him emotionally with her upset expression when he'd found her arguing with Emma in the hallway. And in that second, he would have moved mountains to have eased the distress in that feminine heart.

Sometimes it happened, just like that. And sometimes, when you found the woman who made your heart race and your thoughts turn to settling down, you found out she was engaged to another man.

Sometimes life just wasn't fair.

But then again, engaged wasn't exactly married.

But marriage, to the Sinclairs, was as much a business arrangement as any of their other dealings.

He wondered if she loved this James. And he wondered how James could love her, when he was so obviously trying to change her. Someone had put that harried, worried expression in those blue eyes.

Well, he'd teach her how to cook. Make sure some of that fear left those beautiful blue eyes. She had five classes to go, as his Kitchen Casanova series ran for six weeks. At the end of that time frame, a man would be able to cook several complete dinners for his lady love, complete with spectacular, decadent chocolate desserts. All with the aim of a well-planned seduction.

The class finished the day before Valentine's Day, the last class being given over completely to presentation. With any luck, that next night several of his students would be well on their way to a thoughtful, well-planned seduction.

Nick didn't think of seduction as dishonest. He thought of it as an art and privately believed that most men put far too little thought into what they did for the women they loved. Any little way he could help the cause of romance was fine with him.

Now, he wondered what he was going to do with Jessica. Obviously not distress her by revealing any of his feelings. He had no real right to do that, being her teacher. She'd come to him for one reason, to learn how to cook. To de-mystify the entire process of preparing and serving food. He would do that for her to the very best of his ability.

Nick looked out the window, not really seeing the view of the bay, with several sailboats skimming over the surface of the water, their colorful sails bright in the sunshine.

His thoughts were on Jessica.

"James? It's me. Do you have a moment?"

Jessica sat in the study of her Victorian house, watching the way the late afternoon sunlight came in through the stained-glass windows. Every time she entered this house, her home, she thought of her paternal grandmother. Not that she'd passed away. Mary Sinclair was still very much alive and loved to rile the rest of the Sinclair family whenever she could. "Tweaking them," she called it. "And they all need it. Badly."

She'd given Jessica this house on her twenty-sixth birth-day. "Move out and make a life for yourself," she'd said. Jessica's mother had been adamantly against it, but Jessica had done the one brave thing in her entire, well-ordered, considerate, quiet life and taken a little leap of faith.

It had paid off enormously.

She hadn't really leapt that far away from the Sinclair family. After all, most of them lived only a few miles away. But her home was still her sanctuary. There were times when she had to get away from all of them. Be alone. Think. These were the times when she realized she was somehow different. And the one thing her family—except for her lovely, eccentric and generous grandmother—did not toler-ate was being different.

She settled back in her chair. "I took my first cooking class today, and I did okay."

"Cooking class?"

She sighed. James had to be constantly reminded of what she was up to, but she supposed it was because he was such a busy man. A financial whiz. Her father thought of him as something of a genius and admired him. He'd been elated by the announcement of their engagement.

"You asked me to take a class, to enable me to—"

"Yes, yes, I remember now. What happened?"

Briefly she told him of her morning, proud of the fact that she hadn't stepped down and slunk away when told she couldn't attend the class.

"Wait a minute, Jessica. Do you mean to tell me you're in an all-male class with the emphasis on seduction?"

She lowered her voice, wanting to connect with him. Needing that connection. "Just think, James, I could even seduce you—"

"What's gotten into you?"

She sighed. "Nothing. I was just kidding. But I did learn how to make a Caesar salad, lemon and garlic shrimp, a very nice chicken dish, which wine went with what, and next Saturday—"

"Next Saturday you'll march right over there and cancel. And get your money back."

"What?"

"This isn't the sort of class you should be taking, Jessica. It sounds rather—common."

She thought of Nick, with his twinkling green eyes, the way they danced with merriment as he told them of the various cooking disasters and predicaments he'd skated through.

"James, you can't be serious."

"I am. And you will cancel. Now, don't fight me on this one, Jessica. You know your father wouldn't approve. Seduction. Good Lord."

She sighed again. And wondered why the entire Sinclair family had to work so hard at leaching all the joy and laughter out of life. Everything had to be done properly. Therefore all the joy and light, the laughter and fun, had to be drained away. To be replaced with what she had often thought the Sinclair coat of arms should have really said—"We always did the proper thing, at the proper time, and with the proper person."

Now, talking to her fiancé, she realized James would never understand how important this morning had been to her. All of her life, she had complacently gone along with what others wanted for her. Today, she'd fought for something she wanted and been able to win it. She'd enjoyed the class, Ben, and most of all, Nick.

She'd loved the way he'd taught their cooking class; his enthusiasm was contagious. And at the end of that first three-hour session, she'd come away confident that she could stay the course, attend the entire six-week class, and come away a good, if not totally accomplished, cook.

Suddenly she didn't want James to know any more. It didn't matter what he thought. What mattered was that she have a chance to master the skills that would make him proud of her. He didn't have to know how she would choose to accomplish this.

"All right," she said quietly. "I'll see what I can do."

"Don't see if you can do it, Jessica. Cancel the class."

"Yes, James."

After she hung up the phone, Jessica climbed the narrow stairs to the top floor and opened the door that led out to her rooftop greenhouse. She'd added this on, this one major extravagance, after her grandmother had given her the old Victorian. Now, as she entered the steamy environment, her senses leapt.

Orchids. Everywhere. They had become a real passion for her, and she sent away for new varieties whenever she could. When Jessica was in her greenhouse, hours could go by and she never even noticed.

Now, she heard the thundering of two little sets of feline paws, and looked down to see Stumpy and Hobbs come tearing up. They loved the greenhouse and the adjoining rooftop area she'd completely screened off. There was absolutely no way either kitten could fall off the roof, but they could climb up to the top story, let themselves out the cat door into the bright sunshine and take a sunbath any time they wanted.

The kittens had come to her in a strange way. She'd seen some children crowded around an apartment building during one of her evening walks around her neighborhood, then realized that some of the boys were disturbing a nest of feral kittens. The mother had been walking back and forth along the fenceline, crying and crying.

She'd taken those kittens away, furious at what had happened. Knowing that the mother cat, essentially a wild animal, would no longer accept and feed her young, she'd taken them to the vet, then hand-fed them. A litter of five, all had survived. She'd found homes for three of them, but Stumpy and Hobbs had been different.

Both had been damaged. No one had wanted them. Stumpy had only three legs, the fourth had been broken when she'd been carelessly thrown to the ground by one of the boys. The vet had to amputate it when she was three weeks old.

And Hobbs sometimes had intestinal problems, from being squeezed a little too hard while being tossed around. He had an anxious, nervous personality around strangers, tended to overeat, and was slightly plump.

No one had wanted the two damaged tabby kittens, so she had decided to keep them. They would stay in this house after she married James, and she would still come to her sanctuary when things got a little too rough in the outside world. She would hire a housekeeper who would look after her kittens, and perhaps care for her orchids, too. It would be her secret, this sanctuary, and no one would take it away from her.

Even her family couldn't ask for total obedience.

She would marry James. It had been decided when she'd turned sixteen. He'd just always been there, and she'd always known they would marry. It sounded so unbelievable to the average person, but the Sinclairs did things in a different way. What was good for the family as a whole was the right and respected action.

Her grandmother had told her what a load of hooey she thought that was.

"The only reason you're putting up with all their nonsense is because you haven't fallen in love," she'd declared the last time she'd visited Jessica. She'd stomped into the elderly Victorian, her cane making the most terrible racket, Stumpy and Hobbs flying off in all directions until they realized who it was and then coming back for a game of fetch the catnip mouse.

Jessica hadn't known what to say to that, because the truth was she'd never been in love. Oh, she'd had dreams of it. Dreams in which a man came and took her away, to a life filled with love and laughter and babies. A garden. Time together to think and dream, listen to music. Read. He wouldn't laugh at her orchids and she would encourage him in whatever he wanted to do.

Long, lovely evenings together, spent talking. Or just feeling that contented quietness with someone who knows you so well you don't need words.

It had never happened.

One didn't meet too many men at exclusive Swiss boarding schools. College had been another carefully cloistered, all-girl affair. Then she'd been whisked back to San Francisco and into the bosom of her demanding and controlling family. Often, when she'd gone out to various functions, her father had hired a discreet bodyguard.

She'd been as isolated as any princess in any of the fairy tales she'd so loved as a child. And still did.

Jessica knew each member of her family for what they were. But she also loved them. And knew there were different rules for the rich. She wanted so badly to please them, had wanted to since she was a child. What she wanted most of all was to believe that if she tried hard enough, she might win their love.

Oh, she knew all the psychological buzzwords. She'd been sent to a psychologist once for an evaluation after admitting to being depressed. Even though the psychologist had urged her to break out and become her own person, to do what she wanted and not consider others, she somehow hadn't been able to accomplish that.

The psychologist had no idea how completely controlling her family was. How manipulative. How—if she were brutally honest with herself—much easier it was to simply acquiesce and go along with most of their plans. And if she secretly carved out these little sanctuaries for herself that they had no idea existed, where was the harm?

She walked among the orchids, up on the rooftop of her home, with the two six-month-old kittens racing after her, jumping and fighting with the fluttery hem of her blue flowered dress.

And thought about Nick Kellaher.

Now there was a man who made her feel safe. She didn't know why or how, but he just did. She would have loved to have stayed after class and talked with him. Those eyes. So alive and vital. So intelligent and quick to spark with laughter.

His hands. She'd watched them as he'd torn salad, whisked a dressing, chopped vegetables. Nothing from a can for Nick Kellaher. He seemed almost disgustingly healthy, but what Jessica had really liked about him was his optimistic and adventurous attitude. When he made a mistake, he said, half the time a better dish resulted from the culinary disaster.

He didn't blame anyone. And he didn't diminish any of his students, make them feel less than what they were. And that, to Jessica, made her like him all the more. She touched a pale pink petal belonging to one of her orchids, a very happy plant, in full bloom and thriving.

Nick. He would want a woman as vibrant and colorful and alive as he was. Not a blonde little mouse who had barely been able to balance a checkbook and care for herself when she'd graduated from college. Who had been sent away to Europe for a grand tour and looked after. Who had come back and been given a totally useless job with the family company. She'd known the position in public relations had been created for her, but she'd enjoyed it. The people, the small, not too challenging challenges. Then her mother had arranged for her to take an extended leave of absence while she planned her wedding. But Jessica knew she'd never return.

Being James's wife promised to be a full-time job.

Jessica had only managed to break free from a certain amount of familial control when her grandmother had given her a home and practically shoved her into it. And even then, Jessica knew that her downfall was that she still cared about what the rest of her family thought of her. Every day.

She wished she were more daring. She wished she were the sort of woman who would attract the attention of a man like Nick Kellaher. She wondered if he had a girlfriend. What she was like. What they did in their spare time together.

He seemed like a man who would be comfortable in the silences. And who would also be there for a woman in every way that mattered. He would make a woman feel strong and secure in their relationship.

She grinned, still stroking the soft, pink petal. And she'd bet her last dollar that he'd bake her an incredible birthday cake—probably chocolate—and make her feel so special.

Her hands stilled as she thought of what Nick would be like as a husband. A father.

He'd bake cakes for his babies, too . . .

The rush of emotion that overcame her at the thought of the woman who would give Nick his first son or daughter made her catch her breath, a queer little hitch that made her side ache.

She could picture James with any children they would have and knew he would have the same overwhelming expectations for them that her father had given to her and her four older brothers.

The thought made her sad.

She wasn't expecting to change her fiancé. She'd thought about her future children, about how she didn't want them to go through what she and her brothers had. The pressures. The expectations. The pains in the stomach, the headaches, the tears. Jessica had thought that if she could love them enough, she could offset whatever her father and James would do.

A bright red light flashed by the door and she realized her phone had to be ringing. Walking quickly to the corner of the greenhouse where she'd installed an extension, she picked up the receiver.

"Darling?"

"Yes, Mother."

"I've scheduled your last fitting for next Saturday afternoon. You'll be able to make it?"

It wasn't really a question, but a command.

"Of course."

"Would you like me to meet you there? We could have lunch."

"No, Mother. I—" She thought of making up an excuse, lunch with James, for example. But her fiancé spent more time with her parents than she did.

"That's all right, dear. I just wanted to make sure your dress was ready. You hadn't called Antoine in a while, and I thought perhaps you were becoming overwhelmed by all the details."

Not for the first time, Jessica wondered exactly why her mother had arranged for her leave of absence from the family firm. She had nothing to do with the planning of her own wedding. Her mother had taken over that job.

Nick's cooking class had been such a high point in her life, partly because it was something of her own, something she alone did. And according to Nick, didn't do too badly. She liked the sense of accomplishment even that first class had given her.

I thought perhaps you were becoming overwhelmed by all the details.

How typical of her mother. Of course, she had to make the thinly veiled reference to her daughter's basic incompetence. Correction, she thought tiredly. Her mother's *perception* of her incompetence. Something had happened to her in Nick's cooking class this morning. She was beginning to see herself in a different light.

"Oh, not at all, Mother." For one insane moment she wondered what her mother would do if she simply told her she didn't want to marry James. Not now. Not ever. But she didn't.

"Saturday then, darling. I have you scheduled for three o'clock."

"Thank you, Mother. I'll be there."

❤ TWO

H ER SECOND CLASS proved even more instructive than the first.

"Never, ever," said Nick, "tell your guests what a dessert is called. Here's the reason why. I once told some friends I was going to make a peanut butter cheesecake. I slaved over this culinary masterpiece all day, then the damn thing cracked into chunks when I released it from the springform pan."

"Then what should you have done?" asked Ben, clearly amused by this turn of events. Even Jessica had to smile.

"I should have simply scooped the crumbled cheesecake into parfait glasses, sprinkled it with roasted peanuts, and presented it at the table as Peanut Butter Surprise."

This got quite a few laughs, and Jessica found herself joining right in. Nick's class was so informal, it was impossible not to feel like she was part of the group. She'd disregarded James's little imperative and gone ahead with the second class, all on chocolate. And the creation of the ultimate dessert truffle for that romantic Valentine's Day dinner.

Nick had given them a brief history of chocolate, which she'd found quite fascinating. A bit on vanilla, which she was thrilled to find came from a variety of orchid. A run-through of the various types of chocolate—milk, white, semisweet and bitter—and the plusses and minuses of working with each. The importance of cocoa butter and how to begin to train the palate to taste and appreciate the differences in types of chocolate.

Nick also discussed the various kinds of fine chocolates. Callebaut, Valrhona and Lindt. Tobler and Ghirardelli. Belgian and French chocolates versus American and Swiss. Jessica's fingers flew as she took detailed notes.

Now, with the chocolate already chopped and in bowls at their various work stations, they were about to learn the fine art of tempering chocolate in order to coat their Valentine's Day truffles, for the ultimate in sensual, seductive desserts.

The actual truffles had already been made. The *ganache*, a mixture of chocolate and cream, had been mixed earlier that day. Now it waited, chilled and rolled into small European-sized truffles, all sitting on parchment paper on large cookie sheets. And all inside the industrial-sized refrigerators that lined one end of the large classroom.

"You want to melt your chocolate slowly," Nick continued. "Don't ever let the water below the chocolate come to a boil." He was a great believer in the double boiler as opposed to melting chocolate in a microwave.

"We'll start with the white chocolate," he said, walking over to Jessica's and Ben's work station and taking the bowl of chopped white chocolate off their table. "Let's all gather around the front burner."

Jessica, nervous now that she was one of the first to try tempering—and with the most temperamental of chocolates!—watched as Nick set the bowl of white chocolate over the pan of simmering water.

"Come on over," he said, motioning to both her and Ben. "You need to take a look at what's happening."

She walked to his side, then stood next to him, for some reason terribly conscious of his presence. He worked swiftly, talking to the class as he did.

"You only temper the chocolate you coat things with, and the reason is you're stabilizing the cocoa butter. And remember, cocoa butter has five separate melting points."

"Can you melt it, cool it, and melt it again if you have to?" This question came from Ben. Jessica had already found out a lot about her seventy-eight-year-old cooking class partner. He had a lady love named Elizabeth he was going to impress on Valentine's Day with an intimate dinner just for the two of them.

"Sure. No problem. Now Jesse, come over here."

He'd called her Jesse from the start, and she found she liked the nickname. She suspected he called her that because he found the way she'd infiltrated the class rather amusing. It didn't matter. No one else had ever called her Jesse, and she liked the way Nick said her name.

Now he stood her right next to the burner and asked her to continue to stir the finely chopped white chocolate. The mixture was just starting to melt.

"Truffles are actually very easy," he said, just behind her. So close his breath ruffled her hair. "Here," he said, his arms quickly coming up around her as he lifted the bowl off the bottom of the double boiler.

"It doesn't seem like it's even started to melt," she said. The chocolate still looked chopped and grainy to her.

"This chocolate is the temperamental one, remember? Milk and white chocolate have milk solids. They'll burn."

"Okay."

"Just keep stirring it with your spatula. That's it. You'll see—there it goes, it's melting. The heat will do the rest."

And it was melting. Perfectly.

While some truffle makers preferred using tools to dip their candies, Nick was of, as he referred to it, "an older, much more primitive school. Like mudpies, we'll use our hands."

Soon they were all gathered around the main working area, dipping truffles for all they were worth with one hand, sprinkling on the garnish that would encode the rich candy with the other.

"And remember," Nick said with a grin, "if it doesn't work, if your truffles never come together—"

"Peanut Butter Surprise?" Ben said.

"Just add some Chambord, heat up the whole thing and serve it over some Häagen-Dazs."

Groans of culinary ecstasy erupted from the class members. Jessica couldn't help laughing. The man certainly knew how to improvise.

She was washing her hands just before leaving when Nick approached her work station.

"Enjoy the class?" he asked.

She was touched by the fact that he seemed to be watching out for her. Jessica had the distinct feeling he was deliberately toning down the probably risqué manner in which he usually taught this class. After all, the emphasis had been seduction of the female from the male point of view. Which could, admittedly, get a little blunt. But everyone in the class seemed to be treating her with kid gloves—and enjoying her presence immensely.

"It was wonderful! I felt like a little girl again, playing in the mud. I haven't had this much fun since—I don't really know when."

"Good. That makes it all worthwhile."

She felt her feelings bubbling forth, and knew she wanted to share them with this man.

"Nick, I never would have tried this if you hadn't shown us how! I mean, it looks so complicated, and then you start talking about it and you make it seem like anyone in the world could do this—"

"Anyone can. You just have to have a little faith."

"I know, but it's also the way you teach. You—you instill confidence. You make it fun. You just have this way of—making it not so frightening."

He considered all this, and she could tell he was pleased. "Thank you."

"I'll definitely be back for the rest of the series."

"I aim to please."

She found herself walking along the hallway of the cooking school toward the front door with Nick and reluctant to have their time together coming to an end.

"What's the rest of your day like?" he asked.

"I have to go for the final fitting of my wedding gown."

"Where?"

"Pacific Heights."

"I'll drop you off, it's on my way—"

"I can simply call a cab."

"It's no trouble. I have a catering job in the area. I have to deliver several cakes."

She hesitated.

"Humor me. Look at what a glorious day it is." He smiled down at her. "And I have a convertible."

She caught his infectious spirit. "All right."

She liked seeing his world. The way he chatted with his customers, delivered the three elaborate cakes that had been carefully stored in the trunk of his car, his whole easygoing manner.

She liked the way he was with her.

"So you've lived in San Francisco all your life," he said as they drove toward Antoine's shop.

"Most of it." She hesitated. "When I wasn't in Switzerland going to school." She'd always hated the distinctions that seemed to separate her from the real world. Her education had been one of them.

It didn't seem to bother Nick at all.

"I suppose you toured Europe, too," he said. But Nick didn't make this statement as if he thought she were one of the idle rich.

"I did. You?"

"I went to high school across the Bay. Oakland. I haven't been to Europe yet, but I plan on getting there one day when work slows down."

"How did you become a chef?"

"My mother loved to cook, I picked it up from her. She worked double shifts to help put me through the Academy of Culinary Arts."

"She must be proud of you."

He grinned. "She is."

He told her of his days in cooking schools and working for temperamental millionaires, then found a parking place right in front of Antoine's shop and strolled in with her.

"Ah, Jessica!" The designer was very emotional, sensitive, Italian, and a genius at design. "I have a question for you."

"Go ahead." Antoine seemed, to her, to be in a particularly fragile mood. Sometimes he was extremely temperamental, but he'd never been anything but kind to her.

"There are a few other gowns. All in your size. I did not tell your mother because—"

"Because she liked the original gown."

"Well, yes. But I said to myself, Antoine, you must judge whether the bridal gown is going to wear the girl or the girl is going to wear the bridal gown." He caught sight of Nick. "And now we have someone who is totally impartial, who can tell us which is the better dress!"

Nick started to laugh. "I know chocolate, not bridal gowns."

"Yes, but you are a man, and—chocolate? Are you a cook?"

Nick held out his hand. "Nick Kellaher."

Antoine's dark eyes widened with an air of first surprise and then reverence. "My God. That torte at the Adamson's wedding. I almost wept when I tasted it."

"Thank you."

"*Cara!*" Antoine clapped his hands briskly. "This is the man who will decide your fate! He has the most exquisite taste."

She ended up trying on six different gowns, and Nick saw her in all of them. Antoine fluttered in and out, zipping a zip, adjusting a train, plunking on a headpiece. Sweeping her hair first up, then down. Different earrings. High heels, then flats. Every adjustment a woman could make to look her finest on this most special day.

Finally, exhausted and sick to death of wedding gowns, she came out of the dressing room in a gorgeous ivory silk slip and sunk down into one of the comfortably overstuffed chairs.

"I can't try on another dress, Antoine. You and Nick have to help me decide."

"Mmmm." Antoine tapped his chin with a forefinger. "Of

course, your mother wants you to wear that modern monstrosity. This I cannot allow. That dress is not you, *bella*."

"I've never liked it," she admitted.

"Nick?"

"It stunk."

"Good. Now, about the sheer—"

"Too frail," Nick interjected. "What did you think, Jesse?"

"I—didn't really feel comfortable in it."

"And it showed," Antoine said. "Now, I say we're down to the one that makes you look like a little princess and the other that is a simple slip dress. Which one do you vote for, Nick?"

She turned her head, anxious to hear Nick's reaction, wanting this day to be over. Strangely, trying on wedding gowns for her day with James had only served to depress her. But then she caught the expression in his eyes before he thought to conceal it.

Nick Kellaher wanted her.

The slip was a perfectly decent garment. She'd worn dresses to premieres that had exposed more skin. But now, as she saw the look in his eyes, she finally had an emotional reaction to go with the expression, "he looked as if he could eat her up."

"The princess dress," he said softly. "Her hair down, the medium high heels, and a classic veil."

Antoine sighed with sheer, unadulterated pleasure. "And the pearls." He glanced at Nick. "You're sure you were not a designer in a past life?"

"Positive."

"May I have your number for the catering business? My next show, I want you to make something like that torte. But not too delicious—the focus must still be on the clothes."

Jessica would have laughed, but now she found herself getting up, walking toward the array of dresses, and selecting the one Nick had chosen. Slowly, she approached the bank of full-length mirrors in Antoine's studio.

"Help her back into it," Antoine said, and she realized that Nick had followed her.

The moment was so highly charged. He held the dress up, supported it while she stepped inside. He slipped the zipper up, slowly. She could feel the brief warmth of his fingers against her silk-cooled skin. Then he helped her step into her shoes. She arranged the voluminous skirts, then faced Antoine.

"Your mother," the designer said slowly, "doesn't know what she is talking about. You will take their breath away."

She fought against her tears, blinking furiously. Why didn't that statement bring her any pleasure at all?

He bought her coffee afterward, at a little shop high on a hill, overlooking the bay. The fitting had taken longer than she'd thought, and now lights were twinkling on, adding an almost fairylike quality to the older Victorian houses in the expensive neighborhood.

He ordered a double espresso with a twist of lemon. She had a cappuccino, with freshly grated nutmeg on top. They split an enormous chocolate croissant.

"Do you love this guy?" he said suddenly, out of the blue.

And she gave him the only answer she could. Total honesty.

"I don't know."

They sat quietly for a few minutes. He seemed as if he were in silent agony, and she knew exactly why he'd asked her the question. And admired him for it, putting his feelings on the line.

"I've known James since I was a little girl," she began carefully.

"And it was always assumed the two of you would marry," he said softly.

She stared at him, amazed.

"How did you know?"

"Hey, I've read my fairy tales. I know the score."

So tough, this man, she thought. *But inside, he's soft and vulnerable. Just like me.*

They drank their coffee, watched the lights. Didn't say a word to each other, but Jessica was stunned to find that she liked the silence. With this man.

He finished his coffee before she did and simply stared out over the bay. Thinking.

Impulsively, before she thought better of it and lost her nerve, she covered his warm, strong hand with her own. Drew warmth from it. Courage.

"No," she said softly. "I don't."

"Would you bake a birthday cake for your child?" she asked as they slowly walked the final few steps to her house.

"In whatever flavor he or she wanted. Every year."

"And perhaps a dog?"

"A dog would be fine. And a couple of cats."

"Oh, I already have those." She hesitated. "And you'd like quiet evenings at home?"

"With you I would."

They'd reached the front steps of her Victorian, and she walked up them slowly, Nick right behind her, until they were both concealed in the dusky shadows of her large front porch.

"Nick," she began unsteadily.

He put a finger over her lips, then shook his head. "I have a feeling that this is where you give me the speech about having to do your duty. Your loyalty to your family and to James. And I just can't bear to hear it, Jesse. Not tonight."

She nodded her head.

He lowered his head.

"Do you understand what it is that I feel for you?"

She nodded, her eyes filling.

"But I won't take advantage of you. Not while you're engaged to another man."

She nodded again.

"So—I'll see you in class?"

She lowered her head as the tears spilled over.

"Jesse." He pulled her into his arms and held her while she started to cry. Then sobbed. "Oh, Jesse."

She recovered her composure as quickly as she could, then grasped the doorknob like a lifeline. What could she say to Nick? *I'll call you.* She couldn't. *I'll see you.* It wouldn't be wise.

I love you.
It would have been the truth.

As soon as she was safely inside, he started down her front steps with a very heavy heart.

"Young man!" The voice seemed to come from a large rosebush in the front yard, and Nick glanced around, intrigued.

"Over here!"

He moved cautiously in the direction of that voice.

"Closer," it whispered.

And as if by magic, an elderly woman appeared, leaning on a cane. She'd blended into the garden quite nicely, assisted by her dark cloak, total stillness, and the deepening blue light of twilight.

"So, you care for my Jessica?"

He saw no reason to lie.

"Very much."

"Good." The woman sniffed. "Never did care much for that boob, James."

Nick grinned. He had a feeling that, whoever she was, he and this stranger were going to get along just fine.

She held out her hand. "Mary Sinclair. Jessica's grandmother. I gave birth to her father, and don't think I don't sometimes have very mixed feelings about that."

He laughed out loud. Couldn't help it.

"Nick Kellaher." He gave her his hand and they shook.

"Ah, the chocolate chef. Those desserts you designed for *Gourmet* last month were just sinful."

"I aim to please."

"How did you meet my granddaughter?"

Her questions were curt and to the point. She reminded him, both in speech patterns and inflections, of Katharine Hepburn. This was not a woman who suffered fools gladly.

"She's in one of my cooking classes. James insisted she learn how to cook—for his business functions."

"James is an ass. My Jessica has no real talent as a cook. Her genius lies in growing things. Nurturing. Orchids." She waved her cane in impotent rage. "The entire roof of that

Victorian has been converted into a greenhouse. If she took you inside, you'd swear you'd been transported into another world."

He considered this. Thought quickly. And decided that if anyone could give him the answers he needed, Mary Sinclair could.

"Why are they doing this to her?"

Mary nodded her head slowly. "That, dear boy, is the sixty-million-dollar question. And not an easy one to answer."

He knew a chance when he saw it. Jumped and took it.

"What if I offered to cook you dinner in exchange for some insight into the Sinclairs?"

Her bright blue eyes twinkled. "One of those Kitchen Casanova meals?"

He laughed. "Of course."

"That's the right answer for a strange old coot like me." She smiled up at him. "Brilliant marketing ploy, that class. Saw the ads in a magazine. Wish my Edward were still alive. I would have insisted he attend."

He liked her immensely. And even saw a glimpse of what his Jesse would be in her final years. Beautiful. And spirited.

"Now, take my arm and help me out of this God-awful crouch. I saw the two of you come walking down the street and jumped behind this rosebush. You see, I couldn't believe my Jessica's good fortune. Now, I'll call a cab—"

"No need. My car's just around the corner."

"Better yet." She gazed up at him, those blue eyes smart and shrewd. "A coach and four for your fairy godmother."

At his surprised look, she wagged a finger at him.

"Make no mistake, my boy. They're fierce opponents, the Sinclairs. You're going to need every advantage I can give you."

She told him she liked hot food, so he made her fiery chicken wings with several dipping sauces, a plate of steamed vegetables with garlic, chilies and ginger, and later, over coffee, he offered her slices of a very good lemon pecan pound cake.

"No chocolate?" she asked, on her second piece of cake.

"The truffles are in the freezer. I can set them out and they'll be ready for our second round of coffee."

"Excellent. I so like a young man who's prepared."

They talked far into the night. He told her how he met Jesse and she filled him in on the Sinclairs.

"I don't know where I went wrong with Matthew. Edward and I did all we could, but our son showed a love for the dollar from the day he first found out what money could buy. It has to be from a past life, it was such a strong compulsion. And that woman he married!" Mary rolled her eyes and reached for another truffle. "Annabeth is cut from the same cloth as my son. How they got together to produce the children they did is a total mystery to me. No warmth in either of them."

Nick simply listened.

"There were four little boys born before my Jessica. Matthew and Annabeth honed their skills on their first four sons, so when Jesse was born, they knew how to manipulate her emotions before she even took her first few steps. Do you know she had an ulcer by the time she was twelve?"

She paused, gauging his reaction. He remained silent, his expression calm. The last thing he wanted to do was condemn. He wanted understanding.

"They're not intrinsically evil people. They don't believe what they're doing is bad for her. But it is. If she marries James, I'll have lost my granddaughter as surely as if she'd passed on."

"What will they do to her?"

Mary snorted. "Give her a life so devoid of any real emotion or happiness that she'll probably look for a chance to jump out a window. They won't even let her have her children. She's not at all like any of them, temperamentally.

"Two of her brothers managed to break away and carve independent lives for themselves. Another really enjoys the firm, and more power to him. He has more heart than either of his parents. And the other, Grant—well, let's just say he's still in the making. I'm not quite sure which way he'll go."

Nick saw true worry and compassion in those fierce blue eyes.

"But my Jessica—they've been grooming her from the time she was born to play a very special part in thé Sinclair dynasty. She was to bring home a man worthy of a fortune, who could cast his lot with her father and create a family so powerful that no one would dare destroy it."

"Why?" Nick finally asked.

"I don't know," she admitted. "I've thought, and I've prayed. I've asked for both guidance and answers. When is there enough money for my son to feel satisfied with his life? The answer is, there's never enough. For either him or that greedy wife of his. God knows they were miserly enough with genuine emotion, with any love for their five children. But no matter how badly my grandchildren were treated, they were expected to put duty—God, how I *hate* that word!—and the family first. Always."

Nick considered all this.

"Do you think she'll actually marry him?"

Mary didn't even hesitate.

"Yes, I do. Unless we come to her rescue."

"It has to be her decision," he said.

"Yes, in the end it does. But Jessica's been through hell. She's confused right now and could use a little help. I hope you won't hesitate to give it to her."

"No, I won't."

"Good." She smiled. "Now, if you'll drop me off back at her house, I think I'll go inform my granddaughter that I intend to stay with her up to and during the time of that wedding she thinks she's going to go through with. Oh, and Nick?"

"Yes?"

"Could I take a few of these truffles. for the road? Absolutely marvelous, you know."

Jessica made herself another cup of coffee and took it up to her rooftop greenhouse. Even in the company of Stumpy and Hobbs and surrounded by the lush beauty of her orchids, she couldn't stop missing Nick. There was a decidedly empty space near her heart that actually ached.

It gave her stomach pains to even think about it, but she knew in her heart she couldn't possibly marry James. Not when she felt this way about another man. And the miracle of it was, it seemed Nick felt the same way about her.

So she sat in the lush, steamy heat, amid the jewel-toned tropical plants, and thought about what marriage to a man like Nick would mean. First came the joy as she imagined their love-filled marriage. Then came more burning stomach cramps as she envisioned what her family would think.

Before she could carry this train of thought to its logical conclusion, she heard the faint ring of the front doorbell.

Leaving her kittens to investigate a particularly deep pot, she made her way downstairs, coffee cup in hand, and, after checking through the peephole in the front door, opened it and clumsily embraced her tiny grandmother.

"Put that cup of coffee down before you burn yourself," she admonished fondly. "I've brought us some chocolate, and we can sit and have a little talk."

Jessica didn't have any doubts that the subject of her Valentine's Day wedding would come up. A mere four weeks away, the ceremony was going to be held in one of San Francisco's oldest, most prestigious churches. But one thing about her grandmother, Mary, she would let her bring up the subject in her own time, and when she was comfortable discussing it.

She made a pot of coffee, using the French Roast beans she'd just bought at the coffee house she'd been at with Nick. Bringing a tray into the front room, she smiled as she saw her grandmother already ensconced in one of the comfortable chairs, Hobbs in her lap and Stumpy trying to jump up. Mary eased the eager little kitten into her lap.

"These babies turned out excellently despite their unfortunate beginnings, didn't they?" Mary said as she scratched Hobbs behind his ear. The kitten simply purred as he gazed up into the face of one of the humans he adored most on the planet.

"They did." Jesse set the tray down, asked her grandmother if she wanted cream or sugar, fixed her a cup of coffee, then placed the truffles on a pretty china plate. She fixed herself a cup, selected a truffle, sat back in her chair and saw her grandmother's kindly blue eyes studying her.

One thing about Mary Sinclair, there was no possible way of hiding a single thing from her sensitive heart.

"Oh, Grandmother," she heard herself say as she set down her coffee. "What am I going to do?"

_♡_ THREE

JESSICA TRIED TO breathe deeply and still her racing heart as she let herself into the huge glass doors etched with the name Sinclair Enterprises, Ltd. No one gave her a second glance as she crossed the highly polished marble lobby to the bank of elevators on the far wall.

She pushed the button for the fifteenth floor, knowing that this early in the morning, James would be in. It was only right, she'd decided, to break their engagement in person. It wasn't the sort of thing one did over the phone, no matter how tempting the thought was. She owed him that much.

Once in the reception area, she approached the young woman behind the desk. She seemed all angles and blunt planes, with her glossy black bob and bold red lips.

"I'm afraid he can't see you right now, he's in a meeting."

"Can you tell me when he might be free?"

She checked a leather scheduling book. "This is a bad day. You said you were—"

"His fiancée. Jessica Sinclair."

"Is this an emergency?"

Yes, it is. But James would never think so.

She considered what choice to make, then took the road of least resistance.

"No, I'll wait. But I really do need to see him at the earliest convenient moment."

"I understand."

Jessica settled herself on one of the modern, angular sofas in the reception room area and picked up a magazine. A financial magazine, which she promptly put back down. She thought of Nick and of going to his cooking school with some sort of emergency. Nick could be knee-deep in bread dough, and she was sure if he even suspected she was in any kind of distress he would put the class on hold and be out in the lobby of his cooking school in a heartbeat.

Even Emma, who she'd actually grown to be rather fond of, couldn't stop him.

But James. Business would always come first with James. Never emotions. Never people. He was cut from the same cloth as her father, and she suddenly knew, with that gut-level certainty, that she was doing the right thing. The only thing she could do.

After an hour had passed with no word from James, Jessica got up and approached the receptionist.

"Could you please do me a favor?"

"Of course."

Jessica had already taken off the brilliant diamond engagement ring and put it inside the dark blue velvet box it had come in. Now she handed the box to the receptionist.

"Would you give this ring to James and tell him I no longer want to marry him?"

The woman looked at her as if she'd suddenly sprouted two more heads.

"What?"

"I can't really wait here all morning, and I have to let him know of my decision as soon as possible."

"Wait, I'm sure I can—"

"No," Jessica said as she started toward the elevators. "Business should come first, don't you think?"

She reached home just as the phone started to ring.

"Your mother first," Mary said, dressed in overalls and covered with dirt. She'd been working in the small garden out back, "just puttering" as she liked to say. "She wasn't at all happy to hear I was visiting."

"I can imagine."

"Then your father. He wants you to come to the house for dinner tonight."

"I'm sure James called him."

Mary snorted. "It's the old, 'let's talk some sense into the silly girl.' You know that. Frankly, I think this is the first sensible thing you've done for yourself since moving into this house."

Jessica smiled, suddenly feeling lighter and brighter than she had in years. "I'm free."

"And you stay free, until you run away with that man of yours. Who, by the way, I called right after your mother called. He's on his way over."

"Grandmother! Why did you—"

"Now don't you worry. Nick and I are working as a team. If you don't come home at all today, and God knows I haven't seen you, then you can't possibly go over to their house for dinner, can you?"

"I like the way your mind works."

Nick kidnapped her for the remainder of the day.

He picked her up in his convertible, and they drove out to the beach with the picnic lunch he'd packed. Not one of the city beaches. He drove north, to a private little cove, then settled them in the sand close to the water. Since it was a weekday, they were alone.

"So you did it," he said as they lay back on the light blanket, both stuffed with crab salad, antipasto, freshly baked bread and fruit.

"Yes. Not directly, but I did it."

At Nick's expression, she explained.

"He was busy in his office, and—"

"Wait. You were out in the reception area, asked to see him, and he couldn't take a minute to see what you wanted?"

"Yes."

"He didn't deserve you."

She glanced out over the ocean, watching the timeless rhythm of waves against the shoreline. Here, now, she felt comfortable about her decision. She knew there would be hell to pay later, when her mother got hold of her.

They'd stopped at Antoine's on the way to the beach, where she'd paid him in full for the wedding dress she and Nick had picked out and asked him to hold it for them. And not to tell her mother. Antoine, on their side, had been absolutely delighted.

Then she'd stopped at a pay phone and called the caterers, the church, her priest, and anyone else she could think of connected with her wedding. She'd let them all know it had been called off, she was sorry for all the trouble she'd caused, and she hoped this late notice wouldn't cause them too much trouble. And of course, she'd pay.

The price was cheap, considering what she was giving up. A life so cold, so empty, as to be unlivable.

"Jessica?"

"Hmmm?" She turned toward him, then smiled. She loved just looking at Nick. She had a feeling she would never grow tired of seeing his face.

"Come here." He'd moved the food, repacked all of it into insulated containers, and now the blanket was empty except for his large frame. Nick patted the blanket next to him.

Her heartbeat sped up. But she came to his side, let him put his arm around her and ease her down on the blanket. Looking up into his face, her head pillowed on his muscular shoulder, she had the overwhelming instinct that this was a man who would never, ever hurt her.

She closed her eyes for just a second, feeling the sun against her skin, the breeze off the ocean. Hearing the cry of the gulls. And sensing her life was just about to really begin. At this moment.

She opened her eyes and found him smiling down at her.

"I was devastated when I discovered you were promised to another man," he admitted.

"You were?"

"On my honor. And I also knew you were a woman who wouldn't give your heart lightly."

"I didn't. But I gave it for all the wrong reasons."

The silence between them was comfortable, and her heart felt so full of peace.

"Marry me, Jesse. Today."

That got her attention.

"Nick?"

"We could drive to the airport and fly to Las Vegas. By the time we came back, we'd be husband and wife."

She hesitated. What she had with Nick felt so right, but she didn't know if she could move this quickly into a new relationship.

Her silence gave him his answer.

"Too fast, huh?"

She turned her face into his shoulder, her emotions churning inside her. His free arm came up around her, and he merely held her.

"Jesse, I'm no better than your family, pushing you into what I want you to be. I'm sorry."

"No. It's just that—so much has happened, so quickly—"

"I just got scared," he said.

"Scared?" Nick, scared? She couldn't conceive of it.

"Scared of your family. I have a feeling they're going to do everything in their power to pull you back in. I just thought—if we ran away and got married, there would be nothing they could do."

She remained silent. Thinking.

"Nick?"

"Yeah?"

"I don't think I'm going to cave in on this one."

"How's your stomach?"

She looked up at him. "How did you know?"

"Know what?"

"That I feel everything in my stomach."

He sighed. "I have to confess. I cooked your grandmother dinner the other night and pumped her shamelessly for information."

Jessica laughed. "And you wouldn't have gotten anything out of her if she hadn't wanted you to know."

"That I can believe. Anyway, she told me about your ulcer."

She glanced away from him, toward the ocean. Gulls wheeled and screeched over the cool blue waves.

"Does that bother you?"

"No, I—I don't want any secrets between us."

"I agree." He cleared his throat and she could feel the fine tension in his body. "The thought of you throwing up blood at the age of twelve. Oh, Jesse . . ."

She moved deeper into his embrace and simply let him hold her.

They drove back that evening. She took him on a tour of her house, introduced him to Stumpy and Hobbs, and finally led him up to the top floor, to her greenhouse and sanctuary.

"These are gorgeous," Nick said, examining a pale yellow bloom. "I couldn't grow one of these if someone had a gun pointed to my head."

"It's not that hard."

"It's your gift, Jesse."

"Like cooking is yours."

"Right." He grinned. "Okay, we'll make a deal. I'll do all the cooking, but you're in charge of the gardening."

She simply laughed.

Later, she made them coffee and they sat out on the rooftop garden, the fenced-in area she'd created for her two kittens and their safe sunbaths.

"Why Stumpy?" he asked, looking down at the trusting kitten in his lap.

"I tried all the beautiful names. Belle, Tiger, Fluffy. But people would come over and say, 'Look at that little stump,' and she'd come running up and meow at them. It was the only word she'd answer to. Stump."

Stumpy looked up, as if on cue, and meowed. They both laughed, and Nick gently stroked the kitten's head.

"Amazing that they can trust, after what they went through."

She sighed, so enjoying coffee out on the roof with Nick. "The feline spirit is strong."

Mary poked her head around the door leading out to the roof. "Your father is on the phone. I'm assuming you don't want to talk to him."

Jessica nodded her head. Mary closed the door and descended the stairs.

"You'll have to talk to him sooner or later, Jesse."

"Later. For now, I'm just going to enjoy the evening."

"Stomach all right?"

"Strangely enough, it couldn't be better."

He took a last sip of coffee, finished it, then set the mug down. "I'd better be going. Can I see you tomorrow?"

"I'd like that a lot."

She walked him out to his car, parked out front.

"Jesse," he said, taking her face in his hands. "If you need to call me at any time, day or night, please don't hesitate."

She blinked against the sudden sting of tears. "Thank you. that means a lot to me."

"I mean it. Four in the morning? No problem."

"I may just take you up on it."

The following weeks were the happiest of her life.

She took another three cooking classes and learned how to make a killer chocolate mousse and a cake called "Chocolate Decadence." Along with a few more meals guaranteed to help along the most difficult seduction.

"I was thinking of cooking a meal for you," she said after class one day, teasing Nick. "One evening this week. Then I could seduce you."

Everyone else had left. They were alone in the large classroom overlooking the bay.

"You," Nick said, coming up behind her as she washed the last of her dishes and putting his arms around her, "would just have to show up. That's all the work you'd have to do."

She laughed. "Well, maybe if you promised to make dessert."

He kissed her then, and she forgot about her soapy hands and simply twined her arms around his neck.

• • •

Jessica had never really had the freedom to live like an ordinary person, but now she did. Her time with Nick was magical, opening an entire new world to her.

They went to movies, the zoo, Golden Gate Park. One evening Nick took her to Chinatown and they ate at a tiny little restaurant tucked away among the pagodas and noodle shops. They browsed afterwards and Jessica was fascinated with everything from a fortune cookie factory to the herb stores and t'ai chi ch'uan studios.

But anything—with Nick—was fun.

The only dark cloud on the horizon was the thought of her family. Jessica knew they probably hadn't given up. She was pragmatic enough to know that too much was at stake for the Sinclairs. If anything, her mother and father were biding their time, waiting for the right moment to spring their trap. She just wasn't sure what they were going to do.

She'd consciously chosen not to tell any of this to Nick. She just wanted to enjoy her time with him. In her heart of hearts, she wanted to run away with him, marry him, run so far and fast she'd never have to worry about her family again.

Yet a part of her felt in control of the situation. After all, she'd called off her wedding. Valentine's Day was less than one week away, and there was only one more class left in the Kitchen Casanova series. Nick was going to stress presentation of the seductive meal, along with tips for after-dinner liqueurs.

She hadn't heard from James, other than a curt, formal message on her answering machine. "Jessica," he'd said, not hurt at all but rather patronizing. "When you come to your senses and we can talk about this like two adults, please call me."

She'd erased the message, hoping she could erase James out of her life as easily.

Mary remained at her house, fielding phone calls and usually delighting in telling both her mother and father she wasn't home—and couldn't be reached.

"Run away with that young man and don't look back," her grandmother advised her one evening as she was dress-

ing for an evening out with Nick. He'd been strangely eva-
sive when she'd asked him what they were going to do, but
she didn't mind. Anything at all with Nick was fun. Simply
being with him was an adventure.

"Would they still come after me even if I was married?"

"They might try, but there's nothing they could do that
Nick couldn't handle. I have a considerable amount of faith
in him."

She glanced back at her grandmother as she zipped her
into a pale pink, floaty little dress. Nick had asked her to
dress up for tonight's surprise, and she assumed they were
going out to dinner and perhaps dancing. She loved the skirt
of this dress, it made her feel as if she were light as air. Free.

He picked her up within the hour and they headed out into
the foggy San Francisco night.

He drove toward North Beach and parked his car on the
street near several little restaurants and bistros. Thick fog
floated in the air, and the scent of the ocean was never too
far away.

They walked up the street, hand in hand, until he reached
a doorway. Taking a key out of his pocket, Nick inserted it
into the lock and turned the key. They stepped inside, and he
locked the door behind them.

"Would you stay right here? Just for a moment?"

She nodded.

He walked away, and she stared out the front window of
the dark restaurant into the foggy night. Rain had been pre-
dicted for later in the evening, but nothing could dampen her
spirits. She was with Nick, that was what mattered.

"All right," he said. She'd been so wrapped up in her
thoughts she hadn't even heard him come back into the
room. He'd removed his suit jacket and looked so handsome
in his white shirt and tie.

He led her through several dark, deserted rooms filled
with tables and chairs. The restaurant smelled wonderful;
the scents of freshly baked bread and spices permeated the
air. They turned a corner and entered a room with a single
table in the middle of the floor. Surrounding it were masses

of lit candles and vases of flowers, both filling the air with their delicate scent.

"Dinner," Nick said, "is served."

She felt touched beyond words as he escorted her to her seat, held the chair for her, and handed her the tiny, hand-lettered menu. And she realized he'd fixed her a private dinner, using the restaurant's kitchen.

None of these dishes had been taught in class. From the first course, a delicate lobster bisque, to the last, a chocolate raspberry confection light as air and sweet as sin, each mouthful was simply exquisite.

She leaned back in her chair, satiated. Totally content.

"Don't get too relaxed. The night is far from over."

Now he'd aroused her curiosity.

He left the room for an instant, and when he returned, music filled the air. Frank Sinatra. Those unmistakable vocals. "My Funny Valentine."

"Dance?" Nick asked as he came up to her chair.

"Yes." She went into his arms, knowing there was no place she'd rather be.

He danced well, and they moved together as if they'd been dancing all their lives. Jessica looked up at him, filled with such happiness that she wondered at how she could contain it all. Nick was seducing her, but instead of feeling frightened or unsure of what the night held in store for her, she was filled with a feeling of rightness, of surety. This was the man she loved. This was the man she wanted to spend eternity with.

When the song stopped and segued into another, they simply stood out on the floor, arms around each other, standing very still.

"Jesse," he whispered into her hair.

She closed her eyes. Knew what was coming. Wanted what was coming.

"I love you, Jesse. Marry me."

Her eyes filled. "Yes."

The ring was in his pants pocket. He took it out of the small velvet box and slipped it on her finger.

"I don't deserve you," he whispered.

"Yes, you do," she said fiercely.

He kissed her then and spoke to her between kisses.

"We're from totally different worlds."

"I don't care," she said. "I didn't want the world I was born into. I want my world with you. That's all I want."

He kissed her. She kissed him back, her entire heart in the simple gesture, kissed him until she was shaking with the intensity of her feelings.

"You've got to be sure, Jesse. I need you to be sure."

"I am. I love you, Nick."

She felt his arms come around her, beneath her, then he was carrying her up a flight of stairs and into a small bedroom on the second floor. Nick set her down on the bed as if she were made of the most delicate porcelain, then kissed her hand and whispered, "I'll be right back up, I just have to go downstairs and blow out all the candles."

"Bring one back up," she whispered.

He did. Then he lay down on the bed with her, took her in his arms, and kissed her again. And again. Jessica felt her senses come alive so sharply. Her world had been reduced to this night, this man, this room. This moment.

He undressed her down to her silk slip and had taken the pins out of her hair, letting it fan down around her shoulders before she hesitated.

"What?" he asked.

How this man could read her.

"I—I haven't—I don't have a whole lot of experience with this sort of thing."

"Jesse." Now his green eyes were so warm, so tender. "Are you trying to tell me you're a virgin?"

She nodded her head, knowing she had to look as miserable as she felt.

"That's not a bad thing," he said, cupping her cheek. Brushing a tendril of hair off her forehead.

"You don't mind?" she whispered, looking up at him.

"Come here, you." He pulled her down on the bed, into his arms, cradling her head on his shoulder as those arms came around her. "It's you I love, Jesse. There are no conditions. Nothing you have to do or live up to. Just you."

She sighed, feeling the last little bit of tension leave her body. "I just—I didn't want you to think I was teasing you or something."

"Never."

"Okay."

"Feel better?"

"I do," she admitted.

"It's like Peanut Butter Surprise," he said, playing with a strand of her hair. "You think it's going to be one thing, and it turns out to be something else."

She laughed, and he turned toward her, placing his hand on her stomach. The palm of his hand felt so warm through the silk. So right. She knew it would be wonderful between them and found that, though she needed a little more time, she was no longer afraid.

"Can I ask a favor?"

"Anything." He reached for her hand. Kissed it. "Anything."

"Can we just sleep together tonight? I want to be close to you, but I don't know if I'm ready—"

"You got it, Princess. Your wish is my command."

She wrinkled her nose. "Don't call me that."

He laughed. "Okay."

Nick watched her as she slept.

She was a princess. And though he was a successful man and loved his work, he was as common as one of the alley cats that lived along the wharf and scrounged for scraps of fish when the boats came in from the bay.

He could easily live with their differences if she could. He knew his Jesse was no snob. And he knew she meant what she said. But he also had no doubts her family would not be pleased with their marriage.

He'd wanted to rush things, whisk her off to Las Vegas before anyone was wiser. But he couldn't do that to her. She'd taken huge emotional steps, breaking her engagement to James. Nick smiled down at her. And giving her heart over to him.

His Jesse was a fighter. But she wasn't so strong that too

much too soon wouldn't break her. He didn't want to manipulate her the way her family had. He wanted her to be happy. Therefore, he had to proceed slowly, let things develop in their own time.

Like tonight. Just sleeping. The thought of Jesse waking up in his arms made him happy. He wanted her there for the rest of their lives.

Content for the moment, Nick took her in his arms, closed his eyes, and finally slept.

She woke early the following morning. Blinked her eyes once, then twice. And saw Nick watching her.

"Sleep well?" he whispered.

She nodded her head as she studied him. The slight stubble on his chin. The warm glow in his eyes, even though they were just a little red-rimmed. It couldn't have been that easy a night for him. She wasn't so naive she didn't know she'd had him in a fairly aroused state.

"Nick," she whispered, moving closer.

"What?" But he was smiling.

"It's okay now." She'd remember this moment for the rest of her life. The early morning sunshine streaming in through the windows. The feel of her silk slip against her skin. The warmth of his hands. The look in his eyes.

The feeling filling her heart.

"Now?"

She nodded her head. "Please."

He hesitated, then kissed her with so much feeling that her world stopped. She sighed against his mouth, a little sigh that signaled total feminine surrender, then smiled.

FOUR

H E THOUGHT HIS heart would stop at her sweetness. Lovemaking was so simple when all the emotions were there. When it felt this right. And it was also terrifying. The responsibility of creating her first full sexual experience. The fear that she might not enjoy it. The incredible pressure of wanting it to be right for her. Making sure that her first time making love was a satisfying one.

She gave him so many little clues. Whimpers, moans, and low groans. Her breath caught. Her eyes widened. He took his time with her, enjoying her reactions, trying to keep his own under some semblance of control. Remembering his first time. In a way, she brought back a part of his innocence. It seemed as if he were doing this for the first time as well, because he was with her.

He looked down into that face and his heart turned over in his chest. Those blue eyes. Curious, now. Even puzzled. He loved being the man who could wipe the anxiety from her expression, even if it was only for a morning in a small, closed restaurant in North Beach.

"No one's coming to open this place up, are they?" she'd asked him just before he'd kissed her a second time.

"Not until lunch. Which gives us a couple of hours for what I have planned for you."

She'd looked a little anxious then, so he'd simply laughed

and gathered her into his arms. "Don't worry. You can ask me to stop at any time. I will."

"That wouldn't be fair to you."

"Anything else wouldn't be fair to either of us, Jesse."

He'd eased her along, building passion slowly, and when she'd finally reached her peak, long before their actual consummation, he thought he'd never seen anything more beautiful. Then he'd eased himself up over her, parted those delicate legs, positioned himself and looked into her eyes.

"Don't," he said, giving her a quick kiss on her nose. "You look as if you're on your way to an execution."

She grimaced. "I just don't understand how it's going to—I mean, I looked and—I don't think I can—"

He kissed her then, rolling to the side and taking her with him. Clearly, she wasn't ready. Kissed her again. Knew he had to get her into a physical state of arousal so she wouldn't be up in her head. But more than her body, he wanted to reach her heart.

The next time he began, she welcomed him, opening her body. Her heart. She bit his shoulder at the crucial moment, but he didn't even feel the pain, he was so worried about her own. And then she whispered against his ear, told him it wasn't bad at all, and his heart filled with feeling for her.

Afterwards, they lay in a tangle of arms and legs and watched the sun climb into the sky.

"You're mine, now," he said, playing with a piece of her blonde hair. "I know it's horribly chauvinistic and dated to say so, but I can't help the way I feel."

"I know." She kissed his shoulder, then snuggled even closer. "I feel the same way."

He turned, taking her into his arms. Pulling her slowly against his body. He could have made love to her again in a heartbeat, but he couldn't be so inconsiderate. She'd already made enough adjustments, both emotional and physical.

"I'm glad you didn't marry him," he whispered before he took her mouth again.

He brought her back to her home that evening.

Earlier in the day, they'd gone to his large loft apartment

on the top floor of the cooking school. He'd made her break-fast, then tucked her into his bed and let her sleep. She'd seemed exhausted, not so much from their lovemaking but from all the changes she'd made so recently. Major emotional upheavals.

He went downstairs and taught one class, leaving her a note by his bed along with a few chocolate truffles. When he came back upstairs, he heard water running in the bathtub and smiled.

Nick thought of sauntering into the bathroom, dropping his clothing and joining her in the tub. But he didn't. He had a feeling Jesse might need some privacy, a little time alone to get used to all the changes that had happened this morning. She certainly wasn't a woman who was used to naked men invading her privacy. She might also need the time, soaking in the tub's hot water, to ease any sore muscles.

So he waited.

When she came into the living room, his heart kicked just a little faster. Her blonde hair was slicked back off her face, exposing what he considered to be perfection. Those cheek-bones. That mouth. Those eyes. She wore his white terry robe, and he knew he'd never wear it again without thinking about how she'd looked in it.

"Sleep all right?" he asked.

"Yes. Thank you. I think I needed a little nap."

She was just endearingly formal enough. He didn't care, he'd take Jesse any way he could get her.

"I should probably get back home."

He'd known this moment was coming, even as he'd sensed an almost irrational sort of panic building inside him at the thought of letting her out of his sight. From what he'd learned from Mary, he didn't trust any of her family. But perhaps if Jesse stayed in the safety of her own home, didn't have any contact with them, in the next few days he could persuade her to fly to Las Vegas with him. Or get a license right here in San Francisco.

He had to say it. "You can call me any time, Jesse."

"I know that." She'd raised a towel to dry her hair, and

now the look she gave him, so filled with love and hope, caused his chest to swell with emotion.

She was so beautiful. Inside and out. Her spirit as well as her body. He loved her completely, body, mind and spirit. There would never be anyone for him except Jesse.

"I'll get my car keys," he said, and walked back into his bedroom.

Once at home, Jessica went up on her roof and stared out over the San Francisco skyline. She had an incredible view from her house. The Golden Gate Bridge. The Transcontinental Building. But her mind wasn't on any of it. She thought of her family.

She'd have to deal with them sooner or later.

The question was, should she marry Nick first?

She knew he wanted to. As did she. She didn't even care if they didn't have a formal wedding. She could wear Antoine's gown and stand in front of five hundred guests or wear a pair of jeans and a shirt and walk into any of the small wedding chapels on the Vegas strip. It didn't matter where or how. The only thing that mattered was that she loved Nick and wanted to be his wife.

Sitting in one of the white wicker chairs up on her rooftop, she patted her lap and let Hobbs jump up.

"We'll all be fine, won't we?" she whispered to the kitten. "After all, look what you went through, and it all turned out okay."

Hobbs simply purred, his eyes closed.

Mary had been asleep in the guest bedroom when she'd slipped in the front door, so when Jessica saw the red light flashing by the door, she slipped her arm around Hobbs, stood up, then walked over to the phone extension and used her free hand to pick up the receiver.

"Jessica."

Her mother.

"Hello, Mother."

"Would you mind telling me what's the point of all this? Your little rebellion, I mean."

She took a deep breath. "I'm not marrying James."

"You're not marrying James." She could picture her mother, a thin, ice-cold blonde. As a child, those frigid blue eyes had scared her. She'd gone off to boarding school at a very young age without a murmur of dissent. Even then, she hadn't wanted to be around Annabeth Sinclair.

Now she felt more distant from her mother than ever.

"Don't tell me you're going to marry this—this *cook*."

The way Annabeth said the word "cook" told Jessica all she needed to know.

"Have you been following me?"

"Enough to know there's another man involved." Annabeth paused, obviously waiting for her to comment. When she remained silent, her mother continued. "He's the sort of man who makes for a lovely affair, darling, but don't confuse what you feel for him with what marriage should be."

"You want me to have a marriage like yours," she said quietly, knowing her mother wouldn't catch the irony in her statement.

"I want you to do what's best for the family."

There. It was out in the open. Annabeth had drawn first blood.

"No."

There. She'd finally said it. Throughout all the years, as a helpless child, Jessica had longed to put a stop to it. To the endless, relentless, not measuring up. To the sick sense of never feeling good enough.

Nick had shown her she was fine, just the way she was.

"You're being unreasonable, Jessica."

She took a deep breath. "I don't really care what you think."

Her mother paused, and she could almost sense Annabeth Sinclair gathering her thoughts for another attack.

"So you'd actually give up your share of the family fortune in exchange for a few nights of passion with this Kitchen Casanova?"

They'd obviously had Nick quite thoroughly checked out. Jessica made a mental note never to underestimate her father in such a dangerous way again.

"I'd be content to live out my days in this house with my trust fund. When that runs out, I could always get a job."

Annabeth laughed, and Jesse found the high-pitched sound chilling. "Doing what? Growing those absurd little flowers? Working in a nursery? How long would the charm of living like an ordinary person last, Jessica? I can tell you from experience, you can't live on love alone."

"Mother, please say what you have to say. I'm going to bed soon."

"At least meet with your father and I. He's terribly anxious to talk to you."

She took another breath. "Only if the two of you understand there's nothing you can do or say to make me change my mind about marrying James."

"Oh, I understand. I do think you're giving up a good man."

"In your opinion, I am. But you don't know what's right for me, Mother, and I doubt you ever have."

"There's no need to use that tone with me."

"It's not a tone, it's the truth. Look, I've got to go." Hobbs, sensing her distress, started to wriggle in her arms and she set him gently on the floor.

"Your father and I. Lunch at that darling little French place near Antoine's. Tomorrow at noon?"

She felt she could agree. After all, she'd been more than clear about her feelings toward James. They couldn't force her to do anything she didn't want to.

"All right. Noon."

She hung up the phone and called Nick.

He didn't sleep at all that night.

Something was about to come down, but he didn't know what. And Jesse was being stubborn.

"Don't have lunch with them." He hadn't wanted it to happen. Not until he'd convinced her to marry him soon. Hell, he didn't care if they had one guest or one thousand. If the ceremony took place in a church or a meadow. Marrying Jesse was what was important.

Keeping her safe.

"It's a public place. A little French bistro near Antoine's studio. I think my father just wants one last chance to try to talk me out of breaking the engagement. But he won't change my mind."

"Jesse, I have a bad feeling about this."

"No, it's just that they're used to the old me. The one who would cave in if either of them looked at me with their eyes crossed. They had no idea of what I really wanted."

Nor did they care, he thought after they hung up.

Well, he'd promised not to interfere. But that didn't include trailing her to the restaurant and making sure she got home safely. If he turned up shortly thereafter with tickets to Vegas, where was the harm?

"You can see, Jessica, that this broken engagement places the entire family in a rather precarious situation."

"I'm sorry, Daddy. I don't mean to cause any ill will. But I know you wouldn't want me to marry a man I didn't love."

Matthew Sinclair gave his daughter a look that Jessica could only describe as incredulous.

"Marriage has nothing to do with love. The best marriages act as a form of—merger."

She looked at her father and finally saw the man who had a block of ice where his heart should have been. The only thing he'd ever given her was his chromosomes. And even that had been conditional. He hadn't wanted children, he'd wanted tiny clones, ever ready to do his bidding.

"I'm only going to ask you once, Jessica," her father said in a rather annoyed tone. His gesture imperious, he signaled to one of the waiters, who promptly brought a cellular phone over to their secluded table. Her mother looked on, those blue eyes so cold.

"Now, call James and tell him that the wedding is still on."

She stared at her father, incredulous. And finally got it. Deep in her heart, in her soul. He didn't care what she thought, what she felt, what she wanted or needed. He simply wanted her to do as he wished.

Best for the family. For all concerned.

She felt as if she were choking. Couldn't breathe. The air felt thick and foul. Shaking just a little, a fine tremor that filled her entire body, she got to her feet.

She felt like overturning the table.

You will not create a scene, you will simply leave. And never see either of them again.

"Jessica!" Her father's voice cracked like a lash.

She didn't look back as she began to wind her way around the tables toward the light coming in the open front door.

"Jessica!" The voice was fainter now. She walked on, toward her future. Toward Nick. She'd go to him this afternoon. Marry him whenever he wanted to. And raise their children far away from all of the Sinclairs except for her grandmother.

It was finished.

Nick saw her exit the bistro and let out the painful breath he'd been holding. She was safe, she'd gotten away from them. Not even considering that she might be angry at him for spying on her, he started forward.

What happened next stunned him.

A man in a dark suit waylaid him, a powerful hand closing over his arm. When Nick reacted, tried to pull away, he was punched in the stomach.

He went down, the breath totally knocked out of him. But not before he saw two other men grab hold of Jesse, practically pick her up and bundle her into a long, sleek black limousine.

He struggled to get up, still hearing her screams long after the car had disappeared around the corner.

He didn't know who else to go to, so he went to Mary. She was still in bed, but she answered the door. She would have had to, the way he'd pounded on it.

He didn't have to say a word.

"What have they done?" she whispered, her elderly face paling.

Briefly, he told her.

"Give me a minute," she said, and walked out of the front

room with as much dignity as an eightysomething woman could in her nightgown and bathrobe.

He followed her directions and they drove to the Sinclair Office Complex, in the middle of the financial district.

"She's up there, on one of the floors," Mary said from her side of Nick's convertible. "They've probably given her some kind of sedative. To make her more tractable."

"I don't suppose we could call the police."

Mary snorted. "Matthew has them in his pocket."

"The media?"

"You'd never see her again." Turning her attention away from the imposing, grey granite building, she studied him.

"It's going to take all that you are and everything you believe in order to help her. You're going up against some very evil people. I wouldn't blame you if you wanted to walk away. And if you do, dear boy, I'd advise you do it now."

"Not a chance."

She smiled, and he detected a slight sheen in her faded blue eyes. "Good. My money was always on you, Nick."

"I'm flattered." His eyes narrowed as he gazed at the Sinclair Complex. "What do you think we should do?"

Mary sighed. "This will be the hardest part. For both of us. We'll have to wait and see what they're up to."

Jesse called him that night.

"Nick?"

"Jesse?" He motioned frantically for Mary to pick up the extension. They'd just finished a quick dinner he'd cooked, though neither of them had had much success convincing the other they'd eaten much. It had merely been an exercise in pushing food around on their plates.

Mary picked up the extension just as Jesse said, "Nick, I'm so sorry but I can't marry you."

This hit him far worse than that hired goon's punch.

"Jesse? This isn't like you. Tell me what's going on—"

"Nothing. Nothing is going on." But her voice sounded flat. Dead.

"Jesse, are you—"

"Jessica." Mary's voice was very calm. "Have they drugged you? Threatened you?"

"I can't—" She choked on the words, but rushed on. "I can't marry you, Nick. I'm sorry." The next words were whispered, right before she hung up.

"But I love you."

"Some kind of threat to you, obviously," Mary said. Nick had broken into his stock of premiere chocolate, and now they simply shaved pieces off a good-sized bar of Valrhona bittersweet and drank cup after cup of very good coffee.

He didn't answer. Couldn't. He couldn't get the sound of Jesse's defeated voice out of his mind. His heart.

"Now do you have some sort of idea of what you're up against? My son won't let anything threaten his empire, let alone care about his daughter's happiness." She took a sip of coffee. Even though her tone had been calm, Nick saw those elderly hands shake. "She is a pawn to be manipulated in his world. Nothing more or less."

"There has to be a way to get to her. Somehow."

"There will be. But we can't afford to make a mistake. And I seriously doubt if they'll let us get very close. Matthew wants this wedding—pardon me, this *merger*, to take place very badly."

Nick swallowed another sip of coffee, fighting down the sick feeling in his stomach. "If we should fail—what kind of man is James? Could she be happy with him?"

Mary gave him a long, level look. "James could be Matthew's clone, they are so much alike."

Nick felt his blood chill.

Failure was no longer an option.

Jessica waited until the night nurse her father had hired left the room before taking the capsule out from beneath her tongue and slipping it into the dirt of a nearby potted plant.

A small victory, but satisfying nonetheless.

She'd fought like a tiger until the moment her father had made it quite clear that if she ran off and married Nick he would find a way to destroy him. Barring that, he'd see if there were some way to arrange an "accident."

No matter what happened, she was not to thwart his plans.

The thought of something happening to Nick, the thought of her father arranging to have him hurt or worse, had finally brought her to her knees.

She'd been beaten and knew it. So had her father. The look he'd given her before turning her over to his staff had spoken volumes.

Now, in a comfortable guest bedroom with two burly guards stationed outside the door, she feigned a drugged sleep. She knew better than to fight, that would just earn her the tip of a needle and a far more potent drug.

The marriage was still going to go through, according to her mother. She'd called everyone back, from Antoine to the caterers, and explained away Jessica's earlier calls as a simple case of bridal nerves.

Valentine's Day would find her walking down the church aisle toward James, her future husband.

And dying a little every day, from that moment on.

FIVE

THE WEDDING WAS scheduled for seven in the evening, Valentine's Day. Nick made the supreme sacrifice, considering how he felt, and taught the last Kitchen Casanova class the day before. It wasn't as if he hadn't gone over this material many times previously.

Actually, he could have done it in his sleep. But his mind was on Jesse, so he was distracted. More than anything, he wished he could have been with her. Protected her.

Now, before class, he stared inside one of the large, stainless steel refrigerators at the delicate bouquet of orchids he'd ordered to be delivered this morning. He planned on hand delivering it to Jessica at the church, along with an impassioned plea as to why she shouldn't throw her life away on James when she loved him.

He knew she did.

Nick also knew he had no right to demand a place in her life. But he knew the Jessica he'd talked to on the phone wasn't the Jesse he'd seen laugh and smile. And play at making truffles, with chocolate all over her hands.

So for the time being, he and Mary made their plans. And waited.

She attended his class in Jesse's place, and he watched as an instant rapport sprang up between the sprightly Mary and

Ben. And was glad that, just for the moment, Mary was distracted from what the future might bring.

He discussed presentation but sensed the class knew his heart wasn't in it. At the halfway point, he called a break, then turned on the small, nine-inch television on the main kitchen counter. Perhaps the media had a little more information on the Sinclair wedding.

"We're here at the church watching as Jessica Sinclair gets out of the limousine on her father's arm," the news announcer said, her voice smooth and well modulated. "She's the loveliest bride I've seen in years. Don't you agree, Chuck?"

"What?" Mary's eyes were riveted to the small color screen. "My God, Matthew pushed the wedding ahead one day."

"Damn it," Nick muttered. They'd been tricked. By the time he and Mary made it to the church, Jesse would already be married. If they had her all drugged up, God knows what they could force her to agree to. Furious, he started toward the refrigerator, opened it, took out the bouquet of orchids, then strode to the front of the room.

"Class is canceled."

Every student nodded his head, instant masculine understanding coming to the fore. They'd all seen Jessica, in her bridal finery, on the small television screen.

They all felt for Nick.

"I'll make it up to all of you," he continued, "but right now I've got a wedding to attend."

Mary took a deep breath. "I don't see how we can make it there on time to stop Jessica."

"What's the problem?" Peter, the large, burly, redheaded man who'd wondered if Jessica was single in the very first class, came striding up.

"We need to get to that church and stop that wedding!" Mary said, clutching at Nick's arm.

Peter considered all this in a heartbeat. "I'm a cop. I could ask one of my buddies to come here. He'd get you there in record time."

"Could you?" Mary gazed up at him, furiously swiping at her eyes. "We can't let this happen to my granddaughter!"

"I'll call." Peter left the classroom.

"And I'm coming with you," Ben said, putting his arm around a distraught Mary.

Jessica acted numb as she left the confines of the limousine, but not from any drug. In reality, she was as alert as she'd ever been in her life, her senses on fire. Because she knew this was her absolute last chance at happiness.

Oh Nick, I'm sorry . . .

Her plans no longer included Nick. She knew Mary would care for the house, her kittens, even the orchids. The plan Jessica had was to run away, so far and so fast that Matthew Sinclair's obsessive tentacles could never touch her again.

Her mother had been furious about her wedding dress. Antoine had brought the romantic gown she and Nick had picked out to the Sinclair Office Complex. She'd been dressed this morning, with her mother and a mass of hairstylists and makeup artists in attendance.

Jessica had felt a small measure of satisfaction in seeing how much her mother hated the bridal gown Nick had selected for her instead of the starkly modern style. Yet her mother had still triumphed over smaller details in her appearance.

Her hair felt stiff and artificial in the elegant twist, and the heavy diamond earrings that sparkled in her ears in no way resembled the pearls she would have worn.

Now, stepping inside the massive church on her father's arm, Jessica wondered if she had the courage to go through with what she had to do. If Matthew Sinclair had his way, he'd keep a tight hold of her until he handed her over to James. And James had not liked being publicly humiliated by their broken engagement. She sensed he would find a way to make her pay.

All in all, not a promising future. But it was what she'd been dealt, and she intended to play this particular game to the finish, winner take all.

• • •

"Nick, what are we going to do?" Mary's tense voice broke the silence in the speeding police car.

"Throw all our plans out the window and improvise," Nick said. "Act fast. Go for broke. There just isn't time for anything else."

"Oh Lord," Ben muttered. "Peanut Butter Surprise."

"Park here, around the corner and out of sight," Mary said. "I'm sure my son will have arranged to have guards at the door. We're going to have to think of something." As if on cue, something caught her eye and she leapt out of the car, her movements belying her age.

Nick was right after her, and Ben right after him.

"Father Flannery!" Mary approached the priest as he walked toward the front of the church.

"Why, Mary Sinclair, I haven't seen you in years!" The older man seemed genuinely glad to see Mary, and Nick, right behind her, wondered how they could use this friendship to their advantage. Though he felt a little guilty taking advantage of a priest, they didn't have a whole lot of time.

"Father," Mary began. "Would you do us the honor of assisting in the fight between good and evil?"

He didn't hesitate. "Of course."

"Can you get us into the church?"

He frowned. "I know your son was very particular about who could attend and who could not. He told me he didn't want something as sacred as marriage turned into a media circus. So he has guards posted at the front doors—"

"But there has to be another way," Mary said quietly. "My son and I have had a falling out, and now I believe he's making my granddaughter marry a man she doesn't love. And that, to me, is an insult to the institution of marriage."

"I see what you mean." Father Flannery's expression was thoughtful. "Follow me. There's a back entrance, and I'm sure there are no guards waiting for you there."

She started up the long aisle, her father's fingers digging into the sleeve of her gown. Telling her in no uncertain terms that she was not to be given a chance to cut and run, that she would do her duty to the Sinclair family even if it cost her the rest of her life.

James waited for her at the altar, and she averted her eyes, unable to look at him.

In a shorter time than she would have liked, her father left her at the altar, stepped away, and gave her to James. His hand closed over her arm, and Jessica almost started to laugh hysterically. Both men felt the same, that same controlling touch. She was being passed from one to the other, merely a pawn, a means to bring more Sinclairs into the world—so they could be manipulated, as well.

She almost started screaming, but bit her lip and waited. Bided her time. She would not go into this arrangement gently, docilely. She would fight, and she would choose that time carefully. This would be one wedding that neither her parents nor James would ever forget.

Father Flannery, who had been running late, joined them at the altar.

"Dearly beloved, we are gathered here . . ."

The ceremony had been deliberately shortened by her father, and Jessica caught the glaring omission concerning the part that usually went, "Should anyone know of any reason this man and woman should not be married . . ."

And then it came time for James to recite his vows, which he did, with about as much passion as a head of lettuce. Then came her turn.

"Do you, Jessica Elizabeth Sinclair, take this man to be your lawful wedded husband?"

She paused so long she heard the restless rustles. The whispers. Grasping her wedding gown's voluminous skirts in her hands, she attempted to turn toward the pews filled with family and friends.

James's hand tightened on her arm.

"Jessica?" Now her father was on her other side, slanting her a meaningful look.

Don't you mess this up. Not now. Not ever.

This was her worst nightmare, having James and her father on either side of her. Closing in, preventing her from moving an inch.

"Go on, Father," Matthew Sinclair said, a thread of steel in his low voice.

For a moment, the elderly priest seemed flustered, then he said, "Do you, Jessica Elizabeth Sinclair, take this man to be your lawfully wedded husband—"

"She can't."

Jessica tried to turn her head. She recognized that voice, and her heart sang.

Nick!

He was striding up the aisle toward the altar, dressed in jeans, boots, and a black shirt, and carrying a gorgeous bouquet of pale pink orchids. The goons at the door started to try and stop him, then seemed to remember where they were and how many witnesses were present. So they stood there, impotent, and watched as Nick walked steadily up the aisle.

"Get your hands off her," he said in an undertone to James. Flustered, he obeyed.

Then Nick turned to Matthew Sinclair.

"You, too. Right now."

Her father was red-faced with rage. Shaking. Jessica thought he was almost about to have a heart attack.

"How dare you—" he began.

"I'm pregnant," she said clearly, in a voice designed to carry to the farthest pew. "It's Nick's child."

His arm encircled her waist, pulled her to his side.

"Well then," Father Flannery said as if this sort of thing happened in his church all the time, "I believe we'd better get the two of you married. You're ready to accept responsibility for your actions, son?"

"Indeed I am." Nick smiled down at her while Matthew Sinclair looked on in total fury.

"Oh," Nick said suddenly, turning toward Father Flannery. "Could I have just a word with my future father-in-law before we start the ceremony?"

"Certainly."

Nick turned toward Matthew and spoke in a low, but firm, undertone. "Harm a hair on Jessica's head, and you'll be arrested so fast you won't know what hit you. Harm me or your mother and the same will happen."

"How dare—"

"Oh, I dare, all right. I had the most enlightening talk with one of San Francisco's finest on the way over here, and he let me know that he'll personally keep an eye on you for the first few years Jessica and I are married. If anything should happen to either of us, or to Mary, yours will be the only door they'll be knocking on."

Jessica felt tears start to fill her eyes. For the first time in the last few horrible days she knew her life would unfold in an entirely new direction. Hope, almost nonexistent at the start of her wedding day, now flooded her senses.

Nick turned his attention to her. "Do you want to get married right now?"

She couldn't stop smiling. "I'd be honored."

"Me, too." Nick turned toward the assembled congregation, and the whispered undertone slowed, then stopped.

"There's been a slight change of plans today. Jessica Sinclair is getting married, but not to James. I'm Nick Kellaher, and she's marrying me."

Simple, succinct, and to the point, Jessica thought. Much like the man himself.

"Good one, Nick," Ben bellowed from the back of the church, where he sat with a grinning Mary. "Sort of like Peanut Butter Surprise!"

"Exactly," Nick said, then turned back toward Jessica. He took her hand in his, and she found herself drawing strength from the warmth of his fingertips. Hands firmly entwined, they both turned and faced the elderly priest, who seemed anything but flustered.

"You're doing the right thing, my boy," he whispered as he adjusted his glasses.

"Oh, I know I am. Father, could you wait just a moment?"

"Certainly. Is there something you need to confess?"

"No. Just a few details I need to adjust." And with that, he reached for Jessica's bouquet, a starkly modern arrangement of lilies and ivy. "May I?"

She knew what he wanted to do and smiled. "Yes."

He tossed the flowers to her surprised mother, then handed Jessica the simple and romantic bouquet of pale pink orchids. She felt Nick carefully unpin her veil, then both of them unpinned her hair and let it fall naturally around her shoulders. Jessica slipped off the ostentatious diamond earrings her mother had selected and thought of the pearls she and Nick had decided on at Antoine's studio several weeks ago.

"Voilà," said a familiar voice to her right. She glanced over, then almost laughed out loud at the sight that greeted her. Antoine stood at her side, a pair of stunning pearl earrings in his outstretched hand.

"He asked me to find a pair that suited you," the designer said to Jessica, indicating Nick with a nod of his head. "I picked them up this morning. There are no real accidents in this life, are there?"

"I don't think so," Jessica said, then slipped the pearls onto her ears. She faced Nick.

"Just as I imagined," he whispered, then adjusted her veil so it covered her face. "Ready?"

"Ready."

Together, they faced the priest.

"Dearly beloved, we are gathered here . . ."

Out of the corner of her eye, Jessica watched as her father, mother, James and several of their friends slowly filed out of the church. Not really caring, she focused her attention on the ceremony unfolding around her. When the time came for her to speak her vows, she said them in a clear, emotion-filled voice.

Nick did the same.

Within the hour, they were outside the church, being showered with birdseed.

Nick invited everyone who had stuck around to come back to the little restaurant in North Beach. He then proceeded, with his friend's help, to cook up a very simple wedding feast. Music played, people danced, and Jessica noticed that Ben was paying quite a lot of attention to Mary.

"You know," the elderly man told Jessica as he danced with her, "Elizabeth called to say she couldn't join me for

Valentine's dinner, but I have to admit that I enjoy your grandmother's company a lot more."

"Things happen for a reason," Jessica said, delighted that her grandmother and Ben were having such a good time. "I should know."

After everyone left, Nick took her back to his apartment. They changed out of their wedding finery, her dress and his jeans and workshirt. Then, wrapped in a blanket from his bed, Nick poured them each a glass of champagne and took several truffles out of the refrigerator. They sat on the couch looking out over the glittering lights of the city and the glorious Golden Gate Bridge.

"Happy Valentine's Day," he said, toasting her as the clock chimed softly. "It's just after midnight."

"Happy Valentine's Day," she replied.

They drank their champagne. Nibbled on the truffles. Simply enjoyed the quiet and each other's company.

"Thank you for coming to my rescue," she whispered, kissing him.

"Thank you for coming to mine," he replied. She knew her expression had to be slightly puzzled, because he said, "I could have been a perpetual bachelor had you not insisted on barging into my cooking class and setting me straight." He started to laugh. "I guess I have James to thank for that!"

"I doubt he'd appreciate being reminded."

"No, I guess he wouldn't. So writing him a thank-you note is out of the question." He took another sip of champagne. "Perhaps I could send him a tasteful box of truffles?"

She found this incredibly funny and laughed so hard she had to set her champagne flute on the table in front of the couch. He gazed down at her and she could see so much love in his eyes.

"Happy?" he asked.

"Yes." She thought of all the dreams she'd had as a girl, and later as a young woman. The man she'd wanted to find and marry. That comfort they'd both find in the quiet times. Children. Pets. That absolute understanding that would see them through any of the rocky patches life might throw their way.

And she thought of what she would have had if her father had succeeded. The thought chilled her, and she moved more deeply into his arms.

"Telling the good Father Flannery you were pregnant with my child," Nick mused. "Lying in church. Twenty lashes with a wet noodle for you."

"I could be. We didn't use anything."

He sighed. "It's true. I lose all sense when I'm around you."

"I know the feeling."

They were silent for a time, enjoying the view, the champagne, the truffles. Each other.

"You do want—" she began.

"Of course. But only with you."

"Good."

"But I'll leave it up to you," he said, taking two corners of the blanket and pulling them so he brought her even closer toward him.

"In that case," she whispered against his ear, "don't use anything tonight."

He gazed down at her, his lips almost touching hers. "Jesse. You're sure?"

She looked up at him, knowing her heart had to be in her eyes. "Nick, I've wanted a family for so long."

"Oh, baby." He lowered her to the couch, then lay down beside her. "Whatever happens, you're never going to be lonely again."

Her arms came up around his neck as she kissed him. And then she forgot to think at all.

Years later, she would look back on her wedding night as the moment her life really started. Nick had come to her rescue, championed her cause, taken her out of her lonely, isolated, fearful tower. She would love him for the rest of her life, and their children as well.

This particular tale would have a very happy ending. Love had truly conquered all. And this particular princess would never be lonely again.

Happily ever after. Forever.

George Geary's
French Kahlua Truffles

Yield: 1 pound

Chocolate truffles were the candy fad of the 1980s and now that we are in the '90s, they are going to be around for a long time. Truffles range from $6.00 to $25.00 per pound and sometimes more.

8 ounces	semisweet chocolate, chopped (not chips)
8 ounces	cream
1 teaspoon	unsalted butter
2 teaspoons	Kahlua
4 ounces	semisweet chocolate, melted (not chips)
½ cup	cocoa powder
2 teaspoons	ground cinnamon

In a bowl, place the chopped chocolate and butter, and set aside. In a saucepan, on medium heat, place the cream and cook until boiling up the sides of the pan. Do not stir. Pour the hot cream into the chocolate and stir until very well blended. Stir the Kahlua into the batter slowly. Do not stir too much, as this will create air in the batter. Pour the mixture into a shallow dish and cool overnight on the counter until very firm. Or place in the refrigerator for four hours. Take the paste and roll into small balls; arrange the balls on a cookie sheet and place in the freezer until firm, about five minutes. Handling the paste too much melts the chocolate, so that is why you need to place them back in the freezer again. Dip each of the balls into the melted chocolate and place on a piece of foil to harden. After the truffle has dried, roll into cocoa powder and cinnamon. Serve.

George Geary is a renowned chocolate chef who can be contacted on the Internet at ggeary@aol.com.